KATLYN DEROUEN

TWISTED BOND

CRP

Published by Gilded Rose Press
Printed in the United States of America
First Edition, printed in 2023.
ISBN: 979-8-218-26523-6

Cover Design: Saint Jupiter Designs
Editing: Nicole Zoltack
Formatting: Qamber Designs

To my husband, whom without your constant prodding and excitement, I might have never allowed this to be seen by anyone. I never imagined my story could matter to someone else so much, long before it even hit the pages, but you have proved me very wrong.

Thank you for believing in me and for allowing us to make necessary sacrifices for this story to come alive.

I love you.

PART I

CHAPTER ONE

CAMMIE

It didn't matter that Cammie hated getting up early or that she had slept terribly the previous night. Being in her favorite place in the world made it easier, especially considering she was surrounded by books. It was the only place she truly felt at home in the world. There was absolutely nothing that could make her mood sour.

"Wow. What grave robber dug you up last night?"

Except for Madeline's perfectly timed assessments.

"Do you ever get tired of being such a grump early in the morning? Or do you just figure you'll do it anyway, as if it's a community service?" Cammie retorted.

"Wow...you've never been one to snap back at me. Sassy looks golden on you, *darling*." Madeline failed to execute a perfected British accent.

Cammie rolled her eyes. "It's too early in the morning for accents," she groaned, running a hand down her face. "Actually, it's way too early for anything."

Madeline arched her eyebrows, giving Cammie the once-over.

"I could fall over on this counter right now, but then that would scare away potential customers, and you know Amy wouldn't be happy."

"Believe me, I'd never hear the end of it. My mom would blow up so much she'd die of rage, and then who would be the one to throw the funeral? Me. Who would inherit this bookstore? Me. I don't know which is worse." With dramatic hands, Madeline threw her frustration into the air, and Cammie couldn't help but marvel at her tiny outburst. With honey-colored hair that was always perfectly kempt and a bubbly personality to match, Madeline had a knack for drawing people in. Even for introverts like Cammie, who at one point never would have given the idea of talking to Madeline a second thought. But Madeline took one look at Cammie, with her unruly curls, and deep-set brown eyes and decided adopting an introvert was the best way to make her life interesting.

Cammie's mouth slacked open. "How can you even say that? There's nothing wrong with books! I love them."

Madeline cackled, grabbing a few books on the rack beside her. With the smirk still on her face, she began to stack them side by side. She wasn't organizing them, Cammie realized. She was making a tower.

"You're right. They are fun." She looked over at Cammie, a challenge in her eyes.

"Why do you abuse the things I love?"

Cammie's laments did nothing but egg Madeline on further, and so she continued with stacking the books, and thus continued Cammie's twitching left eyelid.

"Because I can," Madeline sang. "I do it because I can."

That was exactly the stark difference between the two, even though they were both seventeen. Cammie erred on the side of caution, always doing what's right and doing her best to stay low. Not Madeline, though. Not at all.

The little bell above the door gave way to the signature *ding*, and the girls turned at the sound, all sense of taunting gone.

"Good morning. Where would your lore section be in this quaint shop? Is it okay to do some browsing in my leisure?"

The accent from the man in the doorway was hard to place. It sounded like music, a beautiful melodic sound, but it was the man himself who stole the show. He had to have been at least in his early forties.

With copper hair that fell in soft waves at his shoulders, he looked regal. *He looked like the kind of person she read about constantly.*

His clothing was normal, just dress pants and a green button down, but there was something about the way he carried himself that made his attire seem bigger than it was. It was prestigious, Cammie recognized, the rare sight of something she never thought she'd lay eyes on outside of the pages she cocooned herself within.

"What's with the foreign guide standing in the doorway?" Madeline whispered. "Dude forget his passport or something?"

Cammie didn't roll her eyes this time. She wouldn't ever be like that in front of a customer.

"Ahem." Madeline cleared her throat then put on her biggest grin to the stranger. "We. Are. Not. An. Airport. Bookstore." She enunciated each word slowly, her lips wrapping around each word she spoke.

The stranger blinked at her bond then turned to Cammie. "Is my accent too difficult for her to comprehend? She does speak English, doesn't she?"

Cammie held her tongue, but she couldn't keep the laughter in this time. Madeline sent daggers her way, but Cammie didn't care.

"I can speak English," Madeline muttered as she pointed to one of the back shelves. "Have fun taking care of the customer," she remarked as she skipped away.

"Wait, come back—Madeline!" Despite Cammie's protests, Madeline had a mind of her own.

Left alone with the stranger, Cammie did her best to crack a smile. She failed on mass proportions. She always did when nervous or embarrassed, and strangers made her nervous.

"How can I help you, sir?" Her voice faltered, a sliver of the sound crackling. She swallowed a few times then plastered the smile back on.

The man walked from the front door, his boots clicking against the steps. He reached the front counter, letting his palms rest on it. Where most customers would have laughed or snorted at her lack of professionalism, this man merely smiled. It was in his smile, she noticed, that it was genuine. There was no trace of mockery that certain adults had. This man, by all accounts, was not like anyone she had seen before. There was a certain air with how he carried himself, and again, she was reminded of the book characters she adored so much. They all seemed to view themselves in high esteem, which was true for the man, but it wasn't in the way of feeling above her. He was simply compassionate.

Now, Cammie knew she could be very wrong, but one of her talents was the ability to see the genuineness of a person she was speaking to. She wasn't a mind reader, but her mother always said Cammie had a talent for reading others.

The more this man smiled, the more she thought her mother was right.

"Would you happen to know where the books of lore here would be? It seems I scared your friend away." His smile deepened, and his chest rumbled with laughter. It was contagious enough that Cammie couldn't help but laugh too.

"I actually do know where it is," she replied. "It's one of my favorite sections. I love fairy tales." She pointed to an aisle a few feet away from where they were standing. "It's actually right over there, on the back shelf. If you want to follow me, I can show you?"

"That would be lovely."

The man followed her to the back, and Cammie's face flushed red. This job was hard enough as it is, just talking to people. She hated how she wore every emotion on her face. Cammie wasn't graceful like her friend Sabina or strong like her friend Hannah. Cammie was somewhere in between meek and shy, and she could never seem to break out of the mold except for when she felt comfortable with someone. Which would explain Madeline.

Ah. Madeline. That led her brain to get back on track.

"Don't worry about my coworker. Whenever she gets challenged, she loves to question authority. If it wasn't you who made the comment and someone else had, she still would have stuck me up here on my own." She added a little laugh at the end, hoping to ease the tension.

The man didn't respond, however, and her face flushed red once again.

They walked in silence, and Cammie was silently grateful for the halt that came with reaching the bookshelf. She knelt down, her thumbs skimming the spines. She loved the texture of these books. The binding was marvelous in her eyes simply because she knew it would get worn. She was always fonder of the books that were more worn just because it meant that they were being used for the right reasons. She could tell if a book was truly loved due to the pages folded or the spines becoming crinkled.

"Do any of these catch your eye? We have a few titles here that might fit your fancy." As she talked about the books, she began to feel herself relax. There wasn't a need to prove herself. It was just her and her safe place.

He knelt down beside her, and Cammie scooted over a few inches. His fingers also traced the same spines she had before, and they shared a secret smile.

"I see you are a lover of books also," Cammie remarked.

Then, it dawned on her. They were in a bookstore. *Of course, he loves books.*

"I am. Literature is one of this world's finest expressions of life and art. I've found that words can birth many things: passion, despair, intrigue. It's always been one of my favorite obsessions, one I shared with another, a very long time ago."

Cammie wanted to prod more about this "other" person. He spoke with such longing that she was almost convinced there was some epic romance brewing behind the scenes.

"It doesn't seem you have it in stock here. That's quite all right. You must be a fairly newer store. It would be almost impossible to carry this kind of lore without having prior history."

"Has what you're looking for been around a long time? Maybe I can see if my boss has a way to track it down." Cammie's hands waved frantically as she spoke.

The man shook his head. "No, thank you. You've been kind enough to help me. I appreciate it." He stuck out his hand.

It took Cammie a second to realize he was offering it to her to shake. Stuck in bewilderment, she was frozen.

The man looked down at his hand and began pulling it back. Before he could, though, she shook his hand with as much force as she could will into her tiny palm.

"I'm sorry. You just caught me by surprise. I don't do this often." She paused, realizing despite the few minutes he had been in the store, she hadn't even gathered his name.

"I'm Caelan," he responded. He smiled again as he let go of her hand. "And you're Cammie, I presume, based on your name tag?"

She looked down at the one clipped to her shirt and nodded. When her eyes lifted, a sparkle caught her gaze from below. It was a golden band on Caelan's ring finger. She couldn't help her delight.

"It's your wife!" Her words rang ecstatically. "That's who's in your story, right? The person who loved to read with you. You were talking about your wife, weren't you?"

At the mere mention of the word *wife*, Caelan's face lost all its color. He backed away from her as if she were fire itself and averted his eyes. His entire body stiffened, and he barely glanced up at her from behind his eyelashes. "Thank you for your time," he murmured, his voice barely above a whisper.

Cammie opened her mouth to speak, but words did no justice. Caelan was already out the door before she could even call after him, the bell dinging as the door shut.

CHAPTER TWO

SABINA

WEAR A PRETTY SMILE AND *never be ashamed to bend down a little lower to get the eyes upon you, my dear.*

The advice given by her grandmother rang loud in her head as Sabina stared at the sights before her. It was another party, just like all the others her parents loved to host. And just like with all the other parties, Sabina wouldn't follow the advice given last year when she had been sixteen.

The guests were donned in their pretty dresses and fancy tuxedos. They chattered with ease and sipped on wine through clear, long chutes. Laughter rang out from one of the crowds, and little beads of sweat clutched to Sabina's forehead.

She always felt out of place at these parties, despite that it was her birthright, she knew, to be in this room, along with everyone else invited. Her grandfather was rich and his father before that. Her parents carried on the legacy, and they carried it well.

Her mother hovered in the corner of the room, while her husband stood beside her. His arm was wrapped around her waist, and his lips were pressed into her mother's cheek. Her mother giggled, a trait that only her father could bring out in her mother, and Sabina couldn't help but smile. It was one of the only normal things that could exist at these parties. Everything else was loud and far too overwhelming.

All she wanted to do was shrink into a corner like her parents, but then her mother shot her a look from where she was standing. It wasn't verbal, but Sabina understood it all the same.

Stay put.

Her mother's eyes were the color of emeralds, only a shade lighter than Sabina's. When her mother made faces, Sabina wanted to laugh. It was as if watching herself in the mirror making an agitated expression.

People commented on it all the time, how she was the spitting image of her mother and grandmother. They all had fair skin, fiery red hair that was as straight as an arrow, and small-framed, curvaceous bodies. It was a genetic thing, her mother said. Except for the attitude.

"You, Sabina, did not inherit that from me."

Where her mother was short in stature, her father was tall. He might not have had the fiery hair, but he did have the fiery temper. He was known to be stubborn to a fault and had a very hard time changing his mind if it was a cause near and dear to his heart. That same spirit was in Sabina.

That was why it was so difficult to drag her to these parties. She never wanted to stay long, so her parents gave her an offer, a bargain of sorts. If she came to the party, she only had to stay for an hour. Then, she was free to retreat to her safe haven.

Sabina was nearing ten minutes left. She could hardly contain her glee. Only a little while longer, and she'd be free of this madness.

"Why, Sabina! I'm so glad to see you here."

The chipper voice sounded like nails on a chalkboard to Sabina. She had seen this woman many times at these social events, and this was the one woman Sabina could not bear to be around.

"Hello, Mrs. Daniel. How are you this evening?" Forcing kindness into her voice always took more strength than she thought was necessary, but she would do it anyway. It was what her mother had told Sabina to do when she faced this woman. Sabina's mother had plenty of practice with Mrs. Daniel before, a long time ago.

"I'm doing rather well." Mrs. Daniel snottily looked around. "I see your parents took my advice on changing the decor. This gathering room looks so much more beautiful than it did before. Gah, those dreadful drapes. I cannot believe your mother thought the pastel drapes were the right color. The horror of some people and their distaste for fashion irks me."

Due to the constant complaining and making everyone's lives miserable because of the drape hues, Sabina and her family had been forced to change the color as well as the material to please Ms. Royal Highness. These sponsors were the only way her parents were able to throw these parties. The funds helped support the theater they loved so much. *Such a shame that Mrs. Daniel was one of them.*

"Well, you know my parents." Sabina said. "They love to please."

Mrs. Daniel huffed. "Well, I sure hope so. Otherwise, I would be more than happy to tell these people to cut off their funding, and we wouldn't want that, would we?" She smiled, showing her pearly whites.

"Of course not."

The practiced kindness fell easily from her lips, mostly because Sabina knew any second now, she would be far away from this demon woman.

"You were always my favorite out of your family. So sad that you haven't found someone to scoop you up yet. The same thing happened with Martha and Margaret, my fifth husband's daughters. Such a shame they ended up alone and destitute. You won't be young forever, my dear. By how the clock ticks, it looks like time is not on your side. That pretty face can only take you so far, and you're aging every second. Such a waste." She lifted her glass to her lips.

Sabina's face burned. She had never been kissed, not even touched for that matter, and who was this woman to speak? Mrs. Daniel had gone through seven husbands, and each one either died or divorced her. The urge to throw that truth in the woman's face was strong, but the clicking of the clock was more than enough of a reliever.

"I'm very sorry, Mrs. Daniel," Sabina said.

Not.

"I really must be going now. Help yourself to some more champagne." Sabina waved over one of the waiters and turned around. She was fighting the smile on her face, but she couldn't hold it back any longer.

Sabina ran through the crowd, bumping into individuals as she passed. Sabina issued quiet apologies as she went, dutifully playing the part of "perfect daughter." Her heels clacked against the marble floor, and her feet burned with exertion. Even the pain shooting through her toes would not stop her triumph.

Sabina rounded the corridor, sliding into the wall as she did so. She shrieked with giddiness, laughing so hard she thought she would lose breath.

Her shoes continued pounding as she moved, so Sabina did what any sensible woman would do. She ripped them off. They clattered to the ground with a bang.

She reveled in the way the coldness of the floor seeped into her bare feet, and her smile spread even wider. Sabina was feeling undone in the absence of the people her parents adored. She began to yank the bobby pins that held her hair in place until they fell away, her hair cascading down onto her shoulders. With stabbing pain in her toes, she continued running, opening the doors to the garden outside.

It was nice, quiet, and different than what she was so accustomed to. Solidarity wasn't something she often experienced. Not in between piano lessons, theater lessons, family history lessons, and the many other things her family wanted her to do.

Her safe haven wasn't the theater like her parents adored.

It wasn't the mall like her academy friends enjoyed.

It was never what anyone expected, and that was the key.

Her safe haven was never tied to what anyone else thought of her or where anyone else expected she would be. It was wherever the wind took her.

That was her safe space.

Her feet lingered in the dirt. Sabina let the smell of the earth dance in her nostrils and the air kiss her skin. She hiked her dress up by the ends and began doing what she always did in the backyard where no one would witness.

Dance.

The wind seemed to have its own song in mind while her feet moved. Her hips swayed to a silent melody only she could hear. Her hair was ferociously unkempt, and she adored it. Sabina loved the way freedom tasted on her parted lips as rain began to fall. The water droplets stained her tongue and her face. She welcomed it gladly. She ushered in the idea of something so beautiful and uncaged, a part of her that she never bore to anyone else. Not even her family.

As she fell against the canvas of freshly crushed grass, dew tickling her scalp, she began to dream. She dreamed of a world far away from the one she knew, a world where expectations were only what she deemed worthy and not what others yearned from her.

She dreamed until her body stilled in the silence, sleep overtaking her.

Dew dripped softly onto her parted lips.

The cold wetness stirred her, and she shifted her position.

Again, it dripped, and she licked her lips, letting the moisture rest on her tongue.

She heard it before she saw it, shoes rustling against the grass.

When she opened her eyes, the sun stung. A golden haze of brightness made everything blur. Even the figure leaning over her was unrecognizable.

Until she heard the soft laughter.

The butler had found her.

"Blakely," she whined. "Why are you here?"

The blurring figure shook his head. Well, at least she assumed it was his head shaking. It was hard for her to tell with this unreliable vision issue.

"I think the real question is, why are *you* here? It must have been quite an evening for you...here out underneath the trees."

"You must know that I love the gardens," she sputtered.

Words were hard to think of with this light in her face. Shielding her eyes, she peeked up through her fingers. There it was, the unmistakable grin he always wore when amused.

"You might have mentioned it a dozen or so times during your youth," he remarked so matter-of-factly that she narrowed her eyes.

"If you're here to make me the object of your jokes, you can go right inside." Sabina pursed her lips at him, daring him to say more.

"No jokes here, madam, especially not for you. The gathering last night was rather large, and shall I say, your presence here definitely did not go unnoticed."

The statement might as well have left her in a chokehold.

Sabina sat upright, dizziness accompanying her. She hardly registered it, her focus still on what was spoken.

"The guests saw me?" She was able to squeak those words out at least. "How many? It couldn't have been that bad, could it?"

Blakely stared off at the trees.

"Oh, no," she uttered, pressing a hand to her forehead. "Where are they?"

He gestured to the back doors she exited from earlier. "The kitchen."

He gave her a reassuring smile as she rose to her feet. Blakely knew her parents as well as she did.

"Lead the way, then." The words tasted like chalk in her mouth.

Blakely went first.

Despite the slow pace, Sabina wrestled with the impending sense of dread that sat in her stomach nor the realization that her parents wouldn't be as understanding as he was.

Even still, she marched on, knowing fully the reprimanding that awaited her.

There was no sound in the kitchen as Sabina entered the room, shutting the back door behind her. Blakely shot her an encouraging smile before retreating down the adjacent hallway, leaving Sabina to face her doom on her own.

Her palms became slick with sweat, and Sabina could still taste droplets of rain on her tongue as she tried to find the right words to speak. Her brain fumbled with any response that would have been justified before blurting, "I didn't mean to fall asleep outside."

Her father was over the stove, his back to her as he focused on preparing some sort of elaborate breakfast. The morning after a big gathering, her father relieved the chefs. He viewed it as his way of destressing after a long evening. Sabina watched his movements, trying to give her heart time to calm down and stop beating erratically.

Her mother sat at the counter, sipping on a cup of coffee, her body angled in Sabina's direction. Slowly, she set the cup down. The sound alone caused the blood to rush in Sabina's ears.

"Blakely found you in the garden," her mother remarked, as if Sabina had never spoken. She tucked a strand of hair behind her ear and lifted her gaze. The emerald in her eyes darkened, and Sabina's heart skipped a beat.

"Like I said, I didn't mean to fall asleep," Sabina rushed. Her cheeks felt like they were on fire, and her hands gathered more sweat. Cautiously, she moved to the dining table, reminding herself there was no reason to worry and that she would make her parents understand.

They have to.

As soon as she sat in the chair, Sabina took another breath. "I truly am sorry."

Her father turned around then, putting a stack of perfectly made pancakes on an empty plate. He shoveled eggs and bacon on the side before handing the plate to Sabina's mother. She took it with grace, and if it wasn't for the tension in her shaking hands and the earlier expression, Sabina would never have known her mother was upset.

Her father grabbed another plate and began toppling it with food before he sat down in the other chair at the counter. The tension was so palpable one could cut a knife with it. "Apologizing doesn't change what happened. The guests still saw you in the garden, asleep like a fool. What good does that do for our reputation? None." He stabbed a section of egg with such force that Sabina waited for the prongs to cut through the plate, but everything was fine.

"Surely you can understand that things happen?" Sabina was incredulous.

There was another stab at the plate, and her father shoveled more food in his mouth. "Understanding that things happen is a necessity I can justify under certain circumstances, but what you did was no accident. You deliberately chose to sleep in the garden, *knowing* that we had guests there. What did you expect, some sort of congratulations for being idiotic? You will not get that from me or your mother."

The jabs hit her one by one, stinging her eyes with fresh tears. Sabina willed them down, refusing to show any kind of weakness. In this atmosphere, that would only make things worse.

"I didn't mean to fall asleep," Sabina repeated. "It was an accident."

Her father stopped his erratic movements, letting the fork fall to the plate with a *clang*. He turned in the chair, angling his body toward Sabina. "An accident? You went outside knowing you were tired, correct?"

"Yes, but—"

Sabina's father held up a hand. "You went outside knowing you were exhausted and chose to stay there, correct?"

"You're not really understanding what happened." Sabina's eyes were daggers, but her father paid no mind.

"Oh, I think I understand *perfectly*."

Sabina didn't miss the biting in his tone, and she willed herself to be silent, not wanting to make it worse.

"You thought of yourself, like you always do, leaving your mother and I to clean up after you. We had a deal—"

"And I upheld it!" Sabina shouted, her limbs shaking. "Why can't you understand that I do what you ask? I'm still human, so please, just recognize that I try at least. Is that so hard for you two to comprehend?"

At that, her mother scoffed. "Being human is understandable. Falling asleep in the garden when we're already under scrutiny and losing sponsors as it is due to Mrs. Daniel and her dramatic whims is another story entirely."

Sabina could barely control the seething in her bones. The comment flew from her lips before Sabina could even retrieve it. "You act like you've never made a mistake in your life."

A flash of darkness crossed over her father's face, and he rose to a stand, his food forgotten. "How dare you disrespect your mother this way? Go to your room, Sabina," he ordered, nostrils flaring.

"Why can't you just understand—"

"I said, go to your room!" The noise reverberated off of the walls, shaking the lights on the chandelier hanging above Sabina's head.

Her heart held dread as she stood on shaky feet. The tears were close again, and she told herself to hold it together for a few more moments. *I only have to keep it together until I reach my bedroom.*

Without so much as a nod, Sabina walked proudly, the exact opposite of how she felt. She focused on the color of the floor, willing her eyes to latch onto whatever minuscule detail she could until she reached her bedroom.

It wasn't until she was in the comfort of her own room, alone, that she let the tears flow, more than she thought humanly possible.

CHAPTER THREE

HANNAH

WATER SLOSHED IN THE SINK as rough hands moved, scrubbing remnants of food off of the plate.

Hannah watched with pursed lips. Would he be upset?

"Frank told me what you did." Christopher's eyes never wavered from his task at the kitchen sink, his back straight as an arrow.

"And for once you don't have any comment?" Hannah leaned back against the doorframe, letting her head rest on the door with chipping paint. It had been years since the door had had a decent coating, but Christopher paid no mind.

"You expect me to have something good to say about you punching the lights out of someone?" Christopher huffed, shaking his head. "I think you have me confused with another parent."

Hannah bit her tongue and closed her eyes.

He was still scrubbing away, the sound like chalk in Hannah's ears. "Now you have no comment. That's a first."

Christopher's words skidded against her skin like fire, and Hannah let out a breath. His attitude was forthcoming, sure, but it didn't mean she had deserved it.

"You don't know anything about what happened."

Suddenly, the scrubbing stopped. Christopher turned halfway, a flame barely flickering in his gaze. "I don't need to know what happened. What I need is for your behavior to change." His eyes only stayed locked on her for a second before they went back to the sink, and there he was, scrubbing the dishes again.

That was how it always was. Always some task to do, along with one demand or another.

"It could've been in self-defense," Hannah argued.

Christopher barely budged, shaking his head slightly. "I'm not stupid, Hannah. You might be my daughter, but don't doubt my sixth sense. It wasn't protection as much as I suspect revenge. Is that right?"

Guilt pricked her stomach like the tendrils of a cactus, but Hannah held her own. She refused to show her father any kind of weakness. He was like some sort of hound with an uncanny ability to sniff out lies, probably because he had enough practice over the years to recognize when Hannah was being crafty. He was also a cop.

"I will neither confirm nor deny these accusations," she said, shrugging nonchalantly, ignoring the tightness in her gut.

"No need to play word games with me. *I know.*"

A flash of panic ebbed underneath her façade, but Hannah pushed it away. She couldn't let him have the upper hand, so she did what she did best. Feigned innocence.

"Oh?"

"Yes. Frank told me exactly what happened. You and those hoodlums went to Derek Moore's house and asked him for beer. When he refused to give you what you wanted and got handsy, Tony shoved him to the ground, and you beat the living daylights out of him. Tony joined in until he apologized."

"I don't see anything wrong with that statement," Hannah replied. "Derek was a jerk. He got what was coming to him. And don't call the guys hoodlums."

"Do you think I care that you defended yourself?" Christopher completely ignored her last statement. "Of course, I want you to defend yourself, but—"

"But you want us to go about it the 'right way.' I know. You've said this a million times, but what does it even mean?"

"It means I don't want you taking vengeance into your hands. That's why I'm here, to help." As if by cue, her father turned around, his gaze gentle.

It wasn't until Hannah peered closer that she noticed just how worn his eyes were. All of him, for that matter.

Christopher used to be different, and she remembered a time when her dad had laughed more than he corrected. But all of that was gone now, the only trace of who he used to be etched in the lines of his eyes and in the wrinkles of his cheeks. His tan coloring was the only thing that had remained the same as he'd aged. With dark hair turning to silver and frowns in place of what used to be boisterous laughter, ageing had ultimately altered him before her eyes. Hannah just hadn't noticed until now.

Christopher was a strong man, a caring man who sometimes let his protectiveness get too far. Hannah usually appreciated the sentiment, but here he was, calling Tony some kind of troublemaker. Tony was her family too.

"Just because you're a cop doesn't mean I need you to fight my battles." Hannah let the statement hang in the air, watching as his back tensed.

"And just because you're almost eighteen doesn't mean I can't still worry," he whispered.

Hannah had barely heard his words over the running water, but all the same, a lump formed in her throat. She almost felt guilty for what she was going to say next. Almost.

"Well. You're going to have to stop."

Hands stopped moving, and her father held his breath. "What do you mean?"

"I'm taking a trip with Tony and the others. There's nothing you can do to stop me."

"Trip?" her father questioned. "What kind of trip?"

"Derek's father's condition to not press charges was for us to go away for a bit, to give some space. He thinks by staying away, we'll get out of trouble."

The plates fell into the soapy water, and Christopher turned fully to face Hannah. "That's exactly why they should stay away, not you. This is your home."

"It might be my home, but I need to get away. I can't just abandon them—"

"They're nothing but trouble for you!" Christopher's voice rose an octave, and Hannah watched her father's warring emotions flicker in his eyes.

"They're my family," Hannah said. Heat in her stomach bubbled to the surface, and this time she couldn't contain it.

"Whatever you call them, you're not going." Christopher stepped away from the sink and ran a hand over his face. "I'll call Frank, make him change his mind. He has to hear me out. This is ridiculous."

"It's my decision," Hannah stated, her voice cold. "You can't control what I do."

"It's my job to keep you safe." His voice cracked on the last word.

Hannah could feel her father losing bits and pieces of himself yet again. It had been happening for years throughout these arguments. Hannah couldn't stand by and let it continue.

"You can't make me stay," Hannah reiterated.

Christopher's face crumbled. He let out a sigh, closing his eyes. Under the dim lighting of the kitchen, Hannah swore she saw something glistening under his lashes.

"I can't force you to stay. You're grown, as you've said. Go. Be my guest. There's nothing I say that will make you do otherwise." Christopher swallowed, and his face became like a wall. It was so solid that Hannah couldn't read him anymore.

For one night, the dishes stayed in the sink, and her father retreated to the bedroom upstairs. He left Hannah in the kitchen with thoughts that wouldn't turn off. Hannah stared outside the kitchen window, willing herself to breathe through her nostrils and swallow whatever emotion was tumbling in her gut.

She had made her choice, and they would all be better for it.

The van held the constant stench of stale cheese puffs, salsa, and fermented beer. There was also the constant farting in the backseat, but that wasn't her doing.

"Again, Will?" Tony's hand clenched on the steering wheel.

The smell hit Hannah soon after, and she scrunched up her nose.

"I can't help that I'm gassy," Will remarked lazily. His arm dangled outside of the window, his fingers intertwining with the wind.

"Did you have to be an idiot and eat the burrito with beans?" Hannah whipped her head around to shoot Will a death glare. Still on edge from the previous night, Hannah felt herself lashing out more than normal. She hoped no one noticed.

Will laughed. "Hannah, Hannah, Hannah. We both know I can never say no to beans in any form." At this very moment, he let another one rip, and everyone groaned.

"That is it," Marcus let out a growl from the backseat and swore under his breath. "I don't care how on schedule we are. We drop him off at the next gas station."

"Ah, yep. That's five dollars in the swear jar," Hannah protested from the passenger seat. "Go on now. Hand it over." She outstretched her hand with a mischievous grin on her lips.

Marcus mumbled under his breath and handed over the cash.

Will was in a fit of hysterics.

Tony looked back at him through the rearview mirror. "One more pipe out of you, and I actually might take Marc up on his offer."

The chip bag fell from Will's fingers, and his face sagged. "You're kidding," he blubbered. "You can't. I'm an important member of this group."

No one said anything.

"I am," he whined, banging his right fist on the cupholder.

Trevor was the only one who wasn't responsive. He was always the last to be aware of what was going on. Hannah didn't mind, though. Neither did anyone else. It was just who Trevor was—reserved, guarded, and snarky on a good day.

"Could you stop acting like a baby for five seconds? It was a joke." Tony sighed.

"Well, I don't see anyone else making jokes about dropping someone else off at a gas station." Will's southern twang came out.

Hannah cracked a smile. Whenever Will got mad, his accent decided to come out and say hello.

"Maybe they wouldn't offer to drop you off somewhere if you weren't acting so stupid," Trevor piped up.

Ah. There it was, the delayed response that always seemed to creep in at some point. So, he *was* listening.

Hannah peered over to look at Trevor and noticed he had one headphone behind his ear. That explained things.

The van came to a stop, and Hannah turned around to face the front again. The bright red light shined at her, and she leaned her head back against the seat, letting out a breath.

A hand laid on her shoulder, and she looked over. Tony's eyebrows were creased. She realized the meaning quickly. She had seen it enough on his face to know that he was concerned.

"What's with the long face?" Hannah blurted, giving him the side eye.

"You've been quiet since we left. I'm worried about you." Tony erred on the side of honesty. With Hannah, there was no point in lying. She was too good at reading people.

"There's nothing to worry about," she replied, waving his comment away. "I'm fine."

Tony's face didn't change.

"I'm *fine*." She gave a little smile, but he clearly wasn't buying it. "Why do you keep staring? For crying out loud, look at the road."

The light had turned green already.

He shook his head at her, letting out a breath. The van started moving again.

"What?" Hannah's eyes narrowed. In them was a challenge. She pursed her lips.

"I think you should stop goofing around, pick up the phone, and call him." Tony gave her a side glance.

"Oooh!" Will's voice rose an octave as he put on his best imitation of a female. "A phone call? To a male? Hannah has a boyfriend! Hannah has a boyfriend!" He continued singing like a child until he saw Hannah and her facial expression.

"Did we ever talk about whether hitting him cost us money in the jar?" Hannah pondered aloud.

"Hmmm." Marcus scratched his head. "Nope. We didn't."

"I don't think we did," Trevor murmured.

"Fine by me," Marcus said, raising his fist.

"Not the face, not the face. Anything but my face. Girls won't like me if you hit the face!" Will's squealing from the back seat only egged things on further.

"Punch buggy," Marcus shouted. His fist collided with Will's stomach, and the loudest groan filled the vehicle.

"Can you guys knock it off back there?" Tony growled.

Instantly, the noise in the back quieted.

The silence was deafening, and for a brief second, Hannah wished Will would make a stupid comment or do something, anything to stop Tony from bringing it up again. She already had enough guilt for how the conversation with her dad had ended, and Tony didn't even know what happened.

"Like I was saying," Tony said. "I seriously think you should call him."

Hannah didn't look at him. She let her eyes trail out the window, where lonely roads whipped far behind them.

"Hannah?"

She closed her eyes. Maybe that would stop his incessant talking.

"You don't have to look at me, but you do have to listen, okay?"

She still said nothing. Could he not take a hint?

"Whatever issues you had, whatever you said, or he said... just call him. I know it seems like a hard thing to do, but I've been there."

Hannah rolled her eyes.

"I'm not trying to press your buttons. I'm just trying to get you to talk to me. To talk to someone. But especially him. He won't be mad at you forever. You won't be mad at him forever. Right now, in the heat of the moment, it can feel that way, and it's easy to let pride tell you not to apologize. To keep being right."

He had no idea of what her father had said. If he knew, would he still be so open to amends?

"But you never know what can happen," Tony continued. "Life can be a terrible thing sometimes, and it doesn't play fair—"

"Just because you told your father you hated him an hour before he died doesn't mean that my issues are anything like yours," Hannah interjected.

The words flew from her lips before she could grasp them. They settled in the air, a taunting reminder that what was done was done.

Even Will's munching stopped.

The disbelief registered on Tony's face first, and then his cheeks locked. His face became hard, and he turned back to the road.

Hannah stammered, trying to think of words. An apology. Something.

But that didn't happen.

Tony merely turned on the radio and increased the volume.

Music filled the car, drowning everything else out.

Hannah thought over the last words she said to her father, and she couldn't help but wonder if maybe things would be better if she didn't speak at all.

CHAPTER FOUR

CAMMIE

A DAY HAD PASSED, AND THERE was still no sign of Caelan.

Cammie knew it was stupid to wish to see him, as he had only been in the shop once, but apologizing weighed heavy on her heart.

As many customers inquired about books, she wondered if the mysterious man would ever come back. She replayed their conversation over and over, as she often did when she made a mistake in some shape or form, as if that would magically project him here.

"You've been zoned out all day." Madeline's voice caught her out of the trance. "You okay?"

Cammie nodded, but her heart wasn't in it. Her eyes continued to fixate on the door.

"You keep staring off in the distance. I'm not even sure why. It's not like anyone in particular ever comes in here—" Madeline paused. "You're not seriously waiting for that man, are you?"

Cammie's face turned pink.

"Cammie!" Madeline's voice lifted higher. "I thought you said he was married? He's practically forty!"

"He is."

That was all it took for the suggestive smirk to show on Madeline's otherwise calm face.

"Oh, it's not like that."

Cammie hated how fast her words came out. They made her sound practically desperate.

"'It's not like that,'" Madeline mocked, giving a little wink. "There's no shame."

"I'm not going after this man," Cammie assured. "I just want to apologize."

Madeline wiggled her eyebrows.

"You're disgusting," Cammie added.

"I know." The sickly-sweet tone rolled off of Madeline's lips like honey as she puckered up to blow a kiss.

Just then, the bell dinged. It was back to serious business.

The audible gasp from Madeline made Cammie want to shrink in the corner of the room.

There, back at the door, was the man Cammie had been searching for.

This time, Caelan donned a black button down and khakis, with a long peacoat. Though it was summer, Cammie marveled at how the outfit actually looked good. No one else was as odd and seemingly put together as he was. It was fascinating.

"Mr. Caelan." Cammie spoke first, and the simple word made his face erupt with glee.

"So good to see you again." There was no hint of bitterness in his voice.

Cammie hoped he had forgotten their previous exchange.

"Was there something I could get for you?" She was hesitant to ask, afraid of stepping over glass.

But to her surprise, he shook his head. "I didn't need any-thing. I just wanted to stop by and talk to you."

"Talk to me?" she sputtered. "But why? Is something wrong?"

"Nothing's wrong." Caelan smiled. He spoke with his hands, animated, but there was some foreboding in his face. His lips twitched slightly.

"Are you sure?" Cammie didn't want to press the issue, yet she found herself still asking.

"Well, there is one thing. It was about the other day when we met. I didn't mean to frighten you by running off. You just asked a very uncomfortable question about my wife, and I don't fault you for that. It's just hard to talk about. I'm sure you know what it's like to lose someone close to you." His eyes grew somber, and his lip slightly sagged.

The emotion of loss was clear in his gaze. It reminded Cammie of her mother's eyes when Cammie had found out her father had died before she was born. Her mom talked of him often at one point. For a long while now, though, it was as if she preferred to hide him in a closet in her soul, a place where no one could see her pain. While her mom poured herself into writing romances, Cammie kept her father close in her heart, even if she didn't fully know him.

"You understand," he remarked. "I can see it in your eyes. That same familiar feeling."

"It was my dad," she explained. "He passed before I was born."

Caelan's face tightened. "I see. That must have been really hard on your mother."

She nodded. Why would it not be? Her mom's entire world had changed in a matter of minutes.

"It was hard on me too." Caelan's face still had the somber quality.

The shared knowledge of loss made her feel connected to the stranger in front of her, but she wasn't sure what else to say. Not to mention, Madeline was sitting right across from her, wearing a devilish smirk.

As if he could read the girl's mind, he turned to Madeline. "I have no interest in preying on a young girl. You two are old enough to be my children, for crying out loud. If I were you, I'd focus on your job instead of perverting romance for your satisfaction. You both have a lot of growing up to do, but I suggest you be the first before your attitude gets you in trouble."

With the pointed glance he was giving her, Madeline couldn't help but avert her eyes. Her neck became red as she crossed over to a section of books, far away from the conversation.

"I'm sorry." Cammie sighed.

"For her?" Caelan chuckled. "Young adult girls are nothing to be worried about. Her head is getting away from her."

"I just mean everything that happened the other day. I still feel really bad about your wife. Bringing her up, I mean. You apologized in some way. I feel I should too."

He gave a small smile. "You were merely curious. It's not a problem."

Cammie gave a slight shrug.

"You're young and bound to make impulsive statements. I'd imagine my daughter would have been exactly as you are—curious and insightful. It's nice to imagine her like that."

Cammie noted his tense when he spoke of this daughter of his.

Caelan continued before she could respond. "In case you're wondering, my daughter, well, daughters," he corrected, "are gone. They died not much longer after my wife did."

She tried to respond, but all that her body allowed her to do was open her mouth. Her manners lagged. She fumbled for words, at a loss on how to be a comfort in sight of this new revelation.

"Maybe that was too much information. I apologize." He closed his eyes and started to head back toward the door.

"Wait," she called out. "No, it's fine. It's not offensive at all. It just sounds like you've had a lot happen in life. It sounds like you've had a lot of adventures...but a lot of heartache."

He stopped his strides and turned halfway. His expression was solemn but in a way that only made Cammie surer that he had lived fully, enough to be close to both concepts.

"Well, you can't have one without the other." The chuckle rang in the room against the backdrop of the air conditioner.

"Would you be able to tell me your adventures sometime? I'm sure you have a lot going on. I'd love to hear about what your life was like."

One eyebrow was raised, and Cammie couldn't help but wonder if she'd assumed wrong.

Maybe she had made a mistake.

"If you have time this afternoon," he said, "I can meet you at the little café down the road. We can get a muffin or a scone, and I can tell you all about it. As long as you promise to tell me when I am boring you."

"Deal." Cammie couldn't hide the smile.

A chance to learn exciting information, maybe even something she could use or feel inspired by—that was her motivation. Nothing big or exciting truly ever happened in this town she lived in all her life.

But maybe now that was changing.

Caelan smiled, giving her a nod, and then he was out the door again, the little bell dinging.

Cammie couldn't help but giggle.

Things really are changing, after all.

Sweat glistened on her palms as she rubbed them together. The persistent chatter of those around her did give her some relief. It meant she wasn't alone.

The longer she waited for Caelan to return, the more her stomach started to sink.

She didn't know this guy or anything about him. He could be a mass murderer or simply a stalker.

Her intuition on people was usually correct, but she couldn't help but wonder had she made the right choice?

The scolding of a mother caught in Cammie's ears, and for a moment, every worry dissipated.

"More ice cream," the child cried, yanking her mother's leg.

The mother shook her head, giving the child peppered kisses on her scalp, an attempt to soothe. After a few minutes, the tantrum calmed, and the mother and child walked away.

The simple act caused a lump in Cammie's throat, sudden tears leaking out of the corner of her eyes. Cammie swiped at them, a ball of anger throbbing in her gut. She always managed to cry in public, and that was something she hated.

Caelan appeared, a cup and a mug in hand. He set the cup down in front of her, and Cammie almost squealed in delight. She loved iced coffee.

"Is this good enough for you?" he asked, gesturing to her cup.

Cammie was too busy stabbing the straw inside the peep hole and taking long sips. She gave a long sigh.

Caelan chuckled. "I take that as a satisfactory answer."

Cammie nodded and went back to sipping.

"You must really love iced coffee." He tilted his head as he watched her, a small smile on his face.

"What's wrong?" Cammie stopped sipping long enough to peer at him.

"I've just never seen someone devour a drink like you just did. You're almost one third done. I'm still working on mine." As if to prove a point, he took a slow sip of his coffee.

"Sorry," she replied, the sheepish grin on her face. "It's just been such a long time since I've been here. I've missed it. I haven't come here for a while. Not since my mom—" Her words lodged in her throat. A million memories flooded her mind, and she went back to sipping her drink.

"Is everything okay?"

She turned her gaze back to the register. It was easier to focus on the guy taking orders than it was to actually talk and make conversation, especially with everything hitting her all at once.

The little bell by the register dinged as he called out the order number. The sound was shrill, clanging against her nostrils. "Order number three!" The sharpness of it made her clench her teeth, and she grimaced.

Too many noises blended together as Caelan's talking became apparent. She couldn't tell who he was talking to. She was too busy trying to calm the storm in her skull. The cashier's words thrummed in her ears. Every hair on her arms stood upright. Her vision blurred against her wishes, despite how hard she fought it. She shut her eyes, willing it away.

And then, in her mind's eye, she was overtaken.

"Order number three," the young barista called out lazily. He wasn't nearly as enthusiastic as the last time they'd been there.

"You heard him, Cammie." The teenage boy sitting next to her grinned wildly, shoving her arm. "Time to get the donuts."

"And iced coffee," Cammie reminded him.

"And iced coffee," he repeated, rolling his eyes. He wasn't agitated, though he was very good at pretending he was. "I have no
idea why you even drink that stuff. All the sugar, it'll make you
sick." His face twisted in disgust.

Cammie merely shoved him. "You would know, wouldn't
you? With all the candy you steal from the jar at my house?" She
gave a mischievous grin.

"I do not!" he exclaimed, his face growing a particular shade
of red.

The bickering continued, overlapping, until no sound was
recognizable at all.

"Cammie?" Caelan's voice was the only one she heard
now. Everything else was gone.

The boy was gone.

When she opened her eyes, she didn't have to look
around to conclude anything. It was simply obvious. Everyone
was staring.

Her stomach coiled with bile as things came into focus.
She couldn't rid herself of those images. She had never seen the
boy before, didn't even know his name, and here her brain was,
fabricating him as memory.

Her coffee had made a trail down the table, and Caelan
was now crouched beside her, one hand on her arm as he used
the other to hand her a napkin. He was doing his best to wipe
up the scene, but the damage was already done.

Whatever had happened, she couldn't stay here.

Home. I need to go home.

Her labored breathing echoed against the silence of the
café. She stood, her chair scraping up against the floor. Her
bones twinged, and all she could do was try to find the exit she
knew so well.

With stuff in hand, she marched to her destination, even as she heard the footsteps behind her.

The chatter resumed while she exited out the door, and she was grateful that all eyes had stopped viewing her as the main attraction.

But there was one person who wasn't included in the bunch.

"I just want to go home, okay?" She turned around fully, crossing her arms over her chest.

"What happened back there?" There was no falseness. He actually seemed to care.

"I'm not feeling that well. I'm just going to go home and lay down for a bit. Maybe we can have a rain check?"

"Of course." He nodded. "I can at least take you home?"

"No!" It came out with more force than she had intended. "No," she said again softly. "I'm fine. I just need a few minutes."

"Okay, well, maybe we can meet again once you're feeling better?"

She nodded, but she knew she wouldn't be seeing him or anyone else for a while.

They said their goodbyes, and she walked on toward home, leaving Caelan on the street.

But the more she walked, the more she wrestled.

It felt like a dream. It *was* a dream, she told herself. She repeated it the entire way home.

A dream. A daydream.

Maybe if she said it enough times, she would be able to erase the one feeling settling in her gut.

That even though she didn't know him, it felt like a memory.

CHAPTER FIVE

SABINA

T HE HOUSE WAS QUIET. THERE wasn't any noise stirring, except for the music coming from the speakers in her bedroom.

Her fingers clutched the paintbrush. Strokes followed with precision. Her eyebrows were knit in concentration, and her hands seemed to have a mind of their own. They flowed in time with the music.

It took seconds for her to register the rapping at the door. When she was in the trance, she often didn't get back to reality until much later.

She set the brush down, determined to get back to the painting before nightfall.

Blakely stood on the other side of the door, the phone receiver in hand.

"Is it important?" Sabina asked, peering around Blakely. *No sign of them.*

"A friend of yours from the South, she says, and to answer your unasked question, your parents are not here."

Her face fell at the last comment, but she took the phone anyway. "Thank you."

He gave a curt nod and let the door close halfway, leaving enough space to peer out into the hallway.

Sabina raised the phone to her ear and walked over to the stereo, turning the dial down. "Hello?"

There was shuffling on the other end of the line. "Hey, hi…hey."

"Are you running?" Sabina moved to the bed and sat down, listening intently.

"No. Definitely not." The rapid breathing continued.

Sabina rolled her eyes. *Of course, she isn't. Totally believable.*

"Okay, so maybe I am. What does it matter?" The sound of a door slamming resounded through the speaker.

Sabina flinched. "Are you okay, Cammie?"

There was more shuffling and then for a moment total silence. "I honestly don't know."

"So, talk to me."

This was Sabina's usual response whenever Cammie freaked out. It had happened a lot over the years. Helping Cammie usually involved chicken nuggets and maybe a cup of ice cream. Possibly two cups, if it was bad enough.

"You would tell me if I was crazy, right?"

Sabina took a pause. *Where is she going with this?* "I would. You know I would…"

"Something strange happened today, and I don't know what to think about it."

Sabina twirled a strand of hair around her index finger. *One, two, three.* With each pass her finger made, the little nervous bubble in her stomach seemed to expand. "What do you mean?" she asked.

"It felt almost like a memory, but it didn't." Cammie's voice seemed far off and distant.

Sabina's confusion only grew. "I'm not sure I understand…"

The noises on the other end of the line became louder—loud thumps and a huffed sigh.

"Even if you don't understand, I can try to explain it, but honestly, I don't understand it myself. Maybe I'm just going insane."

Sabina shut her eyes, pinching the bridge of her nose. "Why do you do that?"

"Do what?" Her tone was innocent enough, but the shield wouldn't fool Sabina. It never did.

"You doubt yourself. You're so pessimistic all the time, and there's no reason for you to. It's okay to have feelings. It's okay to make mistakes."

There was no response on the other end of the line.

"Cammie?"

"Yeah…" It was barely a whisper.

Sabina wondered if she said the right thing. Maybe Cammie wouldn't talk now, but she had to keep trying.

"What is it?" Sabina prompted.

"Nothing," was the murmur through the phone.

"Be honest, please. What did I say?"

"It's just easy for you to say that. Ever since we were kids, your life has been perfect. Great parents, great school. You're pretty much the definition of 'put together,' so telling me it's okay to make mistakes…it's hilarious, especially when you haven't made any."

Cammie's assumption of her life was a stone to the face. Cammie might as well have stabbed Sabina with a knife. It was the facade she was good at, that was the truth, but it was hard to agree with unknown lies spoken from the mouth of her dearest friend, especially when the bedroom door across from hers had been shut for an entire day. The one mistake she'd made was the reason her parents were avoiding her entirely, and it was hard to feel perfect when her life was really anything but.

"I guess you're right."

She isn't rang loud and clear, but Sabina swallowed it down.

"I didn't even mean to bother you with this," Cammie said. "It's just been a strange day. Ever since I met the man in the bookstore, actually."

"A man? Is he around our age?"

Cammie never talked about boys, not as far as Sabina could remember. Cammie was a lone ranger, just books and all. It was a fact she was proud of, and Sabina found it to be quirky albeit sometimes a little isolating.

"No, he's older. His wife passed away a long time ago, I think. He was coming to ask for a book of fairy tales, and then we just got to talking and we went to get coffee."

"Wait," Sabina replied. "He took you out for coffee, and you just met him. He's older than us, right? Why would he even need to take you out for coffee?" When the words left her lips, she wanted nothing more than to snatch them back and disappear.

"I'm not such a terrible person that people don't want to be my friend." Cammie's shrill tone snapping back made the guilt wrap around Sabina's throat.

"I didn't mean it like that," Sabina reassured. "I just meant that it's better to be careful and safe than to be accommodating and sorry, and you know I never think you're terrible. I've never once thought that. There's the negative self-talk again. Stop thinking that way."

Cammie let out a breath, and everything was silent.

"Is it your mom again?"

"You could say that. Maybe that's what happened with the image I saw. Maybe I'm just getting to be too lonely that I'm imagining people that don't exist. It makes sense, considering my mom has vacated the premises pretty much twenty-four seven."

"What do you mean 'seeing people that don't exist?'"

"It was just something that happened at the coffee shop with Caelan. I had a mental flash, probably because, you know, I've been isolated for so long."

Sabina wanted to ask more, but Cammie was too fast.

"Now that I think about it," Cammie mused, "I haven't really drunk enough water. That could be it too. Dehydration can cause delusions. Lack of sleep seems like another possibility. The last time I truly slept was when Hannah and I went to your parents' bungalow in Florida. It's been busy here. I wish I could go back. It was amazing."

"I can't believe it's been a few months since then. It feels longer." A gnawing grew in Sabina's stomach, and she quieted.

"Hey, what's wrong?"

"I just haven't heard from Hannah lately. She kind of disappeared after the trip. Have you heard from her?" Sabina asked.

"Well, that's strange."

The pause lingered a bit too long for Sabina's liking.

"I'm sure everything is fine," Cammie added. "I talked to her last week."

"Oh." The disappointment fell down harder than Sabina thought it would. "She must text you a lot then?"

"About as much as you'd expect her to, with how busy she is, I guess. Why? She doesn't text you the same?"

"Oh, no, she does." The lie dripped from Sabina's mouth like honey. "I just wasn't sure if she did the same for you."

Another one, her conscience mocked. *You're really getting good at this.*

"I'm just happy to know that things are good between you guys," Cammie said. "I remember how rough it used to be."

If you only knew.

"I'm happy it isn't that way, too."

The sound of a quiet ding echoed in the background, and Sabina shifted the phone to her other ear.

"Oh, pizza's here." The excitement in Cammie's voice was palpating. Her voice even rose an octave. "Could I call you later?"

"Yeah, sure." Sabina forced a grin. "Go ahead. Have fun and eat so much that you get heartburn."

"Isn't that a dream?" The breathy sigh actually made Sabina smile, for real this time. "I promise I'll call you later, okay?"

"If things get worse, please do. Oh, and, Cammie?"

"Yes?" she asked.

"Please be careful with that man. Things are dangerous enough in the world as they are. Don't put yourself in harm's way just to be nice."

"I won't, I promise. Thank you for talking to me."

"Not a—" Before the sentence even finished, she could hear absolute silence. Cammie was already gone. "—problem."

As Sabina sat on the bed, her mind a whirlwind of thoughts, she pulled up messages and began typing. Her brain followed after her heart, and before she even knew what she was doing, the message had been sent.

She hadn't heard from Hannah in several months, and this was the calamity that could only put more distance between the ever-growing divide.

That night, Sabina tossed and turned. Sleep was a luxury far beyond her reach. When daylight hit, though, only one thought was on her mind.

There was no reply about space, no message about being apologetic. Nothing resembling that their friendship of almost ten years meant anything.

It wasn't the tone that broke her. Nor was it the choice of words.

What caused her heart to shatter was the mere fact that Hannah had decided not to respond at all.

CHAPTER SIX

HANNAH

THE PHONE BUZZED IN HER hand, the vibrating noise rumbling throughout the van.

Otherwise, it was relatively quiet.

Trevor and Marcus were asleep, and their snores were playing a wild chorus.

Hannah peered into the passenger side mirror to where Tony was pumping gas. He was behind her, hair flying back in the wind. It gave him a messy look, and with the set of his jaw and how his eyes were creased, one would say he was at war with the world.

And then, they locked right with hers through the mirror.

Her face flushed red, and he immediately averted his eyes. It wasn't the world he was at war with, then.

Not anymore.

"Got a hot date? Never heard your phone buzz like that," Will piped up from the back so suddenly that it made her jump.

"It isn't a date," she retorted. "I don't date."

"Sure you don't," Will prodded.

"I don't. Now leave it alone."

"Just speaking what's on everyone's mind," Will added with his signature smirk.

"That's most definitely *not* on anyone's mind." Hannah bit the inside of her cheek and looked back outside.

Tony was staring in the completely opposite direction.

"He won't be mad at you forever," Will said.

"I highly doubt that," Hannah replied, letting out a breath.

She knew how long Tony could hold a grudge, and yet she still had said something stupid. Mentally, she was kicking herself.

Her phone buzzed again.

"Another love text? Wow, the men just keep running to your backyard, don't they?" Will chuckled and then immediately ducked as a piece of wadded paper nearly missed his head. "You're super touchy today."

"Not touchy. Just annoyed. First, it's Sabina trying to text me, and now this weird thing is on my phone." She shook it in her left fist. "It won't stop freaking buzzing."

"Sabina, is it?" The sultry tone flowed like butter on his lips. "A *special* friend?"

"Again," Hannah muttered, "disgusting. No. Nothing special unless you count a 'childhood friend' special."

"Now that you mention it, I do remember her. You mentioned her a few times. You went on a trip with her a few months ago, right? Oh, and as far as the childhood friend special thing? Most people would consider them to be."

"I'm not most people. You should know that already," she breathed. Her phone continued buzzing, further pressing Hannah into more annoyance. "Childhood memories are nothing but a waste of time. Honestly, the only reason I still talk to her is because of Cammie. Otherwise, I'd have dropped the spoiled princess on her entitled ass."

"That's a swear word. Put the money in my hand now for the jar." As sly as the Cheshire cat, he held out his palm.

Hannah's eyes flared.

"Come on, girly. You know the rules, Hannah Banana." He wiggled his fingers, leaning forward in his seat. His other hand dangled in front of the chip bag as he reached down to get a bite.

Hannah wanted nothing more than to throttle him.

Her phone, ever timely, began the incessant buzzing. She flipped it over, looking at the screen. "What even is this?"

"Give me your phone," Will instructed.

Hannah whipped her head back around, her mouth gaping.

"Why are you looking at me like I asked you to poop out rainbows? Just give me the phone, and I can help you."

She cradled the phone to her chest protectively, away from his grasp. "I will not give you the phone. That's practically allowing you to make stupid decisions on my watch. Nope, not gonna happen."

Will rolled his eyes. "So distrusting. Man, that's something we're going to have to work on if we are supposed to be in a serious relationship together."

"We aren't dating," Hannah said.

"But we're serious, and that, my dear, is something," Will quipped.

Reluctantly, Hannah handed the phone over, and it took all but five seconds for Will to burst out laughing.

"What's wrong?" Hannah's voice rose.

"This is far too easy. Your phone is being tracked."

At that very moment, Hannah's face lost all its color. "What?"

"By the look on your face, I'd say you have no idea who it is?"

"I'm sorry. I'm still stuck on the whole 'being tracked' thing. Seriously?"

"It's very real. I've had it happen before, and it looks exactly like this. I'd say it was your dear old dad who did it."

"What makes you say that?" Her brain was scrambling.

"For starters, you left home on terrible terms. Totally wins you daughter of the year award, by the way." Will began counting on his fingers. "Secondly, refer to the first thing I mentioned, and oh, boy, this third one is really interesting."

"How so?"

"Judging by the way the cop outside of the gas station is staring us down, I'd say dear old dad called in some work recruits." Will pointed outside.

Sure enough, a tall, balding man was speaking into his radio, eyes locked on the van.

"Oh, no," Hannah whispered. "No, no, no, no, no." She shook her head rapidly then looked back at Will. "We need to get out of here. *Now*."

"I'm not the one with the keys." Will shrugged. "What can I do about it?"

Yet another wad of paper flew in his direction. It also missed. Barely.

"I have to get Tony," she realized aloud.

"What an idea!" Will leaned his chin on one hand.

Without waiting for more stupidity to flow from Will's mouth, she fumbled with the car handle until it gave way. She dropped out of the car so suddenly that she stumbled into Tony.

"What the—watch it!" Tony stepped away from her, holding his hands up as a shield. "You didn't have to slam into me to get my attention."

"I wasn't trying to," Hannah protested, putting a hand on Tony's shoulder.

He shied away from her, as if her touch were the very thing that would kill him. "What do you want?" His eyes were looking at anything, everything but her.

She had had enough.

With a force unreckoned, she grabbed his face, angling it until their noses were almost touching. Due to the height difference, it proved difficult, but her straining back wasn't one of the top concerns at that moment.

"This isn't some sort of childish game. This isn't a joke. This is serious, and I need you to listen to me."

His eyes became strained. A million questions were flowing through them.

She shook her head. "There's not much of an explanation, but the one I can give you is right over there." She darted her gaze to the man in front of the store.

Tony's followed, and then it was as if the puzzle came together.

"Who is he?"

"I'm not sure," Hannah admitted, "but I think my dad has something to do with it."

"He's tracking you?"

"Basically," she replied.

"I know we're at odds right now, but we can talk about it later, okay? You just get in the car. I'll follow you."

She nodded and followed his instructions.

He fumbled with the gas pump, and a few minutes later, he joined her, getting back into the driver's seat. He buckled quickly and put the van in reverse. Immediately, her hand latched onto his as her heart skyrocketed out of her chest.

It was as if everyone was holding their breath as they were leaving the little station.

There were no sirens. Yet.

Will let out a sigh, and then Tony shared a grin with Hannah. Her face was scarlet as she withdrew her hand from his. She fully expected him to scold her.

But what she didn't plan on was him taking her hand back.

And then, in that small moment, he said the one thing she had been wanting to hear since a few hours ago.

"What do you need me to do?"

For the next few miles, everything seemed to lessen. There were no cops, no sirens. Nothing was trailing them.

He had stopped holding her hand, but that feeling in her heart wouldn't stop.

"I'm sorry," Hannah said amidst the silence. "I shouldn't have snapped at you. I should have called him. You were right."

"I wasn't trying to be." Tony sighed. "I don't deliberately say things to prove you wrong. I've just been there before—leaving things unsaid, regretting them—and I know what it does to you, how it wrecks you. I didn't want you to feel that way if something happened."

Hannah remembered all too well what he was talking about and how it had stuck. The entire group could recite the night it had happened, the same way one could recite the alphabet as easily as breathing.

"How do you do it?" She looked at him through her lashes.

She had never dared to ask this question. Anything revolving Tony's father was never brought up, no matter the occasion, but there was an opportunity, and it was one she would probably never get again.

"Which part?" He turned to her momentarily and then faced his eyes back on the road.

"All of it," she said, brushing a strand of hair behind her ear. "Do you think I should talk to him? Especially after all of the things I've done."

"I don't think it matters what you've done," he uttered. "I do know that he's your dad and he loves you because that's what dads do. That's how my dad was. I wasn't living the right way after him and mom began having problems. I was drinking, fighting…You remember this part."

"I was the one who snapped you out of it," Hannah interjected.

"Yeah, well, you weren't the only one. He tried too, and I wanted nothing to do with it. He wasn't the best man, even the best father, but he was trying, and I refused to give him even that."

"And you think I'm doing the same?" Hannah crossed her arms over her chest, letting her feet rest against the dashboard. Tony hated it, and that was exactly why it felt all the more satisfying when she caught sight of his left eye twitching.

"I think you're not being reasonable," he stated, "and before you go off on me and yell, just listen for a minute. Your parents loved you. Your mom did, and I know that's why you've struggled with things since she died. Your dad took it hard, threw himself into his job. He didn't have any other option. He had to provide for you. I would have taken that any day over a dad who wasn't really around because he had another family he was building, like mine did. He loves you. If he didn't, why would he call out on the radio for backup or even try tracking your phone? Dads that don't care wouldn't do that."

She couldn't deny his claims, but she couldn't necessarily agree with them either.

"Speaking of..." Tony shot her a cheeky grin. "Where is your phone? I haven't heard it beep for a while. Did you text him while we were leaving and just didn't tell me?"

"Actually..." Hannah cleared her throat. "At the last spot we went to for the bathroom, I dropped it on the concrete. Someone's probably run over it by now."

Tony's eyes narrowed as he turned slowly in her direction. "You didn't."

"I definitely did." She chuckled.

Stirring came from the backseat. "What did Hannah do?" Trevor asked in a low mumble. His eyes were glazed over as he stared at the front. "Did I miss something?"

"You've been out. Missed quite a lot," Tony said with a smirk.

"You've been asleep for a while," Hannah said.

She looked around at the rest in the back. Will was still asleep. Marcus was drooling on his shoulder. She couldn't fight the smile on her face. *How he would love to know his saliva is on the person who annoys him most.*

Trevor's eyes still held the dazed quality, but he was no longer looking at Hannah or anything in the car. His eyes were trained far off in the distance.

"What are you looking at?" Hannah followed the blank stare out the front window.

A huge flash of black was running at the speed of light, right toward them. *It isn't a car or a person. It's something different.*

"Tony." Hannah's voice held a warning. "Slow down. Can you see it? It's right over there."

Tony peered closer and leaned into the steering wheel, but by then, it was too late.

The sky, the roads—all of it began to spin. The circular motion was like a kaleidoscope of colors at the speed of lightning. Hannah's breath caught in her throat as the tires began to skid against the dirt road. She gripped the roof handle in her right knuckle, the texture and force making her hand white.

A few thoughts scrambled into her mind as the spinning became never-ending.

There was no one around for miles.

Since her phone had been tossed, she realized not even her father could help them.

The proximity of death beckoned, and no number of grudges or pride could save her from it. Her own humanity would be her destruction, and there was no way for her to make it stop. There was no remote with a pause button or way to reverse it.

"Hold on," a voice said. It blurred against the screams in the space.

Her head smashed against the window as everything finally slowed. Burnt rubber and dust filled her nostrils, sending her into a coughing fit. She inhaled, but that only accelerated the pain. A rough, burning, searing pain was slick against her throat, but it was a reminder that she was alive.

As movement came from the back, there was a tinkling.

Shattered glass.

"Is everyone okay?" Tony forced off the seatbelt and pushed over the armrest, reaching out for the guys in the back.

Marcus was bleeding at the temple. A shard had gotten through. It wasn't deep, but the color and potency made Hannah gag.

Trevor was unscathed, and Will was coated in sweat.

We are okay was the thought that overcame the shock. *We are okay.*

A mouthful of curses flowed through Tony's lips as he hopped out of the driver's side, slamming the door behind him.

They were in the ditch, but there was just enough space for them to back out onto the road. The realization of how much worse it could have been set in her bones. They were spared.

"It's gone," he said as soon as he got back in the van. "I can't find it."

"But we hit something," Will sputtered. "That black thing, whatever it was, we hit it. Or it hit us. And it's gone?"

Tony nodded. "All gone."

"That doesn't make sense," Hannah stated.

"Maybe it ran off?" Trevor offered.

"Doubtful," Tony thought aloud. "Considering how fast we were going, it should have died. I'm not even sure what it was."

Hannah rested her head back against the seat, trying to process everything that had just transpired. "We need to get Marcus checked out and get the window repaired."

"We can do that as soon as we can find an urgent care. The window, maybe a tarp will work until I can find a good shop to take it to. Is that okay with everyone?"

There were murmurs of agreement.

They got back on the road with a new goal in mind. As they passed the stop sign ahead, there was a shadow in the corner of her eye.

The flash of black.

CHAPTER SEVEN

CAMMIE

THE CEILING, AND ALL ITS little dots, was making her head hurt.

The phone call with Sabina had turned out a lot differently than she had expected. Sabina didn't want Cammie going off the deep end, regardless of how nice Caelan was.

The only problem was, with Cammie, words with an underlying meaning tended to stick. Here she was, a few mere hours later, having trouble falling asleep.

She flipped her pillow to the cold side—her favorite—and turned over. *Maybe that will help.*

The repetition of thoughts spiraled in the quiet room. It was a song, a tempo only she could hear, and it was, by all accounts, an absolute annoyance.

Enough of this. If I can't even get some decent rest, then I might as well do something productive.

She shoved the covers off and leapt out of bed. Her hair was disheveled, and she knew her eyes were stinging, burning, red, but complaining wasn't solving anything. Maybe if she found something taxing enough to do, it would bore her to sleep.

With resolve, she padded her cold feet into warm slippers and flung the closet doors open. Shirts of a variety of colors were scattered among shoes on the floor. Some dress pants were neatly folded and others were tossed.

Her eyes were beheld in bewilderment at the mess that lay before her. She hadn't stepped foot in her closet in, well, how long? It was as if there was some sort of mental block in front of her, dissuading any sort of remembrance. All her outfits for work were freshly pressed and dried in the laundry room, and she had no memory of even stepping into the closet to begin with.

I just haven't been on top of things because there's no way I'd ever leave it looking like this.

She got on her knees and began gathering the clothing into piles. She'd sort through them later. Getting them out of here was the first step. Shoes were intertwined in some of the shirts, and after a few moments of pulling and yanking, they finally gave way, falling back into the wall and landing in a different spot on the carpeted floor.

Sweat beaded on her brow, and she wiped it hastily. *Just keep going. Maybe it'll actually work.*

More shirts begged for her attention, but a sliver of green caught her eyes. It was balled up in the corner and hidden so tactfully that, if she didn't look hard enough, she wouldn't even notice it was there.

Cammie peered closer, her eyebrows furrowing as she grasped the material. She had gotten it on sale back when graduation rolled around. She was lucky enough it still fit. This was one clothing item she truly valued. It was something she had bought when her mom had been in town. *I'd never put it on the floor.*

As she raised the dress up to the nearest hanger, a waft of rose perfume hit. The sickly sweetness coated her nose. The entire dress seemed to dance with it, as if the smell and fabric were eternally attached together.

Her senses blurred on the edge of formidable ecstasy. Colors and people swayed in her brain, rotating until the hint of a whisper, of a noise, came bleeding through.

"Do you think he'll like it, though?" Cammie did a little spin in front of her bedroom mirror near the vanity, eyeing her reflection indecisively.

Her phone was propped against the pillow, and Sabina's smile was as wide as ever. Even though it was through video chat, there was a palpable sense of closeness as if Sabina were in the room. She had that air about her, and Cammie was eating up every second of it as much as she could.

"Why would he not like it?" Sabina switched positions, to her side, leaning on one hand. She twirled her hair with the other, nodding at Cammie's outfit of choice. "That dress looks super good on you by the way."

"Thanks." Cammie turned around and beamed at her, her smile so wide that her cheekbones twinged a little. "I'm just a bit nervous. I got it with my mom about two months or so ago. I never really thought I would get a chance to wear it anywhere, but here we are." The sing-song tone lagged a little as nerves creeped in.

Sabina frowned, concern etched in her eyes. "Hey, it'll be fine. Just breathe, okay?"

"It's just our first official date. We've been friends for two years, and nothing has really happened like this before. We never held hands, never kissed, or even explored being together. Tonight is the night it all could go wrong."

"Or it's also the night it could all go right," Sabina countered. "You're so pessimistic. It's okay to be optimistic sometimes. Not everything will go wrong."

"But—"

"But you can spend all kinds of time thinking about how it could go wrong. That's exactly what's happening here, and it's an easy fix."

"How is it, though?" Cammie crossed her arms over her chest.

"Just don't think of all the things that'll go wrong. Think of it as an adventure. Today is the first day of a new adventure. And believe me, once James sees you in that dress, all your worries will melt away because then you'll see what I'm talking about. The gooey-lovey feeling will be all over his face. Just you wait."

The dress flew across the room at rapid speed. Cammie crawled backward on her hands and legs, her breathing labored. There had never been a video-chat. She hadn't danced in front of the mirror with the dress on. And that boy, the one who had haunted her from her daydream, had shown up again, in passing.

But yet, there it was.

Sabina was talking about him.

This time, Cammie had learned something.

A name.

CHAPTER EIGHT

SABINA

THE AIR WAS DIFFERENT THAN she had imagined it would be. Hearing stories upon stories of how it really was did not prepare her.

Traveling to Louisiana without her parents' approval was not something Sabina would normally do on a whim, but Cammie needed her, so going rogue was necessary.

The air wasn't the brisk coldness she was used to. There wasn't any reeking smell of pollution. Nor were there any lack of trees. The humidity was so thick that she had an inkling of fog in the air.

The streets were crowded with cars on sidewalks and mud in the grass. She had never truly seen the green color this deep unless she was in the garden back at home. It wasn't perfectly displayed among flowers in full bloom here. It simply just was.

Hesitantly, Sabina raised her hand to the doorbell. Her stomach was bubbling with nerves as her finger made contact before she could even take it back.

Standing outside Cammie's door for five minutes was terrifying enough, but Sabina couldn't wait outside forever.

She blinked, taking it all in. The sights and the smells would be enough to mark her memory for a lifetime.

Sabina could hear the sound of shuffling—no, running—as someone raced to the door.

"I'm not sure what it is you want, but I'm not looking to buy any..." The voice died out as the door hit the stopper. "What are you doing here? When did you even—how?" Cammie's eyes beheld nothing but shock.

"I bought a ticket last night, and got on the first flight here this morning. I thought it was necessary."

"But what about your family?" Cammie dawdled in the doorway, the words coming out quickly.

"They're fine," she reassured, putting a hand on Cammie's shoulder. "It's more you that I am worried about. Maybe we should sit down."

Without even waiting for a response, Sabina led Cammie inside the house, making sure to shut the door.

Sabina was smiling and being there for her friend—she knew that was what she had to do—but the smile was glass, and it was on the edge of breaking.

She didn't admit how her parents had reacted. If she did, there was no doubt in her mind that Cammie would force her back on that plane. They were great at entertaining and finding ways to give generously to their supporters but very rarely did they do that for their daughter. How could she crack the facade now? After years of wearing one, it seemed doing that now was of no consequence.

Cammie's hands gripped tightly to her knees as she sat down on the couch. Sabina set down her travel bag and moved next to her.

"I'm sorry." Cammie half-laughed. "I just can't believe you're even here. I think I'm still in shock."

Sabina couldn't help the giggle that escaped her. She wrapped her arms around Cammie, bringing her in for a hug. The concern flowed through her fingers, and she hoped Cammie could sense it. "We just really need to talk about the text you sent me."

Cammie pulled back instantly, her face frozen. "There's nothing to talk about," she stated. Her eyes were creased, and her lips in a thin line.

"I feel like there *is*."

Cammie's eyebrows rose in defiance, and Sabina knew the storm was brewing.

Oh, no.

"Listen, Cammie. You have to understand where I'm coming from. You've gone on about seeing someone you've never met, and to be completely honest, I'm concerned about your well-being."

"But you have met him!" Cammie rose to her feet, the breathy croak higher than expected. "I saw you, in my mind. When I saw the dress in my hands, I saw *you*. You were there. You said his name. I heard you."

Her breathing was shallow, labored breaths. She was pointing at Sabina, and the longer she stood, the more chaos she wielded. Her brown hair was a wild mane, and her eyes were frantically searching Sabina's face as if the answers were written right in front of her.

"I don't know what you saw," Sabina said, standing slowly, "but it wasn't real. None of it was real. I think the stress of being alone is getting to you. That's why I'm here." She reached her hand to Cammie.

Ever so quickly, Sabina was swatted away.

"Don't touch me. Just don't. I know what I saw."

The firmness in Cammie's voice was what terrified Sabina.

She actually believes it.

"I'm not trying to be skeptical of your words, I promise. But...just listen to yourself."

The glare in Cammie's eyes was unmistakable. "You think I'm crazy."

"I never said that. I would never call you crazy." She made sure to smile, just a little, to ease her friend's nerves. "Cammie, you're my best friend. I love you. And Hannah does, too."

"Does Hannah know about any of this?" Cammie whipped around. Her feet pattered against the floor as she began to pace. "Is she just like you? Who doesn't believe me? Or does she actually think—or know—that I'm not lost in the head?"

Her smile was wide, and she was laughing. Unrestrained laughter.

"You need to calm down," Sabina stated. There wasn't any time for games. Cammie was officially slipping, hard and fast. "Come sit down."

"No!" The noise bounced off of the walls. "I know what I saw, and there's nothing you can say or do that will change that. If you want to babysit me because you think I'm having some sort of psychotic break, then by all means, get back on the plane because I'm not." She gave another death stare in Sabina's direction and then headed to the closet.

"Where are you going? What are you doing?"

Cammie shrugged on a hoodie and shut the closet door. "I'm going out."

"But I just got here." She trailed behind Cammie as she headed toward the front door.

"And you can stay here, or you can leave. Your choice. Just like it's my choice to not stay in a room with someone who thinks I have totally lost it. We all have choices, and this is mine."

"Just listen—" The slamming of the front door stopped Sabina from speaking further. The absence echoed in the silence and rang in Sabina's ears.

What do I do now?

As she stood behind the door, she realized, there was no answer. Not the right one, anyways. There were plenty of things she could do, but the only thing that could tame Cammie's fury was the admittance of believing her thoughts.

And that was one thing, one omission, Sabina couldn't—and wouldn't—do.

The water from the showerhead was scalding against her palm as she let the moisture trickle through her fingertips. It had been at least ten minutes, and there was still no sign of Cammie returning anytime soon.

Sabina hated waiting, especially in a house she was unfamiliar with. There was no use calling a driver to come get her to take her back to the airport. She was determined to wait out whatever was plaguing her friend.

The worry nibbled at the back of her mind so much so that sitting on the couch made it worse. She had to distract herself, so she decided a hot shower was the safest and most painless way.

She dug through the drawers and cabinets until she found towels, and she was careful enough to lock the bathroom door. She began taking off her shirt.

That was when she heard it. A distinct ping from her phone.

Instantly, every nerve and muscle froze. *Is it Cammie? Is she hurt? Does she need help?*

Her shaky hands grasped the phone. Her eyes crinkled as the notification registered. Not Cammie. An email from Liz.

The name struck a peculiar nerve of vague remembrance until it hit her. The photographer. The one who had taken the photos of Hannah, Sabina, and Cammie for their trip.

Her eyes skimmed the message, even more confusion piquing.

Sorry it took me so long to get back to you! You guys paid in full already so just disregard the statement below about payment plans. I had a lot of personal things come up as well as a family illness, so I have been away from my computer, but here are the pictures you requested. You guys are so cute together, by the way <3 It was an absolute joy photographing you. If you need anything else ever, please let me know.

Oh, P.S. Tell your friend to give me my hat back!

Sabina rolled her eyes. That made sense, she guessed, Hannah being the one to steal personal belongings. Her edginess sometimes bordered along the same lines as a criminal's. Ironic how her father was a cop.

As Sabina clicked on the first photo, she couldn't help but wonder if Hannah's pose was as out there as ever.

But what she saw was not what she expected.

They were all on the balcony of a restaurant Sabina loved when they were at her parents' vacation spot. Sabina's arm dangled over Hannah, who, for the first time, was actually cracking a smile—a real one. Cammie's face was open, like the camera caught her in the middle of a laugh. Her eyes were bright, and she was pressing her face against someone else's.

Wait.

Sabina's grip on the phone loosened.

Wavy, brown hair, and deep-set green eyes. There were dimples in the cheeks, and the gaze was locked on Cammie as if she were the only person on the planet. The hat was in the hand of said person.

And it wasn't Hannah. It wasn't even a female.

It was a young man.

CHAPTER NINE

HANNAH

THE EARLY MORNING AIR FELT crisp against her skin. The driving was exhausting, but Marcus had managed to find a miracle in a haystack, or for lack of a better term, a mechanic shop. And coffee, another miracle within itself.

Hannah raised the mug to her lips, allowing the chocolatey goodness to linger on her tongue. She savored the honey wisps that stayed behind and closed her eyes against the rising sun.

They had spent their time driving throughout the night. No stops were made until Marcus's internet search found them a gold mine: a mechanic shop that opened before the crack of dawn.

Time was then spent making an appointment, finding the van papers before they arrived, praying the mechanic had the parts to replace the window, and many more things.

Against the hazy backdrop of pinkish, golden streaks of morning, Hannah peered back at the window inside the shop.

Tony was inside at the counter finishing up, while Trevor was sitting down in the waiting area. Marcus was in the chair next to Trevor with his head tilted back, and Will, well, Will was where he always was, which was anywhere that food resided.

He was the only one hanging outside with Hannah, but his morning cheer was absent. Instead, his wild screeching filled the gap.

"Stupid piece of junk," he hollered, grabbing the machine. He shook it, his fingernails clawing at the sides. "Give me my money!"

"Assaulting it won't help," Hannah called out.

Will turned to Hannah. His eyes were droopy and bloodshot, and his lips cocooned in supposed vexation. "At least it won't go on my record. It's just a machine."

The bloodthirsty quest for vengeance overtook him, it seemed, as he faced the machine and began kicking it.

"You're going to hurt yourself, you idiot." Hannah couldn't help the eye roll. *Why is he always so stupid?*

"If I get hurt, it would be worth it. I need my money back."

"We can't afford surgery," Hannah said. She took another sip of coffee. "Even with the money you had, funds are too tight right now."

Will was on his knees now, his arm extended into the slot in the machine. Puzzled, Hannah was about to ask what in the world he was doing until she realized he was reaching for the chips he desired.

"Your hand will get stuck. Please, just stop."

"For these chips, nothing matters more. Not even the aching in my bones will stop me." He moaned in pain as his arm strained, but he never once decided stopping was the answer.

Will was determined. Hannah could give him that.

Determined but stupid.

Before more chaos could ensue, the front door opened. It was Tony, wearing a wide grin. He held a piece of paper in his hands. The scribbles were hard to make out, but it was easy to guess as to what it was.

"Receipt?" Hannah asked.

Tony jogged to meet her, his hair bouncing as he moved. His teeth gleamed. "He charged us half of the price we deserved to pay. I swear, not everyone is a jerk."

"At least some people can overcompensate for rudeness," Hannah replied.

Will took this moment to glare at Hannah. It was as if he was throwing her own words back in her face.

"Do we have a problem?" Tony crossed his arms, making sure Will received the pointed look.

Will rose to his feet, dusting his hands off on his pants. "We don't have one, but she could be a little nicer. Her condescending attitude is really getting on my last nerve."

"And you think your attitude doesn't bother anyone else? We've been cooped up in this car for a long time. Getting out wasn't just because of the window. It was for a break from your antics." Tony's eyes were honest, but that didn't seem to ease the situation at hand.

"You guys always gang up on me. I don't know why, but you do, and I'm tired of it."

Tony sauntered up to Will, their faces inches apart. Will wore rage like a sweater, and Tony's face began to harden.

"And just what do you plan on doing about your anger?" Tony asked. "Are we going to talk about it? Or are you going to use other methods for making it out in the open?"

Tony and Will were very different individuals. It wasn't just how they appeared physically. They were the same height—around five feet eight—but some traits were more striking than others. Will's hair was just like he was, wild and untamed. His locks veered on the murky brown, whereas Tony's were black as night. Their complexions were opposite, with Will being pale and Tony harboring more of an olive tone. There were similarities too. Their tempers were the main component that constantly threw them together, and once again Hannah was caught right in the center of it all.

"It all depends on how you take what I'm saying, I guess," Will said. "I know I'm different than you all are, but being the butt of the joke isn't funny anymore. Calling me an idiot isn't hilarious when you're the one hearing it all the time." Will gave another glance toward Hannah and then turned his gaze back to Tony's stoic face. "How would you like to be called an idiot?" He pushed Tony once.

Tony staggered slightly, his eyes shining. "*Watch it*," he warned.

"Or what?"

The twinkle in Will's eyes was frightening. Hannah had seen it the last time she had been caught in between the spectacle. It had been over a disagreement that had almost broken the glass dining table. Her father had been able to stop it.

But her father wasn't here now.

"I'm warning you." Tony's voice shook, and his hands followed suit as he brought them up to Will's shoulders. The grip was tight and firm.

But in his eyes, Hannah saw the obvious. Fear.

Whenever their rage became synced, stopping it was a hard feat. Regret came soon after. Hannah had some strength in her, she knew she did, but the strength these two men required would be more than what she could offer.

"It seems you've done that already," Will said sardonically. "Do you want to warn me another time, before, you know, you actually do something? Third time's the charm." He added a small smirk, and the tension grew like a balloon.

"I said stop," Tony replied through gritted teeth. His jaw bulged, and the vein in his neck throbbed.

Will, however, didn't listen. He was good at that, at doing his own thing whenever it was the worst choice on the table.

With an animalistic grunt, Will tackled Tony. Their bodies flew in a mangled heap of limbs as they crashed into gravel. Rocks slid on the grass, and the quiet *oof* that came from Tony's parted, shocked lips was barely audible.

Will's fists began flying. There was no stopping it. Left, right.... He even switched hands. One hand then the trade-off. The noise of knuckles hitting face was the soundtrack for the altercation against the backdrop of Hannah's pleas.

Blood trickled down Tony's nose as he held his hands up in protection, but Will didn't let up. He barely took a breath.

Just before he could let one more fly, Hannah had enough.

She charged to the boys, her mind a whirlwind of concern and a tornado of dread. Her friends were idiotic, and they were impulsive, but she couldn't let one of them die at the hands of the rage of the other—something Will would dearly regret.

Her hand latched onto Will's back as she pulled. "Stop," she pleaded. Her voice wavered, and Will paused.

His back was heaving with each breath as he slowly brought his knuckles down.

Tony's face was splattered with crimson. His nose, albeit not broken, was gushing. His eyes held fresh tears and something Hannah recognized instantly.

The shock of betrayal.

"I'm sorry," is all that Will managed to say as he came to a stand, his shoes locking with the gravel and unhinged dirt.

The edge of a sob lingered as he let out a breath and turned around. His eyes lifted from the ground to meet Hannah's.

She expected shame, which she did see.

She expected maybe a little bit of anger. That was also there.

But another beheld her.

Scarlet irises blinked back.

She wanted to shriek, to move, to do something.

But Tony staggering to his feet, his movements wobbly and full of indecision, overrode everything else.

The blood and tears painted his cheeks and disappeared just as suddenly when his hand swiped them away. He winced in pain, and Will turned around, at the ready. He held his arm out, and for a jolting few minutes, Tony's gaze latched on Will. He didn't make any sudden movements.

Hannah held her breath. What would happen?

Tony reluctantly took Will's arm, allowing himself to be led down to sit on the concrete walkway.

As if by magic of its own league, the sound of the van filled the silence. The repairs were done. They could continue on their trip.

As the man got out of the driver's side and handed the keys to Hannah, his eyes rang with alarm when he glanced at Tony's face. His gaze trailed to Will's cracked knuckles and then to Hannah.

She gave a sheepish smile. "He's just really clumsy is all," was the explanation that followed.

The man said nothing, but his eyes lingered for longer than they all hoped. Then, he was back in the shop like nothing happened.

The breath she was holding dissipated, and air was now water on a dry island.

The little shop door *dinged*, and Trevor and Marcus were at the front entrance, taking in every single detail.

"What happened?" Marcus was the first to speak.

Trevor simply stared.

"Nothing." Tony coughed and let out spit. More blood followed. "Just had a little disagreement. Everything is fine now." He fumbled with his hands as he rose to his feet, Will helping him every second of the way.

Hannah waited for them to elaborate, for Will to apologize, but instead, there was nothing—just Will helping Tony to the back. Tony would be the one sleeping, she realized, and Will would be driving. Everyone else quietly piled into the van. All that was left was for her to get inside.

"You ready?" Will asked, halfway inside the van. He lingered, almost as if he expected her to tell him to stay behind.

"Yeah," she finally said. "I...I am. Are you okay?"

He met her eyes this time. The shame wasn't a meniscal component this time. It was an overflowing pool.

But there was no crimson. Absolutely none.

Will briefly nodded and got inside, shutting the door.

What felt like an eternity later, Hannah sat in the passenger seat. She looked at the rear-view mirror. Behind her was a sleeping Tony on Marcus's shoulder. Trevor's music was faintly audible through his headphone speakers. He met her eyes. They seemed to convey the same thing she was feeling.

Dread.

Despite all the convictions she held deeply, she couldn't help the nagging feeling that maybe she wasn't seeing right.

Maybe I'm going crazy.

But deep down, in her spirit, she could sense something. She was on the edge of discovery.

She just didn't know what.

CHAPTER TEN

CAMMIE

Hot breaths of air came from her parted lips. Her legs were screaming in exertion, but the tears blinded her from any sense of time. She had run from the house and made no move to stop. Her lungs were burning, the warning loud and clear.

She slowed to a jog, her knees beginning to buckle. As she wiped her eyes, her focus became clearer. A nearby park bench was perfect, exactly what she needed.

Cammie grasped ahold of the arms, dragging herself to a spot on the right end. She plopped down, pulling her knees to her chest.

The wind was cruel as it shoved air out of her parted lips, and she gasped in handfuls, careful not to inhale so much for fear she might burst. Her brain was a tidal wave that carried confusion and the deepest shade of betrayal. Her best friend had heard her, had seen her, and had denied her all at the same time. The blend of shock was at the forefront, and the conclusion of whether or not sanity was still on the table was right behind it.

Her mother had been gone for weeks, sometimes months at a time. The house was rarely filled with any kind of laughter except for her own. That sound wasn't produced frequently, but tears muffled into a pillow had become the constant. It was a truth she hadn't shared with anyone, which made the sting that much worse.

How many secrets did she have to keep hidden until they finally came to light? How far did her mind have to bend until the reality of insanity became the final authority?

"Are you hurt?" The soft, silky voice startled her.

Her hands rose instinctively to shield herself until recognition came.

"Caelan?" Cammie sniffled, wiping her nose with the back of her hand. "Why are you here?" Her eyes darted upward at him. "Are you following me?" She rose to a stand.

His eyebrows furrowed. "No! No. I was on my way to sit down and go over some paperwork from the office." He gave her a soft smile and waved the paperwork in his hands. The assurance he tried to give her indeed missed as her eyebrows refused to sink. "I honestly promise that you haven't been on my radar. I just saw you crying and thought something was wrong."

She gave a small smile in response but otherwise said nothing. Her eyes darted to the coffee shop a few feet away. *A place to think...alone*, she contemplated.

"If you want to be alone, I can leave you be. I just wanted to be sure that you didn't need help."

"I'm fine," she said, but her voice wavered. The shaking quality that was pushing her to the edge of crying again infuriated her.

"If you want to sit down and talk about it, I'm going to grab a coffee. I can get you something, and you don't even have to talk. If you want to sit and cry, that's okay too." When she didn't budge, he added, "If it'll help, I can try reverse psychology. I cry, and you buy me a coffee." He shut his eyes and feigned tears.

The snorting laugh came from Cammie before she could try to conceal it. She covered her mouth with her hand, her eyes wide, and Caelan's eyes crinkled. Soon, they were both laughing, and momentarily, Sabina and Hannah and weird thoughts were forgotten.

Caelan set the small cup of tea before her. His chair scraped the wood floor as he sat down with a mug of steaming coffee. He brought it to his lips and took a long sip and set the mug down. "This is some good stuff. I didn't know this little hole in the wall had good coffee. A few months ago, I was proven very, very wrong."

Cammie's mind trailed back to when she had sat with Caelan a few days ago. She had been so carefree, light, and curious. Now, she simply felt like a child in a dark room, waiting for the next monster to pop out. How would she go forward?

"You're almost as quiet as you were last time we were here. Is this why you were crying? Did something happen? If I have said anything to you to cause any strife, I sincerely apologize."

Cammie shook her head. "It wasn't your fault. Things have been foggy for me lately, and you can't feel that it is your fault when you didn't cause it. It's been terrifying, honestly. I'm not sure whether or not I can trust myself."

Caelan leaned forward on his elbows. "Would you care to elaborate?"

"I've had..." She paused, trying to find the words that best fit. "...some unusual thoughts lately. It feels almost like memories, but I know that's impossible."

His interest was piqued. She could tell by how he some-how managed to lean in even closer. "Trauma can block out memories. Could this possibly be something you are refusing to remember that could be coming up again? When my wife died, this was something I dealt with a lot. Memories of her, of our time together...it came up in waves of haziness."

"But this is different," Cammie said, slapping her palm against the table. "I know it is. I don't think I've ever met this person before. My mind has been going in circles of its own, and I can't control it. My friend thinks I'm going crazy. It's like my brain is being selective, forming fantasies and many other things, and I'm not sure if there is anything I can do about it. Maybe she is right."

The front door dinged, and a figure was hanging in the doorway.

Sabina, with an open, crazed look, was breathing heavily. She waved her phone in the air, eyes scouring the space. Her gaze landed on Cammie, and she spoke seven words that sent Cammie's heart through the roof.

"I have proof that you're not crazy."

CHAPTER ELEVEN

SABINA

CAMMIE'S EYES WERE LIKE SAUCERS. Her mouth opened and slacked shut as Sabina walked over to the table. As she scooted into the last empty chair at the table, Sabina immediately found her manners. Her friend was not alone.

Directly across from Cammie was a man sipping his coffee. Sabina's first thought was that he'd arrived from the pages of a fairytale and landed there. It wasn't the outfit he donned. More of how he smiled at her. It had a sophisticated air that even the people at parties she had attended never could master. It was as if his entire life had given him enough practice, and this was merely another moment that needed no effort.

"You're Cammie's friend," he said, extending a hand. "It's nice to be acquainted with you. My name is Caelan."

"Cae-lin," Sabina pronounced, the syllables rolling off of her tongue.

The man chuckled and shook his head. He lifted a finger. "Close, very good effort, but it is actually *Cae-lahn*. No *lin*, I'm afraid. I can understand why you would think that, though. Your entrance was definitely inspiring. I am happy you have affirmed Cammie's ability not to be unstable." He stopped speaking, a question in his eyes. "I'm sorry. I never caught your name."

"Sabina," she said, turning to Cammie.

One by one, the dots connected, and Sabina realized this was the man she had, in fact, warned her friend to stay away from. He might have been charming, but he could have been dangerous too. Her heart thumped, and she had this unnerving sense in her gut.

Cammie's eyes remained fixated on the table. With the light reflecting from the lamp, the brown color of her eyes looked almost like it had a golden hue. The redness coated the corners of her eyelids. She had been crying.

"Look at this picture," Sabina said, handing the phone to Cammie.

Reluctantly, Cammie looked up and took the phone. As she zeroed in on the photo, her eyes bulged, and she struggled to speak. "It's.... He's..."

"Real," Sabina finished for her. "You're not crazy. His photo is right here. He's a real person."

"We were together?" Cammie's eyes scrunched as she brought the phone closer, trying to make sense of the image. "But how can that be? I have no memory of him other than the things my mind showed, no idea of how I even met him. You told me earlier that I wasn't making any sense...and now you're telling me there's a picture of him...*here*." Her voice was borderline hysterical and couples from other tables began looking over at the commotion.

"I'm not sure what's happening either," Sabina coaxed, pulling the phone away and putting it on the table.

"What's happening is I'm insane," Cammie shrieked, "or I've lost my mind. Maybe I've been...brainwashed."

"Wait." Caelan gasped. "When did the memories or flashes start? Has it been ongoing, or has it been more recent?"

Sabina turned her eyes on Caelan. "I'm not sure why you are trying to intervene in this. I can handle it."

"I'm an adult here. You are just two young girls. I can offer wisdom—" Caelan's words fell short amidst Sabina's glare.

"Wisdom we don't need," Sabina hissed. "I told her to stay away from you. You could be dangerous or some sort of stalker. Maybe *you're* the one causing delusions by pretending to be her friend."

Caelan's face broke down into crumbles. The eyes that held so much light now withered to a barely flickering flame.

"He's been helpful," Cammie offered quietly. Her eyes were locked once more on the table, and her lips barely moved as she spoke.

The brashness that had flown from Sabina's lips and the crestfallen expressions on the two other faces blended into another realization. She was becoming like the attitude she hated the most—the fist-flying, smart-mouthed girl who didn't care about anyone else.

I'm turning into Hannah.

Even still, she couldn't deny the urge to protect her already fragile friend.

"Maybe he has been helpful," Sabina reluctantly said, giving Caelan the smallest of smiles, "but that still doesn't change the fact that we have no idea what his intentions are. He's older than both of us and seems to want to be your friend. Why should he even want to? It makes me wonder what he has to gain or what he really wants from you."

Caelan held his hands out. "I understand your concerns, I do, but it doesn't mean that I am like who you think I am. Have your opinion of me, but I genuinely care about your friend and you as well. I do not have to know you or anyone intimately to care. It's a trait called empathy. I am not some sort of monster. I've seen and dealt with my own traumas, and I know what it feels like to be confused and not have any solace. I will leave you be. If you need me, you know where to find me."

The chair scraped against the floor as he stood. He rubbed his hands against his shirt and straightened his collar, as if the act itself would rub the embarrassment off of his skin.

His green eyes were warm as they landed on Cammie, and he gave Sabina a parting nod as he headed to the back. Sabina's eyes followed him as he came to a stop at a door.

The bathroom. Okay. He isn't resisting.

Sabina's mind was never more cluttered, but she knew she had to do something, anything to ease the discomfort and confusion her friend was carrying.

"What do we do now?" Cammie asked, her bottom lip quivering.

"We're going to go home, and you can shower and calm down. Maybe we can talk about a strategy after. Maybe we can get in touch with Hannah. She was in the picture with us. She'd know what to do or maybe where to look."

Cammie solemnly nodded and got up from the table. Her nose pinched upward, and then she blinked once, twice.

"Are you okay?" Sabina rose to her feet, arms outstretched toward Cammie.

The color of cherries dotted Cammie's cheeks and splotched her forehead. Little beads of sweat were slick against her eyebrows, small droplets dripping into her eyes. Her hands began to shake. Her eyes were a glass pane that seemed to have no focus, and a small moan fell from her lips.

"Cammie? Answer me. Are you okay?" Sabina's voice was higher than usual, the panic etched into her voice.

It only took a second for Cammie's knees to buckle and her eyes to roll back before she was sprawled on the floor. Within seconds, Sabina was cradling Cammie's head in her hands, crouched to the floor.

Gasps of concern scattered amongst every table, and then the crowd formed.

Sabina tried to lift her, but Cammie's body was too heavy, as limp as it was. And there it hit her.

Cammie was unconscious.

The scream of horror was loud against her ears, and it took a few moments to realize the scream was hers. And then she was crying so much that breathing was like taking skips that never seemed to touch the ground.

An arm yanked on her shoulder, and she pulled her fist backward. No one was going to take her away from her friend.

"I can help." Caelan's eyes were full of horror to the same degree that bubbled in her gut.

"What do we do, Caelan? What do we do?" The words were like a spilled drink, but no amount of wiping would clear it up. "She was fine, and then she stood up, and now she's—is she okay? Is she going to be okay?" The bubbling in her throat was thick, no matter how many times she swallowed. "Do we take her to the hospital?"

Caelan shook his head. "No, a hospital won't fix this."

"How do you know?" Sabina said, her voice above a whisper.

When he turned to her, she could finally see it. His eyes were wise beyond her years of existence, and they could offer an answer to the plea in her heart.

"You're going to have to trust me," he said, hoisting Cammie in his arms. "We need to take her home, where she can fight this in her sleep. It's the only way to go through the process of reclaiming what was lost."

Sabina's head moved faster than her mouth. "Reclaiming? Reclaiming what?"

"Her memories," Caelan said matter-of-factly. It was as if he were discussing something as simple as the weather or what dinner would be. It was as natural as breathing.

"You know what happened to Cammie?" Sabina breathed. "But how?"

"It's like I said," he replied. "You're just going to have to trust me."

CHAPTER TWELVE

HANNAH

THE BRUISING HAD FINALLY GONE down, at least a little. A few hours on the road and a wet compress proved to be the healing factor for Tony.

At least the physical aspect.

Tony was staring out of the window, his eyes ablaze. The one in question was swollen and purple, a tad smaller than when he had first gotten in the car. Dried blood rested underneath his nose. Hannah tried to wipe it, but Tony swiped at her hand, telling her he preferred to leave it there as a reminder, so it wouldn't happen again.

Will didn't make any sound except for the constant coughing or breathing. Hannah wanted to prod, but the worry of provoking stopped her. From what she saw, Will was always one second away from snapping.

"It wasn't his fault, you know," Trevor said. "His anger is a component he can't always control." He was the only one who dared to tackle speaking since the calamity.

The words that came from Trevor's lips felt like a hollow excuse. She wanted to voice as much but decided against it.

"It's crappy is what it is," she mumbled under her breath. "How much farther to get food?" she asked louder. Her stomach rumbled.

"Maybe five minutes," Will said. "And then after that, maybe we can figure out where to go, to actually stay. I guess going home isn't something you want?"

The look Hannah gave him was enough to cause hesitation.

"All right, then." Will let out a breath. "I guess we head some other way, but where do we go? If we go any farther, we'll run out of gas. Or maybe," he added, "we'll die of starvation." His upper lip turned to the sky. "That sounds more likely."

It seemed that a few hours of silence had allowed the sardonic comments to flow again.

"I'm glad you're in a better mood now." Tony's voice made Will stiffen.

Will opened his mouth, his eyes darting back to the rearview mirror. Words were voids that couldn't be retrieved.

The invisible weight hung in the van. Everyone was waiting for the punch to hit the floor.

"Stop staring at me. Keep driving. We need food. Just stop off at the exit here." Gruffness was still evident in Tony's voice, the edge as sharp as knives.

Will's face became scarlet. He faced back at the road, his hands tightening on the steering wheel.

It wasn't the early hours in the morning anymore. Hannah marveled at the way the sun hit just right on her face as she pressed her nose against the window. Warmth spread across her nose and her cheeks, and she let out a sigh. Finally, finally. *Some freaking peace.*

With her eyes closed, it was easy to wade away from the drama of today and of yesterday and all the days before that. It was the first time, in what felt like a long time, that she had allowed herself to breathe.

There weren't any cops. There weren't any dad issues. There weren't any friendship problems or boys with lavish tempers or idiotic words.

It was just her in her bubble, far, far away from the mess that was tied to her ankle. She was always dragging it, always carrying the extra load, but for five minutes, maybe she could sleep it away. Maybe she could float on a cloud, and when she would wake, the troubles would be gone.

The diner was quaint. It reminded her of those '50s movies where people stopped on the side of the highway for food.

But the one thing they didn't make known was the noise.

The little fan click-clacked as the blades sped faster than the ceiling could probably handle. The canopy slanted as each turn went full circle, and she couldn't help but wonder if they could have picked a different table. The last thing they absolutely needed was to have the fan literally fall on them.

But it wouldn't be the worst thing they'd expect to happen after today.

Marcus's lips were in a thin line. He rested his clasped hands on his lap as he shifted his weight. Tony was next to him, his eyes boring a hole at the wall behind them. Hannah was on the opposite side, stuck between Will and Trevor.

"Do you think the food will be good?" Will piped up, his fingers drumming on the table.

Hannah turned to him. "I'm happy that food is on your mind. It's a new emotion. A better one than earlier."

"I said I was sorry." Will's eyes flashed with the semblance of pain. "How many more times do I need to repeat it?"

"Until the bruising is gone. That should be enough."

"That could take months!" Will protested. "Or weeks. There's no telling how long his bruises will stay. Why should I be punished for something I apologized for countless times? I can't change it."

"You shouldn't have done it," Marcus growled.

Several patrons turned to look in their direction, and Hannah's eyes darkened. *Always in public.*

"Keep it down. People are staring," she warned. The earnest stares darting at her were beginning to feel like bugs on her skin.

"So let them stare," Marcus said, his lip turning upward. "Let that be his punishment for being an impulsive idiot."

"Since when were you the judge? You're not the leader of this group." Will angled his body over the table, his hands touching the center.

"And you think you are because you hurt ours?" Marcus was almost laughing. His own eyes were a neon sign, blazing away with the challenge of rebuttal.

"Like you'd do any better," Will spat. "You act all tough, but everyone knows you're just the weakest of all of us. The only time you get any of your strength is when you come to Tony's rescue. He's man enough to take care of himself, but maybe the reason you do it is because you're too spineless to be your own person. You're *pathetic.*"

Marcus shot upward from the table. His fists were balled, and his skin began to redden. His eyes were fire and he aimed the heat in Will's direction.

"Are you ready to order?" The waitress's lips were in a deep-set frown. By the wrinkles in her cheeks and bags under her eyes, it was clear she was at least in her fifties. She wore the world on her shoulders, and loud teenagers weren't at the top of the list, judging by how her nose flared.

"If you could just give us a few moments, I'm sure we would be ready to." Hannah gave a small smile. She hoped it would be encouraging enough.

"By all means, feel free to kill each other outside. I've got a lot of tables, not just yours. You kids would do better to keep your drama outside." Her red lips curled around each word, as if she was worried letting them into the world would cause the biggest explosion of a lifetime. "Or even better, take it to go. You guys can bleed all over your own car. You sure ain't going to bleed onto my floor." She tapped her pen against the pad she was carrying, her wrinkled hands locked tight around the instrument.

"Why don't we take it to go?" Hannah offered to the table.

The rest of the guys murmured in agreement, and Marcus slowly brought himself back down to the booth.

Hannah nodded to the waitress. "We'll take it to go."

With swift hands, the woman got the orders on her pad. She barely smiled as she turned around. The woman walked away, shoving the pen into her hair. Traces of her words found their way back to the table as she left, words that made Hannah's stomach knot.

"Stupid, rotten kids."

As soon as the waitress was out of earshot, Hannah slapped her hands on the table. "Are you idiots out of your damn minds?" Her shrillness caused each and every boy at the table to flinch. "You can't keep trying to kill each other everywhere that we go. You make us look like murderers or people who just want to cause trouble."

"We usually act like this everywhere. Even you. You're no better," Will said with a mere shrug.

"I have my moments," Hannah breathed.

Marcus began slow clapping. "She finally admits it. She finally admits her faults. Gentleman, we have an honest Hannah here."

"But just because I have my moments doesn't make it okay." Hannah inhaled, pinching the bridge of her nose.

"Unless it's absolutely necessary, right?" Marcus asked.

"Why is it suddenly all about what is necessary for me? What about all the times you guys screw things up?"

"You were with us during those times," Trevor mumbled, "and others, well…" He took a breath and then sheepishly smiled. "We kind of had to pull you back."

Hannah narrowed her eyes. "I'm not some kind of violent monster."

"Your punch list says otherwise," Will refuted. "Shall I list the times your fist has left a mark?"

"Please do," Marcus said. He shined his gleaming teeth at Will.

Hannah did a double take. *Is he actually smiling? No way. Not after what just happened and especially not at Will.*

"Ahem," Will cleared this throat. "The first time the boy down the road called you an indecent pig." One finger went up.

"The time he and his friends came back for vengeance after you egged his house," Trevor added.

Another finger went up on Will's hand.

"Let us not forget the time that involved smashing Ian's face with a beer bottle," Marcus was all too eager to share as his smile grew even wider.

"But that wasn't her hands directly. Does it really count?"

Every head whipped to the man beside Marcus.

Tony.

"He speaks!" Will cheered. "He actually speaks." His face brightened like a lamp in a dark room, but his entire demeanor froze as Tony's eyes landed on him.

Everyone at the table held their breath.

Tony broke out into a smile, and Hannah breathed a sigh of relief. *For now, they are okay.*

"It's good to see you guys on some kind of healing terms, but did I really have to be the butt of the joke?" she complained.

"Now you know what it feels like," Will sang. "Doesn't feel so good, does it?"

Looking at the joy on everyone's face gave Hannah a semblance of peace. Whatever spell they had been under, it had finally dissipated. The anger was gone, and she intended to use every moment of this calm to her advantage.

She rose from the table. "I'm going to go wait in the van. Do you guys mind grabbing the food and paying? I just need to stretch my legs for a bit."

Hannah scurried away from the table as quickly as she could. She wasn't going to wait a moment longer in case something went wrong.

It always seems to, but maybe it'll be different. Maybe me being the butt of the joke is enough for their crap to die down. Maybe if I just leave them to their own thoughts with ketchup and fries, that'll keep the calm going.

She marched to the exit, the smile growing on her lips as reached the door and headed outside. Hannah was so lost in thought that she didn't even notice the smell in the air that hit her nostrils until it was far too late.

Her throat burned as if cinnamon was taking a slow ride downtown, the smoke billowing around her eyes. She waved it away, coughing each sting into her balled fist.

"Can you learn how to maybe not blow smoke in people's faces?" She managed to huff the words out, and if her eyes weren't like fire, she would have sent the guy the look of death she so easily mastered.

"Can you maybe learn how to not walk straight into the path of smoke? Watching where you walk actually has been proven to cause less accidents, but, hey, you're one step above those who text and walk. Luckily, I'm not driving a car, and you're not an idiot. Otherwise, that could be problematic."

Hannah couldn't fight back the look of disgust on her face. "And just who do you think you are, talking to me like this?"

The guy leaning against the wall had one arm lazily sprawled across his chest while he brought the other up to his lips. He took another drag of the cigarette he was holding between his fingers. Blue eyes danced with mischief. Tan skin glistened against the darkened grin he displayed. The leather jacket he wore was tight against broad shoulders, and his pants were ripped without a care. He wore his attitude the same way he wore his clothes—nothing short of subtle.

He pushed himself off of the wall, and in the light, his brown hair seemed to almost take on a golden hue. "Take it how you want. I'm here to please. You just happened to be in my way, and you can decide how to go about that. No harm, no foul either way."

"You're disgusting." Hannah grimaced.

The man gave her another smile. "Maybe, but most people call me Nyx."

CHAPTER THIRTEEN

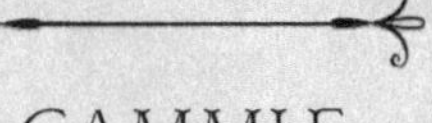

CAMMIÆ

THE WORLD AROUND HER WAS a mirage of colors from violent purples to melancholic blues. As she floated around them, they fought their own war. The colors slowly dimmed before any could get the upper hand.

It was there that she heard the voice calling her to remain awake, to keep fighting.

And so, she tried, but the colors enveloped her. They stuck to her skin like unwelcome glue.

Her mind was fog as she tried to speak, her lips velcroed against her better judgment.

Movements were of no ail.

She once again tried to escape from the condensing hues. Cammie could see the boy's crooked smile as the colors attacked her face.

Before she succumbed, she knew one thing for sure.

It wasn't the lilac or the royal blue that crushed her.

The darkness did enough on its own.

CHAPTER FOURTEEN

SABINA

S ABINA'S HEART RICOCHETED IN HER chest as she rose to her feet, and she swore she could taste the offset of bile in her throat when she inhaled.

Several customers were still staring, but Caelan gave them no indication of importance. Their whispers formed a path as he led the way to the entrance, Sabina following as closely as she could.

His strides were purposeful and much longer than hers. With every single step she took, he was two more ahead. Her breath hitched while she tried to keep up, her shoes slapping the floor.

Caelan opened the door with his hip, sending the little bell dinging. Cammie's neck hung against his bicep, strands of her hair falling across his skin. He was holding her tightly, but it didn't stop the voice in Sabina's head that told her it would take mere seconds for her friend to fall onto the concrete sidewalk they were walking on.

"Where are you taking her?" she blurted.

Caelan was still walking and made no move to turn around.

"You have to tell me this. How convenient is it that she just happened to fall unconscious and you're sweeping in to save the day?"

Caelan halted in his tracks.

Deep, erratic fear wrapped its clever fingers around her clenched heart, adding just enough pressure she was sure she'd burst.

"What your friend is dealing with is no coincidence. I had some suspicion of it, but I didn't want to make any of my concerns known until I was sure."

"And just what are you sure of?" Sabina hurried forward and turned back to face Caelan. She angled her body just enough that she could sidestep any movements.

He can't take my friend. He can try, but I'll fight until my last breath.

"I'm not going to hurt you," he replied.

"How do I know that for sure?" she dared to ask. "And don't say, 'Just trust me.'" She narrowed her eyes.

"I can give you an explanation," Caelan offered.

"The truth would be better," Sabina stated. "The truth."

He promptly nodded. His eyes hardened with resolution, and he took a moment to breathe before he spoke. "The truth is, I did seek out your friend."

Sabina's hands flew upward, as if the force of them could block off anything else he planned on revealing. She lowered her brow as her mind scrambled at his words. "Why?"

"Your friend, Cammie, well, she knows someone I was looking for."

The final puzzle piece slipped into place. All of the stories Cammie mentioned, the meeting at the bookstore, and the coffee shop.... The revelation came crashing too soon, too quickly.

"You've been stalking her, haven't you? Just one of her mother's obsessed fans." Her hand traveled to the phone in her back pocket. Her eyes were animatedly aware of the people walking on the sidewalks. She scanned their faces, gawking, begging for one of them to slow, to help her. This man was absolutely, positively mad.

"I can assure you I'm not crazy, and I very much do care about your friend. That's why, when I noticed she was having the mental flashes, I wanted to help. If I can help her, she can help me."

"You're making no sense. Let me take Cammie. We have to get her to the hospital before something happens." Sabina reached for her.

Caelan shifted back, just enough to where her friend was now seemingly a world away. "What she has, a hospital can't fix. Once a human is marked by the effects of being erased by an Amarian, if not treated within reasonable means and the reasonable timeframe, it's catastrophic."

"I'm sorry," Sabina choked on confusion. "Amara—what?"

"Amarian. It's what my people are called."

Sabina could do nothing but blink. This man was here, standing in front of her with the most serious and earnest of looks, discussing a race that did not exist. He was also holding her friend very close to his chest, as if she had all of the answers that would fix his deranged mind.

He is *very clearly disturbed.*

She began to tread lightly, slowly positioning herself closer, and closer until she felt her fingers brush Cammie's arm.

"It's true. It's why she's remembering someone who doesn't exist, who you clearly saw in the photo. You say you don't want lies, and you want answers. You want her to be fixed? I can tell you how she can be fixed. She needs to come with me to the place where I grew up. There are other Amarians who live there who know how to help ease and reverse some of the effects of the erasing gone wrong. The person you saw in the photo is the person I am looking for. James is what he goes by here. I was never able to get his real name. I was supposed to meet him—he had information about my family, information about me. Information about the world I escaped from as a child. Cammie is the last connection I have to my past, to finding true answers, and she is, from what I can tell, one of the kindest people I've ever encountered." His breath became shorter, laced with the tightness of an emotion that took Sabina a moment to place.

Fondness.

"So, let's say for the off-chance you are speaking the truth," Sabina said slowly. "What happens if we don't get her to the place you mentioned on time? What then? What happens to her?"

"As of now, her body is deteriorating itself. Her mind... it is collapsing within. Her frail human body is fighting the aftereffects. It's what happens when an erasing doesn't go as planned. The memories meant to vanish become dormant until some sort of event awakens them. And then, the mind becomes triggered, trying to make sense of what was supposed to be gone. The mental poison, so to speak, slows every sense. It's like a coma that she can't come out of. She ceases to hear, to speak, to move. As of now, the effects aren't nearly as bad, but you can feel how her skin is fire to the touch. Any longer and..."

"What?" Sabina breathed. "What will happen?" Everything in her body wanted to scream "liar," but something deep in her stomach gave her pause.

"Any longer than a week without being treated...and she will die."

There it was, the finality that halted her breathing. She was frozen at the precipice with no way back.

"How do you know this will work? How do you know she can be healed?" Sabina asked, daring herself to believe the impossible.

Caelan offered the smallest of smiles. She was almost afraid he wouldn't answer until he repeated those same six words, "You just have to trust me."

CHAPTER FIFTEEN

HANNAH

THE MAN CONTINUED STARING WITH his iridescent eyes that held no ending. His smile was on the cusp of lighting a million fires, and the way he gleamed at her was as if Hannah was merely the match.

"I didn't mean to offend you at all," he said.

"Well, you did," she huffed, rolling her eyes.

Nyx didn't reply. Instead, he chose to let his eyes roam elsewhere, anywhere, but at her.

"So no apology?" Hannah shrugged, unable to stop glaring. He was beginning to get on her nerves.

"Saying I didn't mean to offend you should be an apology enough." His eyes were now locked on the ground. With one hand, he brought the cigarette back to his parted lips. He ruffled his hair with the other, a tic that she wondered he was fond of.

"Are you always this rude?"

"And here I thought we had come to an understanding." Silver smoke swelled from his lips, hitting her in the face.

Tears began to slip out of the corners of her eyes, and all she could see was red.

"Is this bothering you?" The sly smile returned, and his eyes trained themselves back on her.

With the smoke still freshly stinging her corneas, it took a second, but when it hit her, it hit full force. *He's trying to see how far my buttons can be pressed.*

White knuckles clenched into a fist at her side. How far was she willing to let him go before she lost it? She was always helping the boys regain their tempers, and sure, her anger had led her into worse situations, but she had done well so far. It seemed all it would take was some cocky idiot with a nicotine addiction to bring out the animal inside.

"I said stop. Is that so hard to do?"

Nyx's eyes softened as his lips went down at the corners. She could tell by the way he licked his lips that another response was ready.

"Is everything okay here?" A strong hand clasped her shoulder.

Her muscles instantly released. *Tony. Always here to save the day.*

"No problem at all," Nyx said as he shot a charming smile Tony's way. "I was just having a little chat with the lady."

Tony did not, however, harbor the same look of fondness that Nyx tried to assuage. Instead, his lips seemed to become thinner, and his jaw locked tightly. "Well, I think you'd better read up on how to treat a woman. I'd say by the looks of it you aren't doing a good job."

Nyx's face twisted, his eyes narrowing just enough to show he was provoked, but then he plastered on another smile. "You seem to be busy or wanting to catch up on other things.

I also have other...matters to attend to." He gave a barely-there nod to Tony and winked in Hannah's direction.

And then, he was out of earshot, walking to the car lot far, far away from her.

Hannah's breath met the open space, and her lungs began to sing.

"What happened? Did he hurt you?" In mere seconds, Tony grabbed her by the shoulders and turned her around. They were face to face now, his eyes full of concern and almost loosened rage.

"He didn't even touch me," Hannah explained. "It wasn't that bad."

The crease in his brows didn't give way. He didn't believe her.

Exasperated, she threw her hands up. "I would have had him."

"Not with guys like that you don't," Tony said, sneering at Nyx's back. The anger he had couldn't be measured in just his face. It was everywhere—in his hands, his fingers, and his knuckles as he clenched and unclenched them.

"Jerks are everywhere we go. What's so particular about this one?" Hannah peered closely at him.

Tony darted away. It was as if she was something that would blind him if he even tried to take a small glance. When she tugged on his arm, he still didn't budge.

"Nothing," Tony said, which made the alarm bells in her head go off even louder.

The door swung open. Several men, all rugged and unkempt, ran out to the car lot. All four of them gathered near the bikes that Nyx stood between. Nyx fumbled through his pocket and brought a cigarette to his lips. One of the men—the one with the reddish hair—leaned in close to Nyx.

Hannah squinted, as if magically she'd be able to understand the words she couldn't even recognize so far away, but even moving mouths couldn't confirm what she desired.

As the man continued speaking, Nyx brought the lighter up and lit the cigarette, making the tip alive with the flame. He took a long drag and blew out the smoke that Hannah had become quite familiar with.

Though they were further away and though she could not understand the spectacle unraveling before her, the one thing she could not mistake was how even as the other man pulled back, Nyx was staring.

He was staring with his deep, prickling eyes.

Right at her.

"I think we should follow them," Hannah said, her eyes trained on the crew of men hanging around the bikes. Her curiosity was getting the better of her. They were up to something; she was sure of it.

Will, Marcus, and Trevor managed to get out of the restaurant a few minutes after the incident and even after several explanations of what had happened were still unconvinced at her words.

"That's not smart," Tony murmured.

"I don't see how following him will solve anything." For once, Will seemed to side with Tony.

"So out of anything you could agree with him with, you choose this very moment?" Hannah was incredulously surprised, shooting Will the darkest of glares. "My idea isn't stupid."

"You're right. It isn't," Marcus shot up.

Hannah beamed. Finally. Her arms reached for the sky because it was some miracle that someone chose her side. "Thank you."

"It's absolutely, ridiculously, entirely dangerous," Marcus finished.

"How come when everyone else has some 'insane' plan, you guys just go along with it? What about me is so crazy that you can't even begin to think it'll turn out fine?"

At this, the guys merely smirked.

"What's the secret, then? Come on. Fess up." She crossed her arms over her chest.

"It just seems, well, every time that we decide to go through on one of your plans, someone gets hurt. This trip, for example." When Hannah stiffened, Marcus paused. "Your dad was one of them. Tony got hit—"

"That wasn't me." The anger was back, coming in fuming waves. "That was most definitely Will. If anyone's to blame for that, it's how you guys have the shortest fuses," Hannah explained.

"And you're no better," Tony stated.

Hannah's mouth slacked open, her tongue tripping over the words lodged in her mouth.

"I'm not saying we're better than you," Tony added, "because, of course, we aren't, but you have just as big of a temper as ours, and the last thing we need is for you to go back to pummeling idiots and the cops finding us again. We were lucky at the mechanic shop, but I can't promise we will be if you get impulsive with this guy. We aren't sixteen anymore. If you want to go stumbling after this guy, I can definitely assure you the cops will be involved somehow, and it won't be like how your dad stopped us from trouble before."

He was being entirely truthful. There were countless times, she vividly recalled, where they had been barely unscathed from the consequences of the law. Her father had done more than enough to help them unravel the situations, as terrifying as they had been at that time. He had done it in the hopes that they would learn and make better decisions. Hannah had failed more than she could count. While they were on the road, she had vowed to tone things down.

As Tony's gaze softened, she realized it was as if he could read her thoughts. She sighed. "You're right. No punching, no pummeling."

The grin that broke out on Tony's face was enough for her to relax. Just a little.

"Where'd they go?" Marcus blurted, cutting through the conversation.

Hannah whipped her gaze around back to Nyx and his crew. Over half of the men were gone, except for Nyx and a few others.

Tony swore under his breath, eyes scouring the parking lot. "We need to get back to the van," he said, gesturing with his head to the lot.

"I'll wait here while you guys go," Hannah said.

Tony scoffed. "Absolutely not. Someone stays here with you, or you come along. Those are the only options."

"I can take care of myself," Hannah reassured him.

With how Tony's nostrils flared, the unspoken response was obvious.

"I'll be fine," she said, giving him a slow nod.

Tony's eyes stirred as he searched her face. For a brief moment, he remained unmoved. Then, he pulled away, turning to the lot. "Let's go," he instructed.

One by one, their friends followed his lead.

Hannah watched their retreating backs before she brought her gaze back to Nyx and the bikes.

Gone. But how? Where did they go?

Hannah nibbled at her lip, her eyes never leaving the now-empty space. Sudden fear stabbed at her stomach in deep, relentless waves while her throat remained tight. She gulped in handfuls of air, hoping that would ease her discomfort, but the feeling only expanded. Hannah started to run, her eyes focused on some random destination in the distance—anything to get her away from there.

Rough hands clasped across her chest from behind.

Instinct took over, and Hannah did her best to jab the person with her elbow, but there was no use. Her hands were captive.

"There's no use trying to run." Hot breath tickled against her earlobe, sending a chill down her back. "Don't bother yelling. There's no use. If you want to survive, you'll be silent, little *Lunar*." Despite the threat in his tone, Nyx spoke the final word so sweetly that it caused an onslaught of bile in Hannah's throat.

Little what?

She looked on wildly for her friends to return, but there was no one coming, no sound of running footsteps. Hannah thrashed, trying to get her chin angled enough to bite the finger that was clutching her collarbone. When that didn't work, she resorted to the second option. "Help! Let me go—" The words died on her lips as she caught a glance of the movement behind her.

Nyx's other men were gathered by the bikes and there were no customers outside paying enough attention to the scene unfolding. For all the rowdiness inside, they probably thought this was a practical joke as Nyx dragged Hannah to where the others waited.

Fiery panic latched onto her heart, and Hannah felt her breathing become shallow. *Where was Tony? Where the hell was Tony?*

Nyx wasn't gentle as he sat her down on the bike before immediately sitting in front of her. The engine revved until it became a deadly roar as Nyx brought the bike to life.

A hollow scream erupted from behind her, and then she heard it.

The footfalls.

Tony was running to them at full speed, his chest moving in exertion as he pushed his legs faster. The rest of her friends were following behind him, the same gazes of panic written in their eyes.

Nyx was faster.

It only took seconds for the billow of smoke to appear behind them as the dust drifted into her esophagus. It felt like they were flying far away from her friends.

Far away from help.

And Hannah knew, deep in her soul, that there was no way that anyone would find her.

CHAPTER SIXTEEN

SABINA

As CAELAN LED HER TO the van, the growing feeling in her stomach shifted to fear tracing her skin. It could have been the anxiety pummeling through her veins as Caelan carried Cammie to the backseat.

It could have been the way he set her gently and buckled her in.

Or maybe it was the way he made just enough room and gestured for Sabina to get in, shutting the door behind her.

Or maybe it was how he professed he was some other-worldly being.

Yes, that is most definitely the reason why I'm feeling like a moth shedding its protective layer.

Sabina kept her eyes locked on her unconscious friend. Cammie's skin coloring was still ghastly white, her chest moving up and down with deep breaths. *She's still alive.* That was the only thing Sabina was sure of as she trailed her eyes away and out to the window.

Caelan had managed to walk around the van, his hair flowing in the wind as he grasped the door handle. With every move he made, Sabina's heart thumped even more erratically. She began to wonder, just maybe, if she were now on a ride that would lead to death itself.

It took mere seconds for him to put the key in the ignition, and then he turned it over. Sooner than Sabina would have liked, the van was already moving and she wasn't sure how—or if—they would return.

The drive was a slow progression. As more minutes began to tick, the more her nerves began to thicken. A deep fog had managed to wind around her brain to the point that her thoughts were hazy and dripped into despair.

Sabina mustered up the courage to speak. "Where exactly are we going?" With one hand, she latched onto Cammie's palm and gave a small squeeze.

Caelan dared to look in the rearview mirror. "We're going to the home of my birth as I mentioned earlier. It's the only way to save your friend."

Sabina kept her gaze interlocked with Caelan's. All she wanted to do was scream. They were getting farther and farther away now from someone, anyone, who could help.

"And like I had mentioned, she needs a hospital. The only reason I agreed to come is because you have a way to get there." As the very words laid bare, paranoia entered the scene. Every window in the van became inches smaller and more condensed.

This time, he went back to face the road.

Her hands immediately went to the door handle. "Let me out of here," she said, yanking backward.

It didn't budge.

"You just have to trust me," Caelan stated, his fingers tightening on the wheel.

"Trust you?" The shrillness wasn't even contained in Sabina's voice. "You're telling me to trust you when you're taking us who knows where, far away from the hospital that can save my friend? You are *insane*."

There was no way he was telling the truth, or if he was... it was a truth only universally believed by him alone.

The road began to dwindle away from a town of lively buildings and people toward a winding line of trees. While the trees stood in formation, towering and long, even they joined in on the spectacle. They were the only witnesses to the sight of fear stemming from the girl in the backseat, and Sabina couldn't help but fume at their selfishness. They would have a front row to her demise, but, inanimate as they were, they couldn't save her.

Which meant one thing.

It was up to her to save herself.

In what she would later describe as one of the most daring moments of her life, Sabina unbuckled her seatbelt and leapt across the space between her and Caelan.

Caelan's grip was sturdy and sure on the wheel no matter how hard Sabina tugged.

"Let go," she screamed, using her elbow to steady herself. Her feet flailed as she scooted closer, leaning her weight against Caelan.

"What are you doing?" His voice was deafening in her ear as he tried to shove her with his arm. With one hand, he succeeded, sending her flying. The back of her head slammed against the passenger side window. *Thwack!* Brain fog followed.

"I won't let you take us anywhere except the hospital." Her voice was guttural and strained, throat thick with the force of impact. It didn't matter that she was beginning to see dots. She had to do whatever was necessary for their safety.

Even if it meant being completely out of her element to do so.

She pushed herself off of the door and leapt again, and that was when it became apparent.

She could hear it so clearly. The sound of skidding tires became the forefront in her mind, while screams and grunts sang in the background.

It only took a second for the dread to plummet to her gut.

The vehicle was spinning, Sabina realized, as the colors blended and burning rubber collided together in beautiful chaos.

It all ended with the slamming of brakes and a distant, unintelligible sound.

Confusion muddled her brain when she slammed back, once again, into the passenger door. The impact had a harder effect this time, sending stars and blurriness to her eyes that were stubborn to fade as she blinked. Sabina had enough strength to look for her friend, breath lodged in her throat.

Cammie was still not awake, and her position hadn't changed since the incident.

That small sight released the nerves that were on Sabina's shoulders, but all it took was one glance at the fire in Caelan's eyes for the fear to return.

He was not looking at her, though.

His eyes were very clearly locked on the road ahead of them.

No debris tainted the passageway, and there were no signs of wreckage, so she began to marvel—almost dangerously so—as to what captivated his attention.

She followed his line of sight. A gray, humongous *thing* was in the ditch.

"What is that?" The breathy curious question flew from her lips without pause.

"It's a problem needing to be fixed." Caelan leaned over his seat, fumbling through bags on the floor.

"What are you doing?"

"Taking care of it," he replied, without giving her a backward glance.

Sabina's gaze stayed latched onto his hands as he continued searching. Caelan lifted an object she couldn't decipher. But underneath the glittering glow of the sun, the light reflected just enough for her to place what the object was.

"A hilt? What are you going to do with that?" There was no sword or blade attached to it, but she realized it could be used as a weapon.

Against her. She flinched immediately as she caught his gaze again.

The hurt bled from his eyes, but just like that, it was gone.

"Please, stay in the car." Caelan's jaw was set. Determined as he was, he only gave Sabina one last glance as he exited the van. "Whatever you do," he added, "whatever you might see, *do not* move. It is for your safety that I am asking this. Please, just trust me."

Sabina pondered his words. He had been speaking a lot of trust, but she didn't know this man in any kind of capacity. How in the world could she trust his intentions?

Caelan said he knew how to save her friend, but there were also other options. He could have been trying to kidnap her. He could have been trying to kidnap Cammie. He went on and on about existing in some other-worldly realm, so any words of "trust me" or "I am honest" were surely coming from a deranged man.

She made up her mind. No more going back and forth on sympathy and self-preservation. She had to be firm in her choice.

She climbed softly, slowly into the backseat. Cammie's face was still pressed against the window, and her chest was rising and falling. She was still breathing.

For now. The pesky thought seemed to have no fear arising in Sabina's mind, and she couldn't help but want to kick herself for not trying to escape sooner.

But beating herself up wouldn't help Cammie. It would only prolong what had been already happening—a delay in help.

It took more strength than she knew she had to get the seatbelt unbuckled from her friend with shaky hands. She knew she had minutes, mere minutes, to get away. She wasn't sure how occupied Caelan was. But curiosity was a weakness Sabina hadn't learned how to tame.

Just one small look, and then Cammie and I will go right to a hospital.

Caelan was crouched to his knees, and from this distance, Sabina could see how the hilt was still firmly gripped in his left hand. The being, from what she could tell, was still unmoving, but one squint of her eyes and one movement from Caelan allowed her to see that it was a huge...wolf.

The gray wolf had ragged breathing, rapid movements coming from the side, and she could see crimson. It had been hit pretty hard, and Caelan made no move to help it. Instead, he only lifted the hilt.

He is going to kill it.

She let go of Cammie, setting her back down gently, and before she could stop herself, she flung herself out of the van and was running. Her legs were screaming for release, and her heart was pumping more blood to her burning joints. Everything was aching and numbing from adrenaline coursing and stopping, but she couldn't let him do it.

"I know you might have some ideas on stopping the pain, or maybe you're just psychotic, but you can't kill it." The words tumbled from her mouth as she reached Caelan, her hand hesitantly lingering above him.

Caelan jumped at her words, the hilt slipping through his fingers. He caught a firmer grasp of it as he glanced at her. His eyes were full of unmistakable rage, and on the cusp of it was... sadness. Sadness coated the edges of his eyes, as soft tears fell down his face. His entire body shook with it as his bones and muscles waded in the deep blue that traveled.

"You don't understand," he pleaded, meeting her eyes fully.

"I don't understand, you're right, but—"

"This thing killed my family." The grief was in his fingers twitching, in the tears flowing, in the breaths he was heaving. He could barely get the words out.

An animal attack is what broke him. An animal attack is what made his mind go into a tailspin.

"I know you are hurt," she said slowly, "and you are grieving, but you...can't kill it. Forgiving it...is what is best. For your health."

Caelan sniffled and let out a haughty laugh. "Humans such as yourself have no idea of the catastrophic things that take place in your world, or mine for that matter. This is none of your concern. Go back to the van." The resolution was firm in his voice, his tone steel as he shot daggers of stone at Sabina.

"But—"

"What did I tell you?" he shouted. "It's for your safety. Now, *go!*" Earnest pleading overtook his angry expression.

Sabina felt her heart thunder in her chest. If she couldn't talk sense into him, now was the time to grab Cammie and run and call for help later.

Sabina turned her gaze back to the animal on the ground. Its brown eyes were looking right at her as it took more ragged breaths.

She could still get away.

The set of deep brown eyes blinked just then, and a small shiver ran down her spine. She couldn't place it at first, still staring at the eyes of the being she attempted to save. The way the eyes narrowed and the corner of the mouth twinged upwards...it was a mischievous smile, one she had seen on shows and movies plenty of times. The edge of a tooth revealed itself, and she heard the throaty, rasping, inhuman sound.

The sound of attack.

"Caelan—" The scream was building, ready to pierce the world as a set of claws swiped in his direction. The thing had been lying in wait, watching for the opportune moment to kill them both.

She felt the hand on her stomach before she could make sense of anything else. The force was powerful, knocking her backward, far away from the wolf. When her back hit the ground, she crawled as far as she could on her hands, using her feet as momentum to push herself. She stood with sweaty palms, fear clutching her chest.

Caelan already had swirled around, moving to a crouching stance yet again. The hilt was still in his hands and he had it raised above his head.

But there was no sword. He had no way to defend himself. They were all going to die, and there was absolutely nothing that could be done to save them.

"You really thought you would try to hurt her in front of me?" Caelan's words were deep, his face contorted, teeth bare. "It was bad enough that she sent you to kill my family all those years ago, but you will now willingly kill a stranger who has absolutely nothing to do with this?"

The wolf's teeth were arched, and a low, cruel sound came from it. It was hard to distinguish, but as Sabina listened closely, she became all too aware of what the noise was.

Laughter. The thing was laughing.

But that wasn't possible. It couldn't be possible. There was no way...absolutely no way...

"You think mere humans are immune to the queen's wrath?"

The grainy words came from the lips of something Sabina never would have imagined in all the years she had been alive. The animal, the wolf, the thing, was talking. The sound was harsh against her ears, like that of a smoker who had finally found words after hours of cigarettes.

"You must not remember your history, then," the wolf continued. "Her ancestors did more than enough damage to these frail, pathetic wastes of life. Killing the girl isn't something our queen deems as necessary. We are merely doing the world a favor by ridding it of such weakness. We have our plans, our motives, and if she gets in the way, then so be it." The wolf changed direction, looking right at her. "Don't worry, little human. I will make your death easy and quick. It will feel like nothing more than a little pinch. And then...you will be gone."

"You're speaking," Sabina said, mouth agape, "but how can that be?"

"You won't touch her," Caelan growled, the hilt shaking in his hands.

The wolf turned its gaze away from Sabina and looked back at Caelan. Its eyes were sparkling with amusement. "You really think, Fallen Prince, that you will stop me? What will you do with that weapon of yours? You don't even have a blade to defend yourself, and yet you speak words of chivalrous honor. Perhaps I should kill her first, in front of you. Her majesty would get a lot of joy from that, I am sure. The helpless one, the prince, awaiting death after losing someone he cared for yet again, but..." The thing paused, lifting its face in the air. It sniffed, and then another grin formed on its face. "It looks like you are not alone. Maybe this other human can join in on the fun."

"I said, enough." Caelan lunged at the wolf, letting out a roar.

The hilt in his hand began to shake, and a golden glow formed at the base. The glow trailed as the sun moved with it, glints of silver appearing and attaching. The glow was too strong, and eventually, Sabina had to shield her eyes. When she opened them, it was then that she realized how majestic Caelan really looked.

Towering above his head was a sword, no longer a hilt without a blade. It was viciously sentient. The battle was a carefully choreographed dance unfolding right before her eyes.

The animal lunged, but Caelan blocked, jumping backward just before teeth clamped on his arm. With a guttural cry, he sliced the blade sideways, puncturing the wound that had finally stopped bleeding on the animal. It cried out in agony, falling frontward, almost on top of Caelan.

But the sword had other ideas. A red glow came from the tip, pushing and pushing until it morphed into a sphere. The weapon was shifting, turning, growing outward until it blocked Caelan completely from the being.

A shield. It's both his sword and his shield.

Sabina had read many times in stories about battles, the length of time it took to dominate the enemy. Each swipe entailed a block. Each block entailed a tumble or different position, but she had never seen a beautiful display of defense such as this.

The sword seemed so lightweight in his hands but sturdy enough as he moved. It was beautifully crafted from a metal Sabina had never seen before, with golden swirls in the center leading to the pointed edge directed right at the beast.

Then, the shield did something that was marvelous in its splendor. It burst, sending the wolf flying backward into the dirty grass. Sparks of light were still floating in the sky, but there was no movement in that patch of grass.

The animal was cornered, laying on its back.

Bloody remnants coated Caelan's hands. Blood from his enemy. He wore the stain proudly as he stomped toward where the creature lay.

"You coward," Caelan spat. "Why don't you reveal who you truly are? It is easy to hide behind this weaponry, but if you dare speak of causing harm, at least reveal your true face." The sweat poured down his face as Caelan angled the blade one more time at the creature.

The animal flinched, its gray fur shifting and morphing. Hair reduced, and paws clenched into what looked like fingers. Wolfish eyes slanted and grew out, and a snout shifted. The coloring changed from gray fur into a soft honey brown tan. Soon, it was no longer the murderous beast who stared back at them but a man with dark, unruly hair clad in barely any clothing. His eyes were deep, set, dark with the same glint of rage.

"What is your name?" Caelan asked, his voice barely above a whisper.

"Lennix," the man said. He let out a laugh, and it was a deep, hollow sound.

"Why did she send you?" Caelan asked, the blade still not moving from its spot.

"You really think I will tell you anything?" Lennix's voice was strained, as if his words were wrapping around something.

"Why. Did. She. Send. You." Caelan enunciated each word, desperation twisting around each syllable. "Who are you with?" Caelan tried another angle.

Lennix resorted to laughing once again, and Caelan raised his sword. "She will find you, you know. Nowhere will ever be safe for you. She will get her revenge, and you, Prince, will be dead. It will be terrible and glorious and a spectacle for her to witness. You...you...will be, forever are, tainted with ruin. Your father's son is what you used to call yourself? That indeed you will be. Marred by death, unable to escape. That is your fate. Long may you perish, and long may my Queen rei—"

His eyes widened in shock, mouth agape as the blade once again pierced his now human flesh. It was an event Sabina did not want to witness, but it was forever marked in her memories.

As the last breath escaped from Lennix's lips, crimson protruding from his lips, Caelan retrieved the weapon from the body. After a moment, the silver metal shimmered and evaporated completely, leaving only the hilt behind.

Caelan turned away, looking at Sabina.

"Are you okay?" He began to walk toward her and held out his empty palm for her to grasp when he reached her.

In her mind, there was now no question of his identity or of deranged thoughts. There was no more madness that he was clinging to. It was simply the reality of loss, of being in a world far from his own.

She no longer had to fight with herself over what was the truth.

So, she took his hand and uttered three simple words that she never thought she would voice, "I trust you."

CHAPTER SEVENTEEN

HANNAH

IF IT WASN'T FOR THE fear clutching her heart, Hannah would have said that the wind felt delicious in her hair at the speed they were traveling.

Alas, in a situation of what could be certain death, enjoying the wind was the least of her concerns.

It wasn't her crew riding the waves of the air. There was no joke from Will or sarcastic remark from Marcus. There was no....

Tony.

His face was now at the forefront of her thoughts, and no matter how she shut her eyes against it, the breeze would tickle her lashes. She was sure it was reprimanding her for her actions of not being smart. She could see him, then, standing at the diner. The shocked anguish was like a fresh coat of paint stinging his eyes.

If only he knew where to find her.

"You're a little quiet back there, *Little Lunar*. Doing okay?" The newfound pet name that Nyx deemed appropriate sent little shivers down her spine.

Hannah didn't speak. She kept her lips zipped tight, and her eyes were still shut against the deep breeze.

"So, the silent treatment, eh?"

She could feel his hair tickling her cheek as he leaned back. He was trying to get a good look at her, but he wouldn't. Every nerve in her body told her to stay completely still.

"You were so eager to jump on my bike earlier. What happened?"

Searing rage pulsed through her veins. That wasn't what happened, and he knew it.

"Is it the speed? Is it bothering you? Are we going too fast for you to handle?" The taunting remarks flew from his lips unapologetically.

Her heart thumped. Each laugh coming from the other men made her jerk. She wanted nothing more than a way to leave this very spot.

"Stop the bike right now," Hannah finally stated, earning a clenched hand around the handle from Nyx, the only response he would allow her.

"Why should he stop?" was the shout that came from one of the men traveling not too far behind them. "Are you getting scared? Is the pretty girl getting scared?"

The catcalls and woops made her muscles stiffen. Another reminder that she had made the biggest mistake of her life by not trying harder in her attempt of screaming for help.

"Leave the girl alone," Nyx rumbled.

She could feel his voice as he spoke, the vibrations pressing against her skin. She was holding onto him for dear life, and yet as her hands interlocked around his stomach, she realized her fate was hanging on him. Literally.

"It's okay for you to make remarks but not them?"

"I really thought you were brave back there, but now you're really showing me just how much you disregard any kind of authority."

His words would have sounded ridiculing coming out of the mouth of anyone else, but they had such a peculiar fascination from Nyx. He seemed...almost proud.

"What I really want," Hannah restated, "is to get off of this bike. Am I not speaking English, or are you guys too stupid to understand?" Insulting him was a risk but something she had to try, nevertheless.

"You're coming through loud and clear, lovely. We will get you off of this bike," Nyx said over the wind.

"Thank you," she muttered. *Maybe he's changed his mind?*

"Let us make a quick little stop first," he added, revving the engine. More gusts of wind whipped through their hairs as he put the blinker on.

Hannah wasn't sure how many miles they had been driving. She had been so lost in the aftermath of destruction that her mind had lost focus.

Her eyes opened slowly, and momentarily, the sun blinded her. Blinking it away, she allowed herself to take in all the things she hadn't seen in so very long.

The dirt road that paved its way to crunchy gravel underneath the tires was like a warm blanket she had forgotten, but once it enveloped her, it was as if no time had passed.

The scent of pine was in the air, and the birds wouldn't stop singing their beautiful little song. The trees that once seemed so gigantic in their size at one time were now somewhat normal in their proportion to her, dark olive leaves brewing from the stems.

She inhaled deeply and knew that if she could bottle a memory, the ones she had made here would be forever captivated in a cylinder jar.

"Do you know this place, *Little Lunar?*" Nyx asked, the first person to dare break her thoughts.

"I came here once, for a week when I was younger." Hannah didn't feel like being snarky. She was in too much shock. "I never thought I'd come here again."

"We needed a place to crash, and it's the closest to the place we need to get to, so we might as well call this home."

Velo's Path. Once was home to me, too.

It didn't take long for Nyx to travel the road. He knew the right turns and where to stop, even the loops that they were destined to follow. He had traveled the road many times, it seemed. After a while, they finally came to a stop.

A small cabin, nestled far in the back of the site, was their destination. There was nothing special about it, other than the fact that it had some significance to both of them.

Nyx got off of the bike, stretching his hand to her. He was a gentleman or at least attempting to be. She took it gratefully, her fear momentarily forgotten as her feet hit solid grass and dirt.

She did a little twirl, letting her hands tickle the puffs of air that leaked through the trees. With each spin, it was like time was reversing, turning her back into the little girl who once dropped to a roll in the grass or the one who giggled behind a closed hand with two other devious little friends.

The trees hold their memories close and seldom seem to want to reveal them to outsiders.

She could feel it, then, without looking. Eyes were latched on her as she moved. Slowly opening them, she saw that Nyx was grinning at her with his lopsided smile.

"I had no idea that this could make you feel peaceful. Much less with us. You had the grip of death back there." He nodded to his bike.

"Well," she replied, crossing her arms over her chest, "as long as you take me back to the diner, I'll be fine."

He flashed another set of pearly whites in her direction. "Not anytime soon, *Little Lunar*. Now, *come*."

Nyx, so soon, revoked Hannah's sense of peace as his hand gripped her wrist so tightly she lost circulation.

The rest of the guys dismounted their bikes, all of them heading to the the cabin. Nyx tugged her in that direction, not caring how her feet dragged behind in protest.

The cabin was a deep copper brown on the outside with rigged paneling and a rickety door that moaned as it opened and shut.

"You're free to stay in the cabin and get some water. It's in the fridge in the kitchen. Don't even think about leaving." The last sentence harbored an unspoken warning as he shoved her up the steps and through the door.

The lighting inside the cabin provided some solace from the sun as blinds were drawn on the windows. The overhead light above the kitchen table flickered on and off, almost in tune with her steps to the fridge.

She didn't realize how thirsty she was until her hand clasped around the bottle and the lid was tossed to the floor. She gulped it down faster than she would have liked, allowing herself to breathe when her lungs couldn't take any more waiting.

With water droplets still dripping down her shirt with each step she took, the little trail from the kitchen led her to the cabin window. Her curiosity was getting the best of her. Without any regards, she turned the little dial, loosening the blinds just enough to peek outside. Would there be enough time for her to run without them seeing?

Nyx was standing in her line of sight, a few feet away from the window. Across from him stood a boy with olive skin of shorter stature. He donned a hoodie and tight jeans, his hands moving in the air as he spoke. With each word, his head moved, sending the array of dark, curly swirls on his head bobbing. The boy couldn't have been much older than Hannah.

He isn't in the group with them.

She couldn't make out the words until she pressed her face closer to the window.

"I need you to tell me exactly what happened and how it happened," Nyx's tone was venomous, territorial, and that of authority.

"I was with him, like you said. We scoured the area, but he said he caught a scent, an older scent. And you know Len... how he can be. He wanted to follow it—"

"Even though he was told not to?" Nyx's eyes squinted as he peered at the boy, whose bottom lip started quivering.

The boy nodded. "He left me on his own. He thought if he followed wherever the old scent was leading, he could find him for you. The Fallen Prince, that's what you call him, right? Len said that we'd be heroes and we'd be in a higher place in the pack...and that you'd be proud, so I didn't think anything of it. And, so, well, that's where he went," the boy finished, stuttering over his words.

Nyx turned his face away for a moment, stone cold at the boy's words. "And where was the last place you saw him?"

"After he left the Colorado border," the boy replied instantly, "but that was over three days ago. I hadn't heard from him since, so I decided to follow his trail."

At this, Nyx's eyes immediately locked back on the boy. "And did you?"

The boy was hesitant to meet Nyx's gaze, one foot shuffling against the other. "Kind of. Not exactly…"

Hannah could sense something flickering behind Nyx's eyes. "*He* killed Lennix, didn't he?"

Solemnly, the companion of Nyx let his head lift. "Yes," he whispered, "but he wasn't alone. There were others."

Nyx stroked his chin, gritting his teeth. "Others? The Fallen Prince doesn't have others. There must be some other explanation."

"Two girls, sir. It was two girls. Lennix's scent led me to Northern Louisiana, but the last trace of his scent in the grass allows us to time frame his death around eight hours ago. The only way I got back here so fast is because of a ride I snagged. I just wanted you to know."

"Tell me more about the two girls," Nyx prodded. "I need details. As much as you can give me."

"I don't know much about one of them. She was unconscious in the van as far as we know, but the other, she was fiery. She had long, red hair and fair skin, but the way she carried herself, it wasn't like a southerner, and based on the fenugreek maple smell that lingered, I would be willing to bet she's a socialite. The last guy I knew who smelled like that was from New York. His home was right on the border. I have no idea why she was traveling with *him* of all people, but I am willing to bet she now knows about us. I don't know if any mind wiping will do any good. I think the damage has been done." The boy finally let out a breath, the tumble of words flowing more smoothly than before.

"You're right," Nyx mused. "The damage has been done." He wrapped his arms around the teenager. "You had one job,

Breckhen. Just make sure Lennix was safe, and you failed me," he whispered.

Breckhen was shaking as Nyx's arms wrapped around him even tighter, his eyes wide with a deep, paralyzing fear.

And then, there was the *snap*.

Breckhen fell to the ground instantly, his neck twisted and body mangled. Lifeless.

Hannah could barely hold the scream back, her heart pounding ferociously in her chest. She scrambled backward, but the deed was already done.

I have to get out of here.

Nyx's eyes were no longer looking at the ground. They were fully, intently focused on her.

"Oh, no," was what she heard. Words were leaping out of her lips, but she was too frozen to register anything except for the stunning, obvious thought that she would die.

Her one idiotic mistake would absolutely, positively kill her.

The door slammed open.

Hannah fell over, tripping on her own nervous feet. She was sprawled on her back with shaky arms barely holding her upright and nowhere to go.

Multitudes of men—the same ones she rode with—entered, right after their murderous leader.

Soon, they were swarming around her, eyes bright with excitement and blood spilled. They were bloodthirsty, and they all angled themselves to the door.

Outside of the window, she could see two others that hadn't yet joined them dragging Breckhen's lifeless body away from the cabin into a patch of trees.

Nyx's eyes were locked on her as Hannah's gaze was locked on the once-living boy.

"Don't worry, *Little Lunar*," he said slowly. "You won't be going to the trees."

She could feel another scream building, but she knew they were too far away from help. Too far away for anyone to find her. She had no idea what they needed her for or why the heck he kept calling her *Little Lunar*.

All she knew was that her head was getting fuzzy the longer Nyx grinned with his beautiful teeth. They were pearly white, the smile was intoxicating, but her head was too out of focus to redirect her vision anywhere else.

A killer's smile was dazzling, but there was something animalistic buried within it.

She could sense it, just by staring. She didn't need to look far.

A hard boot kicked her on the side. Her stomach ricocheted and coiled until her esophagus was consumed with bile. All it took was one exhalation for vomit to pool onto the cabin floor. The stench was enough to make the nausea worse, and she could feel another rush coming.

Nyx crouched down, his hand very softly stroking her hair.

She could hardly keep her eyes open, but she could feel the tightness of rope bound on her legs and hands. *Moving is pointless.*

But Nyx was still smiling.

The beautiful teeth grew sharper and sharper until it was almost undeniably canine. His sparkling eyes became more sinister, and soon, there was nothing but the chaotic, groggy voice that deepened, lulling her to sleep, "You're going to be of great use to me, *Little Lunar*. Just you wait."

PART

II

CHAPTER EIGHTEEN

SABINA

"Are you okay?" Caelan's voice was a hum in the silent van.

The whirring of the air conditioner had been the only sound she had relied on to fill the void of confusion.

"I...think so." It took a second to find her voice, and the searing burn was slick against her throat. It hurt when she spoke. "How...long..." She paused, preparing herself for the sting. "...have we been driving?"

Caelan's eyes met hers in the rear-view mirror. They weren't hard like she expected, or angry, or disappointed. At any given point, she was bracing for the "I told you so" mantra or something about the "I'm older, wiser, and know more than you ever could." That never came. Instead, his eyes crinkled. A soft smile.

"It's been a few hours. Cammie is still sleeping, but the good news is, we aren't far from our destination. The closer we can get to helping her, the closer we can get to finding the answers we both need."

It all seemed so incredulously unbelievable, but it was the truth.

"So, Cammie is really sick?" Sabina murmured. "She's really going to die?" The panic was crawling up her throat as she looked back at her friend's still-sleeping face.

"I promise I will do everything in my power to keep her alive. I will do as much as I can."

The panic still refused to loosen its grip on her throat. "So...you really are a prince, then?"

His cheek clenched, and she could tell she had pressed a sensitive subject. "Under what most would call unfortunate circumstances, yes."

Sabina wanted to know more, to press further. There was so much more to this story than she had heard from Cammie's lips and the answers she sought were right under her nose, in front of her.

"I hate...to pry..." Sabina hesitated, trying to decipher her words carefully as Caelan's face shifted. "But can you tell me something, anything about what really happened back there? I wouldn't ask you if I didn't need to know. I just want this to make sense."

"I can speak in the simplest of terms to start with. That might make all of this easier." Caelan took a long pause before he looked back at the road again.

"Whenever you're ready," Sabina assured against the tenseness in his grip.

"Okay," Caelan took a breath. "Long ago, in what you would call centuries, Amarians were born. Not dissimilar to the folklore tales you've heard of, but there is a big difference in how Amarians were made. If we have time, I can go over that later—"

"We have plenty of time," Sabina blurted. She was on the edge of her seat, not metaphorically speaking this time.

The corner of Caelan's mouth tweaked upward just a smidge, but the rest of his body was still stubbornly stiff. "Maybe just the basic history will be enough. I don't want to overwhelm you. You've seen enough today."

Now, it was his turn to tread lightly. Despite all of her concerns, he had still decided to take his time with her, and she appreciated it all the same.

"Thank you," she said.

"Much, much later," he said, completely passing over her acknowledgement, "there was a group of Amarians who banded together to create the world I was born in. To you, it's just a campsite in Colorado. To me, it's much more than that. It's my home. It's completely oblivious, carefully hidden from you. By you, I mean humans."

Sabina squinted. "But you look human. What's the difference? Surely you guys can't be that special if you still look like us." At the sudden impropriety, she clasped a hand over her mouth. "Oh, my goodness. I am so sorry..."

Caelan's chest heaved with such a peculiar sound she couldn't decipher at first until she saw the sparkle in his eyes through the reflection of the mirror. *He is laughing.*

Quickly, he cleared his throat. "Okay, you are being serious. I apologize. You remind me so much of Leanna with your sarcasm. It might be out of character for you, but, by the stars, was she a bold and fiery woman."

Sabina snorted. "I know someone else just like that." The flickering image of Hannah in her mind was unwavering, and something began pressing on her heart.

"A close friend of yours?" Caelan asked.

"Yeah," Sabina finally replied. "How did you know?"

"Your face sank when you talked about her. I can't pretend to know how the relationship with her is, but my guess is not good. Did something happen?"

"Hey, now," Sabina scolded with a small smile. "The entire point of this conversation was to find out answers, not to change it up to focus on my life."

"And we will," Caelan replied, "but if I can offer a solution to your problem, I would like to try. You and your friend are giving me back my life and are trying to help, so a small detour from our conversation won't hurt anything."

Sabina pondered his words, wondering just how much to share. "Her name is Hannah," she finally said. "She is, well, was, I guess, a good friend of mine." Her eyes trailed out the window, as if they could transport her to another time. "I'm not really sure what happened. We were close as children. And then... we just weren't. She went her own way. I went mine. Nothing I did seemed to make it better, so I'm not too sure what to do about it or her. It's just crazy that we're going to Colorado, and I won't even be able to talk to her, and she's in the same state."

"I think you should talk to her," Caelan stated.

Sabina's mouth slacked open. "Despite everything I've seen or even heard today, this is the craziest. Talking? To Hannah?" The chortled laugh escaped her mouth. "How would that even happen?"

"We would make a stop."

"I think making a stop isn't necessary. Cammie needs help, and you need answers. The last thing on our list should be some kind of friendship reunion."

"You have to make sacrifices for those who make sacrifices for you."

The statement was simple enough, and in it, Sabina could finally see small remnants of what had made Cammie feel drawn to Caelan in the first place. He was wise beyond his years, and now that she had seen some of what was hiding behind the curtain, that sentiment made more sense than just talking of an elder down the street.

A soft moan came from Sabina's right.

Sabina twisted around, gripping Cammie's hand tightly. "Caelan," she said softly.

"What's wrong? Is she okay?"

"She's getting hot. Like really hot. Her skin...is like it's on fire."

Caelan swore under his breath in a language she couldn't decipher. "Tell me more of her symptoms. Don't hold any detail back. It's important."

Sabina searched Cammie's face. "Her eyelids are flashing between colors from white to purple. Her skin keeps shifting too. It's red and white all at once, and she can't stop sweating. I don't know what else to say because I don't understand what's happening..."

Caelan's face was now the one to lose its color. "It's progressing worse. The mind-wiping is deeper than I thought."

"You didn't know where to start earlier?" Sabina huffed. "Start here, right now. Tell me what caused this, what's happening."

"Whoever did this is powerful. With gifts like these, at this strength, my best guess is that he or she has a pretty powerful position in my world. Most likely, the right hand of some sort of advisor or the King's Guard. Worst case scenario, it's someone appointed by the Council."

"All of that is great information, but what does it mean?"

"It means they were either hired or chosen for this specific job, and that means that they are very good at it, very good at not deviating from their mission. Amarians who live in your world don't interact with humans on this level unless they absolutely have to. We don't believe in obstructing your free will of knowledge and choice, so, for this to happen to her, your friend, my best conclusion is that she got too close, got too involved."

"You're saying my friend is dying...purely due to being in the wrong place at the wrong time?" Sabina's raised voice did nothing more than fuel her already panicked state. The vein in her neck started to throb without pause.

Cammie let out a small whimper, and Sabina's rage only grew.

"What I can say is that I am unsure of the true reasoning, but I've seen this before with my wife. Solenne healed as best as she could, and most of it did work, but due to the damage...the full extent just wasn't possible due to time, but I know she can heal Cammie. She will do everything in her power to do so."

"And why would your wife need healing?" Sabina's fingers dragged into her palms, the nausea chipping away at her stomach. "Was she some sort of defective being who wasn't up to your world's standards?"

"It was nothing of the sort. Though it might be hard to believe, my wife, she was human."

Sabina's eyes began to grow like saucers. "How did that even happen? How can that happen? Is it even possible for you to *be* with one of us?"

Caelan dared to look back at the rearview. "I loved my wife. We were together for many years. The story of our union is one for another time. For now, I need you to grab my phone. It should be underneath where I am sitting. I was going to call her earlier, but after the fiasco with Lennix, I was too focused on getting out of there."

The seat belt flew off without a care. Sabina crouched down to dig under the driver's seat. Her hand moved this way and that until she grasped the smartphone. Cold metal was slick against her palm.

"What do you need me to do now?"

His response was instantaneous. "Call Solenne."

For the first time, Sabina didn't ask questions. She went through the contact list until she found the name and pressed the dial button. She made sure the phone call was on speaker and held her breath.

There were several long rings, and Sabina could feel her heart plummeting. If this woman didn't answer…

"Hello?" The raspy, orotund voice wasn't what she expected, but it greeted her all the same.

"Hi, Solenne?"

There was shuffling on the other end of the line, and Sabina could feel the breath coming through the phone with how loud the air was. "Where is Caelan?"

Sabina flinched, and she let herself slowly sink into her seat. "He's here, but he's driving. He told me to call you."

"Let me talk to him," the woman said.

"I—but I can help." Sabina tripped over her words, the strength from earlier slowing fading.

"The one thing you can do," Caelan interrupted, "is tell her we are on the way, and we will be there sooner than expected."

Sabina turned away from Caelan and looked back at the phone. "He said—"

"I heard what he said," the woman responded curtly. "Tell him I understand and that I'll be waiting."

Sabina sat in anticipation of more words, an explanation or some sort of direction, but after a few moments of utter silence, she turned back to Caelan.

"She hung up the phone. What do we do now?"

Caelan's hands tightened as he clenched and unclenched them, rapping his knuckles on the steering wheel. "Now, we follow the plan. We meet Solenne."

"And?" Sabina prodded.

"We pray she can save Cammie, and then, we will find your friend."

CHAPTER NINETEEN

HANNAH

HER ARMS WERE ON FIRE.

At first, sitting in the corner had felt like nothing. It had been easy to have hope then, easy for her to have moments of pure resistance as she'd stared down the cabin door, waiting for her rescue. She didn't back down without a fight this time. Even as they had branded her with straw shackles of rope, she had still flayed and kicked. Even as they had tied the gag around her face, and her stomach had coiled with more bile and searing pain that felt like the force of a thousand knives in her gut, she still had hope.

But that had been hours ago, and this is now.

There was no more daylight out of the window as it spent precious time making way for dusk. When dusk had decided to move on, all that was left was for the darkness to make itself at home.

Aside from the faint glow of the lanterns across the road, there was nothing to keep Hannah company, except for her thoughts.

She leaned her head back against the window, blinking against the sting in her eyes. The air was suffocating and rarely sparing itself all in the same space. No amount of inhaling through a cotton scarf made a difference. Against her teeth, she could taste smooth strings of unraveling fabric. The material was desperate as it slinked toward her throat. While breathing had been a beautiful gift mere hours ago, the gag bestowed difficulty in large doses.

In the time she'd sat there, she'd reached stunning new conclusions about how her life had gone. In no particular order, she was absolutely the stupidest person on Earth, deciding not to defend herself in the first place would go down as one of the most idiotic choices in her short lifetime, and she probably wouldn't live to see twenty.

A loud, instantaneous thump came from behind her. The hairs on the back of her neck stood on end. Her heart leapt to her throat, and her veins made way for incessant blood pumping. Noises were coming from right outside the window.

Sudden curiosity combined with the obstinate voice in her head that liked to make reckless decisions pushed her forward. *If I'm going to die, I might as well have some say in how.*

In movies, being bound and trying to stand seemed so easy. The heroine always somehow managed to look graceful without any sort of struggle, yet all it took was one minute of trying for her to realize how *true* that sentiment really was.

Her knees proved to have the strength of a piece of wood under pressure, sharp pricks of numbness shifting as she moved. Her bound arms did nothing to steady herself when she rose, slick beads of sweat dripping down her forehead. The wetness that was stubbornly clinging to her long mane of hair only beckoned more heat.

More sweat lingered, falling down her cheeks, droplets stinging her clothing. The gag began to make her eyes water. The malodorous, ripe odor from the fabric invaded her senses without permission. Her eyes blurred of their own accord, even as she blinked the stench away.

The constant reek was her undoing. She could feel the sickness starting in her stomach while the putrid smell worsened.

Her legs wobbled until they gave way, her body crashing to the floor. Hannah braced for the fall, but no amount of preparation could have eased the impact. She landed face first, her cheek hitting the ancient, dusty flooring. The muscle around her cheekbone moved in consistent throbs, and she could taste metal intertwined with fabric on her tongue.

Blood.

The urge to spat was great, but no matter how she tried, the persistent cotton wouldn't budge.

Lost in the spiral of her pitying thoughts, the ringing in her ears refusing to quiet, she didn't hear it until it was too late.

"I thought you said he would be here by now," came the barking complaint from the man shutting the door.

Between glimpses of her hair, Hannah could barely make out the face, but she recognized the voice. It was one of Nyx's guys.

"That's the word I got. Are you not satisfied with it? Maybe you should take it up with the boss then."

Though this voice wasn't as familiar, Hannah figured who he was as much—one of many who would participate in her upcoming murder.

"I trust you. It's this guy that I can't trust, but apparently, the boss can. Nyx trusted this entire operation to some second-hand hunter. How do we even know he's qualified to come through for us? What's the compensation? I mean, are we even getting paid for this?" The first man's continuous grievances were more than enough to trigger another gag reflex.

At Hannah's small groans, both heads swiveled in her direction.

She could see pearly whites gleaming at her in amusement as they made their way to her position on the floor. One of the men, the first one who spoke—Consistent Disappointment, she decided to call him—let out a laugh as he shriveled up his nose.

"She smells," Consistent Disappointment stated, waving his hand in front of his nose. He crouched down to be eye level with her, furrowing his brow. "You don't think she crapped herself, do you?"

"Well, whatever she did, we just have to keep her breathing until Nyx decides what to do with her," the other man said. "Nyx said to keep her alive, so we keep her alive."

"But what does it matter if she dies? Not like she can be of any use to us."

Guy Number Two narrowed his eyes. "Nyx gave the order. Do your job...and follow it."

The grave tone only made Hannah surer of this guy's attitude. *Wannabe leader. Definitely his name.*

Both men grabbed her arms, using their strength to hoist her upwards. Their hands were sloppy and careless.

Forget five-star treatment. Even being woman of the hour gets me nowhere.

"Just set her down there," Wannabe Leader instructed with a jerk of his head. "Gentle enough, but no one said anything about being too welcoming."

The sly chuckles filled the room, and Hannah wanted nothing more than to smack both of them so hard they would have to find new names.

Without fail and human decency, they dropped her instantaneously, letting her body *thwack* against the same window she had been at before. This time, her pain tolerance level was wearing thin, even for her.

"Will this be enough room for the other one?" Consistent Disappointment almost sounded concerned.

Finally, Hannah managed to force her head upright. *Other?*

"I don't know what the guy looks like, but I'm sure any space is enough. It's not like he will be sitting there long anyways."

The laughter started up again.

Wannabe Leader shot a smile at Hannah. "Don't worry, fragile girl. You won't be here alone. You won't go out to the woods alone, either. He'll keep you company."

Her gut was now a building, and this building's foundation was beginning to crumble. Bits and pieces of brick were falling, falling, falling into despair, and all she could do was watch.

In the distance, there was a slight, melodic, magnetic noise. It was almost unearthly and unrecognizable in a way she had never heard before.

Both men looked at Hannah and then up at the sound. They each shared the same glint in their eyes and the same Cheshire grin.

"He's here."

There was a sudden pounding on the door. Consistent Disappointment was the first to move until Wannabe Leader blocked him with an arm.

"I'll grab the door," Wannabe Leader said. He turned his sharp eyes on Hannah. "You watch her. Last thing we need is her getting away."

Again, Hannah would pummel them if she could. *Pure idiots* rang loud in her mind as she watched the one man swallow, his eyes thick with nerves as he strode to the door that was hiding someone from her view.

As soon as the door opened, though, she could sense it. *Something's different.*

The man was tall, taller than even Tony, but the entire vibe he gave was what made her curious. A long, black cloak covered his face. Hannah could barely make out any distinguishable features, but that wasn't the strangest part. His garment had several colorful weapons attached to his waist, and on his wrist was a rope...which led to another hand.

Except this hand wasn't his hand.

Next to the man stood another man. Hannah would have been thrilled to know *who* the man was, but, much to her surprise, his features were also hidden by the bag over his head. The bagged head man didn't dress like the other, though. No, it wasn't regal clothing. It was nothing more than a simple shirt and jeans.

"I see you've brought the fugitive," Wannabe Leader stated, his voice up an octave.

The man in the cloak did not reply, but Hannah could see the outline of nostrils flaring. *Is he just as fed up as I am? He literally just walked in. Wow. The guy has great taste.*

"We'll take him off your hands." Wannabe Leader reached for the bagged head man, but mysterious cloak guy held up a palm.

"Not just yet."

Goosebumps immediately danced on Hannah's arms at the sound of cloak guy's voice. Her belly tingled with flutters, and it took a moment to regain her composure. His voice was confident but almost boyish, nothing like she'd imagined.

"There is still the method of payment to be finalized," he added.

Consistent Disappointment decided to speak. "Our boss will give you the payment when he sees you next."

The cloak man's head spun instantly. The bagged head man shifted his weight, and the grip seemed to tighten around the cloaked man's wrist.

"Why is she tied up?" Cloaked Man asked. "I don't remember a human girl being part of the deal."

The words, so openly spoken, sent Hannah's heart plummeting to her feet.

"She isn't," Wannabe Leader piped up, his pompous smirk taking up almost half of his face. "It's a special project our boss has in mind."

"How much did she see?" Cloaked Man asked, tilting his head.

Wannabe Leader and Consistent Disappointment shared a knowing grin.

"Enough," Consistent Disappointment replied.

"For nothing more than the request to be granted, I can do an erasing for you. That would be much more beneficial to you. Less messy for her, and you as well, I can assume." Cloaked Man was demanding but gentle.

Though Hannah knew nothing of what was being said, her gut whispered that he was safe.

"We don't need your assumptions." Wannabe Leader sneered. "We just need you to leave."

He turned on his heels and stalked to the back of the cabin, behind a door that was too far away for Hannah to peer into. It was several minutes before he returned, carrying a single, weighty bag with a tie and wearing a disgruntled expression. He handed the bag to the cloaked man, watching as the recipient merely gawked.

"You said your boss would hand me the payment," Cloaked Man finally said.

"I know our boss well enough to know outsiders aren't permitted to overstay their welcome, so if giving you the cash sends you on your merry little way, then so be it."

Wannabe Leader untied the rope binding the fugitive to Cloaked Man and yanked him from the man's grasp. He tossed him to Consistent Disappointment, who threw the fugitive against the wall without so much as an apologetic glance.

"What about the girl?" Cloaked Man asked.

"She doesn't concern you." Wannabe Leader's voice was stoic and teetering on the edge of vexation. "I will only ask you one more time. Leave."

"Listen—"

"I said *leave.*"

Cloaked Man gave one last look at Hannah as he undid the rope on his wrist and let it fall to the floor. There was no need for it now.

He did as he was told, the cabin door thundering shut behind him.

The newfound companion next to Hannah was breathing heavily, soft groans coming from underneath the bag.

"Do you want to do the honors?"

At first, Hannah thought one of the idiots was talking to her, but one look at the straightforward grins the two clowns were sharing proved her wrong yet again.

Consistent Disappointment, in one swift move, removed the bag from the head of the fugitive.

Hannah couldn't help but wonder what all of the fuss was about. The man looked average. Normal. His hair was on the border of straight and curly, lingering somewhere in the wavy middle. His dark green eyes widened as he blinked into his surroundings. With the light shining on top of his head, his coloring looked almost a sickly yellow, reminding Hannah of the color of vomit. *Fitting for such a normal person.*

To her, nothing was out of the ordinary, but if these guys were willing to pay so much money for an ordinary person who was special to them, she couldn't help but ponder what would happen to her as an ordinary person who meant nothing.

"Water," the man cried out. "I need water, please."

Consistent Disappointment frowned. "I don't think he should get anything. Don't you?" At Wannabe Leader's enriching facial expression, Consistent Disappointment started toward the kitchen. "Water it is, then."

"I'll follow you," Wannabe Leader said. "I think we've earned a few beers."

Their chortled laughter echoed in the space.

The man beside Hannah watched them with a fearful gaze. His eyes were turning red, almost bloodshot, and Hannah wondered when he last slept. She moved to ask him, but there was the beautiful reminder of speech blocked by cloth. With the taste of mildew exhuming on her tongue, she gagged yet again.

The man's head shifted in her direction. His eyes became saucers. "What are you doing here?"

Unable to speak, Hannah merely narrowed her eyes, hoping she conveyed enough in them for him to know she had no idea what she was doing here.

"Did they kidnap you?" he asked.

Hannah nodded.

A sliver of relief appeared on the man's face. "You just tend to get involved in the wrong crowd, don't you, Hannah?" A chortled, strangled laugh escaped his lips.

Every bone in her body stiffened.

He knows my name.

If she wasn't bound and gagged, he would be pummeled. How had he been able to learn her name?

She inched closer, and if looks could kill, the man would be nothing more than a pile of ash.

"I'm sorry," he rushed, noticing her menacing eyes. "I must have misspoken. You just really remind me of a girl that I used to know. Her name was Hannah. You look a lot like her. Definitely not the same person."

More questions lingered on her trapped lips, but the man turned away. She would have reached out to tap him, but the stupid rope held her from any sort of necessary movement. He wouldn't even meet her eyes.

Voices resounded from the kitchen along with the heavy footsteps that would take a lifetime to forget, and soon, the two idiots were back in view once again.

"Don't worry, girly. I got your water, too," Consistent Disappointment told her.

Wannabe Leader gave the man his cup first, and he took long sips, not even bothering to pause for air. Droplets fell down his lips and stained his shirt. The person who wished to be in charge couldn't help but laugh. "Downright disgusting, that you are."

"No, I tell ya, it's these humans who are worse than that. You've got a Guardian," Consistent Disappointment stated.

At the mention of the title, the man next to Hannah looked up for a mere moment, his eyes making direct contact with the person speaking. It was as if there was some sort of unspoken contract between them, a piece that Hannah couldn't fully understand.

"You might be right about that, but she's still useful for whatever reason Nyx has planned. I don't really care about it, but you need to keep her alive until he says otherwise."

Begrudgingly, Consistent Disappointment nodded and held out the water cup to his companion who took it without complaint. He knelt down and began to untie Hannah's gag.

Once her lips met with fresh air, that was all it took.

Vomit trickled out of her mouth until one heaving cough brought it all to the surface. It spattered on the floor, on the pants of the captor, and tickled his shoes.

He rose from the floor in disgust, his fist pulled back at the ready. With blurry, teary eyes, Hannah prepared herself for the smack of knuckles against skin as more vomit kept spewing on the floor.

"Can't you see she's starving?" The captive man spoke against Hannah's heaving breaths. "She needs food."

Both men looked at the man next to Hannah, the challenge thinly veiled in their eyes.

"That's why she's throwing up," he continued. "Humans can't handle hours of hunger deprivation. Plus that rag smells so bad it probably triggered emptying her stomach. She's weak, and if your boss wants her alive, you two aren't doing a good job. That's an obvious statement that even an idiot can see."

Consistent Disappointment moved swiftly, his hand latching onto the captive's hair before the man could move to defend himself. He yanked, and the captive man squinted, not sparing Hannah a glance.

Consistent Disappointment had proud, eager eyes as Wannabe Leader smiled, coming to a crouch. *Anything to please. Maybe he is becoming more and more his counterpart than I thought.*

Wannabe Leader's breath came close to the captive's ear as he spoke in a deep, guttural tone. "The only reason you're alive right now is because the boss wants you alive. If it were up to me, I would gut you like the double-dealer you are."

The captive said nothing in response, but his cheek muscles clenched and contorted. More pain.

"A guardian to the kingdom, a Protector of Natrellum. Such a beautiful title, and the king gave that to you, didn't he?"

The captive didn't respond.

Wannabe Leader tried a different approach. "Didn't he?" he bellowed, the sound making even the blinds shake.

Hannah jolted, her skin dancing with goosebumps, but no one noticed. They were all too entranced with the man who refused to speak. For once in this entire ordeal, she was invisible.

"The entire realm views you differently now. No longer are you a guardian in the king's abode. No longer do you have a say in the ways of the world. You're an outcast, a traitor. A murderer, a treasonous, treacherous being. You can try to salvage your title by caring for a fragile human, but I can tell you this: Nothing you do will ever be able to erase the stain of death that mars you. It's tainted, just as you are, and soon enough, you will realize redemption is too far from your grasp. You can stop reaching for it now." At Wannabe Leader's prompting, Consistent Disappointment released the captive's head.

Though the hardness was removed, the captive's face was still crestfallen. It bore the weight of a thousand untold stories that one had yet to hear, the crushing burden of guilt flickering in his eyes.

"Why are you hurting him?" Hannah's voice was raspy, the roughness of speaking adding to the calamity she was feeling inside. "Whoever he is, he doesn't deserve this. How do I know you're even telling the truth?"

As soon as the words escaped from her lips, a realization smacked her in the face. She had many mistakes, probably just like this man. The worst one had left her here, awaiting death.

Consistent Disappointment stalked toward the Hannah, grabbing something out of his back pocket. A knife.

Wannabe Leader put a hand out, stopping him. "Enough," he said. "There's been enough violence going around. We don't need you spilling more blood. Plus, if you do this, it's your head he's after."

For a brief moment, Consistent Disappointment's brave facade faltered, and his hand had dropped back to his side. "If that's the case...then let me go outside. Otherwise, these two will be slaughtered. I can't take any more backtalk. You're more than welcome to babysit them if you want." His lips curled into the slyest of smiles.

"I think I will go outside with you instead. Maybe it's you that needs more babysitting. You know, in case your temper kills us all. I'll be waiting for you when you're ready." Wannabe Leader gave the most nonchalant of nods and stalked out the cabin door.

No voices filled the room except for Consistent Disappointment's heavy breathing. With an angry roar, he muttered several angry curses, his shoe kicking at the cabin floor. With one hand clutching his hair and the other running down his face, he only gave two glances solely reserved for those also in the room until he opened the door. It slammed shut without so much as a warning.

And then, there was silence.

With Hannah's head near the window, she could hear voices outside as they walked farther and farther away from the cabin until the voices dwindled to nothing but the wind.

The captive moved quickly, not wasting any seconds. Though he was bound, he walked stealthily toward the kitchen area.

"What are you doing?" Hannah questioned, her eyes saucers. She couldn't believe her own eyes, at the complete reckless insanity of it all.

"I'm saving our lives," he said matter-of-factly. "I want to have some sort of say in how I die. Granted, I am over a hundred years old. It's plenty of time for me. You've lived barely beyond a decade. Don't you want a few more good years, or would you rather a pack of Lunar Amarians slaughter you first?"

Her mind couldn't begin to wrap itself around the words *Lunar* and *Amarian* and *over a hundred years old*.

Hannah's heart thundered in her chest. She watched as his retreating form passed the entryway to the kitchen. The ruffling of drawers felt like an echo in the tiny space, and Hannah held her breath.

It took mere minutes for him to start coming back, but it felt like hours.

With the grin covering half of his face, he waved the object—a knife—in her direction as he continued his path across the floor. "Our ticket to freedom."

When he finally reached her side again, he worked quickly, severing the rope that kept him bound for who knew how long. His hands were red and burned by the duration, and he flexed his arms and fingers, breathing a sigh of what Hannah assumed to be relief.

As excitement jumped in his eyes, he practically raced over to Hannah's side, the knife raised at an angle. When she caught sight of it, she couldn't help it. She flinched.

A flicker of hurt replaced the excitement he was feeling but then just as quickly vanished. Soon, the ropes were gone, and she could finally move her arms and legs.

Barely.

There was a small void of feeling from being stiff for so long, numbness coating most of her other senses. Shock was on dial nine, the one protector she could count on. Until now, it seemed.

As he grabbed her hand and slowly helped her up, another feeling bubbled in her stomach.

Hope.

Her legs slowly began to wobble, but the captive was faster, with reflexes she had never seen before. Almost effortlessly, he caught her, hoisting her upward until his hands locked underneath her knees. He shifted his weight, and soon, he was walking.

"James," he finally said as they reached the cabin's porch.

"What?" she blurted.

"It's my name," he replied. "I figured if we're escaping buddies, you might as well know my name."

"Hannah," she said.

Almost instantly, he smiled, a little dimple appearing on his left cheek.

"I know," was all he said, but before she could even ask more questions, this man—James—started running.

CHAPTER TWENTY

SABINA

Her stomach rumbled at the prospect of food. After hours of driving, they had just reached the Colorado border and were in desperate need of gas.

Aisles of the yummiest, health-aversive junk food beckoned as the little shop door closed behind her and the bell dinged. Sabina marveled at the display, her fingers touching the edges of bags as she walked.

"Don't forget...you actually have to pay for things here. We aren't just a touch and go." The gruff voice came from the clerk at the counter, who, with his disheveled hair and bloodshot eyes, looked like the shift was a long one ongoing.

She merely nodded in response, averting her eyes. It couldn't be more embarrassing than him thinking she was a thief. *Well, unless you're Hannah.*

Hannah. The word hit her like a stack of hard blocks. In the time she'd traveled, the name hadn't crossed her mind, until just now.

As she passed through several aisles, her mind aimlessly began to wonder about her friend, but her stomach grumbled of sweetness.

She found her palm grasping for the last bag of assorted cookies hanging on the rack, right around the same time she heard voices talking so quietly she wasn't sure if she was imagining it.

"We've agreed the situation was wrong. We've agreed we're all idiots, and all in the timespan of a few hours, she's far away from us now, but I think she'd be proud."

The voice was so poetically positive, Sabina marveled. How did he manage?

"Proud?" another voice huffed. "Our co-leader got thrown onto the back of a psycho's bike. She's probably dead by now, not proud, you moron."

There was the sound of a small *thunk* and a slight hiss.

"If you ask me," the first voice continued, voice laced with pain.

"But the thing is, William, nobody asked you," a third voice chimed in. "You're always butting in with these unnecessary comments or backstories we don't need to know. You're like the special edition of a novel no one's waiting on, but the editor got stuck with."

"Hannah did what she thought was best, all right?" William said. "It doesn't matter how stupid she was or how she thinks she's a hero. We're family, and family sticks together no matter what. We just need to find her and bring her home. Done. That's it. No other distractions."

With cookies in hand, Sabina decided she had spent too long eavesdropping. She could feel her mother's words in her ears then about manners and decorum just as the slants of her ears started turning pink.

Sabina started toward the register, the small wad of cash in her back pocket pressing in, a nagging reminder of time wasted listening to something that didn't concern her.

A sudden curiosity appeared in her gut. She shifted on her feet before turning back to the aisle she was in. She rounded the corner and saw where the group had gathered.

"Do you need something?" a voice called out.

Frozen, it took Sabina a moment to recognize that the voice wasn't a hushed whisper like before. No longer were their eyes focused on each other. No, several pairs were staring right at her.

She pointed at her chest. "Are you talking to me?"

When the boy nodded, she could feel the blush tickle her cheeks yet again. *Oh, great.*

"I really apologize for staring. And listening. I honestly know better. And this might sound crazy...but I've had my fair share of craziness today, so I might as well ask." Ducking her head down, Sabina could feel her cheeks growing even more red. "I know a Hannah. It might not be the same one, but—"

The boy's eyes lit up with something she couldn't trace. He pulled his phone out of his back pocket with the other hand, tapping on the screen. After a few minutes, he shoved a picture in her face.

"Is this you?"

Before Caelan, Sabina might have been inclined to say no. She would have merely walked away.

But there it was, an image she barely remembered, and even still, the proof it held was undeniable.

Behind the backdrop of sunlight, Sabina stood against the railing, her left arm wrapped behind the waist of an all-too-familiar person she called her friend. There was no mistaking the blue eyes that held the shimmer of a thousand daring ideas or the half-smirk that seemed to challenge the camera or even those looking at the photo. It was the face of a girl who greeted trouble with a big smile, maybe a wave, but never sent a post-card in return. Flickering memories weren't worth her time.

Due to the quality, Sabina guessed the photo's age to be at least two years, and that propelled one more burning question.

"How'd you get the photo?" she asked instead, her palms starting to get sticky with sweat. She rubbed them against her pants to no avail. It only made the moisture grow.

"*Our* Hannah. She sent it to us," the boy said, his gaze beginning to harden. With his messy hair and blue eyes rimmed with bloodshot crimson, he looked like an absolute wreck.

"How do you know Hannah?" Sabina asked boldly.

At this, the boy merely chuckled. "I would be inclined to ask you the same question."

"Is there a problem here?"

Sabina's shoulders immediately slumped with relief.

Caelan had somehow managed to intercept the conversation, glaring daggers at the boy across from her.

"There isn't," the boy replied, sending a pointed glance Sabina's way. "We're just figuring some things out."

"She doesn't have to answer you," Caelan practically spat. He went into a crouch, and his hands went to his belt. Sabina could see—barely—the silver glint of the hilt. He was prepared.

"Caelan," Sabina interjected. "I'm fine."

"There's no need to start anything," another boy piped up, holding his hands to the sky. "We aren't trying to hurt anyone. We just want to help our friend. She gave us this picture a long time ago. And your friend here..." The second boy gestured to Sabina. "...is maybe our one shot at being able to find her." The boy who held his hands in surrender wrapped an arm around the first one. "Will, just drop it. We need to go, to find a way to help Hannah somehow. I don't trust that biker guy and his stupid crew, so let's just go figure it out some other kind of way, all right? Fighting over this is pointless. Finding her is what's important."

"Is she in trouble?" Sabina asked.

Will, the first boy, looked at her with concern clouding his features. "More than you could know."

"We'll help you." Sabina turned to Caelan, and he nodded in agreement. She shifted her gaze back to the group. "She's my friend. She's your friend, too. We don't have long. Another friend of ours needs help, but maybe we can meet up somewhere after we drop Cammie off to strategize?"

"No time," the second guy said. "At least not now. We've got to find this Nyx, get Hannah, and keep her safe. If she can be found."

At the mention of the name, Caelan's hand went to the hilt, his jaw locked in place. His eyes stared off into the distance, his mind a million miles away, consumed by invisible thoughts.

"Are you sure his name was Nyx?" Caelan's words to the group were curt, to the point.

The second one's face lit up with raised brows. "I take it you know the jerk?"

The hardness and tick in Caelan's face was hard to miss. "There's history there. Not the good kind."

Will bumped his arm against the second one's shoulder, and they shared a small smile. Will gestured to the group of young men behind him, and the two young men walked closer to the huddle. "We will give you information if that's what you need and the location. After we get Hannah, that is. She comes first."

Caelan pressed his lips together. "That's all I can ask for. It's what I would do if I were you. I owe you a debt."

"There is no debt you could owe me. All I care about is saving Hannah. That's all I want." The second guy held out a palm to Caelan. "My name is Antonis, but most people just call me Tony."

Caelan's hand met Tony's as he gave another nod. "Caelan."

Tony let out a slow breath, his face making way for a smile. "We've come to an agreement. Hannah, for me. Nyx, for you."

"You don't have to get involved any further from that," Caelan reassured. "My fight with him is not yours. Trouble and my vengeance don't need to be following you around. You've done enough."

"When it comes to one of our own..." Tony locked eyes with Sabina and then Caelan, making sure his words resonated to their cores. "...trouble is never a concern. We don't break promises once we make them. Wherever you need us, after she is safe, we are there. There's no repayments needed as long as you help me make sure she is absolutely safe."

There was no doubt of the steel determination that glinted behind Caelan's eyes. "You have my promise. How will we get in contact again?"

Tony brought his phone out. After a few seconds, he handed it to Caelan. "If you put your number in here, I'll send you a quick text so you have mine. Once we find some sort of idea as to where they are, I'll call you. And whatever business you have to take care of, we're here to help."

Caelan gave one last look between them and then put his arm on Sabina's shoulder. "We need to go now. Solenne is waiting for us."

And so, Sabina and Caelan set off to the car where Cammie waited, leaving behind the lingering group.

The speedometer was barely under the limit that they should have been going.

"How much longer do we have?" Sabina asked, her throat tight. She clenched the seat with balled fists.

"It won't be much longer." Caelan's eyes barely flickered to Sabina before turning back to the road.

"About that...." Sabina trailed off and took in a breath. "How are you so sure? We have to get there in time for Solenne to help."

"Despite what you'd think, I have many centuries of being chased after to know how to avoid unwanted attention. Driving the speed limit will keep us under the radar, avoiding attention from others like Lennix. But I promise, as soon as I am away from lots of eyes, I will amp up the speed."

"I can't believe I'm saying this, but I trust you." Sabina stifled a laugh, turning over how shocking the events had taken in such a weird amount of time.

"I didn't expect us to be stopped for so long at the gas station," Caelan replied. "But we will make it there in time."

After several more torturous turns, Caelan finally hit the brakes, coming to a hard stop and then putting the van in park.

Sabina held her hands out to the dashboard, her heart lurching to her stomach with all of the constant movement. "Maybe you should go back to driving school," she ridiculed with a sigh.

Caelan put a finger to his lips, his eyes surveying the land for what, she was not sure. His eyes were different, though. Golden flecks merged into a violet purple. When he blinked, they shifted into the green and then back to their normal shade. Judging by how the corners of his mouth turned upward, Sabina could only guess the emotion behind the colors. *Excitement.*

Caelan shifted the car into drive, following something that was moving so fast that the outline was barely visible, at least to the human eye. At first, it was merely trees that surrounded them. Sabina was beginning to lose count of how many trees there were when they reached a clearing. *The figure was gone.*

A small, secluded cottage with beautiful wood siding was their destination. A vegetable garden enveloped the cottage, moss growing along the edges of the porch. Silver cobblestones lined the walkway path up until the porch where a woman stood alone, her eyes locked on the van.

As Sabina got out, she couldn't help but keep her eyes trained on the woman. To the human eye, she couldn't have been older than early fifties, donned in a common buttoned-down shirt and dress pants. Her blonde hair with sprinkles of gray held back from her face didn't conceal the wrinkled frown her lips wore. Instead, it accented every feature that came with aging, but the woman wore them proudly.

Caelan gently unbuckled Cammie, his arms enveloping her as he carried her toward the cottage.

When they finally reached the woman, her hardened stare relaxed into recognition as she focused on Caelan's face. "Will you let me in on what's going on?"

"Heal her first," he replied, eyes conveying a message that Sabina could not read.

The woman dared to look at Sabina standing next to Caelan, finally acknowledging her presence. "She can't be here," she said as her eyes drifted away just as fast as they came, interlocking with Caelan's.

"You and I both know she can't exactly leave. It's her friend we're talking about. She deserves to stay." Caelan's voice held no trace of anger but that of a man on his last legs. "I wouldn't ask you to make an exception if I didn't feel it was necessary."

The woman couldn't have been much older than her aunts, and yet behind her eyes held so much wisdom that was barely concealed behind the harboring mask she tried to wear.

The woman's mouth sagged even lower. "Fine." She wearily sighed, running a hand over her face. "Place her in my workroom."

The smile on Caelan's face could not be contained, and the woman's face broke out into sheer joy.

"Thank you, Solenne," he whispered, leaning to kiss her cheek.

She patted his cheek with her free hand, only letting go when he turned to go inside.

As the cabin door shut behind him, Sabina fumbled through her brain for some sort of introduction. "I just wanted to thank you so much for—"

"Nonsense," Solenne snapped. "Your kind has no reason to thank me or even speak to me, much less. I am only doing this for Caelan. You are here as a favor to him. Don't twist it in your mind as anything otherwise."

Sabina's mouth slacked, and she bit her tongue. She merely nodded, and Solenne led the way inside.

The lighting was dim except for the candles that were freshly ablaze along the walls. It made way for a living room complete with modern furniture but scarce of other trinkets unless one counted the trunk of unknown items in the corner.

The kitchen was a full array of spices and seasonings, pots and pans, and dirty dishes in the sink. There wasn't any time to look further, as they had already passed the threshold into the other room.

There was an operating table in the corner and another small table beside it that held many cylinder bottles full of herbs that Sabina couldn't decipher. The liquid was a mixture of amber gold and purple violet, labels marked in an unfamiliar language.

"What is this?" Breathless, Sabina could barely fathom the sight before her eyes. It was unlike anything she had ever seen.

"Have you not told her anything about the process of unsealing an Erasing?" The roll in Solenne's eyes was evident. She strode to the edge of the room where two ornate rolling chairs stood and grabbed one, sitting beside the operating table.

"There hasn't been much time," Caelan said, shifting his weight. Gently, he set Cammie down onto the operating table on her back, letting her arms fall over her stomach. "We've had quite a few instances happen."

Solenne's entire body stiffened. Her gaze darted between the girl on the table and the girl lingering in the opening before her cold stare gripped Caelan. "Were you followed?"

Caelan shook his head. "I couldn't sense anything on the way here. We did have an altercation with a rogue Lunar earlier on our way, though."

Solenne's mouth fell agape as she processed his words. "Was it one of Anwir's group? Or some other one that was roaming this side?"

"I was told it was Nyx Castros who was responsible for another girl's disappearance, another friend of Sabina's. I wouldn't put it past him to be involved in whoever was trying to attack us."

Solenne's face took on a dark cloud, a storm brewing behind her glazed-over eyes. "Makes sense that Anwir's spawn would take over the cause. That family was ruthless in their pursuit of you and in their pursuit of Leanna. The damage...the blood...I just cannot—" She inhaled deeply through her nose, closing her eyes shut at whatever memory sprung forth in her thoughts. When she opened them, there was no trace of the deeply held emotions. Instead, it was pure precision. "Did he hurt either of the girls?"

Caelan shook his head, letting a small smile show despite his tired eyes. "I managed to stop him before he was able to get one scratch or bite in. One would say that he won't be bothering us for a while."

A glimmer of pride shone behind Solenne's eyes, and then, just as suddenly, she turned to Cammie's unconscious form. "How long has she been like this? Not longer than two days, I hope?"

"We drove here as soon as she became unconscious. The tremors have come and gone, but her fever is still there."

After a moment of silence, Solenne finally spoke. "Her body is fighting the Erasing," she murmured.

"What...what does that mean?" Caelan's face twisted, his breath hitching.

"It means that whoever did this was powerful. The gifts we have...are honed as soon as they become known. It seems like this particular individual has lots of practice, but there is something different about this particular type. It is similar... to..." She swallowed, sending Caelan a quick glance before she took another breath. "The simplest way to explain this is that the wiping was quick. Too quick. Almost...as if there was—"

"An interruption," Caelan finished breathlessly, shooting a glance at Sabina. "There is someone in her memories...someone who I was supposed to meet. He had information for me, information that would be helpful for me to return. After all of these years, Solenne, we can finally go home. We just need to find him. If you can locate the memories, there will be a good chance."

Solenne's hands began to shake as she focused on organizing the many bottles of concoctions on the side table. "We cannot go back there," she stated, her voice shifting. Her cheeks flushed scarlet as she averted her gaze. "I made a promise to your mother that night that I would protect you. You've made many mistakes, had many rebellious ideals that have caused so much wreckage. You've run from it so far. I did not tell you anything otherwise than to be safe, but this is different. You cannot go back there. They will kill you."

"You don't know that," Caelan argued. "How can you know that? We haven't been there in over seven hundred years! I don't even know my home. It might be different for you. You were in servitude to my mother, her lady's maid, her confidant. I was barely a few days old when we left. You raised me, protected me even when you didn't approve of things I did on this side of the realm, but I am no longer a child. I am a man. I am a widower, a father to girls who barely got a chance to live, let alone breathe, because of those monsters! I refuse to wait in the shadows any longer. It is my birthright to go back to rule...and you know it."

Solenne finally faced Caelan's alert eyes with understanding. "Feel how you must, but I forbid it. We aren't going back."

"But I am," Caelan huffed. His arms were stiff at his sides, his hands balling into fists. His jaw locked, set in resolve. Then, he glanced back at Cammie. "Heal her, please. Do whatever you have to, so she returns to full health, but know this... me staying is not up for discussion."

He gave Sabina a parting glance as he stalked out of the room, muttering under his breath about needing fresh air and room to breathe, leaving her alone with the frazzled woman.

There was no sound for a few moments, and then Solenne grabbed one of the bottles, undoing the lid.

"What are you doing with that?" Sabina croaked, her throat dry from lack of moisture.

"It's a potion to make sure she stays unconscious while I work with the healing she needs."

The answer was so matter-of-fact, as if beings with abilities and potions weren't something Sabina heard out of stories growing up but merely living and breathing alongside her.

Which, she realized suddenly, they were. *They always were.* It was like some sort of hidden treasure trove that she had stumbled upon, and the more she stared, the more she began to wonder at how much more there was that had been concealed from her all this time.

"Is there anything you need from me? Is there any way I can help you?"

Solenne looked up from her task at hand, giving Sabina the subtlest of glances. Her eyes find the spare chair against the wall at the end of the room. Without speaking, Sabina understood the meaning immediately. *An invitation.*

Slowly, Sabina grabbed the chair and rolled it across the floor. When it finally came to a stop, Sabina reluctantly paused before setting her weight down in it.

Solenne's hands continued moving of their own accord, mixing the concoctions together, pouring from one bottle into another, the colors shifting as bubbles formed at the surface. After putting the lid on top of the last bottle, Solenne shook it gently. When the lid came off, the liquid slowly settled down, and Solenne gestured to Cammie. Sabina stood on shaky legs, awaiting Solenne's words.

"Hold her mouth steady," Solenne instructed Sabina, moving the bottle closer to Cammie's now open mouth where Sabina's palms rested.

Before a drip even fell, Sabina's breath became shallow. "How do I know this is safe?"

"I've done this before," Solenne replied, blowing a strand of hair out of her face.

"But you hadn't saved her, did you? I'm not about to let you pour some unknown substance down her throat that could kill her! There has to be something else you can use."

The shrillness in Sabina's tone was so sudden she could hardly believe it was actually there. It felt like she was drifting, hovering, blissfully aware of the scene before her without any way to actually stop it. Her soul and body were no longer tethered. Instead, she watched without any sort of respite, as if she was merely an outsider in the entire situation.

"Then you must not know Caelan at all," Solenne whispered under her breath. When she looked into Sabina's eyes once more, there was a hint of sorrow spilling from the edges. "He's always had some morbid fascination with humans. I guess it is myself to blame, me being the one who brought him here to be raised alongside them. I thought it would raise less suspicion and that he would blend in better, but I never thought he would sympathize with their cause. They are part of the reason why we slid into hiding, but you must know...as much as he loves your kind, he would not have brought you here unless he thought I was the only saving grace for your friend. I might not entirely agree with your methods or your way of life, but you aren't the first human I have been in close contact with. I have cared before for your kind. In that, you must trust my word, as you trust Caelan's...that for his sake, I will do what I can to save your friend's life."

Sabina had no words left to reply, her tongue dry and trapped underneath anxious thoughts and a million questions, but there didn't need to be a clock in the room for her to realize one stunning truth: time was of the essence.

"Do it," she croaked, licking her lips. "If this...will save her...please do it."

Solenne nodded firmly, letting the golden-purple moisture fall into Cammie's mouth. The room was so utterly silent that you could actually hear the droplets falling with a *drip, drip, drip.*

Sabina held her hopes in her chest, willing them not to swim to the surface until she knew for sure that Cammie would be safe.

"What happens now?" Sabina couldn't stop the question from tumbling out of her mouth despite the heaviness in her chest. Air supply was harder to find here, and she took what she could in grateful gulps even as it burned the back of her throat.

"There will be sudden movement at first. All that I am doing is sending her into the deepest of sleeps. There, as she falls into it, her subconscious will be attacked, so if she jerks and moves, it is completely normal. It's just her body preparing herself for the release of the trapped memories. The human mind usually allows them to be wiped away without even a second glance once an Erasing happens, but due to the rushed job or some interruption of some kind, they didn't vanish like they should have. It's more so...trapped in limbo as your kind would say. I am just merely relaxing her mind enough to where it flows fully sprung, and then there will be no questions. She will just...know." Solenne stood, her hands hovering near Cammie's head. Her eyes danced with a question, but this time, Sabina no longer felt any urge to fight her. Not if Solenne had the power to save Cammie's life.

Sabina gave a slight nod. Solenne's hands, as pale as they were, found their way to rest on Cammie's temples. She exhaled slowly and spoke in a language Sabina couldn't understand. As the mutters turned into a soft musical melody, the hairs on Sabina's arms stood upright, front and center. It was as if she herself was falling into a sleepless trance.

Then, there was twitching, but it wasn't from her. It started at the base of Cammie's hands, traveling until it enveloped her fingertips. Her entire arm followed with it, shooting tremors that rocked her body. Soon, her neck was moving sporadically, her knees fumbling back against the table. Her feet could barely be contained on the table anymore, the movement so resolved that there was no slowing it down, no pausing, no reasoning with it.

"Hold her steady if you can." Solenne's voice cut through the shock that reverberated in Sabina's bones.

Sabina sprung to action. She used all of her might to press down on Cammie's center, holding tight to arms and legs that moved of their own will.

"What do we do?" The shrieking came from her burning throat, and Sabina's heart thumped so loudly that she was sure it was becoming background music. "Tell me what to do."

Solenne fumbled with more potions, her hands steadying just enough to start pouring more of the liquids together. "It probably wasn't a strong enough dosage," she said, still pouring. "We just need to add more. She isn't relaxed."

Solenne moved forward, and Sabina shifted her weight, grabbing Cammie's chin once more. Solenne poured more of the liquid, but she could only get so far. Cammie thrashed once, twice, her hands knocking the bottle out of Solenne's grasp. It fell to the ground with a shatter, the contents spilled all around the wheels of the operating table.

Nothing could have prepared Sabina for the defiance of Cammie's mind.

"Whoever did this...is strong. He's purposeful in wanting her to forget, but he didn't know me. Your friend will make it out of this, do you hear me? Listen to what I say. Do as I say. Keep her steady, try to soothe her however you know how. I will have to go to my garden to get the ingredients she needs. She's broken everything I can use. In my absence, I trust you to help her. Do you understand?" Solenne's eyes were wild with determination, a frenzy of desperation that Sabina herself could feel clawing its way at her throat. It was in the air between them and in words unsaid.

Sabina could only nod.

Solenne rushed out of the room.

Cammie's body still thrashed wildly, unkempt despite all attempts of calm. Sabina's throat felt hollow and strained, hoarseness scratching the back of her esophagus. She didn't realize the cause until she felt wetness staining her cheeks and the sound that bounced off of the wall. *Screaming. Mine. Of course.*

She felt gentle hands on her shoulders and jerked to defend herself, but then she saw the eyes that held so much concern. Caelan.

"What's happening to her?" he asked, rushing to Cammie's side.

"The Erasing, it's too...too...strong." Sabina tripped over words, the entire noise feeling like a hollow gap in the air. "Her body is fighting it too much. Solenne is getting another remedy made up, but I am not sure what we can do." Her body wracked with sobs, and she looked up at Caelan through blurry eyes. "Tell me what we will do to save her. Please, give me something, anything that we can do. Just tell me."

The silence that followed was so deafening that it cracked Sabina's heart in half.

And then, there was nothing but a piercing wail that erupted in the room and Cammie's eyes that stirred open, stuck in place to her own undoing.

CHAPTER TWENTY-ONE

CAMMIE

THE WORLD WAS A BLINDING arrangement of floating colors and much too loud voices. She could hear the faint echo of screaming that somehow sounded a million miles away and right next door all at once. She could see hands moving, feel warmth against her cheek, yet she was powerless to move. Her body and will refused to collide in unison, so she continued staring at the ever-consuming ceiling.

Her tongue was parched, her limbs aching with lack of movement, and her brain was so loud she could barely fumble through the haze. She had no idea who she was or where she was. The one thing she did know was that it was all too much. Too much noise. Not enough freedom.

And then, there was rustling. She didn't know where, but she could feel it, feel the pulse of blood rushing back to organs as the numbness in body parts rose to life. She could feel small gulps of air tickling her throat.

But then came the burning. It was fire from the top all the way to the bottom, as if someone had deliberately set a match to her internal organs and threw away the water. Everything screamed for release, for some sort of refuge from the pain.

And then, she heard a voice.

"This should help her," the woman said. "She just needs to take a few more sips."

She could feel the cold liquid at the base of her lips. As it hit her tongue, she tasted honey and mint.

Sudden clunking filled her ears—the sound of bells. And then, she succumbed to darkness.

When she opened her eyes, there was still darkness. No light presented itself as she used all of her strength to rise to a sitting position. Vaguely, she could sense the outline of her own body in front of her. If she squinted hard enough, she could almost see her hand. Slowly, she stood on shaky legs.

Colors were void of time and space, and nothingness was what echoed.

A giggle. Her ears perked at the sound. She whipped her head around, stunned by the appearance of sudden light.

A cosmic sphere, no bigger than the size of a small palm, floated in what she assumed was air. There was no trace as to what was keeping it airborne, but as she peered closer, it became apparent that it bore color. The only thing that held color.

The outline was a slick silver, little remnants of pink and blue in the center. Glints reflected off of it as if there was light in the space, but the noise...it was coming from the—what was the word?

Bubble.

That was it. A bubble. The epiphany was as sudden as it was comical, simply because bubbles were once her favorite thing.

As the giggling continued, the bubble shifted, morphing until the glints of light faded entirely, replacing it with a picture.

It was so simple she had the smallest urge to marvel at it and even more so when it started changing, turning from a picture to a moving image as if it were no small feat.

Once it became clearer, she could finally see. There was a girl in the moving image, sitting on the porch steps. She had to have been not much older than five years old. A slight breeze caressed her hair. Her little arm shot up with goosebumps, but her hand still moved. As Cammie squinted, the girl's arm came into view. She was holding a bubble wand, and as each bubble formed, the giggling resumed. She was having so much fun, as if there wasn't a care in the world.

To anyone, it would have seemed like a mundane sight. Even to Cammie, it felt like one, but as the picture zoomed out, Cammie barely caught a glimpse of the mud-stained tennis shoes and the bruised eye. Recognition hit her full force, finally shedding some light as to what she was looking at.

It was a memory. *Her* memory.

The more the concept began to twirl around in her mind's eye, curiosity waddled in. What would happen if she touched it?

Her hands had their own mission as they reached for the bubble. When her fingertips touched it, though she could not see them, the smoothness made her entire hand tingle. The tingling shifted, and the bubble began to quake. It moved violently, the exterior leaving streaks in the air that were so white they could vaguely pass as a silvery gray. With the shaking came an explosion of light so bright that Cammie shielded her face with hands she wished were visible. It blocked the light out enough, and when she put her hands down...it was gone.

No more of the bubble but a bunch of particles floating downward were left in its wake. The confusion began to sit in her gut, but then she felt something under her toes. More rattling. And then, there was pressure. She lifted her foot. She could feel it but couldn't see anything.

A sphere rose to the surface and then another and another until there were so many that she couldn't count them all. Sounds multiplied, and images turned to movies until it became a mass of floating ones.

The ones closer to her were easier to grab, and the sounds vanished as they erupted into particles of light, all previous memories of her childhood. Simple ones—eating ice cream for the first time, having her first pet fish, drawing with chalk.

The ones farther away, those were the ones she raced for. Somewhere in her gut, she had a feeling that these were more important ones.

As if the pesky things knew her very thoughts, they began to dart away, defiantly playing some kind of game of catch and chase, much to her frustration.

She raced after them, ignoring the pain shooting up her legs, ignoring the fire that grew in her lungs. The bubbles were floating away in a single formation, but one was straggling. It was at the very end, but it could not keep up with the rest of them. It felt like hours before she was able to break away and trap it in the corner of the darkness, but what she saw made her heart linger in her throat.

Cammie was older in this one, much older than five. By the way her hair was in an updo and the choppy bangs she had, it was easy to figure out the age. Fifteen. She had only worn it like that once and had decided after that it would never be the style she'd wear ever again.

She was in the bookstore, eyes focused and honed on the task at hand: stocking inventory. It was her favorite part about working at the bookstore. She was able to feel the texture of the spines, and maybe she would secretly smell the pages before anyone bought them. She would imagine the lives the authors inhabited to tell such tales of wonder and intrigue and then go back to the cluster of books on her arm. She was so engrossed in her task that she didn't hear the door open, but present Cammie did. The way the image was set, she couldn't see anything outside of where past Cammie was.

Suddenly, a stroke of light shined on the edge of the image, and past Cammie jumped. As her head shifted, the image did too. It was lightning, present Cammie realized.

At the now-ajar door stood a man not much older than she was at the time. He wore torn clothing and a horrified expression as rainwater lapped around his mud-soaked boots. Past Cammie asked if he needed anything, to which he didn't respond.

He was frozen in place with fear, and a bit of confusion fuddled with his features. Against everything Cammie had been taught about being in charge while alone, she went against her better judgment and led the young man inside.

Present Cammie felt her hands go numb as the bubble exploded into a million particles once more like the others. The shock reverberated to her core, and she wasn't sure of how to respond, how to steady herself. *Who was that man?*

As soon as she regained her composure, the rest of the remaining floating bubbles ceased moving. Then, to her horror, they all came moving toward her. No longer was this a game, she realized, as the speed increased. They weren't playing. This was a deliberate charge.

One after the other, the bubbles hit her stomach, her torso, her legs, her arms. The bubbles exploded on impact, sending shards of panic and pain Cammie's way. Movement was once a luxury, and now, paralytic anxiety was her normal.

As more and more bubbles moved, there was only one now in front of her. It didn't rush like the others. It merely paused. It turned many different ways, as if studying the complexity of the human being standing across the way.. A bubble having a personality might have seemed like the most insane thing to experience, but right now, she wasn't going to question the sentiment. She couldn't, not with the fear that lay on her throat.

She almost breathed a sigh of relief until she sensed a different kind of calculating sway of the bubble. She wanted to scream, but how could she? Who would hear her here?

Without sound, she merely watched as the bubble imposed itself, lodging at her face. She couldn't swat it away, but she could taste sweetness on her tongue as it melted, a familiar taste she couldn't quite place. She paused for the explosion of light, but there wasn't one. Then, her vision started doubling, tripling, until she felt more tingling in her hands.

But nothing prepared her for the drop.

"Hey, Cammie? Cammie, you okay?"

The voice speaking pulled her out of her daze, and cautiously, Cammie opened her eyes.

There was no darkness here. Instead, she was back in her room, at home, under the harsh lighting on the ceiling. Her eyes burned as she blinked, taking in her surroundings. There was an array of clothes on the floor, as if a tornado had attacked her closet. In front of her was a mirror, and as her eyes settled, Cammie took in her reflection.

Her hair lazily hung over one shoulder, her brown eyes dancing with nervousness. Behind her, in the reflection, she could see Sabina sitting on her legs on the bed, watching her.

"Why are you here?" Cammie's voice was hoarse from a lack of speaking, but the shock was all the same.

Sabina arched a brow, tilting her head to the side. "Aside from helping calm your nerves before your date? Just sitting here."

This time, Cammie was the one puzzled. "But...what about Caelan? And you...and..." The words died on her lips, and the frazzled feeling was back.

What's happening?

"Okay..." Sabina trailed off, a glint in her eyes. "I'm not sure what happened here. You were fine a few minutes ago, and now, you're in some sort of daze. If your nerves are contributing to the memory fog, allow me to relieve your confusion. My parents had an art convention in New Orleans, and I told them about your date tonight, so they decided to be dears and let me come over to do some styling. I even brought my makeup to help you feel—and look—your best." She held up her makeup kit as a demonstration and then gestured to Cammie. "Now, tell me, how do you feel about the dress? Yes, no, meh?"

Cammie turned back to the mirror. She was wearing a green dress with lots of sparkles. It came to her knees, and it was form-fitting including spaghetti straps. "Is this—"

"—the one your mom got you for graduation? Yes," Sabina finished, sighing. "If you need to have the conversation about how James will go crazy for you as soon as we're finished, we can totally have it again. I just thought you'd be more motivated now. Maybe I should have added more of a kicker to make it better. More encouraging, maybe," Sabina pondered, tapping her chin.

More shock reverberated through Cammie's still-stiff limbs, so sharp she could taste it on her tongue. "You're telling me I have a date?" She turned to Sabina, a million questions in her mind. "Like...tonight? Now?"

The beam that came from Sabina was so bright it might as well have rivaled the sun. "In about an hour, but don't you worry. I will make sure you are absolutely ready on time. That definitely won't be a problem." A mischievous grin formed as she gestured to the bed. "Come. Sit. Make yourself comfy, calm your mind, and let me work my magic."

Cautiously, Cammie made her way to the bed, her stomach turning like a pretzel. She had no idea what was going on, but she was sure she'd find out.

Hopefully.

After what felt like an agonizing long time, Cammie stood in front of the mirror once again, admiring Sabina's handiwork. With hair pulled away from her face, little ringlets of stubborn curls that fell softly by her eyes, Cammie could see the framing. She never fixed her hair, instead opting for the more natural look of versatility and comfort, but the way Sabina used a makeup brush and a palette of colors, she felt like a different person. She *looked* like a different person.

"How did you do this? You made me look..."

"Exactly like you? You're just an amplified version of yourself. I only enhanced what you already had. No need to thank me. A bit of shading never killed anyone. Except maybe James."

At the name, every hair on Cammie's arms stood upright. She turned her head around halfway, anxiety sitting on her skin. "Why would it kill him? What did I do?"

Sabina wore a knowing grin and wiggled her eyebrows. "You look like a knockout. Of course, it'll kill him. You *want* it to, don't you?"

Stuck between not knowing what to say and still being confused about what was going on, Cammie opted for silence, much to Sabina's disappointment.

Cammie refused to ask questions but was somehow begging for some sort of rescue from the awkwardness.

The shrill sound of the doorbell rang throughout the house, and her heart leapt to her throat. Was he here?

"He's here," Sabina shrieked, giving Cammie the once over. "Let me get a good look at you." She turned Cammie around so fast she swore she had whiplash from all the spinning, but she still wasn't too dizzy not to appreciate Sabina's wide grin. "You look so great! He is going to lose it in a good way when he sees you, I promise. No need to be nervous."

Sabina's reassurance, while appreciated, did nothing to slow the consistent pattering of Cammie's heart, even as she smiled and headed out of the room. Her feet felt like anchors to the stairs with each step she took, and no amount of deep breaths calmed the anxious whirlwind in her mind. She had no idea what she was doing here, but there was no way getting out of it, it seemed.

Her palm was covered in a slick layer of sweat as she turned the doorknob.

There, in the moonlight, was James. She had seen him through the flashes she'd had, but it was never long enough to get the full picture of what she was really looking at. Here, she could finally see.

He was taller than her, overpowering her small stature by nearly a foot. He wore not only a casual, dark grey button-down with jeans, but a smile so bright that even if she didn't know him, she would be sure to return it. "Wow, Cammie. You look absolutely amazing! Did you watch a tutorial or something? I've just...never seen you look like this."

Heat rose to her cheeks as she gave a small smile. "It was Sabina, actually. She dressed me up, said it was her duty to do so."

"I'm sure I've told you this before, but I'll say it again. You look amazing regardless of what you wear or what makeup you put on. It's just nice to see you smile. You haven't done that in a while."

At the pure honesty of his words, Cammie was taken aback. She had seen him in mere moments that one would—or could—call fever dreams, but this...felt more *real* than anything else she had experienced.

The way he was smiling at her felt real, and the way his fingers tickled against her palm felt real. She could feel the tingles so sharp that silent shudders traveled up her arms.

I can't be dreaming.

And, if she was being honest with herself, she didn't want to be.

"She didn't tell me where we were going," Cammie finally said. "Did you tell her anything?"

At the crinkle in James's brow, Cammie began to understand some sliver of his personality. He was a teaser of sorts, and though she didn't know much, here and now, she was sure it wedged its way into whatever topic he carried. Even first dates.

"And why would I spoil the fun? Tell you everything? Pfft. You obviously don't know me that well then." He shot her a mischievous smile.

You really have no idea. I don't know you as well as you think I do. I have no idea what I'm even doing here.

"I'm a sucker for surprises," he continued, oblivious to her inner torment. "I know you aren't, but don't you fret, my dear Camille. You'll find out soon enough. That is, if you're ready to go?"

Cammie's head moved faster than her mouth, words coming out sputtered and constricted. "I, uh, I mean, yes."

Immediately, her gaze faltered to the carpet in front of the door, away from his lingering gaze.

She fully expected him to laugh at her, to make some sort of demeaning joke. She had heard enough of it in high school from people who had taken advantage of her shyness or her anxiety-stricken brain. Her entire body tensed with prickling anticipation. She stole a look up at him, despite all of her better judgement.

For once in this entire exchange, there was no trace of laughter on his lips or the evil sparkle in eyes that she had seen from boys her age many times before. Instead, there was a softness that poured out into the crevices and a sweetness like honey in his gaze. He didn't push forward to ask her to hurry out onto the street toward their next destination. Spoken words weren't said. Just patient silence rested between them.

"You must be used to this," she murmured. "I'm sorry. I know it isn't normal—"

"It's normal for you. It's something that you struggle with, out of your control. The least I can do is meet you where you are instead of automatically expecting you to jump over hurdles you can't quite reach yet. I'm in no rush. I know...things are hard sometimes. Things that might come easier for others are like a mountain for you. What kind of person, or friend, would I be if I didn't understand that?"

At that very moment, she felt something in the resolve of her gut. *Respect.* She might have lost her memories. She might not understand what was going on or who this man was before this point in her life, but her mind was trying to tell her something about this interaction. Somewhere deep inside, it was marked as important, meaningful, and engrained so deeply that it wasn't something she could easily forget. And so, for what she could sense was the first time in her life, she allowed herself to close the door behind her and step forward into this new space, where understanding and intrigue bled into normalcy.

The street was busy, as much as she could expect on a weekend night when work was a thing of the past to most on these nights. Plenty of cars honked at nearby pedestrians, willing them to hurry up and get to the other side, so traffic would flow again. As she watched more and more cars go by, the stunning realization of just how impatient everyone was set in like concrete.

"I don't think I've ever seen people be this busy," she commented. "It's like they can't catch a break."

"Why do you think I suggested we walk to Main Street?" James wore a lazy grin, his hand intertwined with Cammie's as his thumb stroked soft circles on her palm. "There's always so much pressure, so much going on. If you don't take a minute, a day even, to shut it all out, it'll weigh you down. It'll be like an anchor that shoots you all the way to the bottom until there's no way out."

"I've never really thought about it like that," Cammie pondered, tilting her head to the side.

"That's why you have me," James stated, a proud smile overtaking his features. "You're the worrier. I'm the voice of reason. We're perfect together."

"Is this something you say a lot? I keep getting the feeling you're forever optimistic."

James's smile grew even wider. His entire face seemed to light up with every ounce of positivity that could be radiated, and it traveled to his feet as he took skipping steps. "What's with the sudden memory loss?" he asked. "Am I that dazzling that your brain has seemed to have misplaced every memory we've had together?"

Suddenly, his feet skidded to a stop as he turned around, jolting Cammie in the process. His grip was tight as he twisted her into a magnificent spin, the ends of her dress flurrying upward, much to the horrific blush staining her cheeks. When she finally stopped spinning, they were face to face, pressed against each other. He stared down at her with a dizzying smile, and for the first time, she noticed he had dimples. It only appeared when he really smiled, and he was dazzling.

His eyes are such a beautiful green.

His gaze flickered once to her lips before becoming trapped under her gaze again. She could have sworn she felt his grip move to her waist, but maybe she was kidding herself. Surely he wouldn't kiss her?

His head lowered, just then, as if her own thoughts were sprawled like a billboard on her forehead. If she only leaned closer, she would be able to feel his breath grazing her lips and practically touch the body heat that consumed his flushed cheeks. If only...

"Cammie...you should know me better by now," he whispered. "Kisses don't appear until *after* the first date. I'm too much of a gentleman to ruin that sentiment. Besides...it's probably best we get food or something first. I'm not a big fan of spoiled dessert. Or special moments, for that matter."

When he moved away, she could feel the heat traveling from her lips, to her cheeks, to her forehead. Her entire face was on fire with embarrassment and how convincing the entire exchange was.

You've got to be kidding me.

The sudden tug of a hand on hers snapped her out of her shell-shocked brain. "I wasn't kidding when I mentioned dessert," James said so matter-of-factly that it shrunk any doubt that lingered in her mind.

Steps that were wild and chaotic became smooth and undisturbed, though her mind began to play in reverse to the almost moment. Here she was, still in the unknown, still struggling with the concept of what she was actually doing here, and an almost kiss was boggling her more than it should have.

Get a grip, Cammie. For real. It isn't a big deal.

"Are you okay with Donny's?"

The simple question made her eyes bulge. "Are you kidding? I *love* Donny's. How did you know?"

"It's because I've been around you so long. The first time we hung out, after you know...well, after you found me and did your best to help me acclimate to the new surroundings, you told me the best place to go that wasn't just the bookstore was Donny's. You said that when you were younger, going there, eating a bit of ice cream made all of your worries go away. Not once did you ever view me as some sort of crazy person." He laughed. "Though I'm sure I looked like one. I had to have been, scaring you like that, showing up at your job. I had no sense of customs here."

"Would you say that you do now? I might have some sort of brain fog, like everything else, but where did you say you were from again? Tonight feels very fuzzy for me."

James looked away from her for a moment, his eyes trailing the outline of the moon in the sky. "I would say there are some customs I might never understand, but that's because what's normal for you isn't always normal for me, and I think I told you about the traveling. My parents did a lot of traveling, so I never really fit in anywhere. With you, it is easier. Not the same but easier."

"Do you ever miss home?" Cammie dared to ask.

James's cheek stiffened as the question tumbled from her mouth. "More than you would know."

His lips curved and dipped into a frown as his eyes seemed to disappear into a world unknown. Cammie desperately wanted to travel there, to know the crevices that lay underneath, but all too quickly, a smile plastered.

"Onward to Donny's. We want to make sure we can get you some ice cream. It isn't much farther. Are you okay waiting outside? I can go grab it if you want to wait outside the door. I thought we could do some more walking, more talking, and then maybe get some dinner later, but that's only if you're up for it."

Cammie nodded, suddenly aware of the rumbling within her gut. *I must really be hungry.*

Soon enough, he reached the little shop, sending Cammie one last smile before going inside.

She stood outside of the establishment, her backside pressed against the wall, letting her head fall against it. Hard bricks rubbed against hair, but she reveled in it. It was something here, right in front of her, that she couldn't deny the realness of.

She dared to peek into the window, and the thought of seeing James made the blush come again, full force. After a few moments, she found him talking to the cashier. Though she couldn't hear him, there was no mistaking the easy-going attitude he carried. He spoke animatedly to the worker, his hands flowing over the tops of the ice cream bins separators. She couldn't help but marvel at the fact that he knew enough about her to go forth and try, yet here she was, knowing nothing, and what was she to do?

As more things appeared in the pondering of her mind, she felt it—a cool chill on the back of her neck. It whispered across her face, like a smooth glove. It struck every nerve she had on her body and willed her eyes open.

There was nothing there, other than the few pedestrians walking along the main sidewalk and the hustling and bustling of cars on the busy street. Even so, she couldn't stop herself from clutching her heart as paranoia thumped in her chest. Her eyes darted, and she peered closer to the edges of the street. There, in the shadows, she could vaguely make out a faint outline. If only she could move closer...

Ding!

The sudden shriek of the bell jolted her a million miles upward, and her hands were out for blood.

"Hey, hey," James said, a soft murmur. "It's just me. It's just me." He spoke slowly and took a deep breath. "Follow with me, Cammie. In, out. In, out. *In, out.*"

As she followed his commands, the pressure in her chest subsided, and the drum in her heart slowed to a barely there thump.

"You're doing great, Cammie. Just one more breath for me, okay? In. Out." He inhaled and exhaled with her, and it had a surprisingly calming effect. He did it effortlessly, like he knew the ritual was written on the back of his hand. "Now, do you want to tell me what happened? Was it an anxiety attack?"

"I think I saw something," Cammie said, voice laced with shaky breaths. "In the distance, at the edge of that intersection."

With furrowed brows, James followed her pointed finger hesitantly.

"Well?" Cammie prodded. "What do you see?"

James squinted, clenching his jaw. "I see...a road with several cars that have drivers with the patience level of a toddler. Those same drivers have a very obvious disdain for walking pedestrians, but if I look really hard...I can see..."

"Yes? See what?" Cammie held her breath.

James's hands gripped the waffle cones of sugary goodness, his mouth barely ajar. "Wait!"

"So, you see it? You see that outline?"

"No." James chuckled. "I just wanted to make you laugh. I know that's the hardest thing for you to do after an anxiety attack." At Cammie's deadpan expression, James offered her the waffle cone in his right hand. "For you. To make up for my idiotic attempt at cheering you up. I am indebted to you forevermore."

He did it again, she noticed. He knew her so well. Even Hannah—Sabina, too—never knew her favorite ice cream order. As long as they've been friends, she doubted they'd even remember her favorite color right away, even though she had told them dozens of times. It took a long time for those things to register for them.

"Why do these things come so easily for you? You remembered my favorite ice cream. You took the time to do all of this for me...and I can't tell you how nice that is of you."

"Well," James said.

Then, his expression shifted. No longer was he focused on Cammie. His eyes were dead set on the space far, far behind where she stood. Without words, he brought the ice cream in his hand to his lips. He took a big bite and swallowed immediately, his cheek jutting out.

"We need to go," he uttered, his face taking on a pale color. "Right now."

"But why? There's no need to pretend that someone scary is out there. You don't have to pretend to make me feel better. I was just being paranoid for no reason—hey!"

The waffle cone she was about to devour vanished from her grasp, and Cammie watched in disbelief as it fell to the ground without warning. James tossed his cone along with it despite Cammie's narrowing eyes.

"You know, I was still eating that," she complained. "If you didn't want to eat the ice cream, then why'd you buy it? That's got to be the most ridiculous thing I've seen tonight out of everything else. You can't just—um, *ow. That hurts. Let go of me.*"

His hand was a steel trap against her wrist, against all of Cammie's defensive words. A grip that refused to lessen as he dragged her away down the street.

She was scrambling mentally, trying to figure out why he was acting so chaotically. *None of this makes sense.*

"Can you just tell me what the heck is going on? Tell me something?"

"Just take my hand, follow me, and *run.*" James's hands were slick with sweat as he led the way down the pavement.

She could hear feet moving behind them, but she didn't dare look back. She couldn't, not if she wanted them to survive, whatever this was. It seemed insane, but if she did so much as question, she was sure he would fall into even more insanity.

James led Cammie through red lights and crosswalks with cars that refused to pause, nearly getting them hit. His strides were sure.

But so were the footsteps that followed just as closely behind them.

James didn't bother with common courtesy as he rounded the corner that led to Cammie's house, his grip so strong that she almost fell flat on her face.

Face red with determination and a blend of exertion, he let go of her hand, reaching for her purse. "Keys," he said as he grasped it, finally, despite her stubborn hands. "I need your keys."

"But what about Sabina? She might be in there. She needs to know—I need to know what's going on."

"She isn't," he rushed, turning the purse over in his attempt to locate the zipper. "Knowing her, she left as soon as she was done with helping you. Her parents probably made a bargain with her in order for her to get here. None of that matters, though, unless I can get this damn zipper open."

His hands shook as he struggled with it, taking several tries until it finally opened. He looked over his shoulder with darting eyes before he finally caught the object he was desperately searching for.

"We need to get you inside," he commanded. "I need you to do as I say. Don't ask questions. Please. I'm trying to protect you." For once, there was no trace of laughter in his eyes or mischief in his smile, only utter, complete fear.

Without waiting for a reply, he merely shoved the key in the hole at the door and ushered her inside. He didn't waste time and was at her side quickly, shutting the door behind them.

"What's going on? Who's chasing us? Tell me something, anything! Don't leave me in the dark."

Frustration flickered across his eyes. "I said, please don't ask questions. It's for your own safety. We need to get you hidden and fast, and no matter what you hear, I need you to stay upstairs, okay? Please."

Tears surged from the corners of his eyes, and his entire face tightened. Pain was dancing all along every curve of his skin to a tune that echoed so loudly she could almost hear it in her ears. When he took a step closer, she could hear his breath hitch in his throat as he grasped her shoulders. His grip clung like a wet T-shirt, and his gaze never faltered.

"I just need you to trust me." His eyes searched hers, as if her pupils held enough power to anchor them both from falling into oblivion. "Can you do that?"

Though every bone in her body told her that this was insanity, and that anything—and everything—he said had to be a lie, Cammie nodded.

Banging and pounding sounded at the front door, sending her nerves flinching.

James let go immediately, turning her around to face the stairs. "Go. I'll be right behind you."

It felt like seconds. It had to be. One minute, he was staring at her with such pure concern. The next, someone had James pinned to the floor. A hood covered the man's face, so she couldn't see much, but she noticed the worn antique boots were caked with mud and some sort of lilac purple.

Grunting resounded from each of the men, and then James's fist went flying. The man on top fell backward with a yelp, his nose trickling crimson with little flecks of gold.

Now that the hooded cloak had fallen away, she could see the intruder's face. He was rugged, with eyes that pierced so deep that if it were nails, she'd be one with the wall. Blond, curly locks fell away from the ponytail that encased his hair, framing a masculine, scarred face. He surveyed her with mere curiosity. Then, his angry gaze flickered back to James, who was now scrambling to his feet amidst the wreckage of the now-broken front door.

The more Cammie stared, the more she was sure that the door wasn't the only thing off its hinges.

"Why are you just standing there? Run!" At James's words, it was as if her body could move again, now removed from the trance of shock.

There was no other sign of humanity other than the three, and as her feet pounded on the carpeted steps, she was sure that Sabina was safe. If she were here, she would have been yelling at Cammie to call the cops by now.

The strides took longer than she wished they would. Because of exertion or fear, she wasn't sure. Soon enough, though, her hands clasped the doorknob to the bedroom. Shoving it open took more effort with shaky hands, but it finally listened, giving way to the messy bedroom she had left behind merely thirty minutes earlier.

A soft push on the small of her back told her she wasn't alone. She mentally geared herself ready to fight, but the breath of air gave her pause. She knew it. She had felt it before.

It's James. Only James.

Quickly, he shut the door behind them, locking it. He surveyed the room once before his gaze finally landed on Cammie. His eyes held a story of untold fears, saying a million things, voicing nothing at all.

"Are we going to be okay?" Cammie whispered. "How do we defend ourselves? Shouldn't we call the cops? Isn't that what we should do?"

"He isn't after you," James stated. "Only me."

"But that's more of a reason to call for help, isn't it?"

He didn't respond.

"Why won't you answer me? Is it because we're gonna die?"

Fresh tears formed in his eyes as he stepped closer to her, little droplets staining his cheeks. "We will not die. You will not die. I can promise you that with all of me. Your memories will die, though."

"What are you talking about? None of this makes any sense! Make it make sense!"

"I can't," he whispers. "I can't make any of this make sense because *it won't*. All of this will fade from your mind as quickly as memories from ten years ago because it will fade to exist. *I* will fade to exist for you. You will go on living your life, your beautiful, long life, and I...will go back to where I belong. I've been running for far too long, but I will never regret running away in time with you."

"You're scaring me," Cammie finally breathed. "I don't understand why you're—"

"We have little time," James said as the pounding resounded. *Thump. Thump. Thump.* Each movement shook the entire doorframe.

The man was getting closer and closer to breaking in, and she had nothing to use to defend them.

James crossed the room with such purpose, with such pride, despite the shaking in his limbs. His hands caressed hers as gently as light rain before they moved to the back of her neck, finally settling underneath her chin. "You are going to forget everything, but I can never, will never forget you. Through this short amount of time since I've known you, you have changed my life forevermore. You've taught me what it means to be human, something I never thought I would ever experience in my millennia of existence. I am so indebted to the choices that led me to you, though they may be my downfall, and though you won't remember me tomorrow, I hope you will grant me the blessing of this next minute with you. I will burn it—and you—into my mind until my very last breath."

Air from his lips mingled with hers as he moved closer, and that was all the nudging needed. Their lips crashed together with such intensity that she stumbled into it. He tasted like honey against her lips and the electricity of a million regrets against the backdrop of time soon to be lost. As his hands found their way into the ornate decoration of her hair, she allowed herself room to *breathe*. The kiss gave way to oxygen itself, to blossoms in the springtime, to the familiarity of a life well-spent, of memories that couldn't be bought by wishing on them, but only by the sheer will of experiencing them.

It ended far too quickly. A force of brute strength, determined as he was, ripped James from Cammie. It left behind a hollow void that traced her lips, and she brought her fingers up to them, still lost in the tingling.

James wrestled against the grip of the intruder, who had such wild eyes, determined and bright. There was no escaping the finality of what was doomed to occur.

"If you stop struggling and come with me, she will not be harmed," the man said.

James thrashed, even as strong hands interlocked his chest. "Who sent you?" he roared, his palms finally becoming trapped.

"If you stop struggling and come with me, *she will not be harmed.*"

"Not unless you tell me who sent you! Who are you working for? I know you, *Tracker*. Tell me...who sent you?"

Despite James's heaving breaths, no change appeared on the Tracker's face.

"If you stop struggling and come with me, *she will not be harmed.*"

Cammie could feel it in the air, the warning that lingered. He had a job, some sort of duty here, and here she was, as ever, getting in the way.

"James, please...listen. Do as he says." Cammie finally found her voice, but it trembled.

James shared a glance with Cammie, eyes holding more words than his mouth could muster to say aloud, and then he nodded.

The Tracker let him go reluctantly but pointed to the corner. "Stand there. *Do not move*," he instructed.

James complied silently, though the daggers in his eyes told another story.

The Tracker stepped forward.

Cammie took a step back. "What are you doing?" she murmured, eyes narrowed. "You said you wouldn't hurt me."

"I won't," the Tracker promised, giving her a small smile. "You are merely an object in the way, and I am simply here to conclude my duty. I mean no harm to humans. I am just trying to erase your mind."

"Erase my mind?" Cammie shrieked. "I'm in a nightmare. I need to get out of here. Yes, that's exactly what's going on. None of this is real. *Sabina! Sabina!* Get me out—"

A sudden, sharp prickling at her temples gave way to pause. The Tracker's palms were on her head, and he was staring at her so intently that everything else seemed to blur.

"You will forget everything that happened here. Every memory of tonight will merely be registered as a bad dream in your mind. Any thought of me or of this gentleman, James, will vanish from your mind. Every instance, every encounter, from the first to the very last one, will be wiped away entirely. All you will remember is that an intruder broke into your home while you were gone. You were lucky to be away, and nothing was stolen or misplaced. It was just a case of mistaken identity. The thief thought you were someone else. Everyone you know, they no longer know him. You no longer know him. Your friendship, relationship—whatever you shared—is nothing more than a whisper of a dream. Your life will resume as if nothing happened. Do you understand?"

All she could utter, despite the screaming in her mind to fight, to be resilient, was, "Yes."

There was the sudden pounding now, and then there was absolutely nothing.

No darkness.

No bubbles.

No sound.

Until...

"Cammie? Can you open your eyes for me? Just one blink. That's all we need."

The voice was familiar. She had heard it many, many times before.

A blinding light paralyzed her eyes, but her limbs were too weak to move, to cover them.

A woman hovered near, but she could make out an outline but, otherwise, nothing else.

"Caelan, you are lucky my herbs worked. Your friend is alive."

CHAPTER TWENTY-TWO

SABINA

Cammie's entire body trembled as she attempted to rise to a sitting position. Sabina was there instantly, helping her as best as she could. Cammie's skin, flushed and red from exertion, clashed harshly with her tear-stained eyes.

"Are you okay?" Sabina asked, hesitantly wondering if approaching her was the right thing.

Cammie didn't speak as her eyes slowly surveyed the room. They glanced over at Sabina once before darting directly at Solenne.

"She's the one who healed you," Sabina said, noting how Cammie's eyebrows furrowed at the woman.

"'Healed,'" Cammie uttered, more to herself than anyone else. "Like a doctor?" Her gaze sprung up then, but this time, she stared directly at Sabina.

Oh, no. How do I even go about this?

"Not exactly," Sabina said, firmly deciding this was the only word choice that wouldn't sound entirely evasive.

"It was an herbal potion of sorts," Solenne said. "Not exactly magic like your kind calls it—though there is that in our world—but it was something to ease the anxiety and pain you were feeling. It allowed me to gather clarity for you to remember."

Cammie's eyes practically bulged out of her head. "'Your kind?' Does she have some kind of ageism issue?" She directed this at Sabina then turned to Solenne. "I'm not sure if you have an issue with young people, but...we aren't that young."

Solenne let out a haughty chuckle. "This one has a lot to learn, doesn't she?"

"Learn?" Cammie's expression was dumbfounded.

Sabina cringed. "There's a lot you've missed since you've been out of it, and believe me, I'd love to tell you about it, but maybe we should get you some wat—"

"Where's James?" Cammie blurted.

"We were hoping you could tell us that." All heads turned as Caelan took his leave from leaning against the wall next to the doorframe. "That's partially why I brought you here. I needed you to remember. It was important...for me to know your memories and where he went. I was supposed to meet him, and when he didn't show, I figured I would go to the person he trusted the most: you. I had a few sources do some tracking, and they told me he was very fond of a girl named Camille Romero, so..."

"So you lied about wanting to be my friend?" Cammie finished, her voice quivering. "You lied...all of those times when you said you weren't stalking me or anything, when in reality, you totally were? You never cared about getting to know me. You just wanted James. For whatever reason, I don't fricking know."

"I grew to care for you. I still view you as a friend, almost like a daughter."

"Oh, don't go on and on about that. Just another replacement because your real family died. I've had enough." With unsteady hands, Cammie moved to a stand. Her balance was rocky but determined as she grabbed Sabina for assistance.

Caelan wrung his hands, an expression pained on his face. "Let me just talk to you—"

"No," Cammie sputtered. "I have...absolutely nothing to say to you. I don't fully understand what's going on here, but I do know that I need a mental break. My head hurts. I'm achy. My throat is dry. I have no idea who *you* are..." She glared daggers at Solenne. "...but the only person I know I can trust here is Sabina."

"Me?" Sabina exclaimed. "Wait...what? But, Cammie, he's not a bad guy."

"Maybe not to you," Cammie uttered, completely avoiding Caelan's desperate gaze. "Besides, you were the one completely against him when I told you about him, and now look at him..." She gave Caelan the hardest of glares before turning back to Sabina. "He's nothing but a *user*. Bad news."

"Things have changed now," Sabina stated, the sudden truth of her statement ringing in the air. The stark hint of surprise reflected in Caelan's eyes. "He's gone through a lot to save your life, to get you here so you can be healed."

"But at whose expense?" Cammie's voice rang higher than any other octave Sabina had ever heard before.

Cammie had been upset in other scenarios, sure, but this was on an entirely different level of upset.

"Oh, that's right! *Mine.* Using me was deemed *so* necessary. I'm tired of being a pawn to other people."

The soft, broken sob was loud enough and deep enough that Sabina was sure it shattered all hearts present. Not just hers.

"Cammie..." Sabina moved her hand to Cammie's shoulder.

Cammie didn't hesitate to shy away from the touch. "Please don't touch me," she whispered, her eyes darting up to the doorway. She walked on unsteady legs toward the exit. "I need to leave. Please don't follow me."

"You could fall. Let me walk you out." Caelan was the first to follow after Cammie.

"I have nothing to say to you. There's nothing you could do or tell me that would make me want to talk to you otherwise. You'll get your information about James, don't worry, but I want nothing—or need anything—from you anymore. No help, no conversation. Just let me be, or is following directions another thing you suck at besides loyalty?"

Stunned into absolute silence, Caelan watched with an open mouth as Cammie stumbled out of the room. There was quiet muttering and the sound of stumbles in the background until a door slammed shut.

So she found her way around, then.

"I don't know what to say." Caelan walked over to the now-empty chair where Solenne was standing and sat down. His head became like stone and sunk into his open palms. "What have I done?"

"You probably shouldn't have done what you did. That's a good starting point. You used a girl—*a human girl*—and for what? To find someone who doesn't want to be found. I don't see him anywhere. What were you thinking, using her like that?"

Caelan's shoulders fell into an even deeper sag. "I did what I had to do."

"You keep saying that." Solenne scoffed, "but the more and more you rationalize this, the more and more that I don't understand. You had to do this—barge into her life, disrupt it.

Why? You could have done searching on your own without her. You didn't *need* her help, yet you sought it. I want to know why."

"I don't owe you an explanation," Caelan replied, looking up from his resigned position.

"Excuse me? I raised you. I cared for you. I made a promise to your family, and I deserve some ounce of respect—"

"But all of that doesn't make you my mother, does it? You were just the lady who took the baby from her dying arms. It's not like she handed you the crown and scepter and the role of motherhood!"

Solenne braced against the words, and the crushing weight of them flickered across her face, settling in her heated gaze. "I don't even know you anymore. The man I raised would have never talked to me in such a manner, but this man...I do not know what to think of him." Without another word, she stormed out of the room, leaving yet another gap of silence.

Caelan's head fell into his hands. For a moment, there was pure silence until he blurted, "Do you hate me as well?"

Sabina shifted on her feet, swallowing the lump in her throat. "That depends on how seriously sorry you are about what you did."

"Will any reason I give be enough?" he asked, finally lifting his head.

Finding her resolve, Sabina shrugged. Her eyes had begun to sting. "Only Cammie can answer that question, and as much as I want to stay here...I can't." Sabina wiped away a stray tear and turned on her heel, leaving Caelan behind as she set her mind on the one person who really needed her more than anyone else.

She found Cammie sitting on the steps that led to the porch. Her hair fell in messy waves, and Cammie mindlessly twirled a section of hair around her index finger. She stared off into the distance, as if she were looking for a way out of this place but reluctantly did not find one.

"How are you doing?" Sabina asked as she sat down beside Cammie. "Are you feeling any better?"

"Are you asking physically or emotionally?"

Sabina gave a small smile. "Whichever you feel comfortable sharing about."

"Well..." Cammie sniffled, wiping her nose with the back of her hand. "Physically, I feel like I got smashed in the head. It's like...this pounding, and I have these things that I remember but don't truly remember happening at the same time. Whatever I saw...it was like I was watching it through a lens that *was* me until it *became* me. Maybe that doesn't make sense, but..." She trailed off.

"I think I know what you mean," Sabina reassured. "Crazy wouldn't define that. I've seen crazy these last few days, last few hours. If I told you I saw a talking wolf, would you think I'm insane?"

Cammie opened her mouth, but all that released was a half-hearted laugh. "Wha—what? A *talking* wolf?"

Sabina nodded.

"Are you sure you weren't the one in a daze? I still feel like I'm in one. I don't really remember anything that happened while I was out. Maybe you can fill me in?"

"Are you sure you're up for the story?" Sabina countered.

"I feel like anything you tell me will seem far-fetched, but I think I'm ready to hear it."

With a wide grin, Sabina leaned forward on her elbows. "Okay, then. Here goes."

By the time Sabina was finished speaking, Cammie just sat there, mouth agape. "A sword? Stabbing the wolf? Who then tried to talk to you? Actually, scratch that. Who actually talked to you? Calling Caelan a prince? You were right. This *is* a story, but the question is, do you believe it?" Cammie's eyes twinkled with their usual sparkle of curiosity.

Sabina felt her heart soar. *She is, at least, for this moment, somewhat like her old self.*

"I think I do," Sabina breathed. "Sure, it seemed out there, but once there was a talking animal, there was kind of no ignoring that. I could've said I was losing it, but I knew I was completely sane before that moment, so that wasn't exactly an option. I don't fully know what happened with Caelan, with his parents. I know, based on what I heard after you left the room, that Solenne isn't his mom. He mentioned something about her not being actually given that title—whatever that means—but it seemed to cause some strain. I know he's caused a lot of issues here, by invading your life and mine, but we have to help him."

Cammie's eyes narrowed. "And just why would I do that?"

"Because he can finally leave. Go after whatever he's searching for with James, and we can get back to our normal lives. That's all he wanted, some answers, and you must have seen something after being in your dreaming state. Anything you have will help."

"Normal lives?" Cammie laughed. "Are you being serious? Nothing about our lives will be normal after this. Even thinking that is completely stupid. Plus, why do I want to just give him what he wants? Surely he has someone else he can go to."

"As far as I know, the only lead he has is James, and we can help him this way. *You* can. He might have answers for you, too, if you have questions—"

"I'll do it," Cammie uttered, earning a pointed look from Sabina.

"You will?"

"Yes," Cammie finalized. "I will but not to him. I will speak to you and Solenne if she has questions, obviously, but Caelan.... No. Not at all."

Well, it was better than nothing. It was a start.

Without waiting for Sabina's help, Cammie rose to a stand. "Where are they?" she asked.

"Uh...not sure where Solenne went, but Caelan is still inside, I think."

"I saw a kitchen table." Cammie was already walking up the steps. "We can talk there."

"Uh—" Sabina watched in shock as the door slammed shut, leaving her in the wake of Cammie's newfound determination.

Caelan leaned his back against the counter, arms crossed over his chest. Solenne stood a few feet away, a respective distance away from him, Sabina noticed.

"Let's get started, shall we? I had a granola bar and some water, so it's safe to say I won't fall over." Cammie was grumbling and grouchy, which wasn't the best way to give them "an olive branch," but it was a start in Sabina's eyes.

She's one step closer to normal than she was an hour ago.

"We're ready when you are," Caelan said, causing Cammie's nostrils to flare.

"As I mentioned to Sabina outside, I'll make it aware for you guys too. Under no circumstances during this discussion will I *talk* to Caelan. Under no circumstances during this conversation will I *look* at Caelan. Under no circumstances—even if he's choking, forbid that—will I give him any of my *undivided* attention. If he wants to talk to me, he will have to use Sabina as a channel."

Caelan couldn't prevent the scoff that appeared on his face. "You cannot be serious," he exclaimed. "Tell me you're joking. Have we seriously lost the functionality of being actual adults?"

Cammie glanced over at Sabina. "Did you hear something?"

"For crying out—" Caelan stopped mid-sentence, growling into his hands. Exasperated, he lifted his head, shaking his palms in the air. "Sabina, will you tell Cammie that I would very much like to work with her to get this done?"

Sabina turned to Cammie, who was sitting across the table. "Caelan wanted me to tell you he wants to work with you to get this done."

Cammie nodded thoughtfully. "I see. Well, will you tell him I am open to these terms and want to accomplish the same goal?"

Caelan's eyelid twitched three times. "Sabina, will you tell Cammie—"

"Enough!" Solenne shouted. "Enough with the bickering. Enough with this childishness. We agreed to meet you here to go over your memories, not to argue like pestilent children."

"Jeez," Cammie mumbled under her breath. "I guess manners are lost on Amarians too."

Solenne squared Cammie down. "What did you just say?"

"Nothing." Cammie cleared her throat. "Anyway...the memories. Where do I start?"

"Wherever you want to is fine," Sabina said.

"It started off pretty weird, if I'm being honest, and then it turned into something else."

"Being more descriptive would definitely be an asset. If that's something you can manage." The sly remark flew off of Solenne's lips like butter.

"No need to be rude, Solenne. Let her talk at her own pace whenever she's ready," Caelan said.

Cammie's eyes held a remnant of gratefulness, but she didn't look in Caelan's direction. "The weirdness came from the memories. It was as if I was experiencing them all in my own time. I wasn't watching them, then. I was actually *in* the memory, which sounds weird, but that's how it happened."

Caelan looked Solenne's way. "Has this happened before?"

She let out a breath. "Truthfully, I wouldn't know. Cammie is the only one who survived this. The others that I've tried to help undo an Erasing for have always died. It could have just been her subconscious allowing her a new avenue to memory."

"Let's say that is the case," Cammie said. "What do we do with this information now? The memory gave me no sense of time. It could be weeks since James—" Her breath hitched on the word.

"Did something happen to James, Cammie?" Sabina was treading carefully, afraid that any word spoken in relation to the young man might break her very fragile friend.

For a moment, Cammie's eyes were glassy as her stare turned away from people and focused on the table. Her breathing was slow, as if one more breath would send emotions all over the surface. "He was taken," she finally said, closing her eyes tightly.

"Taken?" Caelan pushed himself off of the countertop, his entire body tightening. "By whom?"

"I...I don't know," Cammie rushed. "One thing happened. He chased us in the house, and then James..." Cammie's face flushed scarlet. "...kissed me. Then, the guy said I'd have no memory of James, and anyone he'd ever met wouldn't remember him either."

"So he did the Erasing," Solenne muttered. "He was obviously powerful, powerful enough to take your friend."

"But on whose orders?" Caelan voiced. "His? Or someone else's?" Caelan paced, running his thumb over his bottom lip. "We Amarians who live here Earthside have an unspoken rule not to draw attention to ourselves, but if he was so outlandishly bold, bold enough to come into a human's home at that, then—"

"Then he must not be an Earthside Amarian. He's from home," Solenne finished, her eyes locking with Caelan's. "He had no respect for the way of life here, no sense of training on how to approach this situation, but he was on a mission." She turned to Cammie, her eyes bold. "And you're sure there was no kind of identification he could have given you? It could be anything, something so simple that it could seem insignificant."

Cammie sat in silence, her eyes closing shut. She was blocking out the world, Sabina realized. Everyone waited in silence, anticipation hugging their chests, until Cammie's eyes snapped open.

"James called him...a 'tracker.' Does that mean anything to you?"

Solenne's entire body stiffened.

"Are you familiar with this, Solenne?" Caelan asked, his interest piqued.

"It's...an old historic tale. Long ago, before you were born, the royals had a way of dealing with insubordinates. Public hangings, mass executions...it was a bloodbath. Some descendants of those people went off the trails. They didn't live in the inner cities, preferring their own set of rules to live by. The royal family had a truce with them as long as they also held up a bargain agreed upon. When called, this family line would be in service to the kingdom to find other insubordinates—think robbers, abusers. It went up the chain of command until the royals decided that wasn't good enough. The family was called a tracker line, and their new goal wasn't for small crimes. It was to find the worst of the worst."

"Meaning?" Cammie dared to ask, her voice shaky.

"Traitors," Solenne finished, "or, for a better term, those who commit treason."

Cammie blanched, almost falling out of the chair. "So, you're saying that James committed treason?"

"Without speaking to him directly, we can't know," Solenne replied. "As of now, we can only assume he's committed something worthy of being classified as a capital crime. That's reason enough to be wary."

"You can't be suggesting we call this entire thing off," Caelan uttered. "We've done far too much to give up now."

"*You've* done far too much," Solenne stated. "These poor girls got dragged into something they didn't need to be dragged into. Any form of Erasing for them will surely kill them, and Cammie just came back from the brink of death. I won't stand for it."

"So, what do you suggest I do? Give up?" Caelan asked, shifting his weight. His face erupted in anger, but his hands stayed still. "I deserve to know what's going on in my kingdom."

"But it isn't your kingdom anymore. The entire populace thinks you're dead. They surely don't need your input."

"I can't just abandon who I am," Caelan growled. "Why can't you understand?"

"Why can't you understand I'm trying to protect you? The attack on the palace wasn't enough for you to fear going home. The people who murdered your parents are still out there. You're falling right into their trap. You cannot—"

"I have nothing here for me anymore!" Caelan's voice echoed off the kitchen walls. "My wife murdered. My children murdered. My parents murdered. How many more people have to die in order for me to claim my destiny? I say no more, and I am done with your claims of safety. If a king cannot stand for his own family, how can he stand for a kingdom? I fear no evil, for I know what my destiny is and what it will be. You can do your best, but you cannot keep me from it anymore."

Solenne's face cracked.

Caelan stepped forward, touching her cheek. "Everything you have done has prepared me for this moment, to fight to reclaim what is rightfully mine. The methods I chose might not have been the best, but the sentiment is still the same. I *am* going home. Whether you return is your choice. I cannot hide forever. I am going to freshen up, to rest, and I suggest the girls do the same. Tomorrow, I will go looking for clues about where James could be. And hopefully...I can find the answers I'm looking for." Caelan pressed a kiss to the crown of Solenne's head and looked over at the girls sitting at the table. "Have a good night," he said before walking out of the room.

He left them enveloped in complete silence without daring to look back.

CHAPTER TWENTY-THREE

HANNAH

WITH EACH STEP JAMES TOOK, Hannah could feel the anxiety clamping at her heart. It was persistently stubborn in its pace, so strong that she could feel herself gasping for breath.

"Are you okay?" James asked, the crunching of his shoes under the grass so loud that she strained to hear him.

"I...think...so," she said, blinking away at the blur in her vision. She was seeing dots, multitudes of them, and it was as if someone held the wrong prescription lenses over her perfected eyes. "I just can't see."

She felt the roll in James's shoulders. "That makes sense. You, well, humanity has a longer history of having problems when adrenaline wears down. Your body wires down after being in fight mode for so long. We don't really have that problem, not to the same extent."

"What is it with the 'we?' You keep saying that, the idiots back there keep saying that, and it just makes me even more confused. But with this pounding in my head, maybe everything won't be clear for a while. I really don't know."

James shifted suddenly, picking up the pace, sending Hannah's head straight into his chest.

"Ow. Oh, no, not this again," she exclaimed, right as the spinning picked up again. She then felt something else in her stomach, another lurching.

"What?" James was breathless as his pace never slowed, even as he took another turn. "What's going on?"

"I think I'm gonna—" Hannah turned her head away from James and aimed her head at a faraway spot in the distance. She couldn't stop the vomit from spewing, her stomach rolling with each breath as she tried to calm herself.

"Oh, no. Dang—not the shoes. It's okay. I'll get another pair," he reassured her.

The shame hit her next. "But I aimed away from you," she gurgled against the taste of sour apples on her tongue.

"Well, you definitely missed your target, but it's okay. Okay..." James stopped in his tracks, his shoes skidding to a stop. "Let's see. Where can we—ah. There."

"What are you doing?" she asked, the spinning still prominent.

"I am finding a resting place for you so we can deal with your head."

"Do you have an aspirin?" Hannah asked hopefully.

"I don't, but I have something better."

Hannah's surroundings were a haze as she felt herself being lifted out of James's arms and her back meeting dewy grass. It tickled the back of her neck, sending a shiver down her spine.

"What could be better than an aspirin at this very moment?"

"Magical healing?" James offered, his eyes twinkling.

Or at least Hannah thought they were twinkling. Everything seemed to twinkle at this very moment.

"As if that would actually help anything. Magic doesn't exist...does it?" Hannah stared up at the canopy of trees above her. *It's such a pretty green, pretty, pretty pine tree.*

"You keep singing about trees. That's good. It shows me you're still conscious, somewhat. Hey, you got a rhyme despite being exhausted and hurting. That's one point."

"I actually said that? There's no way..." The slur in her words was clear as Hannah felt her eyes shutting against the backdrop of nature. "I don't sing."

James's hands fumbled through the grass. He rubbed something against her head, and on her temples, she felt heat and then a little rush of cool.

"What are you doing to my head?" Hannah mumbled.

"It's what my kind calls inner healing. I don't use this much. I'm not supposed to, at least not here, but there's no telling how long we have to run for, so I'm making an exception. I'll keep watch, I promise, and then maybe we can see about getting Tony or someone else to help you, okay?"

All Hannah could make out was the vague outline of James' face as he stared down at her, his hands on her temples. "How do you know Tony?" is all she got out before she lost her senses completely.

Hannah awoke to violent shaking. It rumbled through her entire body, and her heart pounded a million miles a minute as she adjusted to the complete darkness that she was shrouded in.

Eyes filled with absolute fear stared down at her. "Are you awake? I really hope you are because we need to get moving."

"What?" Hannah grumbled, running a hand over her face. She slowly sat up. "Why?"

"We're being followed. I don't know by who, but I can hear the footsteps. I accidentally fell asleep. I should have done better at keeping watch. I'm sorry, but right now, we need to hurry. If you can stand, do it, but get ready to run."

James offered her his hand. She took it, finally landing on two feet after what felt like an eternity.

As she marveled at feeling absolutely human, she realized two things: the nausea was gone, and so was the splintering headache.

"I feel fine," she uttered, breathless. "How do I feel fine?"

"I told you already," James said in the dark, "but now I need you to run and stop asking questions. It's for your own safety. I'm trying to keep us alive."

"Give a better explanation than 'I told you already,'" Hannah said. "This is stupid to think otherwise."

"If I told you, we'd be dead or right back into the hands of those barbarians, which I very much would prefer *not* to do right now. Can you settle with that explanation until I can give you a better one later?"

"How do I know you're being honest?" Hannah asked.

Sudden footsteps resounded, and James flinched. "I promise. Now can we go?"

She sighed, pondering his words briefly as the footsteps came closer. "Fine, but later on, I deserve to know everything."

James dashed, leaving her with only one option. Hannah followed James as they sprinted away from the person desperate to catch them.

CHAPTER TWENTY-FOUR

CAMMIE

SHE AWOKE WITH A CHILL down her back. Sweat covered her body. Sabina was peacefully sleeping in the twin bed on the other side of the room. A sliver of moonlight cast a shadow on Cammie's feet as they connected against the wooden floor.

As she reached the window, she saw a figure standing near the edge of the road, with hands in pockets. *Caelan.*

With steps quieter than she thought she could ever manage, Cammie slowly headed out of the room, shutting the door behind her.

She reached the kitchen, putting her socks on first before grabbing her shoes. The spare jacket that Solenne had given her was lying on the kitchen table, beckoning to be worn.

As soon as her fingers grasped it, she heard a creak in the floor. With her heart in her chest, she searched the table for some sort of weapon of defense.

"There's no need for that. It's just me. Besides, if you had done that, you would have been dead by now. Amarian reflexes are much faster." Solenne stood by the oven, brewing a pot of coffee. She poured a cup into a small mug then went to the cupboard, grabbing another mug. "Do you need one?"

Cammie shook her head. "I think I'm okay."

"You don't look okay," Solenne remarked. "Your face is all flushed. Couldn't sleep?" She closed the cupboard, bringing the mug up to her lips, the steam heating her face.

Cammie bit the inside of her cheek. "Bad dream, actually. I don't remember most of it." She gestured to the door. "I was just going to head to the yard for a breather."

"Here." Solenne poured coffee into the empty mug. She handed it to Cammie's open palms. A knowing smile on her lips, she added, "Hand this to him while you're out there."

"How did you know I was going—"

"Call it intuition. Call it a guess. I just know humans well enough to know that being angry doesn't suit them for long. At least for you, from the little I've known you, that much I can tell." As Cammie stood there with her mouth hanging open, Solenne gestured to the door. "He won't bite, you know. If there's something you need to talk about, he's the right person for it."

"But, well..."

"Listen." Solenne sighed, picking up her mug once again and taking a slow sip. "I know you guys got off to a rocky start with the truth being shared. I know things are rough, and honestly... humans just seem to cause trouble wherever they go. Not all of them, though," she added, for a moment lost in her own thoughts. "As far as you go, you're stubborn to a fault, but so is he. I know he can sometimes say or do things that are irrational, but his love for his family outweighs any other sense of rationality. Hurting you, I'm sure he regrets it."

"How do you know?" The mug began heating Cammie's cold hands. "He could not be sorry at all. I could go out there, and he won't apologize. I could look like the biggest idiot on Earth."

Solenne held a smile that Cammie couldn't decipher. It brought out the color in her eyes, and for once, made her look more youthful than Cammie thought physically possible. "Worrying cannot change the outcome of the response. It can only prepare you with scenarios that you may never encounter and diminish the one that you will. The biggest answer to the questions you're asking is to actually do them."

The words were like concrete against any defensiveness left on Cammie's tongue. Solenne was right. There was no sort of concern that would make this any easier than just ripping the Band-Aid off.

"You're pretty wise, you know," Cammie remarked.

"That's what happens when you've lived over six hundred years," Solenne replied, a knowing glint in her eyes. "You gain more knowledge. I can't comment on whether all of it was worthwhile, but I can at least say I have much stored in my mind if I need to locate it."

Cammie's eyes grew into saucers. "Six hundred? You're joking."

Solenne merely turned toward the door. "Don't you have somewhere you need to be?"

By the way she turned away, continuing to enjoy her coffee, it became painfully obvious that Cammie had overstayed her welcome in this conversation.

That was that, then. She had no other choice.

She found him by the edge of the property, standing underneath the canopy of the massive pine. With hands in his pockets, his entire body angled in a direction that leaned toward being blissfully unaware, Cammie expected him to not notice her arrival.

Yet, he still stiffened. She could tell by the muscle pulsing in his upper back that echoed so strongly she could see it through his attire. His neck craned in anticipation, as if waiting for her to say the first word.

"I know you probably don't want to talk to me." She sighed. "I completely understand that."

"You were the one who said that it was me you didn't want to talk to. I tried to make amends, albeit they weren't good ones. Nevertheless, I tried."

The words hung in the air with a finality so strong that Cammie had to take a breath. "You tried, but...I didn't take the chance to hear you out. That was my fault."

Caelan's foot tapped the ground so strongly that his entire leg shook with it. "All of this is my fault if we are comparing who is more in the wrong. It was completely and utterly wrong of me to use you. It was wrong of me to see you as a way to get what I wanted simply because you were so much younger than me. Your life still has value, as much of a speck of dust it is compared to the centuries I will have. I forget sometimes how valuable and simultaneously short life is for humans, but there was a time where that fact haunted me daily."

His head sagged, and the memory of how they met flickered in Cammie's mind.

"You're talking of your wife?" Cammie asked, suddenly aware of the coffee she was holding.

She stepped forward, reaching around to give him the cup. He took it from her, drinking a long sip. Cammie moved back to her position, giving Caelan ample space.

"I am," he said after the second sip of coffee.

"Am I wrong in asking again about her? I know last time you didn't want to."

"Last time, I didn't know you. This time is different. This time, I dragged you into my mess. This time...you almost died, so if you want to ask questions, I think saying no would be completely invalid of me."

When her brain refused to come up with anything, she went for the one she had yearned to ask of since meeting Caelan for the first time. "How did you meet her?"

Caelan sighed then sat down. He waved Cammie over, patting the spot next to him. When she was at eye-level, he heaved a breath. "It was in college," he finally stated, as if this one statement was what he built his life upon.

Cammie's brows rose. "But I thought you guys didn't like college, or...I didn't know that was a thing for Amarians."

"We descended from humanity," Caelan said. "I cannot say for sure what the education system is like in Natrellum now, with never actually being there. Solenne could tell you more, but here, it was merely a way of getting away from responsibilities. Solenne was happy to oblige because avoiding my heritage meant never going home in her eyes. I think...I think the assassination scares her more than she realizes." Caelan swallowed. "It's why she never wants to go home. She worked in the palace. She had seen and heard so much already that coming here was like a refuge for her, so me taking some night courses didn't really bother her. I didn't notice my wife the first few days going in. I was too focused on the teacher, mesmerized at how her skill and eye translated even to beginners who had no eye at all.

Then, once I got paired up with my wife, whom I hadn't ever seen paint in action before, I realized the lesson was mainly for her." Erratic chuckles escaped his mouth as he took another sip of coffee. "The woman had no artistic eye. Painting was by far the worst skill she had ever tried, but Lee...she was adventurous. She didn't take the class because she knew that she would master it. She took it because she refused to let failure stop her from experiencing the fullness of life."

"So I take it her adventurous side drew you in," Cammie blurted, her face frozen with heat as she realized just how utterly moronic she sounded.

"Yes. I had observed many humans before. That class was no exception. Most of them had a drive, a desire, but it wasn't like Leanne's. She saw the world through this most beautiful lens that others refused to inhabit. I was drawn to her, and each time she spoke, I wanted more. I wanted more days with her in the grass underneath the stars on campus after our class was over. I wanted a million years with her, when I knew I'd only get a few decades. She made me want more from a human than I ever thought possible."

With emotion deep in his voice, it did not surprise Cammie when his eyes watered.

"If we need to stop—"

"No," Caelan said hoarsely. "This...talking of her is nice. I can't remember the last time I did it freely that wasn't in my head. I avoid it so much, hoping I will forget, but forgetting her would be an injustice." He wiped the back of his eyes with his hand, heaving a breath.

"If you need a minute, you can take one," Cammie assured.

After a brief silence, he closed his eyes. "Loving her was the best choice I made. In the years we spent together, it was easy to forget what I was, who I was. My destiny. I was willing to throw it all away for a simple life with her. Most human men would have hated being tied down so quickly, but with Leanne, I wanted it all. I wanted the house, the children, the beautiful life that even a millennia couldn't have prepared me for. I loved her so much that I wanted to share the part of me that, despite everything I had been told, wouldn't go away, so...I told her who I was and what I was."

Cammie's breath hitched in her throat.

"It was against what Solenne wanted, what every one of my kind wanted. A human to know about us, to love one of us? We respected our heritage to a point, but having one so intertwined with our lives was unheard of."

"So, what did you do?" Cammie asked.

"I did what any sensible person in love would do. I married her."

Cammie was silent, watching him with wide eyes.

"That's right. I called up the college priest. He ironically was certified to do wedding ceremonies outside of the normal duties of working at the college, and then I proposed to Leanne. She loved me despite our differences, especially the biggest one. She told me that a few decades with me was worth more than never having any, so we got married in secret, far away from prying eyes. We confessed our vows in a small section of trees outside of town at the first trace of twilight where no one would find us. It was a beautiful lie. It gave me hope of something different, hope that she would be the one human who could outlive time itself. It was easy to forget about a lifetime without her when the days we shared were so beautiful, but the more she aged, the more I remembered and the more guilty I became of what I was robbing her of. And then...then she got pregnant. It was something we didn't even know was possible for a human and Amarian, but here she was, a miracle in my life, carrying miracles of our own." As the tears continued falling, Caelan rose to a stand, wiping his eyes. "I think… that's enough reminiscing for one day." The finality in his tone was so sure that Cammie didn't want to press.

Cammie sat in thought, going back and forth about what to say. If she *should* say anything.

"I think I'm going to go lie down." Caelan turned on his heel, despite Cammie's mind's inability to move forward.

"Wait," Cammie called out.

Caelan halted in his tracks. "If this is about her, I can't talk about it anymore. It's too painful."

"It's about you. I saw you tonight, in my dream." Cammie wrung her hands together, twiddling her thumbs as she tried to gather the courage to continue.

"Dreams are normal after a stressful scenario. You could've died. It was just your mind processing it."

"This was different," Cammie argued. "It's partially why I came outside to talk to you. I thought you might have answers about why I saw you in my dream because…it wasn't just *a dream*. It was a memory, the same kind of one that I had with you at the coffee shop about James."

"How are you sure?" Caelan questioned, eyes narrowing.

"It wasn't just you in the dream. Solenne was there, too."

Caelan bit his lip and opened his mouth to respond.

Sudden rustling and footsteps resounded from the edge of the forest. Caelan whipped his head around and strode to Cammie's front. He guided her to stay back with his left hand.

"Don't move," he told her, eyes trained on the spot where the noise was coming from.

Two figures emerged from the rustling, along with two pairs of eyes that Cammie was very familiar with.

As soon as the figures came to a stop, Cammie found herself lost for breath.

There, in the flesh, were Hannah and James.

CHAPTER TWENTY-FIVE

HANNAH

Cammie's wild eyes held a million questions as she sputtered out, "Hannah? How did you get here?"

Still stuck on adrenaline, with blood in her veins, Hannah fumbled for words.

Her companion, though, seemed to suffer from some sort of shell shock. "Cammie? Is that....you?"

Cammie's gaze trailed away from Hannah to the person next to her. "James? I don't....How are you—"

"You remember me," James interrupted. "How do you—how can you remember me?"

As the questions kept rolling, Hannah's ears were acutely aware of the nearness of their coming enemy. "Questions are great but *later*. Right now, we're running from someone."

At the mention of enemy, the man in front of Cammie spoke. His eyes became metal. "Who's after you?"

"I don't know who it is," Hannah said, "but my instincts tell me it's some sort of hired job. There was cash involved, but does that really matter when, oh, you know, we're practically going to *die* out here?"

Immediately, the man gestured toward the house. "James, take the girls inside. I will come inside momentarily. There's just something I need to take care of first."

With a gaze that lingered on Cammie more than Hannah liked, James made his way to the house, letting the girls lead the way as he flanked from behind.

As soon as the door opened, Hannah saw a pair of blinking eyes that belonged to someone she hadn't met before. The woman sat at the kitchen table, right in the middle of drinking a cup of coffee, her gaze full of curiosity at the newfound bunch being led into the house.

"Cammie...I thought you were going outside to patch up things with Caelan. What's...going on here?" She set down the mug with steady hands, but her body had a slight shakiness to it.

She had seen things. Hannah was sure of it.

"They...um, well, they needed a place to stay," Cammie rushed, her eyes flickering to James before settling back on the woman. "They were being chased by something. Caelan said he would deal with it." Cammie's cheeks flushed plum, and she scooted closer to the woman, as if a multitude of space could separate her from James entirely.

The woman's gaze landed squarely on James. "You must be the person she couldn't remember. I haven't seen this much avoidance in a long time."

"How could you possibly know that?" James peered at the woman with a raised brow. Then, he turned to Cammie. "How does she know things?"

"She just does," Cammie snapped.

Hannah did not miss how Cammie's gaze refused to linger longer than a second.

The woman looked at Hannah then, her eyes narrowing into slits. "Who was chasing you? Do you know?"

"If I did, don't you think I would have told you already?" Hannah said, her face a mirror against the woman's.

Shock flickered across the woman's features before she turned back to the front door. "I'm going to go see if he needs anything. You three stay here."

Hannah's eyes didn't dare leave the woman until the sight of her was completely gone from Hannah's line of vision. Then, she turned her gaze on Cammie. "Maybe it's weird to explain, but I don't really care about manners. Who is she, and how did you end up here?"

"It's a long story," Cammie said, her face still the same annoying color, "but her name is Solenne. She healed me."

Hannah couldn't stop the chuckle from escaping. "Really? Like crystals and all that other nonsense? That totally makes sense. She's a healer, and I'm a magician."

"Then how do you explain what I did?" James intercepted. "I healed you, didn't I?"

She could feel the fumes burning in her nostrils. "Healed me?" Hannah sputtered. "You're hilarious. I don't trust you as far as I can throw you, and whatever happened back there, I'm not sure of it anymore. You knew things about me before I even knew your name. Consider whatever you did a mercy, but expecting us to be friends?" Hannah's face contorted into a sneer as she leaned into James's personal space. "You can fricking forget it."

"Whoa," Cammie said gently, letting her hands rest on Hannah's shoulders. "There's no need to be hostile. I'm sure he was just trying to help."

The haughty laugh couldn't be held back. *I've had enough.*

Hannah jerked from Cammie's grasp. "How funny to know that you know things, that you hold the answers to the universe. You do not know what I've seen. I witnessed some-one get *murdered*, Cammie. I watched this innocent boy's neck snap. They held me captive for hours. James was the only reason we got out okay without dying."

"But that doesn't mean he has bad intentions—" Cammie started.

"You speak for yourself, not for me. Until you've been bound and choking on your own vomit for hours, you don't have a right to tell me who to trust and who not to trust. I don't know what to think anymore. Live in your own bubble of na-ivete if you want to, but don't throw your stupid views my way. I've witnessed things, and it's clear you haven't."

"I think we all need a breather," James said softly, moving to where he was in the middle of the two girls.

Hannah was sure that she looked practically insane, with bulging eyes and messy hair, but she didn't care. It had been a few hours—actually, scratch that, it had been a few days.

With another retort at the ready on the edge of her tongue, Hannah's fists clenched at her sides, and for once, she was sure controlling them would be a wasted effort.

The sound of a door slamming open caused all three people to bounce away from the middle of the chaos that was about to ensue, and their heads turned to the door.

The man Hannah had seen earlier had a look of doom on his face, his eyes flickering over the group. "It was one of Nyx's crew that was here to come take back what was rightfully theirs," he breathed.

"He was after me, wasn't he?" James asked, his Adam's apple bobbing. "You can just say it."

The man's eyes trained on James, but there was no flicker of emotion lit behind the gaze. "He was until he found some-thing even better."

"You aren't talking about what I think you are, are you?"

This voice was one Hannah knew well.

The ball of rage came alive in Hannah's gut as her head whipped around to the corner of the room where a tall and somewhat sleepy version of the person she loathed stood.

"Don't tell me you made some kind of deal with Nyx?" Sabina's eyes were bloodshot, with dark circles that refused to be silent, accenting the anger that danced in her gaze at the words from the man.

The man refused to meet her gaze, but he met James's. "His fight isn't with you," he said, completely ignoring Sabina's question. "You will not go back to Nyx's or deal with him. I will, and together, we will take you back home."

"But you don't understand," James said, the desperation in his words palpable. "I'm wanted in every city, on account of—" He stopped speaking, refusing to look at the man.

"On account of what?" the man asked, still locked onto James's face.

Cammie's face held so many unreadable emotions as James fumbled with his words, eyebrows furrowed. It was as if he was deciding whether to speak.

"They considered it the highest of treason. They accused me of murdering one of the king's many advisors, but it wasn't the case. I swear that. They said I held the poisoned vial, but it wasn't me. Once word got out about the king's death, I fled. I couldn't stay there anymore. All signs pointed to me. I knew that. Despite something I had never done, the entire country would root for my death. It would have shamed my family's name. I did what I thought was best. And I ran..." James choked on his words, his eyes landing on Cammie. "I just never expected my mistake of being in the wrong room at the wrong time to lead me here. I was supposed to meet someone, to clear my name, some rumors that spread around the castle that I had heard. The prophecy—it was supposed to happen. I thought maybe now would be when it would, but maybe the rumors were just that, rumors. I'm so sorry for dragging you into this, Cammie. What I did was selfish, even to you." He turned to Hannah. "Involving humans in Amarian business isn't the way to go. I'm sorry for that." After heaving a deep sigh, he nodded at the man. "Take me back. I need to clear my name. In front of the Council, if I can. I can't have more people get hurt or in the way of what Nyx really wants. You said his fight isn't with me, but it is. It has to be. Otherwise, why else would he have bought me from the tracker?"

"Maybe because he thought you had some valuable information, like someone who you were going to meet or would have met?"

"But I told you." James sighed. "There was no way for me to meet him. I searched and searched, and this guy, the true heir, he's gone. I'm pretty sure whoever told that story was on their deathbed, trying to give some hope to us, that a way to defeat evil was coming, when in reality, we're just living it now. There can be no prophecy without a true heir, and there can be no three-in-one without some sort of magical breeding ability. It's as simple as that. There's never been one who's existed."

The man at the door stepped away from the threshold. "And what if I told you that sentiment was wrong? Would you believe me?"

James shook his head. "Absolutely not. There's nothing you could show me—wait, why are you taking off your shirt? There's no reason to do that. In fact, I think it's unnecessary."

The man, still not listening to James's practical shrieks, shook off his shirt and turned around to where his back was facing the group. He gestured to his shoulder. "Solenne, are you still outside? Would you mind helping me with this?"

The woman—Solenne—came through the door, her eyebrows piqued as she took in the man's stance. "Caelan, what are you doing?"

Hannah marveled at the name. *Caelan.* It was the weirdest name she had ever heard, but from what she could tell of the guy, it seemed like exotically weird was his thing.

"I'm proving a point," Caelan said, gesturing at his shoulder. "Please, they need to see this."

Unconvinced, Solenne crossed her arms over her chest. "Don't you think there's been enough revealing for one day? Could it be possible that just maybe we could all go back to sleep for once? To me, that sounds splendid, but you're on some sort of revelation kick, it seems. I don't agree with you," she said.

"Never said you have to. I just need your help since you're the one who basically put this on me to begin with."

Solenne rolled her eyes with a flourish that Hannah appreciated. *I officially like this chick.*

Solenne waved her palm over Caelan's left shoulder blade. A sudden shimmering filled the room, so bright that it exploded into a million tiny particles of gold as it fell onto the cottage floor.

As Hannah squinted, she realized it wasn't particles. It was practically skin that exploded off of Caelan's back. With a scream building in her throat, Hannah could feel the anxiety that wanted to squeeze it tight.

"Solenne," Sabina said, "I think she's freaking out. I'm not sure what she's seen, but do you have anything we can give her? Something to calm her?"

Solenne peeked away from her handiwork and nodded to the back room. "There should be something labeled lavender in there. I added a special Natrellum ingredient that produces relaxation and sleep. It should help her find some peace after everything."

Hannah watched Sabina run out of the room. Hannah's veins pumped more blood as she processed everything in front of her. The room was doubling, tripling in size, and Caelan looked like he was a blend of four people.

"She's going into shock," a voice called. "Maybe today wasn't the best day for revealing things."

Caelan, she realized.

"You guys are insane," Hannah heard herself say. "Burning off skin with just a hand isn't normal. Whatever crazy things you guys are into, I am out. Cammie, come with me. Sabina, I could not care less about her. Stay here, or don't. It's whatever."

"I think you need to relax," Cammie said. Her voice was calming but not calming enough.

"They've brainwashed you. I'm telling you..."

"I got it!" Sabina's voice was distant but getting closer. "How many drops?"

"Just enough to calm her. Her drowsiness will do the rest," Solenne said.

Hannah could feel hands trying to open her mouth and arms at her back. Screaming didn't help, not against the liquid that was being poured down her throat. It gurgled against her words, against her protests, drowning them out against the taste of lilac sweetness.

She could vaguely see a marking on Caelan's shoulder, but it was so blurry she wasn't sure of what it was.

They spoke more words into the space.

"I'm going to call Tony, tell him we've found her."

No words came from lips that were numbing, and despite all the fighting against the liquid, there was nothing Hannah could do but fall deeply into sleep.

CHAPTER TWENTY-SIX

SABINA

S̲HE WATCHED AS SOLENNE AND James carried Hannah to the spare bedroom, the same one she had been in not too long ago.

Sabina couldn't help but marvel at the marking on Caelan's back. It looked like a strange tattoo, but one that had to hide under some sort of glamour was enough to send a shiver down Sabina's spine. The outline was of a bird she couldn't quite place until it came into full view.

It's a phoenix with its wings outspread.

"You've been quiet," he finally said as he leaned down to get his shirt.

"Well, practically revealing yourself to the world wasn't necessary. I know some people are proud of the markings, but this is just...weird."

Caelan looked at her with one brow raised. "You think this is just a regular tattoo?"

"With how dramatic your reveals have been, to be honest, I wasn't sure if it was some sort of Amarian gang marking." The starkness of her comment hung in the air, like the edge of a knife that one couldn't pull back.

"It wasn't a gang marking," James said.

Sabina peered around the corner. It wasn't just Sabina that was skeptical. Cammie's arms were hugging her chest so tightly that she was sure it would burst if she moved any further. She kept stealing looks at James, but he was too involved in staring at Caelan that he didn't notice.

"How do you know?" Sabina asked with a tilt of her head. "We've been told a lot of things, things I'm sure are true, but how do we know this isn't just words? Cammie might have memories of you, but I don't."

At James' narrowing eyes, she almost regretted her words.

"You're right," he replied, shocking her. "You don't really know me, but one thing I can tell you for sure is *that* marking..." He stopped speaking and gestured toward Caelan. "...is entirely what he's claiming it is. Everyone knows in Natrellum what the marking is. It's been around since practically the beginning of time itself."

"But how can that be?" Cammie piped up.

"That's a very long story of history. Are we sure that telling them is necessary since the mind wiping almost killed her?" Solenne was now walking into the room, her voice quiet, although it echoed off of all four walls.

"You're constantly reminding me I dragged them into it, Solenne. The least we can do is give them answers," Caelan replied.

"So, by that information, I am guessing we do the mind wipe on them later? Not now?" Solenne reached the far end of the wall, nearly a few feet from Caelan, crossing her arms across her chest.

Caelan's eyebrows rose. "Why are you arguing about this? They're in the room. They deserve to know."

"Bringing up history we will force them to forget about is punishment enough!" Solenne's voice held so much anger that, if it were a bubble, Sabina was sure it would erupt into a million little particles. "But if this is what you desire, who am I to stop you?" She huffed a breath, inhaling for a few moments. Her eyes shut.

For a brief second, Sabina wondered if Solenne had fallen asleep standing up.

Just as suddenly, Solenne's eyes reopened, and in them were a million stories. Sabina could see it by the way they shifted, as if secrets that had been buried for so long couldn't wait to come out.

"The world you know of," Solenne started with a sigh, "is not the only one there is. There may be more that we don't know of, but Natrellum was the first of its own beautiful creation. It wasn't tainted when it originated. It was the most splendidly descriptive world human eyes had ever beheld until destruction from your kind birthed into ours." Solenne's eyes flashed with a murky gray.

Sabina couldn't help but flinch. "What happened?" she asked, wringing her hands. A new nervous habit.

"Humans were the first to enter our world, yet at the time, no other beings in it existed, except for the Forces who were there long before us. There were no Amarians, for the concept hadn't even been coined until after the first two of humanity were invited to exist within it. At its core, Natrellum was founded on the most beautiful of all of the principles: love. Love caused the first Amarian woman to seek help and hope for the one she called her true pair. Her love was dying, and so she called on the Forces that be, the same ones that exist in this very forest, not too far from here. Light greeted her, allowed her to shift and morph into something stronger that could never be destroyed by the fragility of humanity's realm of existence. Everyone was welcomed because no one were threats. They became Amarians, with gifts and talents to grow the community that the Light had offered them. Even their body shifted. Strength came faster. Hearing became accelerated. Their ears changed to slits and points. Healing wasn't outside of the bounds of learning with the help of herbs that the Light blessed them with. They became what your kind calls Fae, creatures that you've based your stories on. Even then, so long ago, Amarians were deeply intertwined with your history to the point that fact from fiction became harder to tell, but it was good then." Solenne paused with a small smile. "Then, Amarians and humans lived in harmony. Some humans even accepting the gift of becoming an Amarian. Back then there was no hiding, not like now when we have to glamour our true bodies here, so we aren't captured and experimented on. We were free to be."

"But I'm guessing something changed that?" Cammie said, her voice teetering toward nervousness.

"Something did," Solenne agreed. A dark shadow passed over her eyes.

It was as if a chill had been invited into the conversation. Sabina could feel it tickling her skin.

"Raif was the one who started all of this," Solenne said. "If we are to trace fault to any of our own kind, it would be Raif who bore the blame."

Caelan's shoulders slumped. So did James's.

"It's true," James spoke softly. "Raif became the downfall of Amarians, and we've been paying for it ever since."

"A lovely courtship of community between the Light and the people it bore new life to slowly burned into something much darker. The Light, or Liseli, as we called it, had plans for prosperity, plans for peace, but the Dark, Onyx, had plans for ruin. Many plans. We aren't sure exactly of the year...but Raif became infatuated with humanity. He became bored with the way of life here. He wasn't comfortable being a part of the world that was created. He wanted, instead, to be a *creator*. In secret, he devised a plan with Onyx on total world domination, and in his lust for life, he became lust. Raif had relations with one human in the village, but he was very good at keeping it secret until the human woman became pregnant with his child. Raif already had children with his wife, Catori, the first Amarian woman, but that wasn't enough. He needed more—more power to thrive. He was determined to use this new child as a weapon to fuel a war that had been long brewing between Onyx and Liseli, but it was too late. The human woman, in a desperate rage, killed Catori while she slept. Just like Raif, the human wanted more than what she was being offered. *She* wanted to be Raif's true wife. When the village awoke, they enacted justice for their ruler."

Cammie's eyes grew bigger, and Sabina couldn't help but marvel. Who knew all of this was hiding in the shadows this entire time?

"They burned the human woman at the stake despite her being pregnant. I can't say that I agree with their methods, that baby didn't do anything wrong, but we could no longer have humans involved in our business. The darkness had already taken them over, and we had to get them out. Those who weren't Amarian were banished, and Liseli gave new gifts, gifts that were used on Cammie here to wipe away her memories of Amarians. Therefore, your kind only has stories of Fae but no real proof. The portal to home is also another thing that came out of this. Liseli wanted Amarians to travel freely, but humanity could never travel into the space again. By the time a new generation was born, our kind became nothing more than legend as days passed, and no true traveling was done. Not until Caelan was born." A wistful, far-off look appeared in the recesses of her pupils, as if by merely looking in a different direction, she could transport herself there.

"I have a feeling we are breaking many rules by being here, listening to you." Cammie's face took on a pink hue, flushing it with revelation as her eyes lit up. "What you did to heal me..."

"Goes against everything we do and know," Solenne finished. "Humans naturally need to poke and prod at things that are out of their realm of control. It's what they lean toward. Exposing this to you puts you all at greater risk, especially for the mind wiping that is to come."

"We don't need to discuss it now," Caelan suggested. "We can bring it up later, when I get back. The girls can stay with you until I get this resolved."

Solenne merely nodded, her gaze flickering over to Caelan. Stones of heat still lingered in her eyes, but her mouth had a slight curve. "You mean *if* you get back," she corrected. "As far as the girls go, I can do my best to keep an eye out for them and make sure they are taken care of as best as I can offer, but I can only promise as far as their own resilience concerns them. Nothing further."

Like a game of tennis, Solenne's emotions were constantly wavering between abhorring and yearning.

"I would expect nothing less," Caelan said, a shimmer of something like gratefulness resting in his eyes. His entire posture shifted as if his body could finally rest after years of holding a weight without end and no destination in sight. "I think that about covers it, then. We prep for leaving as soon as we can."

"When is that?" Cammie asked, biting her nail. Nerves were displayed on every area of her face.

"Tomorrow morning," Caelan stated.

It was as if a pin had dropped. Complete and utter silence filled the room.

Cammie's eyes locked with James's. "But that's only in a few hours..."

"It gives enough time for rest and enough time to prepare as much as we can," Caelan said, "but with a bounty at stake here, there's not much planning we can do if we want to make it to clear names and find out the truth of what's going on. Whomever started this has plans to finish it, but if we hurry, we can beat them at their own game, and I can find out more information about my family with James. That's why he wanted to meet me."

"That's... why I came to meet you," James said with a perplexed look on his face. "The man who died told me you had survived and that he heard rumors of children. Do you have any?"

A shadow flickered across Caelan's face as his mouth twitched. "I did have children."

"Where are there now?" James asked. "Did they move to some other area within the states?"

After a brief silence, Caelan finally let out a choked breath. "They died...along with my wife in childbirth."

"I'm sorry about your children," James uttered, "but as far as your wife, surely you must have had many years with her. As sad as it is that she's gone, Amarians have long lifespans. Those years won't be forgotten, I'm sure."

"The years aren't what you're thinking, dear," Solenne said softly. As she looked at James, there was a gentleness that seemed to evaporate when she turned to Sabina, though she couldn't quite understand why.

"So it was a shorter amount than a few thousand? How long did you have with her?"

"Only four," Caelan replied, regret written all over his face.

"That's so soon." All eyes averted from looking in his general direction. "There's something else you're not telling me. What is it? Surely, it cannot be as bad as you're thinking."

"Not even the fact that she was a human?" Sabina, against her better judgment, let the words slip.

A multitude of emotions ran across James's face as the words laid bare in the room. "You married...and mated with a human?"

"Why do you say that with such disgust? You and Cammie—"

"But that's different," James interjected. "You're held to a higher standard."

Not one person missed the way Cammie's breath hitched in her throat.

James immediately turned to her, contrition glowing in his eyes, but it was too late. She had already turned on her heel, rushing out of the room.

"I...misspoke. I realize though we are on different soil. You still may end me, regardless." As shame colored his face in different shades of rose, he looked over his shoulder. "I need to go after her," James uttered, his face taking on pained constraints. "She can't think that of me, not after our last interaction."

When Caelan nodded, James breathlessly called out a thank you before jutting out of the room, leaving Sabina alone with Solenne and Caelan.

"And you're sure there's no way I could convince you to stay?" Solenne asked amidst the silence.

Caelan didn't meet her gaze.

"Is there anything I can do to convince you? You don't need to clear your name, and *he* isn't your concern."

"He's my subject. That's all the more my concern."

"You haven't ever ruled before. How can you even be sure you're up to defending James in whatever way of order there is?"

For once, Caelan's eyes became one with the stars in the night. "I had a pretty good woman to raise me, so I think it's safe to say that I will manage on my own well. She took everything she knew and somehow could quadruple her knowledge tenfold onto me, and for that, for loving me...I could never repay her." He moved to kiss Solenne on the cheek before pulling away.

For the first time since Sabina had met him, his face was of utter peace.

"I think I'm going to head to bed now, for real this time. I have a small feeling in my gut telling me I can finally sleep."

With one small nod, he left the room.

CHAPTER TWENTY-SEVEN

CAMMIE

"CAMMIE, WAIT," A VOICE CALLED out. Footsteps followed her even as she passed through rooms and ended up outside.

She knew that voice well. She didn't need more healing from Solenne to remember the words he had told her before he'd timelessly disappeared. Nor did she need any kind of reminder of what had just been spoken.

"But that's different," James interjected. *"You're held to a higher standard."* Being viewed as a timeless moment to be treasured was not on the list now, and it was definitely not in his vocabulary of things to define her as.

"Can you slow down?" James asked, practically breathless.

She couldn't sense exactly how far behind he was, but the snarky comment rolled off of her tongue just like butter. "If you're some sort of Amarian like you say you are, why don't you pick up the pace? You have these gifts. Was speed not your inheritance?"

More grumbling flowed from his lips, but the rage was boiling so hot in her chest that she didn't want to keep listening. Blocking him out was easier, but better yet, maybe she could talk to Solenne. Maybe she knew of someone to do the mind-wiping.

Erase it all. Perfect.

"I can't exactly talk to you if you keep speeding up," James said. "If you slow down, maybe I can clear this up."

"Has it ever occurred to you that maybe I don't want to talk to you? Maybe that's why my feet are suddenly moving a million miles an hour?"

"Cammie, please."

His pleading struck a chord deep in her heart, opening an entirely new tune of crimson hurt.

"I said, leave me alone. Go back to the cabin. Prepare to leave tomorrow. I'd rather you go home with your dignity than keep trying to pretend to care about me for a few short hours."

"But I wasn't pretending," James said hoarsely. "Everything I told you that night was real."

Cammie bit the inside of her cheek. His words hung empty in the air like a million promises that could never manage the beautiful effort of landing a delivery.

Without warning, she whirled around, a response ready to fire away on her tongue when she smacked into his chest.

He smelled of sweat and everything musky pine with a hint of cinnamon bark. It wiggled its way into her nostrils and stole the rhythm of her heart. As she stared at him underneath the silhouette of the moonlight, she told herself to remain calm, but there it was again, the persistent disobedience of a heart still latched onto him that enjoyed skipping beats like a rock on a riverbed.

Their history lingered in his hazy gaze, but as she locked eyes on his lips, she was suddenly and completely reminded of his tongue of death that had killed every moment she'd held dear.

"How can I trust anything you say to me now after what you said in there?" Cammie could hardly make out his face underneath the midnight sky, but the twitching in his cheekbone was prominent. "You've made it clear that I am a burden to you in every way that I can't control. I'm sorry I'm not Amarian. I'm sorry that I'm human. I'm sorry that my lifespan of only a few decades is meaningless compared to your millennia."

"It isn't meaningless," he countered.

"It's just meaningless to *you*," she hissed. "To your kind, we are nothing more than a nuisance. We always have been since the beginning. Isn't that the story your people tell? Probably passed down through generations about how humans are abominations, and you guys were just lucky to escape however you could."

Her stomach dipped as they stood. Sound was completely absent. When James refused to move, to even stir, the truth settled in her gut. Despite everything, what was unspoken screamed loudly.

"So, this is what they tell you," she said slowly.

At his blinking eyes, she hoped her stomach would settle, but the lurching was never ending.

"You have to understand," he said. "We have a history, just like you do."

"But we actually accommodate you."

She flashed back to the bookstore, where she had been met by a confused person wearing muddy boots.

"Are you thinking of the night we met?" James questioned.

This time, she couldn't meet his eyes. Not when hers were stinging with freshly shed tears.

"I made you feel at home even when you did not know our culture, of our ways. You knew nothing about what being a human meant—I thought you were some homeless guy..." She swallowed back the salty wetness that was burning her throat and tickling her nostrils. As she moved back a few paces, she mustered up the courage to let her eyes rise. "You were my friend. I cared about you, in ways...that I couldn't or didn't know how. You asked earlier how I remembered you. Solenne went through all the trouble to help me gain my memories back. After seeing the time we had and how it was so magically, effortlessly beautiful, I thought maybe it would be like that now. When I saw you, I was in shock. I was planning to talk to you later tonight to discuss what happened, but you...you had a lot of nerve kissing me," she finished, sniffling.

"What are you talking—"

"You kissed me," she said. "How can you expect me to be so nonchalant after you were the one who kissed me *knowingly*, I might add—" Flustered, she lost her point of direction. Despite her wavering confidence, she continued, "You kissed me knowing I wouldn't remember you. How selfish can you be?"

"I wasn't trying to be selfish," he replied, but he could barely get the words out. She was talking too fast.

"But the fact of the issue is...you were. You knew I wasn't ever going to be part of your world, and that you did this just proves to me I was never meant to be. I thought we were becoming something. I thought *we* mattered. I thought *I* mattered."

"But you do matter," he proclaimed. "You do. I just misspoke."

Her words felt like chalk in her throat, hard to swallow, hard to take in. "If that's true..." Cammie paused, her breath catching. "...then why did you only apologize for what you said after my reaction?"

"But I didn't..." After a moment of silence, he cursed under his breath. "I...did."

"What you said, James, wasn't just a statement in the moment. It was the hardcore truth. Somewhere, deep down, you feel I am a product of your experiences here with no true meaning of your real life in Natrellum. I'm just something you discovered here. Whatever you felt in the moment when we kissed, let it be in that moment."

Cammie gave him one last look, and then she turned around, focused on being anywhere but that very spot. She needed to clear her head. She needed to find some sort of respite far away from the one person who held her heart in his hands.

His grip was firm on her elbow, and it lit her entire arm on fire. She couldn't deny how he made her feel, how the simplest touch made her crave his affection. It was as if her own skin buried memories, and each time skin brushed against skin, they resurfaced.

Her heart and mind were at war, and nothing she did would stop it.

"What I said was wrong," he whispered. "It was impulsive and stupid and just.... Whenever you are taught a certain way, despite knowing differently...it's still something you react to. Humans were a big reason why our world is so messed up, but in the same breath, you guys are the reason we even exist. There's acknowledgment there, but there's still learning on my part. There are still things I need to rewire my brain on. Does any of this make sense to you?"

Cammie held her breath, weighing his words carefully. There were many double meanings within them. She knew what he was asking. She knew it deep in her heart. Somewhere within the realms of the reckless pursuit of love that she carried, there was a settling, too, a resignation that she had to heed.

"You can do what you wish, learn what you want. I respect that. I understand it, even. But..." A shaky breath followed. "Expecting me to wait for you to overcome your prejudice isn't something I can do. Caelan sacrificed a lot for his wife, regardless of what your view is on that pairing, and that's what I want. I don't want someone who loves me in one breath but curses me in another. I want someone who sees me for all of me, regardless of what they were taught or what they're learning or unlearning.... You just aren't what I need. You coming to terms with humanity and the role we play is something you're going to establish on your own because I can't be there to walk you through it. Not on this."

Her feet dragged, and her heart crashed to the ground. It felt like a cement block was pulling her across the grass, but she knew, even with the heaviness in her heart, that it was nothing compared to the weight James was pondering.

Sabina sat at the kitchen table when Cammie came back in, a small mug in front of her.

"Drinking coffee?" Cammie asked as she slid into the chair across from her, gesturing to the mug. " I thought you hated it."

Sabina smiled weakly. "It's tea, actually." Her face was worn as her eyebrows pierced together, as if there was some sort of string interconnecting one brow to the other.

"Are you okay?" Cammie asked, leaning against the table on her elbows. "You're being really quiet."

"If I'm being honest? No, I am not okay. I'm just kind of sitting here processing the fact that I didn't really tell my parents where I was, and the entire thing of going to Louisiana and then suddenly arriving in Colorado and then somehow finding out along how the Fae are practically real and alive and always have been. Oh, did I mention that the guy you dated ends up being super connected to the guy that's absolute royalty in Natrellum? Um, and that Natrellum is even a word. Yeah... that about sums it up." Heaving a breath, Sabina put her head in her hands. "Am I even making any sense?"

For once, Cammie felt a small smile rest on her lips. "You're making perfect sense. I understand, somewhat at least. With James, that part I can relate to. Caelan, kind of, sort of."

Sabina's eyebrows no longer pinched. Slowly, she lifted her head from her hands and gave Cammie a devilish grin. "So, how did that go? Did he apologize? If he did, and if he romanced you with the best kiss ever, I could say I entirely approve." Her face continued lighting up.

The sucker punch in Cammie's gut grew. "There's really not much to tell. No kiss, no electricity, if that's what you're asking."

"Was it because of the comment he made?" Sabina asked. "I'm sure he was just heated. He didn't really mean it, did he?"

Cammie's lips fell into a straight line. "If by meaning it you actually mean his entire population back home thinks humans are the scum of the planet, then yes, he absolutely meant it."

The audible gasp practically shook the table as Sabina's hands clenched the sides. "He. Did. Not. What?" Sabina's voice rose an octave, red heat coated her cheeks as she squeaked. "Sorry, I didn't realize it was that loud, but you're joking?"

Cammie shook her head. "I'm as serious as I've ever been. That's essentially what it boiled down to."

Sabina rolled her eyes. "What an idiot. I don't remember much of him. I'm sure the mind wipe applied to not just you, but all of us. I'm actually thrilled about that now. I'd probably be angrier if I had memories of him being some pleasant fellow."

"Oh, no," Cammie murmured.

"Don't worry," Sabina reassured. "I promise I wouldn't have taken his side even if I remembered if that's what you're worried about." She waved her hand dismissively.

"But what about Hannah? She has the mind wipe, too. She's obviously been through some trauma, of course. I don't know the extent, and I didn't really talk to James to find out. He's leaving tomorrow, so it's not like he can really do much about it."

A look of stark determination was in Sabina's eyes as she gazed at Cammie from across the table. "If he's going to start a mess, the least he can do is help us figure out how to help Hannah without scarring her."

"But there's no telling what she's seen or hasn't seen. How do we even know how to break the news to her if she doesn't need to know? I just don't want her to find out these things, and then, well..."

"Have a complete and utter meltdown?" Sabina offered.

Cammie sighed. "Exactly."

"Well." Sabina took a sip of her tea. "Maybe it's a good thing the mind wiping is happening. Better for all of us to just forget."

"How will any of us go back to normal? Normal seems so...far away after everything that's happened."

"I think it will be like we never knew it happened. That's essentially the point."

Cammie felt her heart sink. "I guess you're right," she said, the words themselves like tingling numbness on her tongue. It almost didn't feel real.

"Maybe sleep will be good for you," Sabina offered. "Maybe resting is what you need. We can say goodbye in the morning, figure out cover stories for our parents, and then, you know, wait for Caelan to return, and all of this will disappear."

As Cammie gave a small smile, she thought—even wondered—if she really wanted it to.

CHAPTER TWENTY-EIGHT

HANNAH

THE WORLD WAS A BLUR of colors as her eyes adjusted to complete and utter darkness. A person hovered in her line of sight, but if she squinted hard enough, she still couldn't make it out fully.

But those shoulders, she had seen them. She knew them well.

"What's going on?" she croaked.

The figure leaned closer, and underneath a glint of light that was coming from a window, Hannah felt her heart relax. It was only Tony.

"You've been asleep for quite a while."

Tony fumbled in the dark behind him until Hannah heard the dragging of chair legs on the floor. No, more like a scraping. Slowly, he moved to a sitting position, now eye-level with her.

"But what about everything? What about... Caelan, and the tattoo marking, and...." Hannah could hardly think straight, and the words that should form sentences all seemed to jumble together. "How did you even get here?" she finally dared to ask.

"I met up with Caelan by accident, but he knew Nyx, said there was some kind of history with him. I was terrified that you were gone. I didn't know how to find you, but finding him? That felt like fate." Tony's jaw hardened as he looked down at Hannah. "Did I ever tell you how stupid I am?"

The burning in Hannah's throat intensified even as she forced the words out. "You've never told me you had such disdain. How great that you're finally sharing it."

"It isn't disdain for *you*," Tony elaborated. "It's disdain for your choices and mine. That's completely different."

The rush of anger she felt every so often clawed its way to the surface. "Then maybe you should have worded it differently."

Her hissing words stung Tony's cheek. She was sure of it by how the muscle twitched. "If you weren't so impulsive and angry and stubborn and let someone stay with you...."

"So, now it's *my* fault? What about you guys? You couldn't even find me."

"You didn't really give us much choice!" Tony ran a hand through his hair, letting the other fall at his side. "How were we supposed to know where you'd be? We aren't mind-readers, Hannah. You could have *died*."

"But I didn't," Hannah interjected.

"You still could've," Tony shot back.

"I'm done with this," she said, shoving the blankets off of her. Whatever that crazy lady had given her, it was enough. All of this had been enough.

"What are you doing?" Tony asked as Hannah's feet slammed against the floor.

"Didn't you hear? Magical beings exist, and I'm smack-dab in the middle of it all. That's who Nyx is fighting against—Caelan. He's a prince or a king. I guess it's the same difference."

"Those are two different things," Tony said slowly, his eyes trapped at Hannah's shrugging shoulders.

"Either way, these things are real. Or so they tell me. I should definitely believe it, right?"

"Do you want to believe it?" Tony asked, taking a step toward her. "Maybe you should sit down."

Hannah jerked away. "No," she exclaimed, her eyes darting around the darkness of the room as she stumbled in what she hoped was the right direction. "I don't need your help," she uttered as her left foot let her down not so gently.

An arm snaked on her elbow, dragging her upward. "Be careful. You don't want to hurt yourself."

"Don't tell me what I should and shouldn't want to do."

The exasperated groan left Tony, and the corners of Hannah's lips turned upward. "You get a kick out of makin' me frustrated. Why?"

Hannah shrugged again. "It's so fun I'm actually considering making it a full-time job. Just let me go and I'll stop."

"I have a bad feeling about this." Tony sighed. His grip was tightening as he continued pulling Hannah back to the bed. "Why should I?"

"Because I'm giving you a headache?" Hannah offered, already feeling more energy in her bones. All she needed was one moment where Tony actually listened.

His hands loosened, and for the moment, Hannah knew this was her escape. She darted to the door, her feet skidding against the floor as sweaty palms grasped the handle. With more strength than she thought possible, the door flew open, and Hannah continued running despite the footsteps she heard coming from behind her.

Sabina and Cammie were at the kitchen table when Hannah tripped into the room, complete shock displaying on their faces.

"How are you awake?" Sabina asked.

"I don't have time to answer that," Hannah told her, eyebrows creasing together. "Plus, I don't really want to talk to you. Frankly, I'm surprised you didn't get the memo when I stopped returning your calls." Even with a spinning head and lungs that were gasping for breath, Hannah was proud that her insults still knew how to hit a bullseye.

"Tell me what I did for you to hate me so much." Sabina rose from the table with shaky hands. "It couldn't have been that bad. We were friends for so long. What is a moment compared to all those years?" Fresh tears sprung from her eyes.

Hannah's stoic, stormy gaze remained unchanged. "I'm so tired of the riddles you speak, as if your scholarly upbringing is so much better than mine!" The bark and bile in her throat were so pungent Hannah could practically taste it.

Sabina's jaw locked, and her gaze was a mirrored image against Hannah's. "Is *that* what this is about? Jealousy. Are you serious?"

Just then, Tony entered the room, shooting Sabina and Cammie an apologetic look. "I'm sorry for her. She just woke up. Caelan let me inside.... I'm just trying to calm her down."

Sabina turned her eyes on Tony, and they softened momentarily. "Thank you for coming."

He returned her gentle gaze with a small smile. "I'm sorry about how all of this is turning out. I'm sure she doesn't mean to be like this..." He gestured to Hannah, moving his hand up and down at the length of her. "It's just an off day. Now, come on, Hannah. Let's go back to bed for a while. You're talking of magical beings and things that probably are all in your head. You need rest." His hands found their way to her waist, and he began tugging her gently in the direction they came.

With the speed of lightning, Hannah shoved him away, shooting Tony a glare. "Don't touch me. Don't tell me what I can and should feel. You aren't me."

Her fingers became slick with sweat, and a droplet fell into her brow from her temple. The more she talked—the more she looked—the more she was sure that she was seeing actual red. It was everywhere, lingering in the air, and it smelled like soot in her clothes and dirt in her nostrils. The earthly stubbornness clung to her skin, and it only sped up as the front door opened.

Solenne stood in the doorway, holding a basket of berries. She tilted her head. "She's up already? What I give isn't light in strength. She must be pretty resilient to fight it off so quickly. How are you feeling?"

That was all it took. With an animalistic roar, Hannah charged from the kitchen. Her feet moved faster than her thoughts could. She leapt, her hands at Solenne's throat. "What did you give me?" she screamed, wetness protruding from her lips and onto Solenne's cheek. The basket was a small barrier but not enough. Little berries skidded onto the wood floor at the jostling. "You crazy lady, answer me!"

Cammie, Sabina, and Tony ran after her. As Hannah's grip on Solenne's neck tightened, Tony moved first, at the ready.

But Solenne held up a hand, the only one she could move. "Give her a second to process," she instructed, her gaze transfixing on Hannah. "I want you to breathe. You are in shock. I need you to take a moment for me. Your human mind is too fragile for this to overtake you. Ground yourself." Though her voice was firm, Solenne's lips shook, barely.

"You insane woman! Fix me. Fix me." Hannah was screaming like a banshee, blinking against the war in the backdrop of her eyes. "Find the key. Unlock the door," she uttered, her limbs trembling.

Solenne's entire body stiffened. "What did you say?" she uttered, her voice now above a whisper. In her eyes, there was fear, a fear so palpable that if one were to be brave enough to reach out, they would surely touch it.

"Find the key. Unlock the door," Hannah pleaded.

And that was the last sentence she uttered before falling to the ground, completely overtaken.

CHAPTER TWENTY-NINE

SABINA

ALL EYES STARED AT THE space where Hannah's unconscious body lay, her chest barely moving.

Sabina heard alarm bells in her mind.

Tony rushed forward to be at Hannah's side. "What happened to her?" He directed the question at Solenne.

Solenne wasn't even looking at him or looking at anyone. Her eyes were glassy and unfocused as her chest heaved deep breaths.

"Can someone get a remedy, get something!" Tony shouted, his hand cupping her face as he rested her head in his lap. "Wake up, Hannah. Wake up." With each movement from Tony's fingers, Hannah didn't stir.

"What do we do?" Cammie asked, her eyes brimming with tears. The anxiety in her body was evident in her hands as Cammie's fingers drummed against her thigh.

Staring into Cammie's gaze was like a vortex of paranoia. So many fears lingered at the surface, but if Sabina kept allowing herself to see, she, too, would be sucked in.

"We need to grab Caelan. Maybe he's seen this before," Sabina said.

"But—" The protest was barely off of Cammie's lips before Sabina put a hand on her shoulder.

"Don't go there," Sabina pleaded. "You can't."

"She could die," Cammie said, her lip trembling.

"We won't let that happen," Sabina said, her voice firm. "If he hasn't seen it, there's got to be something that can be done to help."

Cammie quickly nodded, but the fear was still clear in her eyes. She looked back at Hannah, biting her lip. "Please, we need to find him. He needs to heal her or find a way to."

Sabina took her hand in hers and squeezed gently, hoping words could flow through fingers like pieces of bark in a river. "Go find him," she instructed.

Cammie nodded before rushing out the door, brushing past Solenne who hovered in the way.

"No quick remedy will fix this." Solenne willed herself to speak, but her gaze was still a million miles away.

"Why aren't you doing anything? *Help* her." Despite Tony's pleading, Solenne didn't dare move.

After several minutes, Cammie returned, Caelan in tow.

"What's going on?" Caelan hovered behind Solenne, who was still lingering in the doorway.

Solenne, jumping out of her skin, moved just enough to let Caelan pass.

"Why is she on the floor? What happened?" Caelan rushed to Hannah, crouching down beside Tony.

Cammie made her way back to Sabina, grabbing her hand yet again.

Solenne refused to make any remarks at Caelan's inquiry and instead bit her lip. The basket of berries jostled in her arms, small ones still falling at her feet.

"She just started saying this thing, something about a door and a key needing to be unlocked. She didn't really say anything more. She couldn't. And this lady, whoever she is...just stared and watched." Tony's cautious eyes never left Hannah's face. "I don't know what happened. Someone said something about a remedy, but I don't think that'll work. She needs an ambulance."

"She needs healing," Caelan agreed, "but not the kind you're thinking of." An unspoken word passed between them, and Caelan rose to his feet, walking to Solenne.

Her gaze was unapproachable while a single tear fell down her cheek. "I need to go outside," she finally whispered as she turned to the door.

"Why can't you heal her?" Caelan asked. "I know you're angry at me. I know you will somehow forgive me whenever that is. Our lives are timeless. Hers isn't." Within Caelan's voice, there were so many underlying layers. Some of them were so deep that even Sabina was sure she would never uncover them.

Solenne turned around, silent tears pricking her cheek, and she swallowed. "Her life will be fine, but you will never forgive me."

Caelan's eyes softened, and he covered her hands with his. "Whatever I said, I didn't mean it earlier. You *are* my mother, and life, as long as it is for us, is still too precious to spend all the years we have left angry at each other. I'll be coming home after I help James. I promise you that. You have every right to be concerned and worried and still upset at me. I understand and respect that, but don't let your anger stop you from helping her."

"Not that I won't help her," Solenne said, taking a breath. "It's that I can't. If I do that, then... everything I worked for will be gone."

Caelan's eyebrows fluttered. "What do you mean? You've done a lot for my family. You helped my wife. You did your best to save my children. You did...what you could."

Solenne's voice was hoarse as she finally, truly met his eyes. "I promised her. I promised Leanne. There are just things you wouldn't understand, things as a mother...that you couldn't understand."

A spark passed in Caelan's eyes as he stared at Solenne, and Sabina felt her stomach lurch. *What does she mean?*

"What are you talking about?" Caelan asked, eyes wide.

"I'm saying that I lied to you. I'm telling you that your children are alive."

For a moment, there were no words until a choked laugh escaped Caelan. "You're lying," he said, practically breathless.

"I'm not lying." Solenne did a sweep of the room. "In fact, they're right here in this room."

If there was a hand hovering above the sky with fingers surely set to destruction, Sabina was sure the roof would have caved in at this very moment.

Sabina's breath caught in her chest, anxiety's swift, possessive fingers around her throat. "That can't be possible," she claimed. "I'm not Amarian. Cammie and Hannah aren't Amarian." She shook her head, as if that one movement could push away the confusion that was muddling in her mind.

"Why are you torturing him like this?" Cammie spoke with such hurt that it actually tore Caelan's face away from Solenne. "He's told me things, told me pain about his family, about his children, and you're just sitting here, telling him they're alive? How heartless do you have to be to make up some story?"

Pain flinched in Solenne's eyes, but she turned her gaze to Cammie, complete seriousness in her eyes. "This isn't some sort of trick. As stubborn as you are, you remind me so much of

Leanne. So brave and bold…. You even have a bit of her eyes…. I didn't notice it at first, but I see it so clearly now." Tears now fell onto her cheeks.

Caelan's face became stone as he removed his hand from hers, fire in his eyes. He pointed to Hannah, his voice firm. "Stop doing this. Heal her. Enough of this nonsense."

Solenne remained unwavering in her stubbornness. "The healing will come once I release it. I haven't yet because I need you to tell me you still love me, that you won't hate me forever, disown me even."

Caelan's hands grasped at the air, at nothing tangible. "You're letting her life hang in the balance over something you can't prove? Over some sort of embellished lie? To what? Get back at me for leaving you? That is low, even for you. Heal her. *Now.* I won't be asking you again."

"You need to hear me out first—"

"If you don't heal her, she will die!" Caelan shouted, the entire room shaking at his words.

Sabina felt the chill against her cheek, and every single hair stood upright as if he merely commanded it.

"Cammie almost died earlier," he added. "I won't have you let Hannah die for something so incredibly stupid, for a dream that can't ever come true."

"Do you ever wonder why it was Cammie you were so drawn to, even before you found out about James?" Solenne spoke quickly, completely passing up Caelan's outburst as if it were the most natural thing in the world. "You may not remember her, but I do. We were there when she arrived here years ago at this very spot. She was playing frisbee with the other children, and somehow, it landed in our yard. You, being the kind man you are, offered to grab it for her. I was left alone with her, and that's when she spoke. It wasn't Hannah this time speaking about the key and the door but Cammie. I trained the protection enchantment to where the words would only be spoken once they were all together, but I hadn't perfected it yet. I had to erase what I could from her memory."

Cammie's eyes were frozen as words tumbled from her lips. "You and I drank lemonade together."

Solenne only nodded. "Except yours had the same ingredients I used on you earlier but in different amounts. With enough triggering, it could make you dizzy. Cause only certain memories within the closest time to...simply fade. We Amarians had to learn how to protect ourselves in case of exposure. I just used it to my advantage..."

"So, me blacking out at camp and being sent home early because they thought I had a concussion and suffered from memory loss...you're telling me all this time that it was *you*?" Red, hot rage flickered across Cammie's crestfallen face. "You did something so...wrong, all for some delusion! I'm not his daughter!"

"Camille is your full first name, adopted by Addison and Adam Romero in Louisiana. Birthdate, coming up, is August 18th. The same birthday as Hannah, same birthday as Sabina. Don't you find that coincidental? Your birthdates just collide in the same year, same day, same time? You just met each other at the campsite? No, this is not a weird instance of chance. This is *your* destiny. It always has been. Our people have talked about it for centuries. You are *our* hope."

Uncertainty flashed in Cammie's gaze as she scanned Solenne's face. "You're insane. She's insane." She looked at Caelan with wide eyes. "How do we help Hannah if she won't?"

"You don't believe me?" Solenne flinched as if stung. "Why would I lie to you?"

"Let's say this scenario is real," Caelan started, heaving a breath. "That means that you hid them—my daughters—for eighteen years. You made me believe they were dead for what reason exactly?"

"I had to protect them. Nyx, his family...they would have killed the girls and you. I had to make you believe they were dead. It was the only way to keep all of you safe. It was Leanne's last wish as she delivered, and she begged me to save them, even if it meant lying to you. I took the girls. I hid them at an adoption agency, and I made sure they were taken far away from each other to avoid suspicion. Honoring her last wish was my way of protecting you and them. Please, understand...I did what I needed to."

With a shake of his head, Caelan turned away from Solenne. "It's obvious nothing I say will cause you to give up this ruse. I need to find James. Maybe we can find some sort of remedy from someone who will actually want to help."

"I never said I didn't want to help. I said I couldn't because I didn't want you to hate me without hearing the full story, but if it is proof you want, then proof you will get." Solenne heaved a sigh, looking at all three girls in turn with determination in her eyes. "Unlock the door. I release the key for the door to be unlocked. I release—"

Sudden shattering stopped Solenne's words completely as glass shards from the open window flew all over the floor. Sabina covered her eyes and crouched to the floor, dragging Cammie with her. They huddled together, and Sabina dared to peek through her fingers.

Where Solenne stood was now a puddle of crimson that traveled for what seemed like eons to the kitchen, where she lay clutching her throat, choking on the liquid. It protruded from her lips, little droplets falling onto the floor. She gasped hoarsely, but it was like time itself was frozen, and no one dared move.

CHAPTER THIRTY

CAMMIE

SOLENNE WAS STILL BREATHING, SOMEHOW still alive.

A throaty growl claimed attention, and Cammie allowed her gaze to travel.

Hovering over Solenne was a beast, triple the size of a regular wolf. Cammie's heart issued a warning in a symphony of beats, but every bone in her body refused to stir.

Tony stared, angling his body above Hannah's.

"Take Hannah to a safe place and hide," Caelan instructed, his entire being completely still.

Tony didn't move.

"*Now!*"

With reflexes so quick Cammie almost didn't see it, Tony took Hannah to the room, and Cammie turned her gaze back to the animal with blood dripping from its fangs.

"Did you really think we wouldn't find you getting ready to leave?" The wolf was speaking.

Why is the wolf speaking? What in the world is going on? A sudden realization came upon Cammie. *It's just as Sabina told me earlier. It all was true...*

"You should have kept your end of the bargain and not attacked first," Caelan argued, standing his ground. With fists clenched and the muscle twitched in his cheek, it was obvious he was ready for anything.

The wolf-beast laughed. *Laughed.* "If you can play dirty, so can we, and based on that little conversation I heard earlier, it sounds like the entire party is gathered here." The wolf turned to Sabina, his mouth curving into a smile. His eyes briefly flickered to Cammie. "I wonder which one of you would taste sweeter on the tip of my tongue. The Prince's Daughters' blood in my stomach, the Crown finally discarded on the floor. Has a nice ring to it, doesn't it?"

"But we aren't his daughters," Cammie blurted. "She made a mistake."

"Mistake?" the wolf echoed, shaking his head. He brought a paw up to his stomach, wiping the remnant of red. "You're the one that's mistaken. I can smell the royal blood. The faintness of pine and lilac and rose is hard to miss, but I suppose your half-blood nose can't quite pick up scents that far. Maybe with some training, you would have been able to tap into your animal instincts. Surely one of you belongs to our sector. Such a shame that we won't be able to find out." The animal brought his paw down to the floor.

"You won't hurt them," Caelan said. "Your fight isn't with them. It's with me."

"Oh, boy. For a 'prince', you're pretty dense, aren't you?" The animal incredulously shook his head. "We've been searching for you for years, and now that every person in this single group has gathered...we make our mark."

"Make your mark? You have no purpose here, no fight with them. Leave them out of it," Caelan spat, chest heaving with hard breaths.

"My father talked a lot of how satisfying it was almost eighteen years ago while you were out doing your rounds, gracing your subjects, getting them used to the idea of you returning home. He said the whispers of it were all about your soon-to-be bouncing joys that you so desired to meet." The wolf stepped over Solenne and slowly walked forward, his dark eyes trained on Caelan. "He told me of how the people were so excited about the reign of the true family coming back. I can only imagine how ecstatic you were, names you might have picked out, but a future without your beloved wasn't something you pictured, not for a long time, at least. They always told you she was on the verge of dying during childbirth, right?" The wolf tsked, licking his lips. "What your mother conveniently forgot to mention was how sweet your wife's blood tasted. We watched the life drain from her eyes, and now I can only imagine how much sweeter it will be to drain yours."

With a roar, Caelan charged full speed at the animal, who kept his weight steady. They fell through the open, cracked window into the night, leaving Sabina and Cammie inside to their own devices.

Cammie's wide eyes filled with disbelief that slowly shifted to immense fear. "What do we do?" she asked, breathing shallowly.

"We—" Sabina's words halted. "We take it one step at a time."

"And that step is?" Cammie prodded, the anxiety getting more frantic.

Before Sabina could respond, there was the low sound of growling. More wolves had entered the space, coming into formation around the girls.

"We can't let them get Hannah," Cammie whispered to Sabina. "She's practically more dead than we are."

Cammie turned her gaze away, back to the beings that wanted them dead. All of them were monstrous in size, way bigger than that of a regular wolf. They were in a variety of colors, ranging from browns to blacks to even an auburn fur color, but the one indistinguishable feature that all of them shared was the pointy canines.

"You don't have to kill us," Sabina said, speaking slowly. "Just because that one guy is kind of insane in his pursuit of violence doesn't mean that you have to be too."

The wolves continued staring blankly.

"We could call a truce?" Sabina offered, holding up her hands. "I think we'd all be in favor of that."

"Truces are for people who want peace," one wolf argued.

The surrounding others nodded in agreement, and Cammie felt anxiety clutch her throat.

"But why don't you want peace? We haven't done anything to you," Cammie intercepted boldly, even though every single limb in her body stiffened. Holding herself upright was no easy feat, but she told herself to remain calm. *They can probably smell weakness.*

"Your mere existence threatens everything. That's all the proof we need to kill you. If you die, then our problems are easier."

"Is that what your boss told you?" Sabina asked.

One of them huffed. "Our orders are our business. As for you..." He stepped closer, baring his teeth. "...your time here is over."

All Cammie saw was a flash of fur charging at Sabina. A scream was in her throat, but there was absolutely nothing she could do to stop it. Her mind flashed with concern, with fear, with regret. As she yelled for help, there was nothing but the continued gurgling of Solenne's crimson breathing and a hand shoving Cammie away. *James.*

"Go over there. Get out of the way," he instructed, charging against the animal that held Sabina captive.

Cammie nodded, forcing her jelly-like legs to move. Her knees met the crimson-stained floor where Solenne lay, her glassy eyes focusing on nothing. After a moment, they turned on Cammie.

Solenne spoke so quietly Cammie wasn't sure she heard her right.

"What did you say?" Cammie leaned in closer.

Solenne's breath tickled her ear. "*Heal me,*" she gurgled.

Cammie's eyebrows furrowed. "What are you talking about? I can't."

Solenne gave a small smile. "But you can. It is in you."

Sudden movement caught Cammie's eye, and she turned. Sabina's hair was a wild display, and her entire shirt was tainted with death, remnants of fleshy tissue adorning it like accessories. Cammie bit back the bile rising in her throat as Sabina knelt next to her, grabbing her hand.

"What do we do?" Sabina asked. "Is there anything we can do?"

James followed behind, his fingers clutching the hilt of a bloody knife. He stood next to Cammie, on the other side, and she felt her heart almost evaporate at his nearness.

The rest of the wolves had scattered, but she didn't know where to.

Cammie shrugged, shaking her head. "I can't think of anything. She keeps asking me to heal her, but I don't understand what she means by that. I can't..."

"You can," Solenne rasped. Blood trickled down her lips, continuing the waterfall to her neck where a giant pool already rested. "I released the hold I had. Your abilities are fine now. You can access them to become your fullest self. Your *Amarian* self."

"Don't waste your breath on this," Cammie said. Her face contorted into a frown, and her eyes struggled to keep the multitude of tears at bay. "You need your strength."

Solenne choked out a laugh, a small smile curling at the sides of her lips. "There is no more strength left in me, my dear. Not this time."

"But your herbal remedies," Cammie said, rising. "Surely, with the right combination, there's a way to fix this, a way to make this better. If that's what you mean by healing, I'll do it."

"Not that kind of healing, my dear, and besides, I only asked you to...to make me more comfortable."

Cammie scrunched her nose. "But why would you need to be more comfortable? You need to be healed. Sabina, tell her. Tell her she needs to be healed."

A conflicted expression passed over Sabina's face as she stared at Solenne before turning her gaze to Cammie. "I can't decide that for her, Cammie," Sabina said firmly.

Cammie's face fell. "What do you mean?"

"Only she can decide it. It's her choice. Not yours. Not mine."

"She's right," James said. "It's not any of your choices. Only Solenne's."

Solenne blinked, her eyes out of focus as she angled her head in James's direction. "She has the gift of healing. I know it. I can sense her Amarian blood now. Can't you?"

James looked at Cammie as if for the first time. The way his eyes were searching her face, it was as if he wanted to memorize this exchange and bottle it up for another time. "Do it," he instructed, bending down to Cammie's side. His face was so close to hers that she could practically taste his breath. "Heal her."

"But I can't," Cammie uttered, bottom lip quivering. "What she's asking me to do...it isn't possible. Why can't you do it?" Her eyes were filled to the brim with unshed tears, yet a stubborn few lurched to the floor.

"I can heal smaller wounds but nothing of this magnitude. Solenne believes in you. Now it's your turn. You just need to believe you can," James whispered to Cammie, and for a moment in time, their previous troubles faded away. "Honor this wish for her even if you can't physically obtain it. Honoring it in her last moments will do her some good. She can pass with peace."

James grasped Cammie's hand. The simple act alone of him touching her was enough to set her entire body on fire.

"Even though it's a lie?" Cammie questioned softly. "How does that help?"

"To her...it's the most beautiful truth there is. In what will probably be the last moment you have here...you want to be comfortable. If she thinks you healing her will bring some comfort, out of respect, I think you should do as she asks."

"But—"

"We know the truth," James interrupted, his voice soft. "That's all that matters. And we believe in you."

Sabina looked at Cammie, forcing a smile. "You can do this....whatever doing this is."

"If you three are quite done," Solenne hacked, a spittle of more crimson overflowing from her lips.

"What exactly do you need me to do?" Cammie removed her hand from James's and slowly raised them above Solenne's gushing wound.

"You need to feel the wound," Solenne instructed.

Cammie's face twisted. "How do I do that?" The question hung in the air, and the answer seemed to be on the other end of the world, far away from her grasp.

"You feel the wound with your heart," Solenne added. "You allow yourself to connect with it, the deepest recess of pain, and you bring forth...light. You think of the purest thing you can...and you watch as nature does its course."

With furrowed brows, Cammie nodded then let her hands fall on top of Solenne's wound.

Solenne let out a hiss of breath, inhaling sharply. "Now think of a moment where you felt absolutely wounded, and channel that into the wound."

Cammie's eyes flickered at the thought. It was easy to find.

The moment when he called me beneath him, that will do it. It was hard to forget how her heart had shattered into a million pieces at the hands of the one who had held it.

Another stubborn tear fell, but she didn't wipe it away. "Okay, I'm there. What...now?"

"Now, you channel the light. You channel the peace to that wound, to that moment. I believe you can. You just have to believe in yourself."

Cammie met Sabina's eyes with uncertainty, biting on her lower lip with such intensity that she tasted a trickle of blood on her tongue.

"I believe in you," Sabina mouthed.

Cammie broke out into a slow grin, and she touched the wound with more intensity. As her nose scrunched in concentration, it felt like every organ in her body was putting all of its focus to the wound. Cammie shut her eyes. She could feel her pulse shifting, accelerating as she went back to the moment where her entire heart had shattered like glass.

She could see herself, angry and afraid and betrayed, and she channeled all the peace and love and forgiveness she could muster.

Her fingers thrummed with something indescribable, and Cammie hesitantly opened her eyes.

Beyond her wildest dreams and outlandish imaginations, she never would have predicted this. Underneath Cammie's dainty, bloodstained hands was a golden light. It shone with the force of a thousand suns, peeking through her fingers like an eye in a keyhole wanting to know the mysteries behind the door.

The radiant gold only grew as she removed her hands, dancing around Solenne's wound. It entered the punctured skin with care, gently caressing the tarnished tissue. It didn't need prompting or instruction. The task had been made aware long before Cammie's hands even laid bare to it.

Shifting colors before their eyes, from the golden yellow to the light lilac, the wound was sealed shut. An explosion of light came from it, sending Cammie flying backward and James soon after.

Her head hit the ground with such force that she saw stars. A blur followed as she opened her eyes again, James's face hovering over her.

His eyes pinched in concern. "Are you okay?" he asked.

The sudden nearness made her pulse race, and she nodded swiftly. James moved out of the way, sitting beside Cammie. When Cammie's eyes found Sabina, she was shocked to see that Sabina hadn't moved. She wasn't even stunned by the exchange. She was completely fine.

Cammie focused her eyes back on Solenne, her heart in her throat. *What did I do?*

CHAPTER THIRTY-ONE

SABINA

SABINA FELT A SUDDEN HEAVINESS in her hands.

With slow movements, she looked down, breath in her throat. Where there once was nothing, she now held a circular shield.

Sabina dropped the object, and it disintegrated into the floor, completely gone.

Cammie's hands shook. "What happened?" she blurted. She whipped around to Sabina. "How did you get that? How did I even—" Looking down at her hands with horror, Cammie stopped speaking.

"You are your father's daughters," Solenne uttered with pride. She laid still, but the smile was clear on her face as was the pain in the twinge of her eyes. "You healed the wound. What you could.... The interior damage is too great. But cosmetically...you healed." Solenne turned to Sabina. "And as for you...you channeled a weapon from that same light."

"Impossible," James breathed. "No one of our kind can summon gifts like this. Healing from nothing? Not even a remedy? And you..." His frightened, astonished eyes lingered on Sabina for a moment too long. "You summoned a weapon from nothing, out of emotion. As powerful as we are, we can only conjure from what's physically there. But this..."

"...is the prophecy unfolding before our eyes," Solenne finished softly, the glee in her eyes undiminished.

"But there's supposed to be three," James countered. "Where's the third?"

Solenne coughed again, but this time, no blood rushed to the surface. "I told you who she was. How are you not so quick to believe after everything I've shown you?"

Cosmic horror catapulted across Cammie's face. "You can't be telling me that Hannah is one of you guys? That we are.... Amarian? It doesn't make any sense."

Sudden yelling from outside jolted their attention.

Sabina slowly stood. "What's going on out there?"

James moved and went closer to the window, sparing a glace back to the three women. "The fight's getting worse. More guys joined to help Caelan, but I don't know who they are." He faced the window again, his fist clenching at his side.

Sabina walked to where James was standing, an incredulous smile on her lips. "It's Hannah's crew, the one she's been talking to us about forever. I met them earlier. They're good guys...albeit a little scary at first, but they mean well."

She could make out the faint outline of guys fighting in the dark. The one who was quick to judge her at first—Will—dodged a snarling wolf full of teeth, doing a quick spin in the air before landing on the wolf's back, plunging a dagger into their skin. The sharp howling whine ricocheted through the house, and Will smiled, wiping his weapon clean on his shirt before charging at the next one.

"Are you ready, Sabina?" James asked, a smile tugging at his lips.

She was almost knocked off her feet. "Ready for what? If you want to go help them, by all means..." She gestured at the chaos outside with a grim frown.

"*We*," James corrected. "We are going to help them."

"We?" Sabina sputtered. "What in the world are you talking about?"

"What you did could have been a trick of the eye, but if this is really a gift you have...it could be of some use to us. We could actually win this...with you on the battlefield."

Sabina could barely move then with James's hand on her shoulder. He spoke with such confidence, even though Sabina felt about ready to vomit. She could barely understand what had just happened, and he wanted her to channel it to fight Fae?

"I can't," she replied with a shake of her head. "I don't even know how to fight or how to summon again."

"Then you don't have to," James said, "but we could use an extra set of hands." He turned to Solenne. "Where do you keep your weapons? There must be some here."

She gestured to the closet off the far end of the hallway. After rummaging through it, James pulled out two swords, still in sheaths.

He handed one to Sabina, his face entirely serious. "I hope you're ready to learn some combat, city girl."

CHAPTER THIRTY-TWO

HANNAH

SHE WAS COMPLETELY SHROUDED IN darkness.

Panic gripped her heart as she lurched forward. Her head was pounding, but her gut was completely churning. Something was going on.

Trapped between the blankets and the smothering heat, Hannah grasped for some feeling of where she was. Sweat glistened on her hand from the moonlight shining through the window. A tingling sound rang in her ears, so sharp that it felt like it pierced the eardrum when she ripped off the blankets.

As the ringing in her ears got louder, she rose to her feet from the rickety bed. Louder and louder, it went, and she gritted her teeth against it, willing it to stop.

She stumbled to the door, pulling it with one hand. When it didn't open, she took a breath and released then tried again. She smelled wood in her nostrils, heard splintering against the backdrop of the ringing, and felt something against her feet.

Little pieces of wood lay scattered among her toes, and when she peered closer, she realized then. She had broken the door. It had completely fallen off of its hinges.

A glimmer of light appeared from around the corner as she stepped over the splintered pieces, but the closer she got, the farther away it felt.

Sound was warped, and she could smell copper pennies combined with pungent sweat. Another scent came through, that of roses and lilies. She followed it blindly as she entered the living room, her vision still constricted.

A woman with dark hair sat next to another, but the more Hannah blinked, the more unchanging things became.

Charcoal colored her vision, and the woman's skin became paler as she stared. Her hands were coated with a color so dark it resembled pebbles, but she was...crying.

Noticing her presence, the woman looked up with shocked eyes, asking, "Hannah? Are you okay?"

As the woman's voice flooded her brain, memories upon memories surfaced of brown hair, a deep smile, and eyes so dark it was the color of cocoa itself. Cammie. It was Cammie.

"I can't see anything," Hannah slurred. Panic was brutal in the way it clenched around her nerves, sending anxiety spiraling through her veins.

"What are you talking about?" Cammie asked, rising to her feet. "Are you okay?"

"Color," Hannah said, wincing. The light above burned her eyes, and no matter how hard she squinted, the feeling never subsided. "I can't see color. I went to sleep seeing color, and now...everything is layered differently."

As she cautiously opened her eyes, the words were still true. What was once vibrant, earthy colors had now faded into nothing but a dull gray, with some aspects flowing into shadows. In the corners of her eyes, she could feel the haze of violet against the backdrop of the ringing in her ears.

"Do you need to sit down?" Though she spoke quietly, it was as if Cammie's voice itself was magnified through a megaphone, so shrill it made Hannah jump.

"Stop talking," Hannah uttered through gritted teeth.

"Let me help you," Cammie said, her voice echoing in Hannah's ears.

"Shut up!" Hannah screamed, covering her ears. "Just shut up already."

Sound was now her enemy, and it became apparent that her body would be as well. Layers of sweat appeared on her forehead, and her insides felt like a furnace was lit and the water to cool them was nowhere to be found.

"Solenne, what's wrong with her eyes?" Cammie looked with horror at Hannah, taking a few steps back.

The woman on the floor stared at Hannah, and then the ever-present guilt came gnawing back in her stomach. *Before, I had the nerve to tackle the woman... Did I do this to her?*

"Just...sit down, calm your breathing. I know you're in shock. Calm down, please. Just sit down." The woman sounded like she was on the brink of death, but her face was full of light.

All of it became intertwined, so loud, too much for Hannah to keep containing. "I'm going outside," she said finally.

Maybe there, I'll find light. And color.

"How do I stop her?" Cammie asked.

"There's nothing you can do. Let her go," Solenne said.

The farther away Hannah got from the noise, the more her ears quieted, but the twinkling of glass hitting her foot made her pause. As she looked down and then up, she realized the window had been broken, but had it been broken when she was awake? *No*, she told herself, shaking her head. Overreacting, overthinking was the mantra as she opened the door to the outside.

Her eyes adjusted to the absence of the moon as utter chaos waved hello.

The blur of figures moving would have passed too fast for the average human eye, but this...was different for Hannah. Every move that flowed in her line of vision was slowed down, as if someone had a remote and were toying with the speed. Wolves attacked friends, and in the distance, a few of them were gaining the upper hand.

She couldn't see fully, but she could smell the pine, bark, and hint of lilac. Another scent, then, the smell of sword lilies.

As she entered the fold, to her right, the smell grew deeper. A woman with dark hair moved wildly with another beast, her sword in sync with her body as she dodged and attempted to swing. In one sweep, she used her leg, tripping the animal and leaping to plunge the weapon into its side. With wide eyes, muttering under her breath, she looked up, eyes locking with Hannah.

"You're awake," she said. "Why are you here? Go inside. You're going to get hurt." Another wolf growled behind her, and the woman turned around, unleashing the sword from the now dead animal, swinging it wildly. "Tony," she called out. "Get Hannah inside. She's not able to fend for herself. She's just standing here. I don't want her to get hurt."

The gentle tone was like a wrecking ball to her mind, and memories shattered. Sabina, the girl who would never dare do anything violent, was holding...and wielding...a sword.

Sabina faced the animal now, her back to Hannah.

"Why are you out here?" Hannah exclaimed.

Sabina huffed then stabbed the animal in front of her in one go, a shadowy liquid protruding from its chest. It fell against the weapon limply, and she groaned, shoving it off. The dead animal fell to the ground in a puddle of wetness. Her weapon dripped with blood, but she didn't dare bother cleaning it off.

"If you won't help, then go inside," Sabina said.

A mass of emotions exploded behind Hannah's newfound headache, and she couldn't stop herself from blurting, "What in the abyss was that? How did you learn combat so quickly? All your life prepared you for was teatime and politics."

Sabina rolled her eyes, twirling her sword in the air. "Tony," she shouted again. "Get her inside!"

Before Hannah could process or respond, Sabina was already throwing her sword in mid-air. Hannah watched in awe as it pierced the throat of another wolf, who fell on its back with no warning.

A hard grip on her shoulder sent Hannah reeling, fist at the ready.

Tony gripped a bloody weapon in his free hands. "We don't have time to talk. You need to get inside."

"No," Hannah muttered, the headache growing even stronger.

Tony swallowed, eyes full of something she couldn't read before they went to his weapon. "Are you going to help us or go inside? You only have two options. I can't stand to see you hurt."

Nothing else was said until Tony handed her his weapon.

"Why are you giving me this?" Hannah asked, the words barely leaving her tongue. "You need it to fight."

"There are more weapons in the shed over there." He pointed to the little square building lingering in the distance. "You can get one there since you won't take mine."

Hannah quirked a brow.

Tony shook his head. "Go," he told her. "I'll cover you."

Someone shouted her name, but she didn't respond, instead opting to run to the shed. The cries and whines were loud behind her, but the goal wasn't to stop. It was to keep running. Despite everything in her that told her to go back, to help, she knew she'd be of no help unless she had her hands on a massive weapon.

The charcoals and tints of steel in her vision did not aid her running. It only added to the cumbersome task of trying to navigate while half blind. The trees—what she assumed were trees—blended together. *How can I be of any help to them if I can barely see while running? How can I hold a weapon?*

As more and more thoughts spiraled, Hannah willed her feet to keep moving, unsteady as they were. She needed the weapons. She needed—

A man stood next to the shed, hands in his pockets, but even blurriness couldn't shake away memories.

With a smile so wicked it could kill, Nyx stood there. "We keep meeting like this, don't we?" The dark chuckle danced in the air, sending goosebumps up Hannah's arms.

Hannah turned, searching for Tony. He was in the middle of fighting off another wolf, her presence forgotten.

"I don't know what you're doing here, but you need to leave. You need to stop all of this." Words were like chalk in her mouth. Stupid fear had stolen her breath, and every single muscle locked in place.

"I think you know more than you're letting on," Nyx stated, cracking his knuckles. "Either that or you're just oblivious to the story going on around you, a story that you're a part of."

Hannah scoffed. "The only story I'm a part of is getting kidnapped by you. The rest of this doesn't concern me. I don't know how Cammie and Sabina got tangled up in this, but it needs to end. Leave Caelan alone. Leave everyone here alone. Go home. Let *us* go home."

"You really are oblivious, aren't you?" Nyx shook his head and stepped away from the shed, taking a step in Hannah's direction.

Instinctively, she stepped back, putting more distance between them.

"You know there's two sides to a war, don't you? I'm sure you've heard of the stories in school, stories of war and death and good and evil and all of that stuff. This…" Nyx did a wide sweep of his hands. "…is all part of that. Everything you're seeing here is part of a feud that existed long, long before you were born, long before your father, Caelan, was born."

"He isn't my father," Hannah declared boldly, mouth twisting. "You've confused me with someone else."

"I'm sure all of you had the same reaction when you were told he was your father, but something you do not know about me is that I'm also Amarian. I'm like James. I'm like Caelan. I'm like *you*."

"Stop comparing me to something I'm not. I told you already. *You have the wrong person.*"

Nyx stepped closer, and this time, she could smell the pine, musky scent of cologne, but this time, there was something deeper, so much so that it was an undertone, a sweetness like candy and a blend of cedar.

"You can smell it, can't you? The violet."

Hannah didn't respond, her breath caught in her throat. She shook her head.

"Don't lie to me," Nyx said, voice deep. "I can hear your heartbeat. I can see the blood rushing to your neck before it even fully gets there. You're lying."

"That's physically impossible," Hannah blurted. "No one can tell if someone is lying by hearing their heartbeat. Not without some kind of tool, or—"

"Your doubt will be your downfall."

The words were spoken plainly, but Hannah could sense the meaning behind them. She felt like something had chewed her up and spat her out all in the same breath.

"But channeled through to truth, your destiny could be that much greater."

More words were on the tip of her tongue, but she never got them out, not before Nyx spoke again.

"A Lunar princess hasn't been heard of in a very long time.. The last one there was...she was outlawed, banished to never roam free again, but you, Hannah, with the right training, under the right queen, you could do marvelous, unspeakable things. You could harness your talents, harness your *beast*. We could make something beautiful together, and I'm sure if you took my offer, the queen would be more than willing to gift her favor on you. All that we need is for you to end this nonsense with Caelan. Convince him to live a life of peace. Convince him to give up his throne. It's that simple, really."

"You think I have more control over him than I actually do? You also think that I would willingly follow and believe whatever you say when I don't understand it? You allowed your friends or minions or whatever they are to beat the crap out of me, starve me to where I almost died—"

"And I apologize for that now," Nyx said.

"—and now you're expecting me to just throw that knowledge out completely and bow down to some 'Amarian queen' for your pleasure? No. I don't fully understand what's going on, but you would have to be absolutely stupid if you'd think we'd *ever* work together. And if, for the sake of this conversation, Caelan was my father, I'm supposed to completely abandon him and go on some merry quest to put you and your ruler on a pedestal?" Dizziness was near. As her vision tripled and multiplied, more slivers of violet crept from the corner. "No. You can take yourself, your queen, and your stupid offer and shove it up your Amarian backside."

Nyx's face twisted into a sneer, and he cracked his neck before lifting two fingers in the air. "She made her choice. Bring him out."

Through the opening of the trees, there were figures. Three that she was sure of. No, four. Someone was walking behind the group.

Two men were dragging someone, but his face was so brutally battered that she couldn't identify who he was until he let out one hollow breath.

Will.

With one eye bruised and practically closed shut and the other struggling to stay open, Will hung limply between the two beings that held him upright. Blood dripped from his temple down his chin, lines of pain etched in the creases of his cheeks as he winced.

"We decided that your little friend here got a little too bold for his own good. He stabbed and killed several of my dear companions, so I wanted to show you the present we did to his face. I had been storing up this anger for a long time. Figured I'd put it to some good use."

Hannah could barely hold back the choked gasp. "Do nothing more to him. He's barely standing."

"If you want him to stay breathing, then you will do as I say. Each wrong step you take, he will get another punch. If you want your friend's internal organs to continue staying intact, then I would suggest you listen."

Hannah bit the inside of her cheek, tears threatening to spill. She hated crying, absolutely couldn't stand it.

Willing the weakness away, she stared Nyx down. "What are you suggesting I do? I don't want to join you."

"I think you'll change your mind once you realize we are the only group who can help you channel and calm your wolf in this very moment. Everyone else is busy."

"Man, you really are insane," Hannah said, the chortled laugh escaping her. "I'm no wolf."

"Beggars can't be choosers," Nyx shot back. "Now, do as I say. Inhale, and channel the wolf."

"I don't even know how to do that," Hannah said, panic clutching at her throat. "I don't even know how to do what you're asking."

Nyx raised his hand again, and the one guy lingering behind the group walked to the front, coming to a stop directly in front of Will. "Give it your worst," he instructed.

"No! No! Leave him alone. Leave—"

The screaming and pleading weren't enough as the man plunged his fist into Will's gut.

A shattering sound erupted from Will's lips as a liquid protruded onto the grass. Hannah's eyes were still seeing gray, but she didn't need colored glasses to know the green was now stained crimson.

"Now," Nyx said, his eyes gleaming with a hint of coal, "have you made a different choice?"

Hannah was silent, eyes boring into Will's as one man held his head up by the scalp of his hair. More blood spewed from his lips, his teeth stained with darkness. She still could not decipher color other than blackness, but the pain radiated through his facial features all the same.

"Don't tell them anything," Will said, his words teetering on the edge of groaning and barely incoherent.

The man yanked his head back, and Will cried out in agony. "Did we tell you to speak?" he asked Will, tugging. "Huh? You had something to say? *Speak*, Lunar!"

Lunar.

"Is that what you call the wolves?" Hannah dared to ask, her limbs trembling.

Nyx's smile grew. "Very good. You're learning, and your friend here is one of them."

Suddenly, a very clear memory appeared in Hannah's mind's eyes. The mechanic shop. The fighting. The glowing eyes.

Truth radiated from the pain etched on Will's face, but his gaze never wavered once. "This part of what he's saying is true, Hannah." Will spat again, more blood flowing like paint onto a canvas into the grass. "But anything else? He's a snake. This queen he's talking about...she ruined Natrellum. She's locked behind bars where she can't ever hurt anyone again. He's trying to get you to go along with it. Don't. I know you, Hannah. You're my friend. We love you. Tony..." Will stopped speaking, his breath caught. "...he loves you. Whatever you are, you don't have to find it out. Not like this."

Nyx's smile hardened, his face like glass. "He spoke his part. Now...again." He waved Will off with his hand.

Absolute horror filled Hannah's bones. "No," she shouted, tears actually stinging this time.

Before she could even rush forward, the man used his fist again, a deeper punch to Will's gut. A howling cry resounded, and more crimson splattered. Will couldn't even catch his breath. The hands were too fast. *One. Two. Three.* He dropped to his knees as the man used his left foot and kicked.

Will fell forward in a heap of blood and dirt as it streaked his face like paint. With unsteady hands, Will tried to push himself up, but before he could even begin to rise, Nyx was already there, his foot crushing against Will's backbone. Will's chin met the earth once again, and more blood spilled onto the stained grass.

"I'll let this foot off of you if you cooperate," Nyx said amidst Will's struggle. When Will didn't reply, Nyx let his foot rise and crouched to Will's level. He gripped Will's hair without mercy, his voice near Will's ear. "You've brought this on yourself by speaking. By not aiding her. You can make all of this stop if you help us channel the wolf that she needs."

Will let out a dark chuckle, spitting onto the grass as breathing became more constricted. "I refuse to let you cloud a choice of her destiny because of what your evil will bring. There's nothing you could do to me that would make me feel differently." Will inhaled then turned his head. He let his almost swollen eye lock with Nyx's. "I would rather die."

"Is that so?" The threat lingered in the air, and Hannah could feel the electricity behind it.

As Nyx raised his hand, Hannah dove in front of Will. She felt the cold sting against her cheek before she saw it.

"Such a selfless act. Perfect for a princess but weak for a queen," Nyx remarked, tsking. "If we want you to be a warrior, an ally, we need to channel deeper than selflessness, my dear. We need your rage. Apparently, just hitting him isn't enough. Fear isn't your motivator, but despair...that I can work with."

The one man who was so quick to beat Will fumbled through his pockets. There was a flash of silver. Her gut fell to the dirt as the object, something she could finally recognize, shone under the moon.

A dagger.

"You don't need to stab him," Hannah pleaded. "You don't need to hurt him any further."

The man ignored her words, bringing the weapon higher. The blade slid along Will's neck, right where his vein erratically throbbed, just enough to where it contacted the skin, but it hadn't pierced through. Yet.

"Is that so?" Nyx asked.

"I'll do anything," Hannah said, the truth resounding in her gut. This time, she meant it.

Wicked satisfaction glimmered in Nyx's eyes. "That's exactly what I want to hear." He gestured at the man holding the weapon, who dropped it to his side. "Take him away. Hold him until this entire fight is over, and then we will figure out what to do about Caelan."

The men started moving, yanking Will with them.

He struggled against their grip, his stare desperate against Hannah's. "Please, don't do this. I'm Lunar. I can take care of myself. My body will heal. You don't even know how strong you are yet. It's too risky. A sudden shift, there's no telling what it will do. It could kill you. Please, Hannah. *Don't—*"

One of the men released his monstrous grip, using his free hand to smash against Will's temple. Will's body hung limply as he drifted into complete unconsciousness.

"No!" Rage pierced through Hannah's tears, and she turned her angry gaze on Nyx as they took Will away. "You're a monster."

"And he'll live," Nyx replied effortlessly.

An unspoken condition hung in the air. *Only if I do as he says.*

"Tell me how to do this," Hannah said. The words were simple, but her mind screamed with fear.

"It isn't something that can be taught," Nyx said. "It's something *within* you that needs to come out. It's always been a part of you. It's just your job to find it."

"How full of wisdom you are," Hannah said, the sardonic comment thick on her tongue.

"Sometimes, it is that way. Depends on the day and if cooperation is part of the equation." Nyx clicked his tongue thoughtfully.

"So it can't be taught. You're telling me that all Amarian Lunars are just born with this innate ability to shift? They aren't coaxed into it?"

"From the moment baby Lunars can walk, they find themselves in the best way by learning how to identify who their wolf is. It's an innate part of who they are, and it shows up in their everyday lives long before the first shift. Some wolves have a quieter side, so they're usually more drawn to the isolated spaces. Some wolves are more on the rougher side or the more adventurous side. Do any of those sound familiar to you?"

As Nyx's words settled in her brain, the two rang out louder than the rest. "Rougher and adventurous. Ever since I was a child, there's always been some part of me that can never sit still, as if there's always something...missing. I feel more at home here in the forest than I ever did at home. Not that I felt...like I wasn't human. More like nature knew me better than I knew myself." Hannah turned her gaze back to Nyx, who, for the first time since meeting him, had a softened gaze.

"I'd say you found her."

The gentleness in his tone startled her to her core. There was no malice, no sense of waiting to pounce. Only simple, utter pride.

"Now you channel her, and before you ask me how again, you channel her by connecting with that part of yourself. Listen to your senses. Listen to what your body is telling you. What are you feeling? What are you smelling? All of it, no matter how simple it seems, will take you closer. Lean into it, and take your time."

"Such a stark difference from when you were trying to get me to hurry, otherwise Will was going to die." The anger bubbled to the surface.

"There. See. Channel that. Lean into *that*."

Even though everything in her body told her she was being crazy, that none of this could be real for her, Hannah rolled her eyes and did as he said. She closed them, letting her once defensive hands fall limp at her sides.

Channel the wolf. Where are you? What are you?

In her mind's eye, there was nothing, nothing but the darkness and the sounds of battle cries. She felt stupid, as if the very word was hanging above her on a neon sign for everyone to see, but Will's life was at stake and everyone else's who she cared about. She pushed forward, forcing herself to not be so negative.

She thought of quiet summer days with Tony and the days when her mom had still been around to braid her hair. She thought of the bullies she'd encountered in middle school and the brave boy who had forced them all to run away, and she thought of Sabina and Cammie and a million other things combining with the magnificent scent of pine that lingered in her nostrils. She thought of it all, letting the violet haze grow stronger.

"That's it," Nyx coaxed. "Keep going."

Hannah pushed deeper into it, shutting her eyes tighter until the haze grew so deep that it overshadowed the gray and the charcoal and the silver, blending it all together in such a splendid purple in her mind's eye.

"Hannah…" The voice was heightened, so much so that it sounded like an octave higher than she was used to. "Open your eyes."

The world was different to her as they adjusted to the light. Colors still radiated black and white, but something felt different as she blinked. She could feel the beating of her stubborn heart, but no longer could she feel two feet. *I feel four.* When Hannah looked down, shock bubbled in her throat as eyes settled on paws that could barely fit in her own human palm. The color was so dark she was sure it was black, but there were defined streaks of a color her canine eyes could not pick up. A frightened whine escaped her mouth, and with darting eyes, she started backing away.

"Hannah, it's okay. Calm down. You're going to be okay." With a voice as soft as the barely moving wind in the trees and strong hands, Nyx walked closer, putting his hands up to her snout.

Anger welled up inside, and she couldn't stop herself. The growl exited before she could contain it, and she bared her teeth. *Don't get any closer.*

"You're going to be okay. You just need to calm down." The gentleness in his voice did nothing more than continue to irk her, and she took another step back, a whine at the ready.

"What the hell are you doing?" The voice, so strong and furious, was a voice she could place anywhere. Weapon in hand, there was Tony, stalking across the grass to where Nyx stood.

"I was just helping her," Nyx said, right as Tony's fist collided with his face.

"Like you were. Truly, this might fly with anyone else but not me. Will goes missing, and two of my guys find him with his face barely intact, and you have the nerve to sit here and tell me that this interaction with Hannah is supposed to be helpful? You sent an entire team to kill her family, might I add, and you *forced* her to shift? What kind of monster are you? Huh? Huh?"

Tony's weapon fell to the ground as Tony shoved Nyx. He fell backward on his tailbone, but the fire in his eyes didn't fade.

"One who cares about results," Nyx replied. As he reached his feet, he wobbled, but his gaze still held strong.

"Hannah isn't some sort of test that you can jerk around with. She's never shifted before! You could have killed her."

"She's just fine," Nyx said, gesturing to Hannah.

For the first time since the shift, Tony's eyes turned to Hannah. They lingered, and in it, she sensed and smelled many emotions—love, fear, and...anger. The first was a rose scent that had shifted quickly to an aspen until it melted into charcoal.

Tony tore his eyes away, back to Nyx. "You took her choice away. She's frightened and confused."

"If she's ever to be queen, she needs to have the proper training. She has to learn to push past it, past the fear. Otherwise, she will be nothing more than a weakling. Is that what you want? A weakling for a ruler?"

Tony shook his head, one fist balled at his side. "The queen you worship is *nothing* compared to the queen Hannah will be. If she has the choice, I know she would be just and true, but you? You're doing nothing but trying to corrupt her. Your greed and lust for power might cause you to trip up a few people, start a few wars if that's what you're after, but Hannah is not so easily swayed. She does what she wants under her own authority. No one else's. *Not* yours. Your intentions might seem honorable to you in some twisted way, but true Amarians don't play by bending the rules."

Another sparkle glinted in Nyx's eyes as he found his footing. "I think it might be safe to say that you don't know

Hannah at all. Shifting changes the person. You might be quick to find that she's not the person you thought she was."

Tony bared his teeth. "I guess we'll find out. Right, Hannah?"

With the wind in her ears, tickling her fur like a hand on carpet, Hannah allowed her legs to push her farther than she had ever gone before.

The arguing was too much. She needed to find Will. She needed to get away.

The colors seemed brighter in her line of vision, though they still ranged from the grayish black to a whiteish hue. With her heightened senses, she could hear calling from behind her, and noises shifted and blended until it was just one loud echo of concern.

Her paws clenched against the dirty mud, slick and smooth, as she clambered to find her way in this mass of darkness. More sounds resounded the farther she traveled until one bellowing cry came through the loudest.

Sabina.

In her mind's eye, Hannah could hear it, Sabina crying out in pain. In her head, she knew it was several miles away, but that didn't stop the smells from appearing. It was a tangle of sorts to where she had to wade through each one carefully—rose, lilac, pine, peonies, and a burnt orange. The burnt orange scent was the strongest as Hannah entered the clearing.

A wolf had Sabina pinned down to the damp grass, drips of saliva falling onto her hair as it bared its teeth. Her face was locked in determination, but her eyes—they radiated the fear. Sabina used her hands to push on the wolf, but there was no budge.

With adrenaline thick in her bones, Hannah lunged forward on all fours. Speed became a magnet while she locked her target in place. Her canines met fur as her teeth clamped on the wolf that held Sabina captive, the force knocking them both to a nearby tree.

The wolf whimpered in her grasp, eyes darting to look straight at Hannah. "The...princess...wolf is true," he whispered against shallow breaths.

Hannah wasn't sure how to respond if she even could. Words felt far from her grasp in this form, and with every step she took and every move she made, it felt like learning it would be impossible.

As Hannah stared blankly, flesh still in teeth, the other wolf looked on expectantly, as if merely gesturing Hannah to speak would be enough. She removed her hold on him, stepping away.

"What? Is the little princess too scared to move? Too scared to do anything? Some Amarian leader we have here..." Despite being wounded, the wolf still had a lot of gall, making sure his words pierced Hannah directly in the heart.

She heard another growl, and her eyes lifted. More wolves had gathered, all of their fangs and pointed teeth right at her.

"You don't really think you're as strong as us, do you? Not with *that* being your first shift."

Looking down at her newfound form, Hannah could feel the fear rising, but something entangled with it, something like courage. She let her tongue slide against her canine teeth and then slowly opened her mouth. It felt foreign, an obstinate idea in the face of danger, but she knew from her experience on two legs that stalling in a difficult situation could usually put the fire to a mere blaze, and if nothing else, she *had* to try.

"You...don't...know...me."

The four simple words took more effort than she intended to flow freely, the sound coming out in a weird blend of chiming bells, blending with a softness Hannah had never heard in her voice before. *This talking thing will take some getting used to.*

For a moment, there was complete silence, and Hannah felt a shrill of pride in her gut. Maybe she had gotten through to them?

And then she heard it, the sound of raucous laughter, all in unison from the beasts who held their heads back like they were beckoning the moon to appear so the howling could begin.

"Wow, such a statement. Should we all bow down to the princess who has such a complex? You heard her boys. Let's bow."

Mockingly, all the animals bent forward on their legs, their eyes shining with malice.

Hannah felt her eyes watering with angry tears, but she blinked them back as the wolves rose back to a stand.

"She's crying," one wolf howled, slapping his paw on the wet grass. "She's actually—"

Words died in his throat as blood bubbled to the surface of his lips, and he fell limp to the ground, the other wolves staring in shock.

Hannah's eyes narrowed, trying to find the cause of his demise.

A single arrow in his side.

Hannah lifted her eyes to the sky. Underneath the covering of a canopy of trees, she could vaguely make out a shadowy figure standing on a branch, arms raised to his face. Another arrow flew, landing in the side of another wolf. The ones gathered around Hannah scattered, but so did the arrows.

One, two, three, four flew as fast as Hannah could blink, their aim true as more wolves fell to the ground with pained howls. Even the one Hannah had pinned to the ground found his footing and scrambled away, barely missing an arrow. Sabina was long gone, no longer pinned to the forest floor.

Through the running, Hannah could make out three figures. The first was Sabina, back in combat, the earlier fear forgotten. The second was Tony, running through the clearing with another at his side.

Nyx.

Nyx stared with an open mouth at the multitude of his crew running with their tails between their legs, far away from the flying arrows, and at those who had met their untimely demise far sooner than he had planned.

Even Caelan had the upper hand, his sword running clean through one wolf he was sparring with. As his eyes lifted to the new chaos that was unfolding, a smile appeared at the corner of his lips when gaze found Nyx. With strong steps, he cleaned off his sword and made his way to his enemy.

"You've lost, Nyx," Caelan said, breath heavy with exertion. "You might as well give it up. We've already won."

Stubborn determination lit itself ablaze in Nyx's hardened gaze. "I'd be pressed to say that so boldly. I can still win this."

Caelan spread his arms out wide. "Look around you. Your group of soldiers have fallen. With the group we have, all sparring and the savior who stepped in, you don't stand a chance. Stand. Down."

Nyx let out a chortled laugh. "You're seriously asking me to abandon my pursuit? For you? You can't be serious."

A sudden *whoosh* sounded from the trees as hard boots hit the ground. All eyes turned to the sound, where a man with blond hair and disheveled clothing held his weapon like treasure—the bow.

"Ah. If it isn't Rigel, here to save the day. I'd be tempted to bow, but you don't possess the crown or any kind of title I could respect. Not anymore." Nyx's lip flickered in disgust as he sized Rigel up and down. "The only good thing you did was deliver James to me unharmed. As far as him escaping, I can blame that on my own idiotic members. But tell me..." Nyx's eyes beheld something like fascination as Hannah watched the entire exchange. "...what triggered you to change sides?"

Rigel's bow never strayed from Nyx's position as he stared with wide eyes. "Maybe because I realized I was wrong to be bought, and I finally see what evil you really are. You told me this man was evil and that he would bring down dominion to the kingdom. The more and more I've watched this entire display, the more I realize the Crown and you...were wrong."

Hannah could smell the guilt in his words, in his tone as he spoke.

Nyx pouted, his bottom lip hanging. "Such touching words. I almost feel tempted to cry and surrender, but beating you offers too much of a reward." The slow, cruel smile spread out over his lips as he stretched out his fingers at his sides before balling them into fists.

"If you take one more step, I will shoot you." Rigel's words were firm, his hand never shaking. "I've already shot and killed half of your crew, and after all the damage you have inflicted, I won't hesitate twice to let this arrow fly. Disobey my words, and just like that, you're nothing. I'd think carefully before you make any sudden movements."

For once, Hannah saw something on Nyx's face that had never appeared before.

Absolute fear.

"And if I listen, what will become of me?"

"You will be taken back to the castle to pay for your crimes," Caelan instructed. "Treason against the true Crown should be fit enough of a punishment."

Rigel aligned his gaze with Caelan's. "I'd be inclined to agree. We shall let the Council decide what to do with the likes of you. Now, kneel."

Nyx bared his teeth. "Absolutely not. I pledged my allegiance to the true queen. Not this abomination walking on two legs."

Rigel let his one hand rest on the stem of the bow, fingers tightening. "Kneel."

And so Hannah watched as Nyx's eyes, full of defeat, blazed brightly with contained rage at Caelan, right as his knees hit the ground.

CHAPTER THIRTY-THREE

CAMMIE

T HE SOUNDS OF HORROR OUTSIDE of the house slowly descended from their crescendo, becoming nothing but quiet.

Cammie stayed at Solenne's side, her hands on her stomach. If her healing gift was clear in this moment, Cammie could not see it.

She wasn't sure how many of the enemies had fallen or what had truly taken place outside of this small refuge, but judging by how many cries had erupted into the night, she was confident that there were many.

Her heart practically climbed out of her chest as shadowy figures approached the house. It was so dark she couldn't make out faces, and momentarily, she wished she had Sabina's gift, the ability to conjure weapons from nothing. She wasn't sure what Hannah's gift was yet, if she even had one, but Cammie trusted Solenne's claims to be true. With the abilities they possessed, they were for sure Amarian.

As her mind drifted onto how close she could get to the weapons closet, Solenne let out a heavy breath. "You can relax, child. It's only your friends."

Sure enough, two figures came into view—Tony and another guy who Cammie wasn't familiar with. In between them was another whose face was so unrecognizable that Cammie did a double take.

"You must be Hannah's friends," Cammie remarked, her eyes never leaving the one in the middle.

Tony nodded, shifting his weight as they stepped over the threshold into the house. "Sabina and James told us you can heal. Do you think this is something that you can do for us?"

Hesitancy rested on Cammie's tongue as many things, but especially the word *no*, wanted to flow from her lips. She had no idea if she would even be capable of reconciling such damage.

As she formed the words aloud, another face appeared in the corridor. She knew those green eyes anywhere. A memory so recent, still so fragile, flashed in her mind. She knew words, unlike the many things told as a child, hurt. Sometimes, the damage of things said could leave a wound so deep that repairing it could take eons, or maybe there was *no* accurate amount of time. As he stared on from his place near the door, she could see something in his gaze that warmed the coldness in her heart.

Belief.

"I can try," she said, to which James gave a soft smile. Her eyes flickered back to Solenne. "If that's okay with you?"

Solenne's breath was shallow, but she still gave a small smile. "Delve into this. It's your gifting. I...will be fine."

Another came to the door. With red hair and worried eyes, as she moved around the group. A shocked gasp escaped her when she took in the man's form in the middle.

"What happened to Will?" Sabina uttered, bringing her hand to her mouth.

Tony's eyes flashed darkly. "Nyx had a brilliant idea to get Hannah to shift. I'm guessing he thought torture would be a good place to start in such a vulnerable moment."

"Shift?" Cammie asked, the word like electricity on her tongue. "Wait, Hannah's one of *them*?" The distaste was clear in her words.

Tony shot her a grimace. "One of us," he corrected. "We aren't savages."

"I didn't mean—"

"What you think of us doesn't matter," Tony interrupted. "Will needs our help."

With Will sporting a face so battered and bruised, Cammie was surprised he was even alive.

"Don't...fight...guys." The hoarse gasp came directly from Will.

Cammie held her breath. He lifted his head weakly, and in the light from the moon, Cammie had to bite her tongue to keep the tears from falling. Bruise after bruise. Blood stained his cheeks. Pain painted over his eyes, and every movement was an effort that someone else would take for granted.

Urgency was near and needed.

"Set him on the floor," Cammie instructed. The sudden stark realization of Solenne in her arms hit her, and she scrambled for a solution.

"I'll hold her," Sabina offered, moving to where Cammie knelt.

"I'll help you." The voice was quiet, but it echoed throughout the room all the same.

Caelan stood at the door in crimson-stained clothes, with tears in his sleeves, but none of that compared to the absolute horror that wrecked itself in his eyes.

Caelan strode across the room with shaky steps until he reached Cammie. He crouched low, his hands slow and purposeful as he reached around to grasp Solenne. Hoisting her ever so gently, he let her rest in his lap as he cradled her head.

"How are you still alive?" he asked, his voice barely a whisper.

More tears flowed from Solenne. "It is Cammie's beautiful gift. She is how I have... survived this far."

Cammie rose to a stand, hugging her arms.

"But the only way you would've—" He stopped speaking, looking over at Cammie. "Healing. You can heal?"

Before she could answer, Solenne said, "Let her show you."

With all eyes on her, Cammie swallowed, doing her best to shove the nerves down. *How am I going to do this with these people watching?*

Tony and the other guy laid Will down, who groaned in pain as his back hit the floor. With cries of agony, Cammie felt her heart pierce. What kind of monster did you have to be to do this to him?

"Whenever you're ready," Solenne said, her voice cracking. More energy was being taken out of her than she needed. Nevertheless, her voice radiated such pride.

Cammie did her best to block out the noise. Even the sounds of breathing felt like too much pressure. It was an ever-constant reminder of prying eyes, eager to see this newfound ability that even she was sure that she couldn't control or even fully conjure.

Cammie slowly brought her hands to Will's core, and he cried out. Guilt prickled her stomach, but she knew she had to keep going.

If he's going to be healed, I need to be brave.

The sentiment rang in her ears as sweat dripped down her skin, anxiety riddling left and right with no kind of relief.

Closing her eyes, Cammie honed her deepest feelings of light into her hands. She thought of peace, of reconciliation as a chill appeared on the back of her neck. Hair raised, but she continued.

Behind her closed eyes, she could feel the heat—light, glorious light—in front of her. Audible gasps filled the room, but Cammie didn't dare lift her hands. She couldn't. Not yet.

She let her hands press even deeper into the wounded area, channeling more light into her hands, and then there was complete silence.

"You actually did it," Tony breathed.

Cammie slowly opened her eyes. All the boys crowded among her, with eyes full of shock and amazement. Cammie had read about spectacles like this, but never in her lifetime did she think she'd be living it.

"She's really Amarian," the other boy said, his eyes alight with something Cammie couldn't decipher. "I knew Hannah was, and James said something about Sabina, but...all three of them—" A sudden expression appeared on his face, and he turned to Tony. "You don't think—"

"The marking is the only way to tell," Tony replied. "As far as I can see, I don't see it directly on her. Without that, we can't jump to conclusions."

"You just aren't looking close enough," Solenne butted in, her eyes fluttering shut. "You can't let your mind wander away from the truth that's right in front of you."

Caelan was staring at Cammie, his eyes practically burning a hole in her head.

Nervous heat lit her cheeks ablaze, and a suddenly familiar feeling arose within her, the same one she'd get as a child whenever she felt uncomfortable in any situation—the urge to hide.

"Why don't we give her some space?" James spoke up, and Cammie met his eyes from across the room. "She did her healing, and by the looks of it, she's been through a lot today. Learning a new Amarian skill takes a lot out of you. I'm sure you all remember your first shift. It's similar here." Giving a pointed look to the two men, he gestured toward the back room. "Let's take Will out there to get some fresh air, see how he's feeling, and give these three some privacy."

With eyes that radiated gratitude, Will shot Cammie a glance before allowing himself to be brought to his feet. He hobbled to the back room, with Tony and the other guy at his side.

James was the last to leave, and his eyes lingered on Cammie for a moment longer before he retreated, following the others.

Sabina and Cammie were the first to make eye contact, and in them, Cammie saw something that mirrored her own tears.

"Just because they have gifts doesn't make them my daughters," Caelan uttered, his cheek twitching. Unshed water pooled at the recesses of his eyes.

"You're so stubborn to the truth," Solenne whispered, her breathing becoming more erratically interrupted.

"I've lost them once already," he choked out, quiet gasps erupting against the stoic facade he carried. "I can't lose them again."

"They will need you to guide them. They will need you to lead them against the ways of the enemy, of the Council's stubborn refusal. You know…they won't take it lightly to you returning home. But like...you have said...it is your destiny. It is your children's destiny. Your biggest role will be to love them, so love them well." Solenne opened her eyes finally, and in them were a million things that couldn't be said in the mere moments and space in this cabin.

"Mom?" Caelan gripped her form tightly, his eyes panicked and stricken.

"I love you, my son," Solenne breathed, heaving one last breath.

A single tear made its way down her cheek, and all that Cammie could make out was the sound of grief clawing its way out by the multitude of weeping screams.

CHAPTER THIRTY-FOUR

HANNAH

Bloodcurdling screams.

That was the noise Hannah heard first once paws became feet.

A sudden chill filled her body and her bones when the air met the skin. Heat flashed across her cheeks as her eyes made their way down. She was completely bare except for the blanket that had been thrown onto her back.

Hannah gripped it tightly, goosebumps forming underneath the fabric. She wasn't sure how much time had passed. A part of her felt like she had been asleep, and she had just now awoken, but there were still certain things she couldn't deny. She had, in so many words, transformed.

What once was human flesh becoming fur and then back again, and her familiar toes wiggled in the dirt. That fact was astounding. She had shifted.

She had shifted.

If she repeated the words enough times, she could almost tell herself she was thinking of another person, of someone more or less like a character in a novel that Cammie loved reading.

It was still pitch-black outside. That alone gave her some idea. It was still night, but even with that small realization, it couldn't stop her from seeing the truth.

Hannah was no ordinary girl. She wasn't human. She was something else entirely.

It would've been so easy to run from the idea. She had done it many times before, but something about this was so tangibly real that she just couldn't. The evidence was plainly staring her in the face. There was nothing left to do but watch.

"She's finally awake," a voice said.

Hannah felt every hair on her neck stand upright. He had had commands to make, and her hair was attentive to it. With each little strand raising, the high-wire emotions became more intense and fluid: fear...and something much deeper.

As she watched his sardonic smirk, a red, hot blazing fire came far too quickly onto her cheeks.

Even though he had caused chaos and ruin far beyond reparation, his demeanor was still intact. Even though he had fallen onto his knees, agreed to a ceasefire and a stubborn sur-render, his grin still held the power of a thousand torches that would willingly burn the world to the ground.

"How can you smile after everything you've done?" The words were hollow and foreign, rage barely containing itself through the words she uttered. Ringing resounded in her ears, and colors were far too bright as she stared at the man who deemed destruction so valuable, like a toy to a child.

"I can't exactly move, can I?" Nyx sneered back at her, his eyes dark with something she couldn't place. His clothes were bloody, torn, and ruffled.

As Hannah's eyes adjusted to the human eyes she didn't know she missed, another figure stood next to Nyx, his face stone. She had missed him entirely, her anger clouding the fact that Rigel was standing there.

From the exchange Hannah witnessed, there was a history there, but whatever history there was, it was long gone, dead and buried.

"Maybe you being unable to move is of your own doing," Rigel replied, his grip on Nyx absolute. On his back rested a pack that held glorious weapons, another set of the bow and arrow that he wielded with ease.

"I'd say it's because of the man who is holding onto me like I have somewhere to go," Nyx retorted. "Definitely not of my doing."

The cabin door swung open. All eyes looked over, and Hannah's eyes met another pair, one that was hollower than hers.

Fresh tears fell down Caelan's face as he stood silent for a moment. No words were needed. Blue grief mangled in orange embers that adorned his cheeks and his eyes. He clenched his fists and before anyone could stop him, he stormed down the steps.

"I should kill you," he shouted.

His words were trembling over themselves. Caelan spoke to no one in particular, and he couldn't even bring his eyes to Nyx.

So much pain. All at the hands of an absolute monster.

"Are we done with formalities now?" Nyx cocked his head at Caelan's display. "Usually, you're the first to stare me right in the face, to tell me my position, my place, and now...you can't even turn to face me with a threat so bold?"

Caelan's head snapped upright, his eyes shining with more than just tears. Wiping his eyes with the back of his hand, Caelan took a breath and then charged.

"Stop!" Rigel cried out, his voice stern. "Think about what you're doing. There's a right place and time and channel for his punishment. I will see that it gets done. I promise you that. After all..." He paused, a flicker of emotion against his harsh mask. "You are my king."

Caelan stopped moving, as if Rigel's words were a force field that held him bound. "He killed my mother," Caelan told him, shooting daggers at Nyx. "His entire legion is the reason my family is dead. He killed my wife, he killed my...mother... and now..." Caelan stopped speaking, his face blank against the words coming out of his mouth.

As if he finally recognized his surroundings, Caelan's eyes met Hannah's vulnerable form. His eyes never lingered on her face for more than a second, as if even looking at her being here, alive in front of him, was too much.

"Rigel," Caelan instructed. "Give Nyx to me. I need you to do me a favor."

Rigel turned to attention. "Anything. What can I do?"

"Take Hannah inside. Have the girls get her some clean clothes, a shower, whatever she needs, and then grab James for me. We have some business to discuss. Tell him he needs to get his goodbyes ready."

Hannah felt her heart quiver. *Goodbyes?*

"What do you mean?" she asked.

Caelan barely spared her a glance. "It's none of your concern. Follow Rigel. Rigel, hand me Nyx." Caelan held his hand out to Rigel.

"No," Hannah said, squaring her shoulders. "I'm not leaving until you tell me what's going on." She pulled the blanket around herself tighter.

Caelan's eyes flashed darkly. "Stop being defiant," he commanded, staring her down. "You're completely unclothed, and it's indecent. Not to mention you're probably freezing. Go inside, please. Do as I say."

"Just because you're angry doesn't mean I don't deserve an explanation," Hannah challenged. "Why does James have to leave?"

"Because I have to do what I need to in order for you to be okay," Caelan shouted amidst the tension in the space.

Hannah, frozen, looked on with a tight lip. "Who told you we needed you to make the choice for us? There's no reason for you to need to leave so suddenly. There's a lot to process—"

"There's nothing to process," Caelan interjected, spittle flying from his furious lips. "My true parents, dead. My wife... also dead, and my mother just died in front of me." His eyes were a storm of darkness that refused to be contained, and pain was its master as he let his gaze linger on Hannah. "You're asking me to just pretend like none of that happened? Or to just look over it?" Shaking his head, the incredulous response came faster than Hannah expected. "That, I cannot do."

"But there's still hope for you," Hannah proclaimed.

"Hope...died for me a long time ago," Caelan said.

Before Hannah could find words, Caelan already grasped Nyx, and Rigel was heading her way.

With apologies in Rigel's eyes and words that fumbled on his lips, Hannah felt herself being dragged away back to the house.

"Wait," she cried out, struggling against his grip. "What are you doing?"

"I'm taking you inside," Rigel replied. "Just like Caelan asked. You're going inside, and you're going to tell James to say his goodbyes."

"You can't just decide for me what the choice is. I need to process, and all you're doing is forcing me inside..." Her mind scrambled as to the reason, and she looked wildly at her surroundings before glaring at Caelan. "What are you doing?" Hannah screamed. "Why aren't you telling me what's going on?"

"Because his plan is to wipe all the memories of everything that happened," Nyx said despite the roaring silence. "Isn't it obvious? You will not remember this by tomorrow."

Hannah felt her gut drop. *What? What is he talking about?*

"Whatever she knows, it won't matter now," Caelan said, his gaze distant and unchanging. "Tell James to gather the others and then get them all in the living room. I will meet you there after I find something to tie Nyx down with. Then, we'll begin the Erasing."

Erasing. No memories of this. I will lose...everything.

"No!" Hannah screamed, the noise deep and guttural despite the dragging she felt on her elbow. She was sure with all the tugging that the blanket would fall off, but at that moment, she couldn't bring herself to care. "Stop. I don't want my memories to be wiped!"

"What the heck is going on?"

The voice snapped Hannah's screams in their tracks, and she lifted her eyes to the cabin.

James stood with his arms crossed in the door's threshold. There was still glass shattered in the blades of grass from the window, but more and more people followed him out of the cabin, murmuring something that Hannah couldn't quite hear.

"Who said they would wipe your memories?" James stared incredulously at Caelan. "You—you're *actually* going to wipe her memories? After everything that happened?"

"This doesn't concern you. Apart from you saying your goodbyes, the only thing that should be of any consequence is you gathering your bearings." Caelan's words were curt as he spared a half glance to James.

"You're erasing our memories?" The broken tone could have come from miles away, and Hannah would have still recognized it. She had heard it many times growing up. Cammie, always the softie, did not do well keeping her emotions in the cheek.

"There's no other option," Caelan argued, shaking his head slowly, as if he, too, were weighing the many options that lay at his feet. "If there was, I would have gone for it already, but there isn't. So, by this time tomorrow, you will all be at home, with no recollection of me or what happened today or anything that's happened in our time together."

"You can't do that," another voice cried out, and Hannah had to stop herself from rolling her eyes. *Always the one to play the hero.* "Cammie almost died because of the last mind-wipe."

"Because it was rushed," Caelan snapped. "I will make sure it won't be. This time, there won't be anything stopping it from actually following through. All of this will be far from your minds—"

"You mean, far from yours," Cammie growled.

Hannah turned to look at her, and her heart jolted. Cammie's hair was a disaster, and her brown eyes were bloodshot. She was exhausted, but she was still showing her heart, a trait that Hannah had never truly mastered, but it shone through in Cammie.

"This entire time, you've only been concerned about yourself. *Your* family, *your* truth," Cammie continued. "Well, what about *our* truth? Just a few days ago, we all thought we were just humans. We didn't think that anything revolving Fae or Amarians was even real. We literally just found out our entire lives were lies. Whether losing Solenne was painful for you doesn't change how our entire destinies have been completely altered, and you think that wiping our minds will solve it for you?"

"Having you here is a constant reminder of everything I've lost," Caelan retorted, clenching his left hand. "Because of you, because I dragged you here to sift through your memories, it caused my mother...to die. You're a constant reminder of the fact...that I am, and forever will be...a failure. I couldn't protect her. I couldn't protect my children—"

"Solenne believed we are your children. Are you saying she's a liar? That she's wrong?" Cammie pressed, lifting her brows.

"Amarians are not all-knowing. We make mistakes just as humans do. My mother was not bound to truth the way you seem to think she is. Whatever happened to you had to result from some other Amarian's mind tricks. Not hers. She just felt responsible, like she always did." Caelan gripped Nyx tighter and spun on his heel, heading in the opposite direction.

"Where are you going?" Cammie asked Caelan's retreating form as he reached a tree directly across from them.

"Tying Nyx up because this conversation is over." Caelan gestured to Rigel. "Get me some rope, will you? Something strong enough to keep him down."

Cammie's fists balled, and Hannah couldn't help but marvel. Cammie...actually taking after her for a change.

"When will you wake up?" Cammie asked, her voice hoarse.

Caelan froze from his position at the tree, and he barely lifted his head as an acknowledgement of hearing her words.

"When will you wake up and stop letting fear run your life? You let it stop you from living, and when you do finally decide to crawl out of that stupid hole, all it does is send you spiraling back into it! It's the same cycle over and over again. You might not have your parents back, and yes, Solenne might have died, but if what she's saying is true—and we *are* your children—then you have us here already. But if she's wrong, and we aren't, then congratulations, Caelan, you've succeeded,

succeeded at letting people leave your life before they've even settled. Is this what you want? To always be alone? Because you're sure doing a great job of it!"

Caelan didn't speak, and Hannah herself was frozen in shock.

"So now, after commanding our choice for us, you have nothing to say?" Cammie challenged.

This time, Caelan could not even meet her eyes. He angled his body away to Nyx and shoved him down against the tree. "Rope, Rigel," he commanded.

Rigel's grip was now nonexistent on Hannah as he choked out a mumble of obedience, running to the distant forest. Hannah spared a glance at Sabina and then at Cammie, who was now not trying to keep herself together. With words that refused to bulge from her tongue, Hannah found herself at a loss.

But then she felt it...the thrumming. It was on her back, traveling up her shoulders. It sang a song that she was sure only she could hear, but the stark shock that rested on the faces of Sabina and Cammie told her all she needed to know. She wasn't alone. Not in this, at least. A mirage of colors appeared before her eyes, and she wasn't sure at first where they had originated from.

It was a blend of the rainbow, an iridescent green, a lavender, a rose gold, shifting and interchanging until the colors were merely a kaleidoscope that floated around into a circle. No number of words could do the beauty in front of Hannah justice, even as it glowed brighter in her midst. Swiftly, it changed yet again to a sphere, the colors changing to form an outline, a shape.

Hannah could not make any firm connection yet, and a look at the surrounding others proved they were just as conflicted at deciphering it.

With a howl, wind flowed in through the trees, whipping hair into faces. Her skin flushed with goosebumps as golden rays appeared from underneath the shifting, secretive shape.

Hannah squinted. "What is it?" she asked.

"It can't be," Nyx uttered, completely breathless.

Hannah whipped her head around to Nyx, but Caelan's eyes captivated hers. In them, so many emotions reflected such beautiful things, but the one that shone the brightest of them all.

Hope.

The burst of light advanced, and finally, the outline came into view.

A single phoenix hovered above them all.

It erupted into a thousand tiny particles that shimmered in the air as the form hit the grass. Mouths were agape, and eyes filled with what Hannah could only describe as awe-struck wonder, same as what she felt inside of her soul.

"What does this mean?" she dared to ask, turning her gaze back to Caelan. "Surely...someone's seen this before."

Sudden thumping resounded from a few feet away, and Hannah whipped her head around.

Rigel stood with his hands empty, and his mouth open wide, eyes consistently blinking. "The prophecy," he blurted, "unfolding before our eyes. No mere human/Amarian blend. No, this...this is...what we've been waiting for."

The discarded piece of rope rested near his feet, and Rigel's knees buckled. They hit the forest floor so quickly that no sound erupted, except for the weeping breaths from Rigel's mouth.

"My family, we were loyal to the Crown for our punishment of a crime that happened so long ago. And Caelan..." Rigel swallowed, blinking away tears. "I followed him out of a duty of what was right, but this marking, this...was prophesied long before your births, and yet here you are. Right in front of us. The true royals."

More shifting sounds came from behind, and Hannah turned. James was kneeling. Tony and the entire gang had gathered together, all in the same position.

They were kneeling...for her.

Sabina and Cammie clasped hands.

Not her, but them.

Wetness protruded from Hannah's eyes. *How can this be possible?*

Footsteps sounded, and out of the corner of her eyes, Hannah sensed someone else was also on their knees.

With unkempt hair and his body wracking sobs in a way she had never seen before, Caelan was practically face-first on the ground. Dirt coated his cheeks and streaked his eyelids as he lifted his face. He was no longer holding onto Nyx.

Panic gripped her throat as she met eyes with the unstable green. He had every reason to run, to save himself after the stunts he pulled, but would he?

"Get to your feet," Nyx instructed as he crouched to Caelan's twisted form on the ground. "Get to your feet. Do it."

Caelan finally nodded before standing. Though his face was coated with the grimiest of dirt, his eyes radiated with delight. "My daughters," he choked out. "You're finally here."

Hannah knew she wasn't sure about modern miracles or whether she could claim this as pure heresy, but what she had seen with her own two eyes, that couldn't be something she denied.

Amarians were real. Solenne had spoken some truth over her, and she was sure of the other two girls as well.

Something bigger was brewing, something that involved her and Sabina and Cammie, and with the way everyone was looking at her—at them—hoping they would change the world, Hannah couldn't help but marvel.

Maybe they could.

That thought only grew as Hannah watched Caelan step forward to envelop her in a hug. Sabina and Cammie were pulled in, too.

Though everyone else kept an eye shut, Hannah dared to open one. An entire circle formed around them, a circle where everyone—save for Nyx—was on one knee. They held their heads in the most solemn respect, as if these three women could and would forever alter the fate of the world.

CHAPTER THIRTY-FIVE

HANNAH

THE FLOWERS WERE ROSES, PEONIES, and lilac. Hannah hadn't known Solenne long, but she wondered if this was a combination of her favorite colors.

The grave itself was unmarked, except for the flowers. For once in his lifetime, Hannah was sure, Nyx was being kind as he stood quietly and didn't fight. He had even *helped* Caelan by forcing him to his feet.

Behind the crowd, whom was still paying their respects, Nyx was in the back with Rigel, his hands bound by ropes. He wore the devious smirk as usual. Hannah sauntered to where they were standing.

After a shower and a fresh change of clothes, she felt fully refreshed and ready with vengeance. "What game are you playing at?" she whispered to him, leaning in to speak as close as she could get to his ear.

Nyx leaned his head over, adjusting his position. "Whatever do you mean, *Princess*?" he asked, a small chortle escaping his dark smile. "I'm just trying to pay my respects."

Scoffing, Hannah shook her head. "That, I seriously doubt. You *hate* Caelan. You have *no* integrity. You're the same man who requested I be abused at the hands of your men to serve some great purpose, or maybe... maybe you just like inflicting pain on innocent people."

A dark sparkle glittered in Nyx's eyes. "Very perceptive, and after such somber events. I have high hopes I haven't seen the last of this, I surely hope not, but to answer at least this one question, I can say...there are greater things at stake here than a mere funeral. Your entire existence will turn Natrellum on its head. Tell me, are you ready for such consequences, Princess? Or are you simply feeling the pressure above your head to be too...shall I say...daunting?"

Hot, rich rage flickered in Hannah's skin as she met the gaze of a monster. "You just never give up, do you? Do you really think threatening me is the answer?"

As he stared down at her with those emerald eyes, a slow, deep smile appeared at the corners of his lips. "Oh, believe me, Princess, this question wasn't a threat. It was an honest question, one that I think you'll do well to heed."

More words seemed to flicker behind Nyx's gaze, but before Hannah could prod him, a booming voice resounded at the front of the crowd.

"I know not all of you here knew my mother truly, but all the same, I cannot appreciate you being here enough today. It has simultaneously been the hardest...and the most blessed day of my life." Caelan donned a black jacket and dress pants, and he had styled his hair—messily—but Hannah knew he had tried his best. His shaking hands had been proof of that fact.

Near the front of the crowd, Hannah could make out the back of Cammie's head. Flowers adorned her messy bun like a crown, and she was pressed close together with Sabina. Bubbles made their way in Hannah's stomach at the sight, though she couldn't quite fathom why.

"Is someone jealous? Why don't you join your sisters up front instead of bickering with me?" Nyx's words were as sharp as knives.

Hannah could feel the pinprick deep in her gut. *Sisters.*

"This'll take some getting used to," Hannah mumbled. "It almost doesn't feel real." She sighed, pushing a strand of hair behind her ear. Lost in the moment, she had almost forgotten she'd said the words aloud until the haughty chuckle came from lips she despised.

"Your life is now a fairytale," Nyx rebutted. "For all of you, that is. Your entire lives were lies, and now, you're finding out your true heritage. You're no peasant. No bottom of the food chain for you, no, ma'am. You are an exquisite princess, and your life is now altered in the best way possible. High rise living indeed. Ballgowns, Amarian food that you've yet to taste...all of it at your fingertips. There's a lot to love."

Hannah scoffed. Caelan was still giving his speech, but Hannah couldn't be bothered to listen. Not when this guy was an absolute, imperious idiot.

"Just earlier, you said I had more than I bargained for. And now you're telling me I'm being handed Sabina's lifestyle on a silver platter with a fantastical, ancient twist. Sounds contradictory, don't you think?"

"I think you're reading into my words too much, maybe projecting your own fears, possibly. Or..." Nyx's lip twisted upward into a crooked smile. "...maybe you're actually enjoying these conversations, and I don't exasperate you as much as you think. But, for conversation's sake, let's be honest with each other. There are two sides to a coin, and where you're headed, it could go many ways. Do you really think the people will welcome the original family back with open arms, especially with how things have been running for the past few hundred years? It could definitely end with champagne and roses, I won't deny that, but don't be surprised, Princess, if the people end up wanting your head on a platter."

"But I saw people kneeling earlier. Everyone did. *Except you.* But that doesn't mean the people will hate us. It isn't our fault we just found this out. I mean, all of it doesn't seem real, not to me, but to people who have been around this their entire lives...they have enough sense to look past it, right?"

Another questionable smirk tugged at the corner of Nyx's lips, but he said nothing and turned his head back to the front where the procession was still ongoing. Caelan, so lost in his monologue, thankfully did not know Hannah's position by Nyx.

"I think you should continue watching the funeral. You're being quite disrespectful," Nyx uttered, watching Hannah with such intensity that she felt her face coat with heat.

With more rage beginning to rise to the surface, Hannah took a deep breath.

Nyx's eyes twinkled. "Better watch that temper before it gets you in trouble."

"I'd say you're the one stirring up trouble," came a voice from behind.

Hannah felt her breath catch she caught sight of her friend. *Tony.*

In any other situation, one would say he was being disrespectful, but because of Nyx's chaotic schemes and blatant disregard for life itself, Tony wore the same bloody, torn clothes from the night prior. His eyes shone with alertness, though Hannah knew exhaustion had to be layered in there somewhere.

"Tony, here to save the day. Just like before. How predictable." Something like annoyance flickered in Nyx's face as he gave Tony the once-over before turning his gaze back to Hannah.

In the background, Rigel tightened his grip on Nyx. He was so silent that Hannah almost forgot he was there. The sudden realization caused the flush to deepen. *He was practically a witness to it all.*

Nyx wiggled his fingers absentmindedly, rolling his eyes. "How nice of you to remind me of your presence, captor."

Rigel let out a breath, grinning. "Doesn't feel so good on your end, does it?"

Nyx shrugged. Well, tried to, as best as he could, despite bound hands. "Not really. Never thought this day would come. Never in my wildest dreams."

"Maybe you should take your own advice about respect and be quiet and listen. Caelan's talking, and seeing as he's the King of Natrellum, I'd advise you to stop talking." Tony's voice was stern.

"Look who's rising in position. How amazing. You've gone from handy sidekick to king's advisor in only a matter of hours. If I ever want a rise to power, I know who to talk to." Nyx winked.

Tony gritted his teeth and grabbed Hannah's elbow, tugging. "Come on, Hannah. Let's get you away from here."

Tony led the way through the small crowd that had gathered, several people who Hannah didn't know murmuring as hands collided against skin. She wanted to apologize, but in the same breath, she kept feeling a tug to turn, to look into the same eyes she had retreated from. Unfinished business had a stealthy habit of following her like prey.

The crowd wasn't as big as the ones at funerals Hannah had heard about on the news, but it wasn't the smallest she had seen either. In the wake of the prior evening, Caelan had rallied people who had known Solenne for far longer than she had. They held onto his every word, and as Hannah batted away the distractions in her mind, she forced herself to hang onto his words, too.

My dad's words.

"There have been many years of longing for all of us, I feel. For you, years ago, your families left their homes after destruction raided your cities. Hellfire rained on our homes, and several families perished. The Light blessed us with survival. It blessed us with sanctuary and a promise of redemption. Solenne was not my birth mother, but she was my mother all the same. She kept the promise to my birth mother to keep me safe, and then, years later, she made the same promise to my wife, Leanne...for our children. I didn't understand it at first when she lied to me. She lied and told me that my children perished at the hands of Nyx's barbaric father. For years, I fear I walked in darkness because the grief was too overpowering, but Solenne knew what she was doing. Solenne believed in the prophecy's power, in the power that my girls could bring, so while I was defending my bride, she took my children and hid them until they were ready to be found."

The crowd, captivated, held its breath as Caelan's words fell down on them like a blanket, and Hannah watched in amazement while shock tickled her fingers.

"After several moments of doubt where I didn't want to face the truth, the truth made itself known to me in such a way that denying it would be heresy itself. I now can confidently say that these are my daughters, and our place...is no longer Earth, Colorado, whatever you want to call it. Our place is where the skies combine blues and purples and trees grow such beautiful cherry blossoms even in the coldest of winters. Our rightful place is on the throne in Natrellum, where my daughters will rule with peace and justice. Now, I know many of you had the hopes that I would rule—"

Cries of outbursts erupted in the crowd,.

Caelan raised his hands out. "I understand the frustration, but I am not as young as they are. I know they will bring about change in a way that I cannot. The decision is final. I will be their advisor, and I will guide them as much as I needed guidance when I was their age. I will prepare them the best way I know how, and we will brace the Council together. Hopefully with our truth, it will sway them to allow these conditions, but—" Caelan paused, eyes searching the crowd until he found each of the girls. "Please, allow my girls to come up here. I want to show them to you. My beautiful, strong daughters who were here with me all this time. Fate and irony are stubborn siblings, but I wouldn't trade this journey for anything. I found the other sections of my heart, and I just know...they will do us proud."

As his speech ended, there was nothing but complete silence as Caelan held his hands out to Sabina and Cammie. They took it, rising to stand next to Caelan. Hannah felt her feet dragging as she found a place next to Cammie. Hannah could feel the heat of Sabina's burning gaze, but she didn't dare look.

Multitudes of strangers were staring at her as they erupted into cheering. Hannah couldn't help but wonder what the outcome would be of them going "home," but one thing Hannah was sure of—Caelan spoke like a true king. He had been trained since birth how to return to his rightful place. Solenne had done him well, but how much training could one prepare for if their entire heritage was foreign?

As more questions swirled in her mind, Hannah finally found the one she had been desperately trying to avoid.

With the glistering in his eyes that he wore so often, Hannah was sure that if his hands weren't bound, Nyx would be toasting, raising a glass of the finest alcohol he could fit into a cup at Caelan's speech. But as his smile grew, so did the sinking feeling in her gut.

Nyx was no saint, and she knew he would toast regardless of the two options he had presented.

Even if it meant her head on a platter.

CHAPTER THIRTY-SIX

CAMMIE

As CAELAN'S WORDS RANG OUT over the crowd, Cammie felt something swell in her stomach as she tightened her grasp on Sabina's hands. *Pride.*

He spoke with such love and honor for his people, and Cammie knew he was meant to be their king, but here he was, being selfless, and allowing the girls to take their true place.

Nagging questions of how the other girls were handling this nibbled at the back of her mind. What would their lives be like now that everything had come to the surface? What would become of her mother, or Sabina's artistic-driven wealthy parents, or even Hannah's cop dad? Would Cammie remember her? Would Cammie even *miss* her?

It was like a carousel of anxiety, just circling around and around until she felt a tap on her shoulder and the clearing of someone's throat.

"Can we talk?"

She turned her head. James stood with his hands in his pockets and an unreadable expression in his gaze. Cammie had qualms, and different decisions of how she could respond danced in her brain.

She nodded, licking her lips. "Sure, we can talk."

James glanced at Sabina and then to Hannah. "I was wondering if we could talk in private. I think...it would be better that way."

Sudden tightness hugged her chest. Cammie released her hand from Sabina's. "I'll be right back," she promised.

Sabina said nothing, worry dancing in her eyes as her eyebrows pinched together.

"I'll be fine," Cammie mouthed before turning back to James.

She followed him through the patch of woods, a different angle from the prior bloodshed of the night before. She hadn't seen it. Caelan didn't want them to have any more reminders, so the funeral had taken place deeper behind the property.

Cammie wasn't sure of the total damage, but she was sure he had gotten their help to clean up whatever dead bodies had stained the forest floor. The thought became louder as she stared at the dewy grass. Rain must have fallen the night before so stealthily she hadn't heard it.

"How are you holding up?"

The question startled her out of her thoughts, and she allowed herself to meet his eyes. In the middle of the forest, standing across from each other, it was easy to pretend nothing had happened. She actually wanted it to be true, to escape from the reality of consequences she had never asked for.

"Is that a real question?" Cammie opted instead.

James brushed the back of his neck with his hand, looking down at the ground. "Probably not the best question or even the smartest one, but I figured it was one I should ask after everything. It can be a lot to take in. At least I imagine it would be."

She felt dust in her dry mouth. A tornado of emotions swirled in her stomach as she let her eyes fall back up to the sky.

"Finding out your entire life isn't what you thought it was definitely feels...different." No other words were doing her justice, even as they settled into the air.

"You're an Amarian royal," James said. Beaming pride radiated into a smile as James finally brought his gaze back to her. "That's a big deal, and I know adjusting will be scary, but—"

"But what about my family? Sabina's family? Or Hannah's? What happens to them now? Their memories become wiped, and our entire existence fades from this world. How are we supposed to fit into a world that we don't understand? I just..." Cammie paused, grasping for words. "I don't know what Solenne was thinking, hiding us. She said it was for our protection, but how can that be? And...all of it seems a bit much. We've been best friends for so long and find out we're sisters? It's something straight out of fiction. Not real life. Not for me."

A twinkle appeared in James' eyes. "That's a lot of words for different."

At his sudden newfound expression, Cammie's face slacked. She turned on her heel, ready to be finished with this conversation, but before she could leave, she felt a hand on her elbow.

"Wait, don't go. I was only joking. I didn't mean any harm."

"Joking in any other situation, sure, that I could excuse, but there's a lot going on now, a lot...that I have to figure out, that Hannah and Sabina also have to figure out."

Frustration was in the air, in her spirit, and in the words she spoke. It was slowly clawing up the surface no matter how hard she tried to bottle the feeling. Slowly, she turned back to face him, and the guilt slapped her in the face.

Hurt was written all over his gaze, and he licked his lips, as if there were more words that wanted to spill without warning. "I need to apologize," he said finally, huffing out a breath.

Cammie raised a brow, letting her arm fall away from his grasp. "What are you talking about?"

"I had no place to talk to you like I did earlier. No place to disrespect you or humans. My culture, they have ingrained it in us since the beginning. And despite what you are, half of what I am, you're still human, and you taught me so much in the time that I was here. Even if you hadn't..." His breath hitched as he let his eyes flicker to something in the distance. "...I still had no right to disrespect you. Or Caelan. And I know asking this is a long shot, but I wanted you to know the truth. I meant...what I told you that night. If you remember—"

"I remember," Cammie interjected, her words forcing James to look back her way.

Declarations of love rang true in her mind as she peered into his eyes. What he was saying was true. But what he said earlier... was also true.

"Can you ever forgive me? Can we ever get back to whatever we were? If you just give me a chance..." Hope cracked in his voice as the words rushed from his lips, and it was so poignant that if she could, she would have reached out and touched it.

But uncertainty ruled all her decisions. At least they did now.

"I don't know," Cammie breathed, tears threatening to spill. The wetness stung, and she blinked it away. "I can't think that far ahead. Please, if you understood at all what I'm dealing with, you wouldn't ask me that. At least not now." She swallowed the ball of guilt in her throat and forced herself to pull it together. With a resolved nod, she looked back up at James, wiping her eyes. "What's done is done. You've apologized, and I've forgiven you. I don't want to be angry. I'm just not sure how I'm supposed to move forward with you—with us—until things get resolved."

For a moment, there was no reply, but words didn't need to be in the open air for her to *feel* them, *see* them.

His face moved in edges, pain dancing across his eyes, and he gave her a resigned nod. "You're a royal. Whether or not the Council appoints that, the fact still stands. You're under different orders, different rulings than I, and in terms of romance, I'm sure you'll be paired with someone in a higher standing than that of a guard. It's better I just embrace it now." He sniffled and wiped his nose with the back of his hand, taking two steps backward. "Take care of yourself, Cammie," James uttered breathlessly before turning on his heel.

Despite the mass of tension Cammie felt in the air, he never looked back. Not once. He left her in the forest like a discarded animal, left her alone with a gaping wound in her heart that even she was sure couldn't be rescued.

Hot, stinging rage was in Cammie's eyes as she blinked away the tears. Being stuck in the forest like some damsel wasn't the answer. No more waiting. No more confusion. No more apathetic or passive dismissals. Cammie was going to finish this once and for all.

She pushed up the sleeves of the dress and forced her feet to move. She willed the anger to the side—if only for now.

With determination in her heart, she set her eyes on the clearing where James had just exited. He wasn't getting away that easily. Not if she had something to say about it.

CHAPTER THIRTY-SEVEN

SABINA

WORRY WAS LIKE A CONSTANT needle in her arm. It was ever persistent and a constant annoyance that wouldn't dissipate.

The crowd conversing among each other after Caelan's speech was a small distraction, but it wasn't enough. His words still swirled in her mind, along with the constant anxiety that stuck to her palms in the physical state of sweat. She wiped them on her dress, one she had borrowed from Solenne's closet.

The material was like nothing she had felt in her life of being a "high riser," but it was so exquisitely woven that Sabina couldn't help but marvel about the fabric used in Natrellum. It was soft and sturdy, giving her a reminder of silken ecstasy for comparison. With a flowy skirt, the dress conformed to her body, shifting and molding against the backdrop of nervous antics.

"Can you stop moving? Your energy is giving me a headache. I can feel the anxiety in waves from here.

Your dress keeps hitting my ankles." Hannah's angry tone cut through the air.

Sabina stopped moving, shooting her a glare. "I'm worried about Cammie and about all of this, so I pace." She continued moving again.

"And is it helping?" Hannah asked, raising a brow. She crossed her arms over her chest triumphantly, as if this conversation were merely a game and she was taking the winnings by storm.

"Why are you such a pain? Is everything some sort of challenge?" Sabina asked, narrowing her eyes. *I'm sick and tired of her attitude.*

"It's not exactly a challenge if you're failing at it. Anxiety and you are not good friends, so I suggest you stop pacing and maybe talk to the person in charge, *sister.*"

Sabina had always hated being an only child, but her parents had never decided on another. She always considered herself close with Cammie and maybe at one point Hannah, too, but this? This was pure betrayal, the truth behind those words displayed for all to see.

"You're heartless," Sabina spat, angry tears prickling her eyes. "You know *just* how to cut people down. I don't need your hatred or your judgement. For once in your life, would it kill you to be nice to me?"

"Being nice to you would include me actually caring about you. I stopped a long time ago, Sabina. Any sort of interaction we have now is just me tolerating you, for Cammie's sake. Expect nothing else. Maybe once I'm on my deathbed, I'll change my mind, but for now? This is as good as it's going to get."

Sabina was ready for more—more anger and more defiance—but before more could be spoken with no retrieving them, footsteps resounded behind Hannah.

More nerves fired as Sabina forced herself to stop pacing, her eyes becoming wide as Caelan cleared his throat.

"I'm sorry it took me so long to get to you. I was lost in conversing with the others about our journey. I wanted to touch base with you, see how you were doing?"

Words themselves seemed to fall short as Sabina took in this man, who was once a stranger, now turned father. The phrase felt weird on her tongue, the same feeling she would get when she'd eat something out of the ordinary to please her parents or when she had been forced to give a speech.

"We're okay," was what Sabina finally settled on after a brief interlude of silence. She had trouble even looking him in the face because all of it didn't seem real.

"Speak for yourself," Hannah interjected with a huff. "Little Miss Entitled here can't seem to stop pacing, and she's concerned. Worried. Whatever word you want to use." Hannah's careless attitude was clear in her tone, and she rolled her eyes. "I have some things to catch up on, and it might be better if you take care of her worries. I have people to talk to."

Without a care, she bumped shoulders with Sabina before going around her, heading to some distant place in the corner where Tony and the others had gathered.

Caelan furrowed his eyebrows, concern flittering over his face before he swallowed. "She said you were worried. Is there anything you can tell me about that? If you want to, that is." His words were rushed, harboring on the border of awkwardness and confusion.

This new territory was becoming harder to tread for all of them, Sabina realized.

"A lot of it is just the newness of all of this," Sabina started. "It's been hard to adjust to this life, this reality."

"We will provide everything you need to know and learn," Caelan remarked, a soft smile appearing on his face.

So sure of a reality he hasn't yet grasped himself.

"But how can you possibly provide training when you haven't been back there since you were born?" The question was something weighing on her heart since the mere hours where she had realized the truth, but there was more to it. "And not even just that," Sabina added, "but there's also the entire issue of our families here, of our lives. What are we supposed to do with that?"

The smile that had appeared so quickly on Caelan's face faded, and he was silent. "I'm not sure what you mean. You're Amarian. You're my daughters. This is the truth for all of you, and this is in the blood in your veins."

"We might be those things, but we also have duties here. I know I do with my parents. We have lives outside of this new...realm. I can't just throw that away."

"The prophecy has spoken of you for centuries. You've all been what we've been dreaming of, the force that will finally eradicate the Darkness. It's been in our history, in our hearts. In *my* heart. I've searched for you for so long—" Caelan stopped speaking, taking a breath. "The point is, you're here now, and you're alive, and there's an entire world, an entire heritage that's been waiting for you. It's part of who you are. Ignoring it will only give you more grief."

So much yearning was in his words, in his gaze. He had spent his entire life searching for something he wasn't even sure existed anywhere else other than his heart, but it was alive *here*. That part she could sympathize with, but there was another part of her that told her to just turn her back. How could an entire kingdom be split between three shoulders, a kingdom that might be entirely different from what Caelan had conjured in his head? How would she even be up for the task?

"Maybe what you're saying is right," Sabina said, "but also...maybe you could be wrong. Maybe the world is different. Maybe we're the wrong people to be in this position. There could be another set of three who will be the answer."

"Every hero has a struggling phase, a phase of doubt. I ran from my destiny when I was younger. It doesn't surprise me you're feeling tempted to run from it too. Just take a day.... Really think it over."

"But—"

"That's all you need to do," Caelan replied. "Let your destiny speak above the fear, and then let me know your choice. If you really want nothing to do with this, then I can't force you. As much as I want you to come with me, I understand that might not be feasible for you. We are different people. I don't expect you to morph into who I want you to be but to be *who you already are*."

Sabina's jaw slacked at his words. She bit her lower lip, stunned, pondering, until another question hit her square in the face. "But what if I don't find the answers you want me to?"

"All I ask is that you take the time, truly. The rest, I will leave up to you." With a look in his eyes that was faraway but not fully distant, Caelan gave Sabina a nod and turned on his heel.

He had a belief in Sabina that she had never seen before, and if she allowed herself to be truly naïve, she might believe in it too.

CHAPTER THIRTY-EIGHT

CAMMIE

T REES AND NATURE BECAME BLURRED while she walked, her tears still fresh, her feet heavy with purpose as she kept her eyes steady on the clearing.

She blinked the stubborn blur away as the small crowd came into view, but James was nowhere to be found. If only she had some sort of razor-sharp vision. Maybe that would be a new Amarian talent she'd inherit.

In the corner of her vision, she saw Sabina standing alone, Caelan's retreating form leaving her. She made her way to Sabina's side, who startled as she approached.

"You and James are done talking already?" Sabina asked, rubbing her arms. "I wasn't sure when you guys would be finished."

"It didn't end how I wanted it to. It isn't important, now. Why are you here by yourself? I saw Caelan leave. Is everything okay?"

Sabina blanched, her face taking on the unusual pale instead of the brightness it usually possessed. "I'm fine," she said with a smile that didn't quite reach her eyes. "It's just something we should...probably talk about."

With raised brows, Cammie took in Sabina's averting eyes and nervous hands. *She's hiding something.* "Do you want to talk now?"

"No," Sabina rushed. A hint of red coated her cheeks. "I don't think so. I think we should find Hannah, regroup somewhere else. Somewhere less...crowded." Her eyes flickered to the gathering of people before settling back on Cammie. "If that's okay with you?"

Cammie nodded.

Sabina turned back to the crowd. "I'm going to find her," she said, wringing her hands at her sides. "While I find her, if you can meet me behind the clearing? Same place you went to with James. I don't think anyone will hear us there."

Before Cammie could even protest, Sabina was on her way on a mission to find Hannah.

Cammie wasn't why the meeting needed to be so secretive, but something in her gut told her it would not be pleasantries or a recap.

Something told her it would be definitive.

If she listened hard enough, she could still hear the excited chatter. These people were ecstatic, hopeful, and ready for change.

For *them* to be the change.

It seemed like a lot to swallow, and as Cammie allowed glimpses of their words to fall over her, a shadow appeared from the corner of her eyes. A very annoyed shadow.

"She dragged me over here. So, what's the occasion other than listening to Sabina cry her eyes out about how hard her life is? That's usually what the whining is about, anyway. Things we just *won't understand*, etc. Etc." With an eye roll, Hannah plopped herself on the ground next to Cammie, who piqued an eyebrow. "What?" Hannah retorted. "My legs hurt. You try shifting into an animalistic being for a few hours and then tell me how you feel."

Stomping resounded from the far corner of the forest, and Cammie turned. *Sabina.*

"Here comes *Her Highness* herself," Hannah scoffed. "I can finally call her that now and it is not a lie. For once, it feels like life is smiling at me. Even my insults can now have some sort of truth to them."

With Hannah's long, ebony hair and deep-blue eyes, and a smirk to kill, Cammie always thought she was strong, but in these moments, Cammie could clearly see an unmatched hatred for Sabina. It was lathering itself, as if it was its own personal bubble bath.

"Your attitude never goes unchecked, does it?" Sabina growled uncharacteristically, balling her fists at her sides. The anxiety from earlier dissipated, nothing but blind anger in its place.

"For you?" Hannah put a hand over her heart, a devilish grin on her face. "Never."

"This...this...this is so out of control!" Sabina threw her hands up in the air, absolutely exasperated. "I mean, we're *actually* sisters, for crying out loud!"

"And how unfortunate that is," Hannah drawled, looking down at her nails. "I sincerely wish that I could have talked to our mother somehow through the womb and convinced her to drop just you on your parents' doorstep. I honestly feel that Cammie and I would have been much better off without you."

"You're heartless to hate your own blood," Sabina spat. Her face contorted as her nostrils flared, her arms practically shaking as the emotion traveled through her body.

"It's called freedom, Sabina." Hannah sighed, throwing her head back. "I'm surprised your aristocratic parents didn't teach you that." She slowly brought her head back down, a twinkle in her eyes. "You know, I think I misspoke. What I meant to say was 'your *false* aristocratic parents.'"

At such stark, cruel comments, Cammie couldn't help herself. *I have to do something before things blew up.* "Let's all just take a minute and cool off. Sabina brought us here to talk to us about something. Let's focus on that."

"Yeah, Sabina, what did you have to talk about?" Hannah asked with a challenge in her eyes.

"Hannah," Cammie warned. "Stop."

"What?" Hannah shrugged. "A little question never hurt anyone."

"I'm not doing this," Sabina huffed, throwing her hands into the air dismissively. "I'm not arguing with you. We can talk another time. Take a break and regroup." Turning on her heel, she hugged herself and took a few steps.

"Why? Are you scared?" Hannah taunted.

Sabina clenched her fingers, stopping in her tracks.

"Sabina, say nothing," Cammie said, her voice shifting. "Don't let her get to you. Just...walk away."

But it was too late.

Sabina had already turned around, her steps sure and true as she reached her destination—a few feet away from Hannah. "You say my parents are fake? Sure, all of ours are, but at least I had the decency to see my mother alive. You lost two mothers, and you're such a shrew that I bet they did you a favor by dying early! It's not like you have anything to offer them other than your freaking temper!"

Hannah's eyes flashed violet, and her face became stoic. For a minute, there was just silence.

Cammie's chest heaved. *Did she really say that? There's no way.*

"Hannah, I'm sorry," Sabina blurted. "I didn't mean it."

Hannah said nothing but rose to a stand, her entire body trembling. "Oh, you meant it, all right. Your innocent act might fool Cammie, but I see you exactly how you are: calculating, bold, and cunning. You might be almost as bad as I am, but at least I can see it."

She was seething but never moved an inch, never raised her fist, but her eyes—those were the fury. If Sabina was a target, and Hannah was the gun, Sabina would have been shot down.

"Can we just calm down?" Cammie asked, treading carefully. "Sabina brought us here for a reason, so maybe let's circle back to that again. I know things were said, and you both were wrong...but...let's try to talk, maybe?"

She held her breath as something flickered over Hannah's and Sabina's faces. *How will they get out of this?*

"Speak," Hannah finally instructed after the tension was so palpable Cammie felt it squeezing her throat. "Whatever you have to say, just say it."

"Not until you accept my apology and tell me why you're angry," Sabina told her, letting her arms fall to her sides.

"I don't have to tell you anything," Hannah uttered, taking a few steps back. "I can listen because you dragged me all the way out here, but don't expect me to tell you anything that I don't want to. So go on, then. *Speak.*"

After a moment's hesitation, Sabina swallowed, averting her eyes. "It's about what Caelan offered or, well, asked us to do."

"You mean going to Natrellum?" Cammie prompted. "Isn't that kind of a given?" She looked to Hannah, who was expressionless.

"But what if it doesn't have to be?" Sabina blurted, raising her eyes to meet Cammie's. "Who said we actually need to go?"

"I can't believe you're actually considering this," Cammie muttered under her breath. "We have to go.... Don't we?"

"Think about it, guys. I mean, I get what happened earlier. We all saw it—the explosion of light, the phoenix—but it could have been a trick of the light or...or some sort of joke. I mean, maybe whatever we saw, it wasn't for us. It could be for some other *chosen* one."

"Oh, cut it out," Hannah cried out. "Here you go again with the 'poor me' act."

"It isn't an act," Sabina defended. "I'm merely speaking the truth."

"What truth is there to anything you just said?" Hannah uttered. "Do I need to change into a wolf again for you to believe anything that's happened? This is for *us*. All of this isn't some coincidence. I had to practically beg Caelan not to wipe our memories, and last I checked, you wanted the choice to not forget either."

"I wouldn't be forgetting it," Sabina said.

"So you'd just be avoiding it, then? Pretending everything that happened didn't? That's such a cowardice move, and you know it," Hannah fumed, her jaw tensing.

"But if we're not up to the task, then what point is it in even going? A lot has gone on, a lot of revelations, and those are great, but—"

"No," Hannah interrupted. "I have hope for the first time about something that isn't the scraps life threw my way. This is an entire chance to grow, to shift, and to learn more about who we are, who we *truly* are. Just because you don't feel up for the task doesn't mean Cammie and I are going to willingly go along with your argument. Solenne *died* for this, for us. I didn't know her that well, but I can't take that lightly. I thought you would feel the same, but I guess not."

"But what about James? Things seem pretty rocky with him, and—"

"Cammie's practically an adult. She can make her own decisions about who to love and what to do. She doesn't need you to mother her, and neither do I. This conversation—at least for me—is over." Without even a backward glance, Hannah moved around Sabina, heading back in the direction she came from. "This is my choice, Sabina, and I choose yes."

At Hannah's retreating back, Sabina called out, "Wait, just think about this. Please!"

But Hannah never turned around. She kept walking, leaving Cammie and Sabina alone in the clearing.

Tears appeared in Sabina's eyes, and her bottom lip quivered as she turned to Cammie. "Please don't leave me alone in this. We have families here, like my parents, your mom. Hannah's dad, even. We can't just leave them to forget us."

"I'm sure Rigel will make it as painless as he can," Cammie stated, her throat tight.

The thought of her mother going on existing as if Cammie didn't caused a sharpness in her heart. A sliver of it cracked, and Cammie held her breath.

"But they will *forget* us," Sabina repeated. "Do you get that? *Forget* us. It'll be as if we never existed here."

A sudden thought of clarity appeared for Cammie. It was so translucent that she didn't have a chance to shove it back into the corner it came from. The sharpness in her heart faded slightly.

"Sabina." Cammie sighed, tucking a strand of hair behind her ear. "Don't you see it? That's how it was *always* supposed to be. Our lives here were never meant to be so simple. Our destinies are so much bigger than residing here. Even our friendship—so beautifully orchestrated—was meant to draw a path...a path that led us right here." Cammie could feel the weight of her words on her shoulders. Speaking them seemed to make the burden lighter. The truth had a way of doing that, of making the way straight and narrow to where there was no other option.

"So I take it you have your answer then? Just like that?" Disappointment overtook Sabina's features in such a way that she almost looked unrecognizable.

Cammie couldn't let Sabina's distress hinder her answer. "It's yes for me. There's so much here that we should lean into. It's who we are, and isn't it exciting to dive in, to experience it? There's so much we don't know, but that phoenix didn't shine for just anybody. It appeared to *us*. We'd be fools not to listen and reach out to take it. Aren't you tired of regrets? I am, but take your time. Please, don't let the fear of failure stop you. I promise you will regret it."

Her heart heavy with grief, Cammie left Sabina in the clearing. For the first time, she wasn't fully focused on James and his stinging words or the magnificent talent he had for tearing her heart into pieces.

She was focused on her future, one where she might have finally—after so many years—found her *true* home.

CHAPTER THIRTY-NINE

SABINA

THE TIGHTNESS IN HER THROAT didn't give way as she balled her fists, bringing them to her sides.

Cammie and Hannah had long gone, leaving Sabina to her own devices and her own incredibly ruthless thoughts.

Still spiraling, Sabina realized she only had two choices.

I can stay.

Or I can go home.

With everything she had seen, it would have been easier to just give in, to just do as he asked, but he hadn't asked her to come. He only asked her to think about it and make a choice that way. He only asked her to find the truth—face the fear—and continue on.

He would understand if she said no, surely?

What of her parents?

If I can even utter that anymore.

The sudden reprimand of guilt gnawed in her belly. It ripped away at her core, taking its time pulling and ripping at the edges. She hugged her stomach, willing the ferocious emotion away, trying her best to blink back stubborn tears.

How am I going to decide what to even do? I can't ask my parents. They'll know something is up and force me back home, but how can I just abandon them?

Mulling over different options in her mind did nothing but add to the cataclysmic ball of chaos of thoughts. With stones in her shoes and on her shoulders, Sabina sank to the ground, putting her head in her hands.

"This has become an absolute disaster," she muttered under her breath. "What am I ever going to do?"

Sharp ruffling sent the hairs on her neck upright, and Sabina felt the sudden rush of goosebumps as a chill touched her skin.

"I never picked you as the type to sit here in the forest alone," the person said.

Forcing the sadness away, Sabina raised her head. "What are you doing here, Will?" she asked, shocked. "Shouldn't you be with Hannah and the others?"

As if she had mentioned she had given birth to a cow, Will's face twisted, and he scoffed. "Hannah doesn't own me," he stated proudly, crossing his arms over his chest. "She just likes to think she does."

Her lips threatened to burst into a full smile, but she held it back, cocking her head to the side. "Is that so?" she asked, on the verge of laughter.

"Hannah might like to pretend she's alpha, but we all know it's Tony. Now that the cat—*ahem*, wolf—is out of the bag—ha, get it? Wolf? Because she shifted, and well, you can't exactly let that stay hidden anymore."

Sabina stared blankly, and Will's cheeks turned a slight shade of plum.

"So…" She sniffled, wiping her nose. "Does this mean no more chocolate at all? What about chew toys? I can definitely run over to the pet store for some. You look all about out of those."

Will's deadpan expression was the end of her. No longer could she hold back her laughter, fresh tears in the mix as she doubled over, clutching her stomach.

"It isn't funny," he said, above her roaring laughter.

"Oh, Will." Sabina sighed. "It really, really is."

With frail fingers, she wiped the new tears from her eyes and smiled a real, *huge* smile. If she was being honest with herself, it had been an eternity since she had done so freely. *So accustomed to party smiles I've forgotten what the real one feels like.*

"I'm glad to know my wolf-form amuses you," Will grumbled.

With his wildly tousled hair and bright eyes, she could easily forget how lifeless he had been only a few hours ago until Cammie's healing touch had brought him back from the brink of death.

"I just really needed a laugh," Sabina said quietly, dusting her legs off. The dress was soft against her skin, but she still felt like a layer of shame attached to it, despite her rigorous brushing of it to go away. *I've never lost control of myself like this before.*

Will raised a brow. "I take it you haven't in a while?"

Her tongue was ready to smother down the truth like she always did, to cling to some sort of false pretense, some fake smile, or some meaningless words.

"I haven't," was what she decided on instead. "With my kind of lifestyle, I couldn't really afford to do that."

"Well," Will drawled, "the only things I really know about you are that we met at the gas station on the same journey, and you're now the chosen royal. Also, when we get thrown into a fight, I can count on you to have my back. You're telling me in your life back home things were very different?"

"I guess it depends on how you define different," Sabina replied. "I know I didn't have any kind of martial arts training. Everything you saw earlier was all James and, I guess, adrenaline and pure instinct coming out. But with my parents, it was about showing to a crowd. It wasn't about honesty, or morality, or any of those things. My parents loved beautiful things, and I think that's why they adored me so much. I was loyal to making sure their lives stayed beautiful even if it was a disaster on the inside." The lump in her throat returned, and she swallowed it away, before taking a breath. "So, no, I haven't smiled in a while," she rushed, "and I don't think I'm the *chosen one* at all."

"You say that, but did you not *see* the phoenix? I mean, I thought it was pretty bright, but maybe it really wasn't for you."

"I *saw* it," Sabina clarified. "I just don't know if...if it's me you're thinking of."

"Someone told me you also conjured weapons from nothing. You're saying that's a trick of the eye too?"

Baffled, Sabina fumbled for words. "I'm not—"

"You can poke holes in anything if you look hard enough. That's all I'm saying, and from what it sounds, you have a crappy enough life with your old family. Why would you want to crawl back into that when your true destiny is right here in front of you?"

"Crappy or not, they still deserve my goodbye," she whispered.

"You don't have to stay loyal to something unhealthy for you just to gain their favor. You have a right to leave and form your own family. That's what I did when I left Texas. I miss my mama and my brothers, but they knew it was my turn to shift and to join my own pack. Nothing was wrong with my family back home. I just needed space to find myself, and now, I have. You can, too. Don't let the fear of change stop you in your tracks. This break and change in destiny might be exactly what you're needing, but if you need closure first, I can't say that I blame ya." Will fished through his pockets and shoved a shiny object in her direction. *A cell phone.*

With shaky hands, Sabina grasped it, her heart like thunder in her chest.

Will pointed to a spot in the clearing, far away from where she was. "I'll give you some privacy to call them. Just come get me when you're done."

He retreated, and Sabina waited there, frozen, staring at the phone. She could barely control the shaking in her fingers as she pressed the buttons to dial her parents.

For a moment, there was ringing. Then, an annoyed voice answered the phone, "Who is this?"

Sabina was used to the breathless tone as she had heard it on many an occasion, but it had never been a context like this one. "Mother?" she said, releasing a breath.

"Sabina! Your father and I have been worried sick! Blakely wouldn't tell us where you had gone because he didn't even know! How could you just leave us like that, without warning? I don't even recognize this number. Where are you?" There was shifting on the other end of the line, like her mother had changed which hand was holding the phone. Sabina could see it now, a nervous tic her mother often did when having a serious conversation.

"I'm in Colorado," she answered.

"Colorado?" her mother shrieked. "Why are you there? Are you with Hannah again? I know you've gotten along when you were younger, but, *honey*, she is a terrible influence on you.

I don't know what she's got you roped into, but you need to come home."

Sabina's breath hitched at her mother's patronizing tone. *Would I ever hear it again? Am I making the right choice?*

"That's why I called you. I'm not coming home. I don't think I can. Or that I should."

There was a moment of silence on the other end of the line, and Sabina felt her stomach drop.

"What do you mean you aren't coming home? Are you in trouble? Sabina, are you alright?" Her mother's voice cracked at the last word.

Sabina forced herself to breathe. She couldn't cry. She had to keep it together.

"There's a lot going on here. I'm needed here in a way you can't understand."

"You're needed *at home*. Whatever you've gotten roped into, you need to end it. *Now.*"

"I can't," Sabina said, her resolve finally faltering. "I won't be coming home. My family needs me here."

"But what about your *real* family?" her mother asked.

Sabina wanted to say more, but she knew anything that was said would fall on deaf ears. "You won't remember me, I don't think, soon after all of this is over. I just wanted you to know that I love you, that I love Father. I'll never forget you."

"Sabina, you're scaring me. Honey, listen. If you're in trouble, we'll find a way to take care of it. Just come home."

At her mother's insistent pleading, Sabina felt her soul shatter into a million pieces. No longer could she hold the tears back as they streamed down her cheeks.

"Goodbye, Mother," she whispered, shutting her eyes against the tearing of her heart.

"Sabina, wait—" Her mother's voice was no longer in her ear as Sabina hit the end button.

She clutched the phone tightly to her chest, her entire body wracking with sobs. The noise ricocheted in the forest, bleeding against her own ears. Her cries were a symphony of grief in an otherwise empty space, and for once, she wished she could be anyone else. This burden was too heavy for her to bear.

She didn't know how long she had stayed on the ground when she felt a reassuring hand on her shoulder. Will had found his way back to her, lifting Sabina to her feet. She wiped her eyes and handed him back the phone.

"Are you okay?" he asked, his eyes full of concern.

Sabina gave him a small smile. "I...think I am."

"Are you ready to head back?" he asked her.

She looked to where everyone had gone to and felt some of the grief in her stomach dissipate.

"Lead the way," she said.

CHAPTER FORTY

HANNAH

"I CAN'T BELIEVE WILL LEFT AFTER what I told him," Hannah grumbled, rolling her eyes. "He's such a stupid softie."

"Well, you were a jerk to Sabina," Tony replied with a sigh. "Will always roots for the underdogs. You know that."

"Just because he's at the bottom of the barrel doesn't mean he needs to wave a flag every time someone is having a hard day," Hannah huffed. She crossed her arms over her chest.

Rigel still stood at attention, as if at any moment Caelan would rush to tell him, "It's time. We need to leave, fulfill our duties."

Well, maybe not that wording.

She wore a crooked smile. Rigel was just too eager, filling the exact spot of hero's sidekick. It was enough to make her barf.

And there, just in front of Rigel, was the most roguish grin she had ever seen on the face of a person who should have most definitely not been wearing it.

"What's your deal with him?" Tony asked, voice gruff. As she turned his way, Tony's eyes flickered between Nyx and Hannah before settling back on the enemy. "He's been obsessed with you, I think. He sits there, watches you like prey, and then smiles like he has all the answers to whatever's on your mind. You can't tell me this isn't strange to you?"

"He's Nyx," Hannah answered, but she could feel the heat so prominently on her face. "What can we really say about him that can be true? He's a liar, and he causes trouble. Every word out of his mouth can't be trusted."

She waited for the ball to drop, for Tony to chastise her, for his entire face to erupt with disgust and frustration, but that never came.

He merely smiled, giving her arm a shove. "I'm happy you can see through whatever words he's putting into your mind. He beat you, kidnapped you. He hurt Will. I just feel so relieved to know his stupid charms haven't worked one bit on you."

As he turned away, beginning to talk to the others, Hannah let her eyes waver back to Nyx. His smile remained like a fixture, his gaze dancing with mischief as he looked at Tony and then back to Hannah. He skimmed her over, and Hannah felt like some kind of painting that was being criticized as his eyes took their time to make their way across her face.

"Can't keep my name out of your mouth, can you?" Nyx mouthed from across the way at her.

Hannah felt her cheeks blaze with the heat of a thousand fires. Nyx was bold enough to wield the match, but she couldn't dare let it continue to be fanned.

She could feel the heat traveling across the tips of her ears as she jolted around, making sure her eyes didn't dare wander back. The gang was so engrossed in conversing that none of them picked up on her heartbeat thundering wildly in her chest, though she was sure if they listened closely, it would be as loud as sirens.

"Guys! I got her! We're golden, baby!" The hooting and hollering came from none other than Will, who was rushing from the clearing with his hands in the sky to victory, gallivanting like a child.

Hannah's eyes narrowed into slits. *He never grows up, does he?*

Behind him, a shadow appeared under the covering of the clearing as a woman walked out, a bold smile on her face. She looked like she could conquer the world, and Hannah wanted nothing more than to squash that idiotic grin off of her stupid, little face.

"What changed your mind?" Tony shouted through his cupped hands that reminded Hannah of a megaphone.

The other boys were hooting along with Will, causing a bashful blush to appear on Sabina's face. *Obviously a fake one.* Sabina was having fun playing a show to the others, but Hannah was too smart to fall for it.

"It turns out Will is better at giving pep talks than you think," Sabina replied, her eyes wide with something that sparkled like hope. "You guys should listen to him more often."

"Sorry," Hannah interjected. "I think our crew has enough input from the ones already part of it. We don't *need* your input, too. There's no room for a rich girl, and it's such a shame for your sake."

Sabina's eyes shifted from hopeful to something much darker, but she turned her attention to Will as she reached his side. "Thank you," she said, resting a hand on his arm. "Your kindness means more than you know. You didn't have to drag me out of the woods."

"Of course, I did," Will proclaimed. "You're a princess now. It's our duty to make sure we can help you fulfill yours."

Hannah had to bite her lip to keep from screaming. *Here. We. Go. Again. With. The. Poor. Me. Act.*

If Sabina continued, she could have her own reality show about how every knee should bow at her feet. It was enough to induce nausea and trigger bile.

"All the thank yous are totally great and appreciated, but if we're gonna go, then we need to go tell Caelan and find Cammie." Straight to the point, Hannah watched as the gang took in her words and then looked back to Sabina.

"Let's do it," Sabina replied, her tone suddenly stark. "If you're in such a hurry to get out of here and have all of your bearings, then be the person to lead the way."

Hannah flinched. Sabina was becoming more and more bold. *That's how it was going to be.*

"Fine," Hannah said. "If you'd stop gawking and playing damsel in distress, maybe we'd finally get somewhere. If you're ready—"

"Oh, I've been ready," Sabina interrupted. "Since you're so adamant, let's get a move on already."

Hannah's cheek twitched, but she reminded herself to remain calm. She couldn't lose it in front of everyone, not while Sabina was still playing princess. Hannah swallowed down the urge to scream. Instead, she did the diplomatic thing and turned on her heel.

She could hear people following behind her, but if she wanted to play her part, she had to go through with it. With eyes on the prize, she scoured the crowd until she landed on someone in particular. Was it the someone she wanted to see?

No, not at all. Would he provide answers? That was one thing Hannah was pretty sure of.

He was staring off in the faraway distance when Hannah approached him, as if his worries were a world away and he couldn't reach them quickly enough.

"Where's Cammie?" Hannah questioned when she reached him.

James jolted, a confused look in his eyes. "We went our separate ways,'" he replied, as if it were the most obvious thing in the world.

Hannah bit the urge back to eyeroll. "You're entirely free to mope on your own time, but right now, you're in the way of what could be an entire kingdom at stake, so do you know where she is?"

With wide eyes and a mouth that couldn't—or wouldn't—quite close, James shook his head. "She has a tendency to take walks when she's upset, or sometimes, she'll go to an area that's her safe place. I'm not really sure which one it would be here."

Hannah was silent, pondering his words. "I hope whatever it is you're going through, you resolve it. I know Cammie seemed to really care about you. Thank you for at least telling me something. That, I can work with."

With a nod toward the house, Hannah led the charge in that direction. She climbed the steps first. Slivers of glass rested on the porch, but Hannah did her best not to look at it. She'd heard enough of what'd happened last night, and she didn't want flashbacks.

A sudden noise resounded, so quiet that Hannah craned her neck to hear it. *Sniffling.*

"I'm pretty sure she's in there," Sabina said. "We need to go in there."

Tony and the gang started moving to follow them inside, but Hannah held a hand up.

"I think it should just be Sabina and me," Hannah said. Despite everything that yelled for her to handle this on her own, Hannah knew Cammie and what she needed. *She needs both of us.*

The boys all nodded.

Sabina had a flash of confusion in her eyes. "Okay," she finally breathed, nodding. "Let's do it."

Sabina entered the house first. Though the lights were on, and it was still day outside, Hannah felt a sudden chill down her back when she crossed the threshold. The house itself, as beautifully chaotic as it was, felt wrong. The eerie heaviness clung to the walls, and for a moment, Hannah pondered if she was violating some kind of unspoken rule by entering. Solenne embodied her house—and with her gone—it seemed the life of the house was gone too.

"Cammie?" Hannah called out. The sniffling grew louder as she turned the corner to where the back room was, and then she heard hiccups.

"H-Hannah?" Cammie's voice was hoarse, but she still had enough strength in it for her words to not sound completely hollow. "What are you doing here?"

"We're here to come get you," Sabina said before Hannah could utter anything. "We're here...to make sure you're okay. We couldn't find you after you left the forest earlier."

"I'm sorry," Cammie wept, the sound becoming louder as Sabina and Hannah moved closer.

Hannah's eyes adjusted to the lighting in the office, and Cammie's position became clear. Huddled in the corner near the chair, Cammie sat with her knees to her chest. Her hands covered her face while her entire body wracked with sobs. Her fingers left a bit of space in them where she could peek through. Hannah stopped walking.

Cammie's hands shook as she brought them down. "I'm trying to keep it together. I don't know why it's hitting me now," she said, her voice barely a murmur.

Without hesitation, Sabina knelt down next to Cammie, resting her hand on Cammie's snot-stained arm. "You don't have to keep it together, Cammie. Not with us. We love you, okay? You can cry if you need to. You can talk if you need to. Or don't," she added, giving her a small smile. "It's whatever you need. We're here."

Cammie let out a big breath, her eyes wandering to the ceiling while the air released from her lips. "What I need is to stop crying." She wiped at a stray tear. "But more than that, I just need to process and move on. I just.... It's hitting me that Solenne has just...that she's...and I...I feel I could have done more. Maybe if I knew about my gift beforehand, or if I had trained enough in it before, maybe she would have still—"

"You can't think like that," Hannah interjected. "You can't blame yourself. You didn't know about the gift. None of us did, and the further you look back, what does it really change? Does it bring Solenne back? No. All it does is cause you more pain, and you've had enough pain, Cammie. We don't want you suffering when you don't need to."

"She's right," Sabina said.

Hannah felt herself freeze. Were they actually agreeing on something?

Sabina met her eyes, and this time, there was no fire. No rage. No unbridled urge for revenge. The only thing they embodied was a solemn understanding of what needed to be done.

Hannah felt extremely out of her element as she let her feet take her downward until she was kneeling. A few feet away from Cammie would be enough. Sabina was already close enough to do her job. Cammie didn't need two people hovering so closely, and Hannah didn't need more uncomfortable situations. Nevertheless, she embraced the unnerving nature of how her knees fell against the floor despite the thunder in her heart that refused to quiet.

In that moment, there was absolute silence except for the quivering breaths from Cammie's lips. "What happens now?" she asked, licking her lips as her eyes focused on the far-off wall.

"Now, we just try to move forward," Hannah told her.

"And how do we do that?" Cammie asked.

"We can't ignore the past," Sabina whispered, her eyes shining, "but in that same breath, we can't avoid our futures either. We have a choice to make. I know we had that conversation earlier...and I was wrong. What I said was wrong. I shouldn't have been mean to you, Hannah. What I said...is unforgivable. I know it will take a long time for you to even think about forgiving me."

"You're right about that," Hannah chimed in, "but we can handle later issues. Right now, a joint decision needs to be made. Caelan is counting on us, but we can't do it alone or just with two people. They need all three of us to come to a choice. I made my decision, but you guys could have changed your mind. I don't really know."

"I know what I want," Cammie uttered, nodding. She looked more as if she was trying to convince herself. "I want... to go to Natrellum. I want to see the world, to find out more about who we *truly* are. There's an entire world, an entire story waiting for us to explore, and as absolutely terrified that I am, I don't want to miss it." Fresh tears appeared in the recesses of her eyes, and she wiped them quickly. "Does that make me sound crazy?" She lifted her face, streaked with tears, looking at each of the girls. "If it does, just tell me. I'll understand—"

"You're not crazy," Hannah said, determined to somehow, someway, make Cammie see differently. "We've gone through a hell of a lot. If you didn't have some conflicting concern, I'd probably think *that* makes you sound crazy."

Hannah shook her head, the true meaning of those words hitting her full force. Sabina had concerns. How could Hannah fault her for that, at least?

Sabina perked her head upward, meeting Hannah's eyes. "Everything okay?" she asked, her gaze creased with worry. "You're lost in thought."

For the first time in Hannah's life, she did something she had never done before. She swallowed her pride. Her throat felt trapped by a lump she couldn't diminish. "I'm fine, but...if we want to do this right, then we need to do it right. I can't say that I fully forgive you for the words you told me. If I'm being real, I'm still pretty heated, but you were confused, and Cammie's been confused, and maybe somewhere deep down, I am too. So...I can't really fault you for being confused."

No more words allowed themselves to tumble out of her mouth, and for a moment, Hannah wondered if what she said even made sense or even was enough of an explanation.

Sabina's gaze softened, an inner glow radiating as she blinked. She ducked her head, turning her face away, as she whispered, "Thank you."

"Does this mean you guys are okay now?" Cammie's once hollow face now came to life with the light in her gaze. Her smile was so wide that Hannah wondered if her skin would crack underneath all the pressure, but her grin was so wholly exuberant that it took Hannah by surprise.

Hannah could feel her resolve fading into a soft smile as she nodded, unable to stop the feeling from captivating onto her face. "I think it's a step," she decided on.

With a force Hannah didn't even know she had, Cammie grabbed Hannah and Sabina and tugged them in. It was the strangest hug Hannah had ever experienced, but she couldn't imagine that another one would do their new situations justice.

"I'm so happy," Cammie said, her voice straining with tears. Her grip tightened, and Hannah hugged her back, letting out a chuckle.

"I can see that," Hannah replied.

Soon enough, they were all laughing together softly. Something so traumatic had birthed something beautiful, even if the beauty was only for this moment.

Loyalty was hard to find, and if these were, in fact, her sisters, Hannah was sure of one thing. They deserved her loyalty most of all, despite how much every single bone in her body told her to run, to discard them, and fend for herself.

That voice in her head was getting louder, the one that spoke of self-preservation, and even Nyx himself seemed to think that everything would fall apart. Hannah might have tended to think negatively about this new world they had yet to explore, but she knew Nyx was nothing but a liar. She had to prove him wrong.

That was the thought she clung to as she led the girls out of the house, past the clearing to where Caelan stood. That was the same thought she repeated in her mind even as Nyx's eyes found her and sent her heart spiraling into a million tiny beats.

She could not—and would not—let him win.

CHAPTER FORTY-ONE

SABINA

HER HEART FELT WEIGHTLESS. HER steps felt lighter, as if she were drifting on clouds. The smile was impossible to kill even though her stomach flipped nervously as they walked the steps to Caelan. It was a feat that felt like hours, though she was certain it only took a few minutes.

He was, once again, surrounded by people who were still enamored.

Soon enough, he saw her. Caelan quietly excused himself and turned to face the girls. He gestured to a section of forest that wasn't overrun by people. "Did you three decide so quickly? That didn't seem to take long."

"Not that long," Sabina agreed, eyes flickering over to Hannah and Cammie, who still wore soft smiles. "There was some difficulty, but we came to the same decision."

A spark of hope lit itself ablaze in Caelan's eyes, followed by a grin so wide he could barely contain himself. "And would you mind sharing what that is?"

"We've decided to go," Cammie blurted. She was practically bouncing on her own two feet like a child, her eyes sparkling with what looked to be excitement.

The ecstatic shout was louder than anything Sabina had ever heard as Caelan shook his hands in the sky. He, too, was doing a little dance of his own until his feet skidded to a stop. Pools of wetness fell from his eyes, and without warning, he lunged forward, pulling Sabina and the other two girls into a bear hug.

Squished between the other two girls, Sabina couldn't help but chuckle. *I can see where Cammie gets it from.*

"There's no more time to wait, then. Let's get things packed and head out. I've yet to see Natrellum, and I'm so grateful to be sharing this experience with you three. Rigel, of course, will be with us, leading the charge." Caelan gestured behind him, where Rigel was walking toward them, Nyx in tow.

"Leading the charge along with the villain, you mean," Hannah sputtered out, shaking her head dismissively.

A Cheshire grin appeared on Nyx's face as Rigel stopped walking, pulling on the ropes that held Nyx bound, coming to a stop. "I'm so flattered to know you think of me as the villain."

"You're happy to be known as evil?" Hannah questioned, crossing her arms over her chest.

"I'm happy to be known by you in any regard because it gives me some sort of satisfaction," Nyx countered, his grin never fading.

"And what sick satisfaction is that?" Hannah scoffed, leaning forward, her lip curled upward into a sneer.

"The satisfaction of knowing you think of me at all."

Hannah's mouth fumbled as Nyx's grin simply grew, and Sabina felt her face go hot. *No way is he flirting with Hannah.*

"Stop talking," Rigel instructed, shoving Nyx forward. "No need to cause any more problems. You've harassed them enough."

A stubborn smirk stood its ground on Nyx's face as he tilted his head back to Rigel. "You've really grown to enjoy being in a new position of power, haven't you?" he tsked, his voice barely above a subtle whisper as he added, "Such a shame how the tables have turned, the one I hired to bring me to my death."

"There's nothing we can do to determine whether you survive death at the hands of Aamir. You surrendered to the True King. *That* was enough for us to not kill you. I can't say so much about the prince. I have known him for his rough exterior, and so have others, and judging by how you poached me from under his thumb, I cannot promise how well he will welcome you, a son of one of Natrellum's most problematic families, with open arms and forgiveness."

"Well, isn't that fitting?" The gasping laugh turned breathless as Nyx's eyes shifted. "The very one who accepted my deal suddenly exempt from punishment? It pays to have friends in high places, I see."

Rigel's grip tightened, and he yanked the ropes until Nyx was face to face with him, Rigel's lips inches from his nose. His face was susceptible as he hissed, "I have no friends in high places, only allegiance where allegiance should lie. Aamir might very well kill me for throwing away someone I was supposed to capture and return for mere coins I was stupid to accept, but I have no qualms about it. My own mistakes allowed me to see the truth for myself, and I have *his* acceptance, and I'm sure I have James' forgiveness. Petty threats of demise that you drop from wicked lips will do nothing to my resolve. It only affirms the difference we have, and that you, my adversary, are nothing but a snake."

It happened so fast that Sabina was sure she was exaggerating, but it was there—the flaring nostrils, the breathless expression, and the eyes that were usually full of mischief turned dull, then shifting to a magnetic gleam as Nyx's lips tightened. Before long, the expression vanished, and no words erupted from the lips that usually boasted so proudly. Nyx jerked away, his back facing Rigel as the quietness loomed.

The silence sent chills down her spine, and Sabina's gaze settled on Hannah, with her pursed lips and clenched fists. Sabina was sure Hannah didn't feel the fear that was so prominent in her stomach at Nyx's impassive expression. No, Sabina was sure Hannah was feeling something much deeper, something much more red. Something that glowed like anger and burned like rage.

"There will be due process," Caelan said amidst the strain.

A sudden breath left Sabina's lips. All the knots she held in her shoulders loosened. With one look at Hannah, Sabina could see the tension leave her face, and her hands stopped clenching. *She is calm too.* Good. At least for now, there would be no bloodshed.

But with how they were speaking about the prince, how could Sabina be sure that bloodshed wouldn't come? Would he slaughter them, too, for claiming a throne that he was sitting on?

Sabina wrung her hands together, clutching tightly as if the mere force was the only thing holding her upright.

"You speak of due process," Nyx replied, eyes narrowing at Caelan as he turned his head, "but what you cannot recognize is that the kingdom has changed eons since they presumed you to be dead. How can you honestly expect to have any sort of control over something when no one even thinks you exist? You promise me a peaceful—or maybe *fair* is the word you would use—trial, and yet can you deliver on the promise? Tell me that, *King.* Just tell me how much of this you can deliver, and maybe my sworn allegiance will mean a little more than just *words.*"

With fire in his gaze, Nyx was clearly determined, and in his eyes, he was looking a lot more like the man she had gotten used to seeing, but there was another element that blended itself within his gaze: the look of complete helpless fear.

Caelan swallowed, and something passed over his eyes as he stared Nyx down. For an interlude, there was nothing except the gaze that kept Caelan in place, his hands stoic at his sides.

"Sire, you don't owe him anything—"

"I do," Caelan said, nodding, cutting Rigel's statement off completely. "He might have killed my mother, his father might have killed my wife and also have tried to kill my children, but who am I as a man, a king, if I cannot be impartial? What does that say about my character as a ruler, as someone who will provide guidance for these girls, if I cannot do what I must, despite what physicality might scream at me? No." Caelan shook his head violently, turning around, beginning to pace. "These girls deserve better, and so does my mother. She would be furious if I handled justice in my own hands when it wasn't my place. I've let his family sit in the trenches of my mind for far too long. I cannot allow them to sit idly by anymore, not when I have much bigger things to lay claim to, my family included, so I will do my best to swallow my anger." He stopped moving, angling his body just so to where he was facing Nyx, a solemn smile on his lips. "I release you from my anger. I release you from the clutches of revenge. I am far too exhausted to keep fighting for it to pass. Instead, I will keep hope in my heart for you...hope that whatever may come of this, that you, too, may find the peace your soul so desperately craves."

"Are we ready?" James, seemingly unaware, decided to greet the group. *He did have a habit of arriving late.*

At least, that was Sabina's impression. Aside from the interaction James had had with Cammie earlier when Will was being healed, he seemed to avoid Cammie like the plague.

Cammie's face flushed a slight shade of pink, and she averted her eyes. *So awkwardness will be their constant now.*

"Is there anything else that you need to take care of before we leave?" Caelan asked.

James shook his head quickly.

Hannah piped up, "Tony and the guys aren't here yet. We can't leave without them."

"We can wait so long for your friends, but if they aren't willing to come along, I can't force them," Caelan stated matter-of-factly.

"We're ready to go," a voice chimed.

As Sabina turned her head, she realized she recognized the voice more than she thought. *Will.*

More footsteps followed, and as Sabina's eyes trailed the group—Marcus, Tony, Will, and Trevor—she realized all were accounted for.

Is there anything else we need before we step through to our new destiny?

Caelan looked at them all in turn before he dipped his head. "We're all set to leave, then." He gave one more glance to Rigel before letting his arm fall in front of him. "Lead the way, Rigel."

Rigel nodded then said, "I need to grab my horse. Nyx will be seated there, where I can monitor him."

"I can't exactly leave. I'm bound," Nyx retorted with a snort. "You guys seem to worry so much about me leaving. I don't even have room within these ropes to shift into wolf-form as much as I'd love to conjure it willingly, so no need to fret. I will be dragged to my impending doom without a fight. Will

I go happily? Absolutely not, but beggars can't be choosers, right? If I would have known today was the day that I would get dragged to my demise, maybe I would have had a glass of some liquid courage. Alas, I can't do anything about it now. So, lead the way, *Hunter*." The retort dripped off of Nyx's lips like honey, effortlessly.

Nyx was the first to walk, leading the charge. The horse seemed to be momentarily forgotten until Caelan walked off to retrieve it.

Left in the silence as Nyx and Rigel continued walking, Sabina turned to Cammie and Hannah. "He needs a horse?"

"I've seen it," Cammie said, her eyes wide. "It was honestly pretty shocking. It glowed. I'm not sure if it's something that's normal for Natrellum, but it was the most breathtaking and the scariest thing I had ever seen."

"So far, we have people who turn into wolves, myself included, and now, we have horses that are like glow-in-the-dark lamps. This new world just keeps getting better and better. Maybe our food will float." Hannah smirked, jutting out her chin.

Sabina held back the urge to roll her eyes, and Cammie's stayed glued to where Rigel was heading toward.

"Why are you staring?" Sabina asked.

"Because it's hitting me that this is real, that it isn't some kind of joke. Hasn't it hit you?" With eyes ablaze with excitement, Cammie was in her element. It was as if the mere prospect of something new was no longer frightening.

Not if they were doing it together.

Bracing herself to bat away the nerves, Sabina let out a breath. The physical weight of turmoil from not getting along was no longer there, but the weight of responsibility? Oh, that one had just emerged and didn't look like it would leave soon.

"We can do this," Cammie assured her, reaching for her hand. "We just have to trust that, together, we will be okay."

With Cammie's hand firm in her grasp, Sabina let herself become braver. She did what would have once been unthinkable—she also reached for Hannah's hand.

When it appeared like her heart would break down and fail her, Sabina felt it thunder wildly as fingers latched onto hers. *We really are in this together.*

"Are you ready to go now?" Caelan had come back, the horse's reins in hand. The horse was glowing, just like Cammie had said.

"Yes, we are," Sabina finally answered him, completely sure of the candor in her words.

The trek seemed a lot farther than it was in reality. What was mere minutes felt more like hours. Time blurred, completely held captive by the nerves within her frayed thoughts.

Unlike the others, Sabina moved slowly. Cammie was quick to linger, and Sabina felt her nerves loosen slightly at the kind gesture.

The place they were going was secretive, Caelan had told them. They couldn't draw any unnecessary attention by taking a car. If they did, they risked other humans finding the location.

Hannah was determined to keep walking as Sabina watched her linger close to Tony's side. They were among the few who were leading the charge. Rigel was first, Nyx on the horse. His back was straight as an arrow, but he never dared to look behind him.

"What do you think that was about?" Sabina leaned over to Cammie, whispering against her hair.

Cammie flickered her gaze over, her expression pinched. "What are you talking about?"

"Nyx," Sabina stated matter-of-factly. "He's totally flirting with Hannah. You can't tell me you didn't see it."

"I saw nothing," Cammie replied, facing back to the front.

"You can't be that oblivious," Sabina muttered, rolling her eyes.

"Relax," Cammie instructed, her face light and easy with a soft smile. "I was only kidding with you, but you should've seen the look on your face. Absolutely priceless."

The look of pure mischief in Cammie's eyes gave her pause. *She hasn't been that happy in a while.*

"It wasn't just me?" Sabina asked.

Cammie shook her head, as if the question was the most ridiculous thing she had ever heard. "Definitely not just you. The reason I said nothing wasn't because of you. It's because there's nothing there to see. Nyx is a traitor, and he's going to face whatever punishment the Council throws his way. I'm still not sure what that means, but I know Hannah is not that stupid. Nyx could be the last man on the planet, and Hannah still wouldn't be desperate to choose him. I know that fact in my gut." Something unrecognizable passed through Cammie's eyes, and she faced the front.

Sabina dared to ask the question that was lingering between them. "And would you?"

"Would I what?" Cammie's eyes darkened, a shadow casting over them as she met Sabina's earnest gaze.

"If James was the last person on the planet, would you still choose him?"

Cammie was silent, although her hunched shoulders and rosy cheeks spoke volumes. Sabina had touched a nerve.

"Things are rocky right now," was all she said, turning back to their journey.

Cammie's cheek muscle twitched as she continued walking. Sabina wanted to probe, but soon enough, there was no time. The clearing was right in front of them.

Everyone came to a stop. It was such a normal section that if you didn't know it was there, it would have been easy to miss.

Two large oak trees reached for each other in a magnificent arch, the branches and stems inches from touching. It was as if they were attempting to hug, but there was a gap that prevented them from closing the distance. Purple shimmers tickled the edge of the gap, and Sabina felt her heart clench.

This is really happening.

"Is everyone ready?" Caelan asked.

There were several murmurs of agreement, and everyone in Hannah's friend group's gazes held something like wonder and excitement.

"I've only heard stories of this," Marcus said, his breath hitching as he stared at the enormous trees. "I always knew it was real, but to know that it's right in front of me is something entirely different."

Nyx wore a scowl. "The world is unlike anything your small brains can imagine. You've lived full Amarian lives here on this side of Earth. I can assure you this new world is unlike anything you've experienced here, though I can't pretend I am not the slightest bit intrigued to see how all of this will go down."

"I am not sure you'll be taking part, Nyx," Rigel tsked, shaking his head. "For all we know, the Council will have other plans for you after a trial. And, on that note..." Rigel turned his attention to Caelan. "If it is all right with you, I'd like to go first. I can make sure that Nyx doesn't try to escape."

"How many times do we have to go over the fact that I won't be leaving soon? Or, for better words that seem to fall on deaf ears, that I can't? What will it take for you guys to take me seriously?" Nyx groaned, looking up at the sky.

"Seeing you in custody will be enough," Tony spat. "Caelan might be big on forgiveness, but I'm sure not. After all the stunts you pulled, that's the last thing you'll be receiving from me."

"It's a good thing your approval isn't the one I need," Nyx declared, focusing his gaze on Tony and giving a small shrug.

"Enough bickering," Rigel ordered. "We're here to seek justice for Caelan, not settle your petty disagreements. Nyx, you'll take heed to the Council's ruling regardless of the outcome."

"As will you, I'm sure," Nyx exacerbated. "For your treachery to the Kingdom, who knows? Maybe we'll be cellmates." Nyx's smile was callous. He turned his eyes back to the enormous oak trees. "Lead the way."

Rigel's eyes stayed on Caelan. "It's your command," he said. "Whatever you want me to do, I'll do it. If you're ready for us to go in, we can go in."

Caelan was silent, his stare hauntingly tender. His face was set, and his lips trembled, though his entire body remained stoic. "I'm ready," he whispered breathlessly.

This was new for all of them. Even Caelan had never laid claim to the land he had originated from.

Rigel didn't hesitate. He nodded and yanked on the reins. "Come, Azzura," he called to the animal that glowed, leading her onward. She snorted at the command, propelling her hooves forward. Rigel gave one last parting glance before speaking. "I'll see you on the other side, then. I'll be waiting."

When he stepped through the space, at first all that Sabina could see was the materializing fragmentation of legs becoming invisible, the horse following closely behind. A bright light blinded her vision, and she shielded her eyes, blocking the glow from penetrating through her hazy vision.

When she reopened them, what once was a threshold was now nothing. Nyx and Rigel had disappeared.

Sabina could barely hold back the audible gasp from her lips. "They really went through," she breathed. Sudden shakes erupted from her once-steady hands, and her breathing became slower, deeper.

This is real. This is happening.

Cammie's face became alit with wonder, and she clenched her hands, once, twice, before looking over at Hannah. "Are you nervous?" she asked her.

Hannah scoffed, crossing her arms over her chest. "I'm past scared, Cammie. I left scared a few hours ago when I almost crapped my pants after turning into a wolf. I think it's obvious enough to say I'm just ready to dive in. I want to see what all of this actually is." Hannah shifted her neck from side to side, shaking out her arms. "Let's get this over with."

Hannah didn't wait for clarification, for the okay. Instead, she grabbed Tony's hand and jumped through—literally—the space. Her entire body disappeared in seconds, Tony behind her.

Marcus and Trevor urged Will forward.

"No!" Will screamed, even as they pulled him closer and closer to their destination. "I don't want to lose an arm. Or what about my face? I can't lose my face!"

With a hand as fast as lightning, Marcus smacked Will upside the head. "You'll be fine," he said, despite the shrieks that came from Will. Before there could be any more protests, the three went through the portal. Soon, only James, Cammie, and Caelan were waiting with Sabina.

"This is insane," Cammie squealed, jumping on her heels. "I can't just wait here. I mean...I know it scared me before, but...I just need to do it."

Squaring her shoulders, Cammie closed her eyes, inhaling deeply. Without warning, she jolted, heading straight through the portal, leaving everyone behind in her wake.

James swore under his breath. "I'm sorry. I have to go in there. There's no telling what trouble she's getting herself into. I'm not sure where the others are, but I know you'll be okay."

That was all it took before James evaporated through the space.

Sabina's breathing became more labored, and the tunnel vision started. It was as if a hand had decided her throat was a culprit and was squeezing relentlessly. "I—I—I—I can't breathe," Sabina cried out, her hands clawing at her throat, at a force she couldn't see but could most definitely feel.

"Sabina, take a minute. Sit." Caelan's voice sounded a million miles away, drowned out by the erratic thumping of her heartbeat in her veins.

More blurriness consumed her vision, and strong, steady hands grasped ahold of her, pulling her close. Caelan felt different from her earthly, adopted father. The hugs she received from the artist were scarce and only achieved through some sort of unimaginable feat that she had conquered, like winning first place in the piano competition in high school. This hug was different. Her Amarian father had a uniquely compassionate air within his arms, one of the few places Sabina had ever encountered warmth.

As his grip stayed constant, Sabina felt the tightness in her throat loosen until it fell away completely, but Caelan never let go. His arms remained until she pulled away completely.

"I'm sorry," she muttered, wiping away at stray tears that had left her eyes. "I don't know what's wrong with me."

"You're scared," Caelan said. "It's okay to be scared. I know I might talk highly about being brave...but if I am being honest, I am scared too."

Sabina furrowed her brows. "You? Scared? But this dream has been in your heart for a long time. How can you be scared?"

Caelan gave a small smile, and she noticed little circles under his eyes. "Just because a dream settles into your spirit, it doesn't mean that fear will let go so easily. Every new choice comes with a cost. Fear is only there to remind you of the journey that lies ahead. Change is exorbitant, but only you can decide if it is worth the price to pay."

"I have no idea what lies beyond there. I've seen many things, been to many places, but even Cammie...she got over her skepticism quickly. Why is it so hard for me to just go through?" Self-doubt crept into her words, and Sabina averted her eyes, the red-hot flame of embarrassment lighting a blaze in her stomach.

Caelan's gaze stayed intact on her face. She didn't need to lift her eyes to feel it. The burning gaze she sensed outside of her peripheral vision was enough.

"Because you aren't like your sisters, and that's okay. It's clear in the way you carry yourself, but that child-like curiosity is still there. It is okay to take your time to come to terms with this new reality. I'm not asking you to perform all the Amarian duties now. I'm just asking for your hand, so you can claim your true destiny. I've asked you before, Sabina, but I'll ask you again: Will you come with me?"

Caelan extended his hand out to her, and Sabina watched it with trembling breaths. The feeling of being closed in was back, but this time, instead of willing it away, Sabina leaned into it. She let the fear warn her away from a potentially dangerous path, and in the same breath, she hugged it tightly, instead of letting it envelop her.

As time went on, the feeling left again, instead replaced by butterflies. *It is a new start, a new beginning.*

With her palms still shaking, Sabina reached out and grabbed Caelan's invitation. His grip was firm as he led her to the portal opening.

The ground was rough under her feet, and with each step, it felt like an anchor was bringing her under.

Sabina couldn't see the land beyond. It was completely obscured from her half-human eyes, only allowing her to see what other non-Amarians would see—the other side of the clearing where trees and dirt stood.

But Sabina knew better.

Caelan went first, still not letting go, and Sabina was no longer immune to the pull.

PART

III

CHAPTER FORTY-TWO

SABINA

THE COLORS WERE MAGNIFICENTLY BLINDING, a beautiful blurred array that was so intertwined Sabina almost couldn't tell them apart.

It was unlike any canvas she had seen before under her parents' roof, where everything that was splendid could be bought without question. *This* fell under a different category.

Time seemed frozen, almost, like a stagnant pause as her foot stepped over the threshold, a threshold that mere humans couldn't see.

As her fingers connected with the shimmering portal, a tingling feeling zipped through the tips to her elbow. The shock reverberated through her body as her feet hit solid ground.

The blurring colors dissipated into nothing, and the tingling feeling stopped completely. Sabina dared to open her eyes. The ground was luscious, a beautiful emerald green. Flickers of lilac blossomed from the ground, the stems a lighter hue of purple. Brown specs were smeared into the grass, little traces of mud. As Sabina stepped forward, the smell in the air was fresh, the last remnant of dew from a sprinkling of rain.

The space was vast before her eyes, and Sabina turned her head around for one more glance at the home she'd left behind. Her eyes met nothing but more of the beauty of the expanse she was in. *My home is long gone.*

It seemed the others were also stuck in the enamored state as Sabina finally found where they were. Hannah and the gang were walking in circles, talking amongst themselves, their heads looking up to the sky.

As Sabina followed their line of sight, she bit her lip, holding back the breath that desperately wanted to meet the air. A purplish hue was forming amidst the baby blue she was used to seeing back on Earth. If she peered close enough, she could see tiny sparkles of yellow in the atmosphere.

"What is that?" Sabina questioned, squinting her eyes to focus on the object so far away.

"What your kind calls stars," Rigel replied. "The stars help tell us the time, too." He paused, pointing upward with his free hand, using his pointer finger as a guide. "It looks like, right about now, twilight is almost upon us. That means the curfew will be in effect shortly. It is best for us to keep moving. If we want an audience with the prince, we should do it quickly." He pulled on the reins lightly, leading Azzura forward.

Sabina shared a look with the others then looked at Caelan.

Slowly, he let go of her hand and nodded in Rigel's direction. "He knows best. Do as he says."

Barely visible, Caelan's hands shook. He blinked a few times, a glistening of sweat appearing on his brows. Cammie and James followed Rigel, and Hannah and the others weren't far behind.

"You okay?" Sabina asked, reaching out for Caelan. "You're shaking."

Caelan grimaced but nodded. "I'll be fine. All of this is just new, and what kind of father would I be if I couldn't follow my example? I have spent my entire life trying to fill the void that your absence left. I haven't the faintest clue about how to do it correctly, but putting my best foot forward and showing you how to have courage seems like a good place as any to start." Caelan accepted Sabina's hand and gestured to where Rigel and the rest of the gang were walking. "We should listen. We don't want to be here when it gets dark."

Hand-in-hand, they walked behind everyone. Her feet glided against the grass as she moved, the feeling like smooth glass under her steps. This terrain was nothing like the rocky one she had left behind. It was as if there were no blemishes clutching the ground and no crevices to make her trip.

As far as her eyes could see, there were nothing but tiny specs in the distance, the colors a moldy brown. Even trees were absent here, making the journey feel even more hollow.

"How much farther?" Caelan asked, his voice booming in the silence of walking.

"It shouldn't be too much longer," Rigel replied, turning his head back to Caelan with a soft smile. "We're nearing into the outskirts of town, and we're going to have to regroup before we arrive. There might be some kind of a problem."

"What kind of problem?" Tony asked, voice gruff.

A dramatic sigh appeared from the front of the group, and Nyx shook his head. "Maybe he's talking about the fact that you are all—save for Rigel, smart man— dressed for a certain world. Ever thought that might be an issue? At least Rigel had the decency to wear a cloak."

"How are we supposed to blend in if we're standing out so much?" Cammie blurted, her brows furrowed in thought.

"I'm glad you asked, Cammie," Nyx boomed. "You'll see that—"

"You've done enough," Rigel interjected. "I'll take it from here. That's where the market comes into play. What Nyx was referring to was *stealing*. It makes sense that someone of his caliber would go to that extreme, but what we will do is rely precisely on what I'm under the influence of doing."

"What exactly will you be doing?" Will piped up. "Does it involve snacks? I had no idea that traveling to another world would make me so hungry." He clutched his stomach, a whimper escaping.

Tony groaned, shaking his head. "Why is food at the top of your concerns right now?"

"Maybe because I have no idea if we are going to eat? Is anything even edible for Hannah and the girls? Maybe they'll starve to death. How do you think that makes me feel?" The rambling flowed like honey from Will's nervous lips.

Sabina felt her own stomach growl. When was the last time she had eaten?

"Food doesn't sound like a bad idea," James mentioned, "but maybe we should find something to eat at the market." At Hannah's quizzical glance, he cleared his throat. "Something tame, of course. We don't exactly want another attempted murder." He chortled.

The entire group went silent.

A plum-colored blush coated James' cheeks. "I did not mean for that to turn out as bad as it did," he murmured, turning toward Caelan. "I'm sorry."

Caelan waved him off with his one free hand. "You're fine."

"Mentioning the entire massacre of the original royal family in the same breath as we're about to reveal the true heir to the current nobility on the throne? That is definitely not fine. In fact, I'd be blunt enough to say it was done in terrible taste." Rigel shook his head dismissively, tsking under his breath. "Where are manners anymore?" he muttered.

"I don't know." Nyx sighed. "I think I'd be biased to say it was a job well done. Food poisoning is an old method of dealing with someone. For James to even have come to that on his own since it's basically outdated, I will say, for one, that I'm proud. You've paid attention to history lessons. Can't get much more Amarian than that."

Rigel scrunched his face as if a foul smell appeared in the air. "Leave it to you to find the most pleasant statements in the midst of absolute horror."

Nyx let out a sly smile. "I didn't make it to where I am without being a little ruthless."

"And that 'ruthless attitude,'" Tony said, drawing quotation marks, "is getting you into prison."

"Innocent until proven guilty, remember?" Caelan remarked effortlessly, causing a groan from the others. "I promised the Council would give him a fair trial. As fair as I can offer him."

The tone in his voice was final, and no one dared to speak against it.

They continued their walk in silence until Rigel cleared his throat. "Permission to speak, sir?" His eyes flashed to Caelan with nervous beats.

"You can speak freely. You should know that by now. You have a plan, and I would love to hear it." Caelan gave a smile that rivaled diamonds, and the more Sabina saw, the more she was sure of just how charming Caelan could be. It seemed effortless.

"Once we reach the market, the girls should hang back, as you all should. I'm going to do something that might seem outlandish, but I will need you to trust me. Is that something you can do?" Rigel's earnest eyes searched Caelan, and then he shifted his gaze to Sabina and the others, the weight of it piercing through her.

Sabina swallowed, willing the brick in her throat to subside, and she looked to Caelan for confirmation. *He knows more than we do. What should we do?*

"You do whatever is necessary to get us where we need to be...safely," Caelan instructed with a curt nod. "If you do that, then I trust you with every fiber of my soul."

Rigel genuflected, his eyes becoming more relaxed with purpose. "Then I will do what I do best, sire. I can assure you of that."

After Sabina's feet felt like rocks were dragging her under, hope blossomed in her chest. She could finally see it—the market.

There were loads of chatter, and people were seated at their respective booths. She could hardly make out any faces, as they were still a great distance away. Still, it was finally within reach.

"The plan is coming into place now." Rigel kept his voice quiet. "I will need you," he said, directing his gaze to Tony and the other men, Caelan included, "to huddle around the girls. Grab them, if you can. Not too forcefully, of course, but do as I say and please don't ask questions."

He averted his eyes, turning back to the direction of the market. With a click of his tongue, Rigel pulled on the horse's reins and walked forward. His steps were sure, but there was one thing that Sabina noticed. Whether it was because of nerves or something much more, she couldn't decipher, but Rigel's hands were shaking.

"What is he doing?" Sabina asked, just as the guys crowded around her, dragging Cammie and Hannah in the throes, too.

"Ow!" Hannah shrieked as her head thwacked against Will. "Watch it, you mutt," she snarled, punching Will with her fist.

"Hannah-Banana, coming from anyone else, I'd be angry, but something about you calling me a mutt brings joy I never thought possible to my heart." Will feigned a love-sick sigh, fanning himself with one hand.

Tony whacked Will upside the head. "Stop acting like a lunatic. You can't do that here." He jerked Will's arm roughly, leaning in close. Tony focused his eyes on Hannah, a warning in his pupils. "*Behave*," he said, voice on the edge of a growl.

Hannah scoffed, rolling her eyes.

Sabina shook her head. Too much was going on, too fast. It was on the verge of spiraling, and nothing had started yet.

Tony released his monstrous grip, and Will let out a breath of relief.

Sabina looked over at Cammie for any kind of inclination, any kind of emotion, but her face was impassively blank.

Then, Sabina vaguely heard a voice from afar.

Rigel had finally reached the market.

CHAPTER FORTY-THREE

HANNAH

"I NEED A FEW CLOAKS," RIGEL said.

Hannah was sure the others could barely hear his voice in the distance, but it carried as if it were right across from her. Unruly blond waves blocked his face from view as he leaned over a booth, his elbows taking over most of the marketeer's space.

Hannah supposed the supernatural hearing came from the Lunar gift. The more she tilted her head, the clearer the sound became.

She couldn't tell much about the person, but by the height and build, she was sure it was a woman. But the age? She was definitely unsure about that. The woman wore tattered clothing that looked like it was on the verge of falling apart, the color a blend between sea foam and midnight blue. The sleeves were there, little sections missing that left tiny holes in the seams.

"That'll cost money," the woman said, rising from the stool she was sitting on. Her height didn't match Rigel's by any feat, but for some odd reason, Rigel took a step backward.

"I don't have any coins on me right now, but I can assure you—"

"No coin, no cloak," the woman interrupted, her voice an edgy steel. A slow smile paved the way on her lips, and she leaned forward, her face almost melding into Rigel's. "Ye mostly flounced around in the clearing. It isn't my fault that ye didn't bring the right clothing or the right payment." The woman cocked her head to the side then looked over at the group in the distance.

It was as if the woman could see right through Hannah. The intense gaze sent her heart galloping to her throat.

"Ye can take yer friends and go," the woman instructed. "If ye aren't gonna buy, then begone with ye."

Rigel stood silent, gawking at the woman. For a moment, Hannah wondered if he would actually be so stupid to turn around and make this a lost cause.

But Rigel never moved. He shook his head, an incredulous laugh escaping his lips. "You're mistaken," he said, gripping the reins tighter.

"Is that so?" the woman murmured.

"I'm on official kingdom business, a special order from the prince himself."

"The prince, eh?" The woman stared, unblinking at his words.

And then, the deafening, rich sound stung Hannah's ears—the sound of laughter bleeding into the square. It was as if it were on a loop, unable to stop. Over and over, the noise scratched against Hannah's ears, like chalk on a board.

The woman clutched her stomach, doubling over. Spittle flew from her parted lips onto the dirt, and she rose from her position, glaring daggers at Rigel. "You must take me as a fool to believe something so incredulously ridiculous. Special orders from 'the prince,' my behind. Go on with ye!" The woman shook her head once more. "I won't tell ye again!"

"And I won't tell *ye* again," Rigel demanded, his face like stone. "I have orders, and if you are so incompetent as to heed my words as I tell them to you, then who else do I need to speak to? Guards?"

At the mere mention of the word, several people looked in their direction, quiet mumbles falling over the several booths. Rigel was causing a scene.

The woman was as stubborn as he was, never moving an inch from her position. "If guards will suit ye demands and get ye away from my booth, then send all the men. Bring them here and get out me sight! Ye're nothing but poison to potential customers."

The sudden scent of a musky rose entered Hannah's nostrils. Clanking of metal resounded, and a horse snorted. *That's what the smell was.*

The customers who were standing in front of nearby booths jumped, moving out of the way to form a path for the person to walk through. It was such a hazy blur that Hannah couldn't make it out at first, but soon, the glinting stopped blurring her eyes and her stomach fell to her knees. It was a member of the palace guard.

Donning gleaming armor that rivaled the sun, the man held his head high as his horse traipsed through the space until he came to a slow stop at the booth where Rigel and the woman stood.

"Is there some sort of conflict going on here?" the man asked, his voice a combination of soft and metallic.

Hannah felt her pulse speed up in her neck, and her throat became parched.

"The problem is that he is scaring away good paying customers. He asked for a cloak and refused to pay—" The woman's words fell short as the armored man held up a hand, no words escaping his lips at the woman's expressive complaints.

Instead, he turned his eyes on Rigel, surveying the other horse and the person sitting on top of it. "Is this true?" he asked, his words clipped.

"It is true, but—"

"If you will not do the honorable thing, then ye should do as she asks. Or, if hearing it from better lips would serve ye better, hear it from mine: *Leave*." The man's upper lip curled, but the man's hand never left the space by his side.

The silver glinting didn't disappear from Hannah's sharp eyes. It was a sword.

"If ye refuse to do as I say, I will have no other choice but to escort ye. Ye're causing a scene when there was not one present before ye arrived. There is better business for me to attend to than the childish whining of a non-paying customer—"

"Then, escort me," Rigel said boldly. "That's exactly what I need. We are on the same page."

The guard scoffed. "And what page exactly would we be on together?"

"I was sent on a mission to the Earth realm, special orders from Prince Aamir. They recruited me."

"Telling more lies will not make me have any sort of favor on ye." Disgust dripped from the guard's lips, and his hand latched onto his side, pulling upward. Silver gleamed in the slightest haze of sun that was still lingering.

Rigel raised his hands in surrender. "There's no reason to be testy. I am on the same page as you—*to get justice served in the right hands.*" He gestured behind him. "The reasoning you seek is back there, where the people are in that circle. They're trying to protect the females, rightfully so, but..." Rigel chuckled, clearing his throat. "...no amount of protection can stop the justice from flowing."

The guard shot Rigel an inquisitive look.

"I have found the one you have been seeking. He is known as James, but there might have been another name you have called him?"

The guard shifted position, and his entire body turned in the direction of where the girls stood. More appeared behind the first, and Hannah's gut churned.

"What is Rigel doing?" Cammie whispered under her breath. "Why—why is the guard coming this way? And why are more guards following him?"

The first guard charged, his sword in the air as the horse propelled him forward. Several hooves clamped on the ground behind him as more guards on horses followed suit, all heading to the spot where the gang was gathered.

"James Asaiah Bastian, you are charged with the upmost disgrace that one can bring to Natrellum and to the Kingdom of Eleisa: treason to the high king."

Soon enough, the protection around the girls was dismantled, and James was now face-first onto the ground as a rope was being tied around his wrists. There was no stopping this. What had Rigel done?

"Stop, please, there's no need to do this," James cried out, spitting out pieces of dust and dried mud that had found its way into his mouth.

"Save yer words for the prince," the guard growled, dragging James to his feet. He had no other option but to heed their instruction as their hands prompted him to walk.

It wasn't long until they went after one of her sisters. Sabina's hands were bound.

"On with ye," the guard yelled, pushing her back with so much force that she stumbled. At his instruction, she moved forward.

All the while, Rigel averted his eyes as guards dismounted their horses, and Hannah couldn't stop the roiling sickness that came with the stinging betrayal.

The force of the man's hands felt like a thousand tons, the skill of someone who had been in combat for longer than Hannah had been alive. No matter how hard she tried to wrestle against him, there was no use. She could not break free.

He wrapped her hands in the rope behind her back and pushed her onward. *This is dangerous. How are we expected to get out alive now?*

Tony wasn't handled gently, either. None of the boys were, but James, by far, received the worst. With mud staining his face and unfiltered rage in his eyes, he was dirty and worn and trapped, just like all of them.

Sabina was hard to read except for the shock that reverberated through her pupils. Hannah felt it, too, deep in her core. Traitors hid in the grass like snakes, waiting for the right moment to strike. Rigel had done exactly that. He had intertwined himself in their group to where denying his help would be impossible, and here he was...going back on everything he had said he would do.

Hannah couldn't hold back the clench in her jaw, even as the motion sent shock waves of pain in her mouth. Up ahead, she could see the guards continuing to push James several paces. His legs shook with each step, but the guard paid no mind.

Hannah had enough. "Stop hurting him," she called out to the guard. "You don't need to be violent."

As if her words were merely a whisper of air, the man kept walking.

Hannah's heart thundered in her throat. *He ignored me. Completely and utterly.*

"Hey!" The bellowing croak made her vocal cords burn.

Her entire body shivered with goosebumps as she realized what she had done. He didn't know her or her true lineage. What was stopping him from slaughtering her right there?

At the screaming command, the guard who was pushing James held up a hand, and everyone came to a stop. Slowly, he turned, and for the first time, Hannah got a good look at his face. He did not look much older than she, at least twenty, but Hannah knew better. An Amarian benefit was the lie of aging. He could have been a few hundred years for all she knew, and that was the beauty of it, wasn't it? She could never for sure know where she stood, not with beings who were so easily camouflaged that predator and prey became blended and hard to distinguish.

His hair was like Rigel's but a different shade of blond, teetering edge of a sunflower in the last days of summer before fall came to swallow it whole. His eyes, though, were calculating. The purest blue looked on at her, but the meaning within them contrasted starkly with the type of color.

"Who are ye to tell me how to do the duty assigned to me?" The guard handed his reins to another who had not mounted a horse. More had gathered in the time they were being bound. Hannah just had not seen them. Another got ahold of James, and soon, there was nothing separating the guard from walking Hannah's direction.

Hannah's hands felt like fire as the rope rubbed against her skin, and the person holding her arms captive tugged her backward, her back to his chest. She was bound, unable to move at all now.

"Speak," the guard commanded. "I'm sure ye have a good reason to yell at me, don't ye? But ye do not know how much pain this person has brought. Ye have yer reasons, but ye do not know the true story of what happened here."

The guard's words rang in the air, and Hannah's looked to someone, anyone, for guidance. Caelan's eyes found hers, and she hoped the meaning in them was crystal. *Should I tell him?*

Caelan shook his head, mouthing, "Not yet."

Hannah felt her nerves spiral. She shouldn't have opened her mouth because now, the guard wanted answers. She had no idea how to provide them.

She closed her eyes but could still hear his boots resounding on the ground as he stepped forward. A shadow crossed over her face, and she could feel the breath, hot like ashes, on her cheek.

"What is yer name?" he asked, sending her heart skyrocketing.

"Hannah," she answered instantly, still not opening her eyes.

"Why do ye defend a traitor, Hannah? Is it because ye align with his cause, for the masses the king deemed worthy to die?" The tone was almost haughty.

Hannah had to bite her lip to stop herself from speaking. The metallic taste stained her tongue. The man's perspiration held a scent similar to peeling onions, and Hannah had to bite down even harder to keep from gagging. More crimson spilled into her mouth, and Hannah swallowed, finally allowing herself to meet the man's eyes.

"Maybe it is you who hasn't opened your eyes enough to see the truth," Hannah said softly.

The hot breath came faster, and Hannah practically choked on it. His eyes darted, anger flared his nostrils, and she saw the hand raise before she could say anything more.

When it made contact, her entire body thrummed. Her cheek stung with the force of a thousand bees, and the crimson wetness rattled in her mouth at the friction, splitting her lip open even wider. She saw splatters of it stain his clothing like an offering of war, and pools of tears appeared behind her eyes as the wind stroked her lashes.

"Ye side with someone who killed our people, yer own people, and ye see nothing wrong with that? I wonder why that is—" His words halted as Hannah brought her face back to him, her hair dangling behind her ear. "Yer human," he breathed, his mouth dropping open.

"And you somehow think that makes it okay to hit someone? What a world this is," Hannah said, words garbled with blood. It trickled down her chin.

The guard's angry eyes turned from Hannah to James. "How dare ye involve humans in our worldly matters? Ye dared to get involved with the likes of these...creatures? Our entire existence has stayed safe because of the separation, and ye just had to disobey even more orders and blend yerself into the world that was not, and will not, ever be, yer home? Yer not just killing our Elite with yer treasonous actions, yer killing the entire world of Natrellum. For that, I hope Prince Aamir will not spare ye. I hope ye face judgment that only the royals can give, along with whatever else the Council deems fit to charge ye with."

The pompous guy was getting on Hannah's last nerve.

"Hey, jerk," she called out.

The guard turned his face back to Hannah, and that was when she let it fly.

Spatters of blood flew from her parted lips. She made sure her aim was direct enough to where saliva and crimson dotted his face like a tie-dye T-shirt.

Waves of fury trembled in his nerves as a muscle twitched in the guard's face, and he wiped his face quickly before turning on his heel.

"Anders," the guard called, his voice hoarse and strained.

The grip on Hannah's arms tightened as recognition filled her brain. So the guy holding onto her was Anders.

"Yes, sir," he replied.

"Bring her up front with me," the guard instructed. "I want to keep a watchful eye on her. Unlike the others, it looks like she will be a continuous headache for me, and I'd like to minimize it as much as I can."

"Don't you touch her. Don't you *dare* move her," Caelan said, jerking against the grip that held him bound.

Anders said nothing in response, but merely gripped Hannah even tighter.

Sudden dread filled Hannah's stomach, and she met the eyes of the others. Tony was barely containing his rage, thrashing this way and that despite the guard holding him captive.

Caelan's eyes held nothing but a burning flame, and she knew, without a doubt, that if he could get out of the binds, she was sure that Anders would miss a head.

Cammie was strikingly silent, her cheeks burning with red heat as she stared at the ground. She was completely and utterly hopeless. Sabina said nothing, but the worry in her wide eyes was clear, and it latched onto Hannah's heart.

Anders did as he was instructed, shoving her to the front, right next to Nyx, and by Nyx was, well...

"Please know I didn't mean for this to happen," Rigel implored.

She could barely see him through the tears in her eyes, his figure nothing but a blurry, untrustworthy haze.

"Stop talking," Hannah growled, averting her gaze.

Anders' grip tightened, and Hannah bit her lip to keep from screaming. *We are being treated like absolute animals.*

"I need you to know that I didn't mean for it to get this bad—"

"What did you think selling us out was going to do? Did you think they'd just march up here with good intentions? Don't you see they intend to kill us? Or at least me? And not just me but James too."

"I promise I'll get you out of this," Rigel said, his voice shaky.

"Save your words," Hannah barked. "You've already said enough lies. I really don't need to hear more of them."

Rigel's face fell. He shook his head before blurting, "Please, you have to believe me."

Without bothering to respond, Hannah turned her face away, lifting her chin.

Rigel was completely and utterly dead to her.

CHAPTER FORTY-FOUR

SABINA

Sweat clung to the back of her neck without ceasing, and her stomach felt like it was on the verge of recoiling. If she didn't control her breathing, she knew her last meal would be on the guard's uniform that was in front of her.

Her feet felt like they carried lead with each heavy step, and she kept her eyes downward. If she even so much as looked at someone or something the wrong way, who knew what else could happen to them?

She could feel shadows of stares the farther they kept walking, and as each booth came closer into view, several patrons and booth owners became severely quiet, leaving Sabina with nothing but the pounding of a resistant heart and the breathing of her fellow captors.

Quiet whispers followed suit, and Sabina felt her face burn with embarrassment as some of the words caught wind in her ears.

"Did ye see her ear? I cannot believe it. Humans, here?"

"How did they get to Natrellum?"

"The portal—"

"But I thought it didn't work?"

"They told us humanity could never pass through. Were they lying?"

"There's nothing but filth on them!" a man cried out, his words guttural against the depth of the crowd.

Sabina felt a slight wetness against her cheek and dared to lift her eyes. Saliva pooled down the bold man's chin who sent insults her way. He had spat on her as if she were nothing.

"Walk faster," the guard ordered, pushing her forward.

Sabina stumbled on her feet, and a chorus of chortling laughter filled the air. These people could not stand to see her walk, much less see her survive. If she died in front of them, they would most definitely cheer.

She couldn't help but wonder how far their hatred could go while they continued walking. It was almost incinerated into her brain as something that would never burn out.

It occupied her thoughts feverously until a sudden flashing blinded in front of her eyes.

Metallic shimmer with a bronze glint blurred her sight. It was strikingly bright and caused a yellowish haze on the outskirts of her vision that refused to dissipate until she rapidly blinked it away.

The animal was fierce and unafraid, even in stenciled embroidering on a shield that would not let it come alive. It was so majestic she had to look twice to fully grasp sight of it.

With black wings spreading outright to the sky and a blood orange hue at the feet that erupted into flames, trickling into the feathers, the bird stood high and proud, without shame. The fiery gaze gave way to a challenge, as if anyone who dared to stand against it would surely perish. Sangria swirls outlined the animal, entering the edges of the shield to where silver and red mixed.

A phoenix.

"Stand at the ready," the one holding the shield said.

As Sabina took her eyes away from the shield, she was soon met with a multitude of guards who were holding onto similar shields with their lives, with honor. They held onto them proudly, blocking the armor, and their eyes focused somewhere far off into the distance. Behind them, a huge gate blocked off a walkway, the same walkway that led to a castle far behind it.

The castle was sumptuous and inspiring. It looked like something straight out of a medieval book, and the building's form could have rivaled that of an ancient architect. Gray stones that were melded into a golden hue made up the bulk of the castle, with pointed roofs that stood all on their own.

A flag, with the same emblem, stood proudly, with words in Latin that were unrecognizable in her eyes, even with years of proper schooling.

Sabina pondered how much history resided within the walls of such a magnificent piece of framework.

She felt sudden hands on her back, and goosebumps appeared at the touch. What was going on now?

The group stopped moving.

The guard at front gave a slight nod at the ones standing in formation before the gate. "We found James and his associates of death," he said.

Sudden flashes of anger appeared on several faces, but no one spoke.

"Request an audience with Prince Aamir immediately," the guard continued, his voice gruff. "He will decide what to do with them until we can get the Council involved."

The one guard nodded quickly, turning on his heel before moving his attention to the gate. After several minutes, two other guards called out, and the gate opened inward, allowing the one to run across the drawbridge to the castle doors.

Sabina marveled at the machinery, wondering what sort of contraptions Amarians could have used and created.

It didn't take long for her to be pushed forward again, in the same direction as the guard.

Hannah was silent, blood still dripping onto the ground as she continued walking. Sabina could see the splatters leaving a trail of dots. Even James wore a face etched with pain, and he was forced to walk as fast as the guard deemed worthy.

When Sabina found her footing on the drawbridge, the thundering in her heart started again. Were they going to die?

The creaking of the gate closing behind them echoed in her brain, another sudden reminder that there was no way out of this.

Her eyes searched until they landed on Rigel, who was still staring downcast at the ground. He had brought them to their deaths. They were really going to die unless Caelan found a way to plead their cases. For all she knew, this prince could very well think they were involved in some sort of sinister plot to bring the kingdom to its knees, and yet no one knew they were the ones the throne really belonged to.

The irony. Sabina huffed. A subject would kill the true heirs and not even know it.

Two guards near the doors pulled on the handles, and Sabina found herself peering into the open archway that could lead them to their demise.

Several servants went about their duties as they entered the space.

She wondered what her life would have been like if this had never occurred. Would she have gone forth with her parents plans, owning an art studio, or would she have strayed the path, doing something completely different?

And what of Cammie and James? Hannah, the others?

Sabina pushed herself forward. Her feet clung desperately to the carpeted walkway, and if it wasn't for the guard's persistent urging, Sabina would have listened to the voice in her head that told her to run, but she knew she couldn't risk her friends and family dying for the sake of self-preservation.

The group changed direction, turning the corner instead of continuing down the long hallway. Lanterns were alight along the wall, casting the room into a gloomy glow. Several portraits hung alongside them, from artists that Sabina would never possibly know.

More doors began to open, and servants quickly bowed out of the way. Surely the ropes branded them as guilty of a crime, a feat that the servants wanted no part of.

If she were them, she would have done exactly the same thing.

The walking continued, with more doors and lengthening hallways without end, until the guards rounded another corner. The doors at the end of this particular hall were ornate and massive—a charcoal color with silver swirls that led to the elegant double door knobs.

Two servants waited for the signal. At the first guard's nod, the double doors swung open, leading to a room large enough for at least a hundred people.

Shields and swords hung on the wall, and a large glass window revealed the sun had fallen the depths of the sea, leaving no light present save for the lanterns that were in the room.

The doors slammed shut, and several guards, steady in formation, parted like a wave, leaving a walking path for their group.

Sabina's eyes fell back to the ground, where a velvet carpet led the way to steps of the royal throne.

As her feet got closer and closer to the steps, Sabina's mouth went dry. This was real. She wasn't dreaming.

"Corellon told me that it was urgent, that there was a need for an official meeting. What have you dragged me here for, Lashrael?"

The words sent shivers up Sabina's skin, and she dared to raise her eyes.

There, sitting comfortably on the throne, was Prince Aamir.

CHAPTER FORTY-FIVE

SABINA

THE PRINCE HAD COLD EYES that accentuated his jacquard embroidered overcoat. He wore his house colors with pride. The plain, black buttoned vest blended with the red and gold swirls on the coat itself, reminding Sabina of some crimson-colored mirage.

His hair was neatly in place, along with his frown of distaste, as if even a terrible mood would never go unpolished. Golden chains attached itself to the sleeves he wore, jingling as he brought his left hand up to rest under his chin.

With his dark hair and ivory skin, Sabina could have almost mistaken him for another human, but there was one tiny detail that blew that out of the water.

His ears were slanted, pointed upward in a way that hers never would.

Caelan and Solenne had mentioned something about a glamour, a way that Amarians could blend in with humanity in the Earth-realm, but she had never seen it fall away in front of her eyes in real time.

"I have found the one ye've been desperately seeking, sire," Lashrael replied. "I figured that fact alone was worth getting ye here and out of Darrian's hair. Ye have been busy preparing for the ball later tonight for the King's Celebration of Life ceremony, and I knew seeing justice served would be just the thing to set yer mood right."

Prince Aamir shifted on the throne, his eyes scouring the room until they landed on James. His expression altered from indifferent to a storm. "Bring him closer," he said, words spewing nothing but complete venom.

Lashrael complied, dragging James forward. Within seconds, Lashrael shoved James to the floor. James cried out in agony as his body fell with a resounding thud. Weakly, he lifted his head from the carpet, meeting Aamir's hostile gaze. "Prince Aamir," he called out feebly.

The prince held up a hand, and James stopped speaking. "I don't need to hear apologies or excuses because you left. I already know that you did. Otherwise, there would be no reason for a bounty hunter."

At the word, Rigel stiffened before walking to the throne. His movements were trembling and lagging, even as his knees brushed the carpeted stairs. "Prince Aamir," he breathed, "I have done as you have asked. As you know, it is my family's duty to take care of the Crown's needs without question. He is now delivered to you."

The prince beckoned with his hand, tilting his head to one side. "If you have more to add to this, please complete your sentence. Otherwise, I think we are quite done."

Rigel swallowed, turning his head back to the group. He met Sabina's eyes, and in his gaze, she could see something that resembled fear. "Sire, I must be honest with you. You need to deal with me and what I've done."

The prince merely waved away Rigel's comment with his free hand. "What you've done is fulfill your duty by bringing me this...traitor." A satisfied smile appeared at the corner of the prince's lips. "Now, he can no longer hurt anyone else—"

"I didn't hurt anyone," James pleaded. "It looked like I did, but I promise you, he was already on the verge of death by the time I found him."

The prince turned his eyes on James, his smile slowly fading to a thin line. "That is just what a traitor would say, is it not?" Prince Aamir rose suddenly, running his hands over his shirt, as if doing so would rid himself of the conversation. He turned his eyes to Lashrael, his eyes stern. "Take him to the dungeons. Take the others as well, whomever they are. Do what you must. I have had enough of his lies. He will say anything to get out of punishment, but it's far too late for that."

Prince Aamir started down the steps, his hands resting on the lapels of his coat. His eyes were trained on anywhere else but the crowd that was gathered at the foot of the throne, and Sabina felt another imaginary hand squeeze her throat. *Is he really that callous?*

A memory of how the soldier had treated Hannah flashed in her mind, and the sick feeling in her stomach grew. If he peered any closer and saw underneath her hair, he would, along with the rest of his kind, let her die without having a reason. *Yes, he really is that callous.*

"You can't just take him away without due cause," Caelan called out.

"He murdered someone in the King's Circle," Aamir countered with a brief look over his shoulder, but he was still walking to some far-off destination.

"And your proof of that is what, exactly?" Caelan barked.

The prince stopped walking, and even his breathing halted as he turned on his heel. His eyes were wild while he surveyed Caelan up and down. "The proof is evident by how he ran and how the deceased was found. It doesn't take an imbecile to put the facts together." With a raised brow, the prince took a step closer to where Caelan was still bound. "And just whom are you to talk to me this way? Do you not hold the respect for the heir of Eleisa?"

Caelan did not quiver. He held his head high, and his eyes shone with the stubbornness and force of an impenetrable wall. "It is hard to have respect for a title that you did not earn by birthright alone."

A muscle in the prince's cheek twitched. "You dare disrespect your ruler in the face of his men?"

"There is no disrespect involved if I am the rightful heir they built this very kingdom on."

Veins strained in Prince Aamir's hands as he clenched and unclenched them, moving to a crouch near Caelan's position. "And whom are you to label yourself the true heir?"

"Unhand me, and I will show you," Caelan replied, sending Sabina's heart into a pitter-patter.

For a moment, Prince Aamir didn't speak. Sabina held her breath, waiting for him to strike Caelan clear across the face.

"Do it," Prince Aamir said, gesturing to the guard that held Caelan's hands tight.

Sabina let her eyes wander to the others. Hannah's expression was unreadable amidst the crimson that had stained her lips after the wear of time. Tony revealed nothing in his gaze as he clenched his jaw. Marcus and Trevor both had the same glazed expression. Only Will showed emotion—fear that was lingering like the perfect resting place. Cammie's panicked eyes never left James, even as he rose to a sitting position despite the chaos that was unfolding.

After the ropes had left Caelan's hands, he rubbed his wrists before beginning to shrug off his shirt.

Prince Aamir's face became white as Caelan took one arm out of the sleeve. "Why are you undressing?"

"I have to show you for you to understand."

Disgust curled on Prince Aamir's lips and his nose scrunched upward. "You are merely making a mockery of me with your outlandish claims. I won't stand for it."

"You don't have to," Caelan replied, still continuing to remove his other arm out of the sleeve. The shirt fell to the ground without so much as a sound, and the surrounding guards shifted their position, their hands going to their swords. "You just merely have to let me turn around and show you the proof you need."

Prince Aamir let his hand fall to his side, and the guards slowly relaxed their bodies, but their hands stayed put, loyal to their ruler. "Show me, then. Stop stalling and raise your hands to where I can see them."

Caelan ducked his chin, slowly raised his hands above his head, and turned in a slow circle until his back was facing the prince. "Tell me you see it," he said.

"An inked design on your body proves nothing. There have been several others who offered the same notion to me and my father before me years ago. Do you know where those claims got them? Right in the dungeon. Depending on the severity of the claim, sometimes, they ended up staring at their eventual demise before they even pleaded their case. You've come here, engaged in some kind of nefarious plot with this terrorist..." Aamir gestured to James, who was still frozen in place, and then turned his eyes back on Caelan. "...and you will do anything to save face."

The guards straightened their backs, and, without even a command, they withdrew their swords from their sheaths.

So this was it. Caelan's boldness would get them killed.

But maybe she could stop it.

"Wait," Sabina shrieked. "Don't kill him, please." Her feet were practically digging into the floor, and she was losing feeling in her legs after all the walking. Her hands felt like pins and needles as she tried to adjust her balance.

Prince Aamir turned his cold eyes on her, moving away from Caelan. Several guards charged forward and grabbed his elbows, leaving him immobile.

"Why should I not?" the prince asked, his steps slow and sure, as if he had done this a million times before. "Give me one reason, and I will consider it."

With icy eyes that seemed to peer into her soul, Sabina weighed her options. Her heart fluttered against her chest as she opened her mouth to speak. Her throat felt like chalk from lack of water and moisture in the air, but she still croaked out what she could. "Because he's my father. I just met him."

A flicker passed over the prince's eyes. Amusement, Sabina could finally place it after staring blankly for several seconds.

"Go on. I actually want to see where this is going."

Sabina licked her lips, desperate to stop the burning as much as she could. "He's all of our dads," she said. Her gut churned with anxiety as her words spilled out, but she forced herself to continue speaking despite the fear palpitating through her bloodstream.

A chortle escaped Prince Aamir's tight lips. "Siblings, you say. That is indeed...a mighty convenient reason to give, considering he—and all of you—are on the brink of death. If I wasn't already so skeptical of you all already, I might actually consider it."

"Dang," Nyx breathed, a contemptuous laugh escaping him. "He's even crueler than I am, and that's saying a lot."

"Quiet," Lashrael ordered, and Nyx complied, but his gaze never left Sabina.

Suddenly, she was starkly aware of how many pairs of eyes had to be on her at that moment, the prince's included. What would she do now? What even could she do now?

"Are you saying there's nothing I can do to make you reconsider?" she asked.

The prince didn't wait a beat. "Unless you can have some way to make weight to his claim, my answer is no. With all the evidence in front of me, you all are involved with a known terrorist to the Crown, and for that, you will be punished. I don't play favorites, not when it comes down to the safety of my kingdom."

A shuddering gasp escaped Sabina, and she felt it down in her core. "No," she whispered. "Please."

The prince surveyed her, his eyes blank. "Take them away," he ordered, turning away again.

He was leaving, Sabina realized, as the heels of his dress shoes clacked against the velvet carpet walkway.

Panic clawed in the recesses of her chest while guards swarmed the group. James was the first to be grabbed, his arms being lifted by several guards who were hauling him to the far-off room despite his protesting screams.

Tony and Hannah began struggling against the harsh grips, and Sabina soon was seized in spite of the screams bubbling in her throat. They weren't listening. Their heritage didn't matter. Caelan's view was a fairytale. His diplomatic approach would be the end of them all. It was the end of them all.

"Stop struggling, and obey the prince," one guard ordered Sabina as he pushed her closer and closer toward the exit.

She had to find something, do something. Her fingertips laced with sweat and her mind scrambled for a solution. Prince Aamir was almost out the door.

A sudden tingle zapped up her arm, and a vibration thrummed in her ears, letting the sound drop to a faint echo. Time seemed to slow, even if it was only in her mind's eye.

It was there, in her core, like Solenne had instructed.

Find the light. Sabina willed it to come, shutting her eyes against the noise.

The humming grew louder, and behind her shut eyes, Sabina saw the outline of lavender gold. *It is here.*

Sudden screams from the guards caused her to open her eyes, and her heart galloped to her throat as shining silver glinted in the absence of light in the room.

All of the guard's weapons were levitating. Shields, swords and all had been removed from their grasp and were hovering in the air as if they were weightless. And then, despite the shock on her tongue, they started moving straight toward her.

But the swords never touched Sabina. They merely shifted until the hilts were in her vision, aiming the blades directly at the guards.

"Sorcery!" one guard screamed, letting go of Caelan.

The others scrambled like madmen, and Sabina watched in confusion as the others dropped her companions as if they were cursed.

Footsteps resounded, but Sabina couldn't see anything beyond the multitudes running across the room. Even the guard who had held her close had dropped her and was nowhere to be seen.

Before she even grasped her breath, a sudden jerking on her arm gave way to panic as she met the eyes of the person who gripped her so tightly.

"Tell me who taught you how to do this *now*, and maybe I can work out a deal for you to survive." Prince Aamir was back, his hold on her like a viper, but his eyes were terrified. It was a fear unlike anything she had ever seen. His hands were shaking.

A sudden feeling settled into Sabina's gut. He knew something.

But Sabina had no idea what he was asking, if the answers would even be worthy enough to try.

"Please, it's about my father," Prince Aamir choked out.

And that was when all the weapons crashed to the ground as the telekinesis wore off in her mind, the connection lost. The clashing was thundering amidst the silence, and Sabina felt her gut plummet.

What did he mean by his father?

Prince Aamir barely spared a glance as he moved, brushing past his guards as he gestured for the girls and the others to follow.

"Sire, what shall we do with Nyx?" Rigel asked as he sauntered past.

With a darkened gleam in his eye, the prince turned to Rigel. "I think we can call it satisfactory punishment to put him in a holding cell. Surely, it'll be fit to his liking."

Nyx sputtered. "Your Majesty, I think there's been a grave misunderstanding—"

"And I think you have been nothing but a grave headache for everyone involved," Prince Aamir said.

With a flick of his wrist, several guards found their wits, grabbed Nyx, and walked in the opposite direction.

Rigel stood, dumbfounded. "And what of me, Your Majesty?"

Prince Aamir gave another small smile. "You, Rigel, will sit in this very chair until I give more instructions as to what to do with you."

Several guards grabbed the man at the prince's words, bringing him to a wooden chair. It took three men, but they were able to restrain Rigel with several attempts.

Prince Aamir gave one more glance-over before he seemed to be satisfied. "Follow me," he instructed, leaving no choice but for everyone to follow.

CHAPTER FORTY-SIX

CAMMIE

THE WALLS WERE PAINTED A luxurious purple, another shining symbol of royalty for all to see. Enormous bookshelves lined the walls, filled with multitudes of books with names that even Cammie couldn't pronounce. Her time in a bookstore proved to be helpless in this scenario.

A servant handed her a cup of tea, and Cammie quietly thanked her. The woman paid her no mind, exiting swiftly.

The steaming hot liquid thawed Cammie's already frozen hands, and she cupped them together, hoping to withdraw more warmth. Caelan had been bold enough to ask for tea, and aside from them two, no one else had accepted the offer, but that didn't make Cammie any less grateful.

Her wrists were burning from the friction of the rope that had held her hands captive for what had to have been hours, and with each subtle movement, even something as simple as trying to bring feeling back into her hands, caused a sting of pain.

Ten minutes earlier, there had been no possibility of even having a conversation with the prince, but at that very moment, he was more eager to speak, even if it meant dragging them into his private study room to do so. Guards were absent in the room. At the prince's instruction, they were waiting outside of the study doors.

Prince Aamir's eyes were focused solely on Sabina, his white knuckles clenching the edge of the desk. "You can speak freely," he said, his voice above a mere whisper.

"You fully expect us to believe that no guards will come in here, topple us over, and carry us to whatever dungeon you planned on putting us in earlier? Nope, I call bull on that." Hannah was sitting on the chair beside Caelan, stained blood still on her upper lip and chin as she stared down Prince Aamir with a fathomless scowl.

Sabina was on the far left, and Caelan on the far right, leaving Cammie, conveniently, right in the middle.

Prince Aamir's brow furrowed in confusion, and he looked to Caelan for clarification.

"Ahem." Caelan cleared his throat, sending a look Hannah's way before turning his gaze back to Prince Aamir. "Apologies for her," he stated, a sheepish blush appearing on his cheeks. "In the Earth realm, the word is to mean something that is false, so to preface what she is saying is that your claims of peace are not true. If I am being honest, I am not sure if I believe your claims to be true also. You put us in this room far away. How are we supposed to believe that you won't kill us here?"

"Because I won't," Prince Aamir said so matter-of-factly that Cammie craned her ear closer. Surely that wasn't his reasoning.

"You can't exactly fault us for not trusting you," Tony piped up. He was near the doorway along with the rest of them.

James was smack in the middle, an unreadable look on his face.

"I'm with Hannah on this one," Tony continued, a glint in his eyes as he stared the prince down. "We'll need more than 'I won't' to believe anything you say."

The prince straightened in his chair, letting his head raise high. "Very well," he replied, tone stiff. "If it is proof you want, then proof you will get." He swiveled position, his index finger pointing directly at Sabina. "I won't kill you because of her."

"Me?" Sabina squeaked, her milky-white complexion turning scarlet. "Why me?"

"You shot dozens of weapons into mid-air without so much as a verbal command," the prince retorted. "That alone is very valuable to me."

"My daughters are not toys for your amusement," Caelan growled out, his easygoing demeanor gone.

Shivers ran up Cammie's spine as she watched Caelan's eyes bulge and the muscle in his upper lip twitch.

"And they are not toys to me," Prince Aamir replied. "They are merely answers to questions I seek, important questions that have to do with all of you, especially James."

James's features hardened. "You're talking about why I left?"

The prince nodded. "Precisely. I need to know every detail, down to the second, until you came back here."

"Why do you even care about what happened with us?" Sabina asked.

"Because, like I mentioned, it's all connected, and there's no need to hide behind the glamour anymore. We're in Natrellum now. I don't know why I didn't do it earlier." Prince Aamir waved his hand, and Cammie heard a faint tingling in her ears that slowly absorbed itself back into the atmosphere. "Wait. Why didn't the rest of you shift back?"

"Because there's no reason for them to shift," Caelan replied.

As Cammie looked over at him, her heart clenched. The Amarian features were in full bloom.

"A human alone cannot conjure weapons in that matter. I've heard of the weapons of the Dark One. Maybe spoken curses, and if there was any form of levitation, it wouldn't be for objects but for people, but power like this has not been seen ever. Not in eons, not in centuries. I have only heard of it—"

"—in prophecies and legends," James finished, his voice ringing with pride.

Cammie felt his eyes on her, but she kept her gaze trained on the prince. She couldn't afford to let herself think of him romantically. Not with everything that had happened and with everything that was going on.

Prince Aamir's face flushed. "But the prophecy can only apply to one of the original line, and the only way that prophecy can be fulfilled is if..." He halted his words, slowly turning his eyes on Caelan. "...if your claim were true," he finished slowly, the syllables echoing in the tiny room as he kept his gaze on Caelan.

"It is true," Caelan uttered breathlessly.

Cammie felt a hollow gap in the space, as if the weight of what they had spoken had rested on several shoulders for a long time and was now finally coming to fruition.

"So, your mother—"

"My mother was Amala, the late Queen of Eleisa, and my father—"

"The late King Malik of Eleisa," Prince Aamir finished. "Let us say that this part is true, that you *are* the rightful heir to the throne. How did you survive the assassination? We were told that everyone who was in the castle had perished, the baby prince, included."

A flash of pain echoed across Caelan's features, and Cammie's stomach flipped somersaults. Of course, he would think of Solenne. Even Cammie herself wasn't sure when the ache would go away.

"My mother's lady-in-waiting protected me. As my mother lay dying, she instructed her to take me far away, to a place where the Darkness couldn't destroy the legacy of my line. She did her best to keep me safe Earth-side, but she couldn't stop choices I made that might have been frowned upon."

The prince's eyebrows flinched. "You're talking about your children," he remarked quietly, finally letting his gaze drift to Hannah, Sabina, and Cammie.

"You look at us like we're abominations," Hannah said slowly, her eyes resembling something close to daggers.

"Not abominations," the prince replied, peering at Hannah, "but more so...like a fascination. I've never seen humans this side of Natrellum. We have the same ancestral line, but there's a difference, obviously. Where we were graced with new abilities and a new form, humans seemed to stay stagnant, stuck in their ways of absolute abandon for morality."

Hannah guffawed, a long, rough sound that caused tingling in Cammie's ears. "You want to talk about abandoning morality? Your guard punched the life out of me before we got here, and they've handled us with nothing but *absolute care*."

"Humanity simply cannot be trusted to do what is good for Natrellum. Ever since we got into business with them, it was *their* woman who invoked the Darkness with her dark magic that infected our kingdom, *their* woman who had swayed our originator to go cold and abandon his wife and his family, *their* woman who—"

Caelan held up a hand. "You speak of all of humanity as if one person defines them all. That can't possibly be true."

Prince Aamir scoffed, shaking his head dismissively. "You might be the 'heir,' but you still have a lot to learn. You have spent your lifetime in the Earth-realm, which, openly speaking, I was not aware we could travel the portal back and forth, as I am also sure my father did not know. Otherwise, I am sure someone would have opted to search for you. We have customs here that you could not possibly fathom due to your lack of time in this world."

Cammie had to bite her tongue to stop herself from speaking. Did this wannabe prince seriously just insult her father right to his face? Knowing he was the rightful heir?

"This is not me trying to be undiplomatic," Prince Aamir continued. "It is merely fact. Just because you have a birthright does not mean you are fit for the title."

Sabina's mouth slacked to the floor. "And yet you wanted us to help? You implored us to help you find the connection to your father's death."

Prince Aamir's eyes narrowed as he turned his gaze on Sabina, a flicker of a brewing storm in his irises. "I have also returned favors to you in case you have forgotten in the past ten minutes of the things I have done for you that weren't mandatory."

The memory of seeing Nyx taken to the dungeon flashed in her mind's eye. Cammie couldn't suppress the smile this time. And Rigel, *poor Rigel*, was bound to a chair while they discussed the next steps until Prince Aamir gave his position on where the sorry guy would be going. James was also under discretion but no longer was he going to a chamber of absolute misery and violence.

Sabina was silent, her face still the blooming red as she closed her mouth. She would be complacent, then, but that didn't mean that Cammie had to be.

"You might have done us a favor, but are you really willing to put your 'knowledge' above the rightful heir to the throne? That seems a little...unfair and biased."

Prince Aamir stroked his chin, a thoughtful gaze in his eyes. The venom hadn't fully vanished, but at least it had lessened. "I can say that I will always put my kingdom above other matters. Whatever is best for its survival will be what I do. Thankfully, for your sakes, I cannot make the final decision on the matter. It will be up to you to plead your case to the Council when they arrive, but until then, you will be under my watchful eye." The prince cleared his throat.

The door to the study opened, revealing a man well-dressed and of tall stature. He had to be at least the size of Caelan but someone much older. His Amarian facade benefited him, as Cammie couldn't quite pinpoint his age. He wore the palace seal inscribed onto a jacket, the color resembling the one Prince Aamir was wearing, but the shade was one or two off.

"Darrian will be here to help guide me through the party tonight, and everyone who has seen you will be sworn to secrecy until the Council can make a well-informed decision. He has been debriefed by one of my guards and is caught up to speed already on what has gone on. There is no one I trust more with this knowledge. Nevertheless, you will stay here, under my protection, with several servants to help you. I have another task for you that will include you blending in."

"What are we, errand boys?" Hannah stood, her hands slapping on the edge of the desk. "I won't be here at your beck and call as you take your time ringing the bell while we wait for the Council. We shouldn't be in servitude of you. We're the ones you should be listening to! Not the other way around."

"Watch your tone, girl," Darrian barked, coming to a stop at the prince's side. His eyes held a dark contrast to Prince Aamir's quiet expression. "The prince is doing you a favor by keeping you in the castle, a favor he does not have to do by any means. The outside world hates humanity already, and by your valor and talents alone, you might be part Amarian. As far as looks, you cannot pass for anything other than human. With that being said, you should be grateful for the resting place the prince has offered you, but if that should not be to your liking, you are more than welcome to find refuge outside...where you will surely be slaughtered."

"Being here is fine," Caelan interjected, his voice soft and soothing.

A smile of satisfaction appeared on Darrian's lips, and he nodded curtly to Prince Aamir. "It is settled. You may call for me once you are finished talking, so I can escort them to their rooms." His eyes turned black as he gave Hannah one last glance before turning on his heel. He walked slowly to the door, and his hand gave pause as he went to grab the doorknob, as if waiting for something to erupt. "Let me know if they give you any problems," Darrian finally said before exiting the room.

The door echoed as it shut behind his retreating back, and Cammie flinched, the sound like knives in her ears.

"You still haven't told us what you need from us to find out what happened to your dad," Hannah interjected, as if the previous interaction did not faze her at all.

Honestly, Cammie was sure that it did not. Hannah was bold like that, but her boldness could be classified as idiotic under certain circumstances.

Prince Aamir's eyes narrowed slightly, and he held his tongue before letting out an exasperated sigh. "I thought that having a place to stay would be higher on your list of gratitude."

"I am very thankful to not be in the dungeon," Hannah said slyly, a smirk tickling her lips, "but that doesn't mean that your allowing us to stay here will change the fact that you want us to owe you." She sniffed, wrinkling up her nose as she leaned over the desk, her face inches from the prince. "But I can't figure out why. Tell me, Prince, what can we offer you that no one else can?"

"Hannah, sit down," Caelan ordered, his voice lingering on a warning.

Hannah ignored his request, still keeping her position at the desk. "Just answer me. It can't be so secretive that you won't even voice it to us. Do it. I dare you."

"Hannah!"

The eruption from Caelan caused every nerve in Cammie's body to tense, and the hairs on her neck stood upright as she slowly looked to Hannah.

"Know your place," he said, his words coming out soft and slow as his volume drifted from overbearing to barely above a whisper.

Hannah's skin was flushed, and momentary panic robbed her eyes of the usual cunning glaze they beheld. She quickly straightened from her position at the desk, her hands moving stiffly to her sides. She averted her gaze, and as it contacted the ground, Cammie swore she saw something shining in the corners of her eyes.

"I'm sorry about that," Caelan said, his tone clipped, "and I also apologize for my tone earlier. I had no right talking to you how I did. Until things get sorted out, you are still the heir of Natrellum."

Prince Aamir parted his lips, eyes unblinking, as Caelan looked on at him earnestly. "It...is all right," he murmured, going back to the stroking of his chin. He looked at the girls thoughtfully. "I suppose I can continue as to the reason why I need your help—"

"You can do that without me," Hannah chipped in, shifting, backing away from the desk.

"Sit down. We need to discuss this," Caelan said, his hands moving wildly despite Hannah's determination.

"Just fill me in later—"

"We don't have time to fill you in later," Caelan protested. "Why can't you just sit down, and we'll—"

"Darrian said he'll keep an eye out and he doesn't want any trouble, right? I've done nothing but cause trouble. Oh, and where was this enthusiastic defense that you have the nerve to give our *natural enemy* when my face was the new bloody canvas for a ticked-off guard? You sure were silent then." Hannah's chest was heaving with wild breaths, baring her teeth. She looked like an animal in her human form.

"I'm sorry," Caelan said softly, his eyes shining with unshed tears. They had appeared suddenly, and it had exploded all over his face, in the creases of his eyes, and in the frown in his lips. "I'm new to this. I am going to make mistakes."

"Do you think I really give a drat about mistakes right now? You let me get hit by a guard, and you treat me less than someone who undermines the authority that you—we—have. Kiss butt if you want to..." Hannah started toward the door, not even daring to look back. "...but I'll be cursed if I do."

"Hannah—" The name died on Caelan's lips as the door shut promptly.

The sound ricocheted in Cammie's ears, ringing louder than the heartbeat that was doing its stubborn beat.

With a huff, Caelan rose from the chair, his face flushed with embarrassment. "I need to go see her," he said as he started toward the door in pursuit.

"No," someone interjected, and after a moment's hesitation, Cammie placed the voice as Tony's. "I'll go," he said, looking right at Caelan. His words harbored the edge of steel as he cracked his knuckles, his face impassive to read. "Sit down, please. She needs someone she can trust right now, and if it helps, I've seen her like this many times. She just gets riled up, and the only thing that really stops it is someone putting some common sense into her thick skull."

Something flashed over Caelan's eyes that was gone as quickly as it appeared. "As her father—"

"You said you're still learning how to be a father," Tony replied. "You're not in the right mindset to know how to care for her in these moments. And I get it. Hannah is a wild breed of a person. It's better if I do it. I can calm her down, get her to see the true side of things instead of what's spinning in her head. That is, if *His Highness* is okay with this?"

Prince Aamir took Tony's words in thoughtfully, taking a beat. "Go," he said, waving his hand. "Find her and make sure she doesn't damage the castle."

A flash of anger sat in the pit of Cammie's stomach, a feeling that only seemed to grow the more time she spent in the Prince's presence. *He embodies the sentiment of pompous.*

She didn't notice how her nostrils flared until a comment spilled into the quiet room from Aamir himself.

"Do we need to send you out for fresh air as well?"

The comment, to anyone else, would have seemed innocent enough, but from the prince's lips, all Cammie could see was red.

"No," she replied, after debating whether to let him have it. "I'm fine right here."

A slow grin spread over his face, and as Cammie stared, the smirk on his lips never fading, she put pieces together about the prince. The first being that he was too arrogant for his own good, and the second being that he was afraid. The constant switching between easy-going and vulnerable to a wall of impenetrable steel was a never-ending feat. It didn't lessen by any means as the conversation continued.

"Then we should continue," Prince Aamir said, clasping his hands together and setting them on the desk. "Unless any of the rest of you feel the need to leave?"

The room was so silent that one could hear a pin drop.

Prince Aamir, ever satisfied, nodded before clearing his throat. "Very well. To the task at hand, to be so blunt, my father died. I am sure you have gathered that. James knew that fact at the time he left, so I assumed, with the timing, that it was not a coincidence." He looked at James, an unreadable expression in his eyes as he continued, "But...I am humble enough to admit my wrongdoings. I had assumed you had answers, and you did. It just was not the ones I was hoping for. You brought back someone who could be the true king. What I need now more than anything...is to find answers about who killed my father."

A puzzled look fell over James' face at the prince's words. "Killed?" The word came out jumbled, as if it wasn't fully formed before it erupted from his parted lips.

"After you had long gone, the Failer came back to me and told me my father had not passed from natural causes as we all had expected. I had assumed it was naturally organ failure or rupture or something of the sort as he had choked on his own blood, but his findings revealed it was from some sort of curse. The only person possessing this kind of evil magic is locked away. Most people call her The Queen of Darkness, but…" Prince Aamir paused, letting out a dark chuckle. "…it is kind of hard to do anything of the sort once someone trapped you inside a cave with a magical cessation barrier."

Perplexed, Sabina furrowed her brow and gestured to Caelan. "Not to interrupt your story, but how does any of this concern us? You still haven't told us exactly what you want us to do."

The prince tsked, raising one index finger in the air. "Very perceptive," he said, a hint of humor in his voice, a trait that Cammie was unsure he had until this point. "After the healer gave the news, I started thinking about everything that happened even before my father had passed. Several of his associates had died, all of them through what the healers had said to be natural causes. Some had slit throats caused by suicide, died in their sleep…. You name it, it probably caused their deaths."

"But now you're not so sure," Sabina remarked, earning a wide grin from the prince. He seemed all too pleased with her, and Cammie did not like that one bit.

"You are catching on fast. It all seemed too odd how these people were dying. It almost seemed like certain people had been targeted, and the more I thought about that, the more uneasy I felt. If it were true, then who? Or how, or even why?"

The worry laced itself so deeply on Aamir's face that Cammie almost felt a twinge of sympathy. Almost being the key word.

"Then why not go searching it out?" Marcus asked.

For a moment, Cammie had forgotten they were still in the room. Without Hannah, they were as silent as a quiet wind.

The prince's gaze flickered, and he licked his lips. "I did, but there were only so many places a prince can go unnoticed. There are whispers within the castle, and there are many things that only these very walls know. As inanimate as they are, they have borne witness to things that no one else has laid eyes on, but they are stubborn and unable to voice the truth in this light. I had thought James would be the answer. I had thought he was the killer of some of these people because, for a while, things stopped. Until a week ago. They found another associate dead, his throat slashed, but the angle of the cut was different this time."

"How so?" Cammie asked, leaning forward on her elbows. This entirely piqued her interest.

"A left hand did the cut. The associate who died was completely right-handed and not ambidextrous. The others who died, they were all the same—right-handed and a right-hand slash."

Cammie felt her stomach lift to her throat, and she swallowed to keep the nerves down. "So, he was murdered."

"In fresh blood," Prince Aamir said sharply, a flush of red flooding to his cheeks, "but before you get all defensive and ask why the person wasn't caught, whoever the person was had long gone by the time they found the body. They also took the weapon with them, so aside from the cut, there were no other lingering pieces. As to why, I don't know. Regardless, the evidence vanished without a trace, but it left fear behind. It's been mingling in the cities, and the people are restless, wondering who will be next."

An incredulous laugh escaped James, and Cammie whipped her head around. His face was the pristine image of unchecked rage. With his bulging eyes, his breath that came too fast, and his pursed lips, Cammie knew to brace herself. James was ready to let his words be a loaded gun.

"You've got to be kidding me," James rasped out. "*Now* I know why you want them to do the dirty work for you."

Prince Aamir's eyes rose in what looked like a challenge. "Do tell us, James. I'm sure we'd love to hear your improbable theory."

James' lips twitched, and his eyes narrowed. "You've been in this castle just hoping to catch me because you assumed I was behind it all. You were hoping it was some kind of rebel clan or something else that seemed too far-fetched, something that I would surely be involved in. You were all too pleased to send the Hunter after me. Surely, he would stop it, right? No. When more people started dying, the damn panic set in, not just for the city *but for you*. And here you are, talking to *the* last true heirs to a throne you haven't earned. You want to throw them into a trap, don't you? You want them to be here, to cause a distraction, hoping whoever is killing off your father's associates doesn't come after you. Now tell me, does any of that sound right?"

Prince Aamir's face paled, and guilt flashed across his eyes. James had found out the reason, and it was there staring them all in the face.

"You can't be serious," Caelan said, shock reverberating his words.

"He's dead serious," James stated plainly. "Your life for his isn't something he's willing to be honorable about."

"I told you before I will always put my people above others, and that's what I am saying now. The way I see it is that you have two options—do what I am asking and wait for the Council to appear to make your claim to the throne or leave immediately and let the people have their way with you. They already know you've committed treason, or at least in their eyes you have, so if you go there, surely you will die at the hands of civilians. Ultimately, it is your choice." Prince Aamir said the words so casually that Cammie felt a knife pierce her gut.

There really was no other option. Death was the only true outcome, either way, no matter what was chosen.

One way or another, death would come for them all.

CHAPTER FORTY-SEVEN

HANNAH

THERE WAS AN ACHE IN her bones that couldn't be lessened. It grew with each heavy step, each clenched fist, and each stubborn coil that her stomach would muster.

It was white-hot, invisible, barely contained rage. The way Caelan had talked to her, as if he were so righteous had sent her blood boiling. How he had the nerve to claim good things in his name, or their name, in the face of that complete idiot was beyond her.

But Hannah had been around men long enough to know that self-preservation was always in their "best interest." She had seen it with her father. Or should she say "fake father?" Shaking her head, Hannah pushed the thought away. She was still trying to wrap her head around the right terms.

"Hannah!" a voice called from behind her.

She didn't need to turn around to know who it belonged to. Every nerve tingled on her back, but it burned with something more furious than defensiveness at being approached in a castle after the last encounter she'd had.

Hannah kept walking, biting the inside of her cheek. Focusing her eyes on some random door in the distance as her arrival point, Hannah didn't notice the tug on her arm until it was too late.

Her elbow was red with pain as her entire body jerked around, coming face to face with Tony. His usual expression of seriousness was ever the more present, and if Hannah was completely honest, the look on his face made her sick.

"I don't need a lecture," Hannah barked, unable to conceal the steel in her voice. "In case you missed it, Caelan gave me one earlier. Two lectures kind of defeat the point, doesn't it?"

Tony's expression never wavered, and his clutch didn't lessen. "I'm not here to lecture you," he told her.

"Your grip on my arm says otherwise," Hannah countered with a raised brow.

Tony released his fingers from her arm, and Hannah peered down at the marks left on her skin. Maybe it would bruise, just like she was sure her lips would. *Thanks to Caelan.*

"I'm just here to warn you," Tony said, as if she had never spoken. "I figured you would take it better from me."

His words held more truth in them than Hannah had heard in a while, what with Nyx lying, Rigel betraying them, and Caelan disappointing her. She couldn't pretend that it wasn't nice to hear someone care because it was, but that wasn't the point.

"Go ahead then," Hannah said, sweeping around the hallway with the arm that wasn't pulsating with the rush of fresh blood returning to her veins. "Tell me whatever it is I *need to know*, and then let me go in peace."

A spark of anger flashed in his eyes. "Why can't you just calm down and listen? I know you hate instructions, but this is for your own good."

Hannah bit her tongue to stop the next remark from flying.

"Look," Tony breathed, his nostrils flaring as he took a moment to compose himself. "All I mean is that things are different here. You can't go throwing yourself in the fire when you don't even understand what's going on."

"I understand enough to know humans are hated here, so it doesn't really matter what I do, does it?"

"It does when lives are at stake and there's a different target on your back," Tony shot back.

The words made Hannah freeze in her tracks, and she raised her brow. *What does he mean?*

"You're right," he conceded. "There is a risk of being a human-Amarian here, but you're not the only one. There's Sabina and Cammie too. Before you let your anger get the best of you, I am only asking you to think of the others."

"Thinking of the others got me in this position," Hannah countered, her mind flashing to what she did for James. "No matter what I do, it's always the wrong choice." She didn't bother to conceal the bitterness in her words, even as Tony's face furrowed in concern.

"Hannah—" Tony reached for her arm again.

Hannah stayed stoic, knowing there had to be ears and eyes everywhere. She wasn't so idiotic in that regard at least.

Then, she heard it again—her name—but the sound came from different lips, and it was very far away. Combining that with the sound of heavy footfalls, Hannah sensed what was happening before she saw it. *Someone is running.*

The sound was garbled until it finally floated in front of Hannah, no longer bound by the force of far distances.

"You've found her," the person said, huffing several breaths as he leaned over on his knees to steady himself.

Hannah narrowed her eyes at Tony. "I thought I was done with being followed."

"I swear I knew nothing about him following me out here," Tony said, his eyebrows furrowing as his mouth clenched.

"It's true," Will quipped with a shrug. Even with the world jump, his accent never faded. "I jumped at the offer to come grab you. Prince Aamir instructed me to fill you in."

There was that word again. *Instructed.* The arrogance of the idiot was enough to make Hannah's insides burn.

"You can get mad all you want, but he's still in charge," Will said as if Hannah's words were strewn all over her features.

"For now," Tony added.

Hannah's narrowing eyes turned to slits. "Well..." She swallowed, forcing the burning ire down her esophagus. "What did the *prince* have to say? If it's so important that you had to chase me down, just say it."

Will fidgeted nervously, his neck turning a particular shade of red, and Hannah bit down on her tongue yet again. She couldn't lose composure, not after Tony had at least tried. Hannah would try, too. Even if it was killing her.

Before Will could even speak, a door opened at the far end of the hall. Several people exited at once, all faces that were far too familiar. James led the charge, his expression blank, Sabina not too far behind him, with Marcus and Trevor walking insanely slow. As Hannah craned her head to peer closer, she realized starkly what was happening. They were creating space between the people behind Sabina, who, according to Hannah's calculations and perception, were Cammie and Caelan.

Caelan gripped Cammie's hand, but that wasn't what captivated Hannah. It was the mere look on Cammie's face that undid it all.

Cammie's face was paler than usual, harboring on a shade of almost green. Her lips were set in a thin line, and her eyes held a million thoughts and worries that Hannah couldn't decipher.

Hannah didn't care about what Will wanted to tell her. She knew it was best to hear it from someone else directly. *My sister.* The word, like father, felt foreign on her tongue, in her mind, but it was the only thing she could cling to as the stark anger resurfaced in Hannah's gut.

Without so much as even a backward glance, Hannah dashed down the hallway, not caring about how improper running sounded on the stone floor as she made the distance to Cammie.

She didn't ask for permission when she took Cammie's hand from Caelan and put it in her own grasp, and Cammie's expression never wavered. It was still the same blank, haunted stare.

"What happened?" Hannah breathed, her words coming far too fast for her liking. "Is she hurt?"

"No," Caelan responded, his tone ringing with the same authority she had heard him convey many times before.

Hannah was still too angry to look into his eyes, so she kept her gaze trained on Cammie.

"She's fine," he said, releasing a small sigh. "Physically, she is fine."

"That doesn't tell me anything useful." Hannah half-laughed. "It only vaguely tells me something bothered her in there."

Or someone. As the thought hit like lightning, Hannah's defensive reflexes came back, and all too quickly, her eyes scanned the room. As if the prince was dead set on making her life miserable, he exited the room with his head held high, his gaze transfixed. He was pleased with himself, all too pleased.

Hannah didn't stop the impulsive flow this time. She let it fly from her thoughts to her feet. Before she knew it, she was jumping away from Cammie, her gaze steady on the one man who had caused them so much pain already.

"What did you do to her?" she shouted, the noise so loud even to her it caused a sharp pain in her eardrums.

Several hands grabbed her elbows, and she felt herself being tugged backward, but that didn't stop Hannah from seeing many shades of red.

The prince stopped in his tracks, the stone-cold expression overtaking half of his face. His eyes were coal as he surveyed Hannah up and down. His upper lip curled in a slight sneer before he peered around Hannah, directing his gaze on Caelan. Several unspoken words passed between them until he uttered, "Keep her under control. Remember our chat. Unless you're completely satisfied with the choice her actions will bring."

The warning was evident in the prince's words, and despite every single nerve in her body telling Hannah to let him have it, her eyes flickered over to Sabina.

Sabina's face held the same seriousness it usually did, except this time, it was higher than usual. She was on a completely different plane, so Hannah let her body slump.

The prince apparently was satisfied with that response as he gave a tight nod before continuing his trek down the hall.

And then, it was quiet, far too quiet in this unfamiliar hallway with this unfamiliar castle that was full of mostly unfamiliar people.

CHAPTER FORTY-EIGHT

CAMMIE

SEVERAL HANDS RELEASED THE DEATH grip they had on Hannah, and she rubbed her arms, her eyes wild.

"Can you please try your best to not blow up? We can't afford any more outbursts. We are already treading on thin ice," Sabina said, exasperated. She pinched the bridge of her nose.

Hannah's apathetic expression erupted. "Wow. Even after everything he said, *that's* your reaction? You watched as I got slapped, Sabina! What did you expect me to do? Just sit there and watch?"

"Justice and revenge are two very different things," Sabina muttered, averting her gaze.

Cammie could barely keep her head above water, their argument seeming to fade into the background amidst her spiraling thoughts.

"But what if what I was doing *was* justice?" Hannah proclaimed boldly, her hands across her chest.

"This is frustrating," Cammie blurted out, forcing herself to look past the dark cloud she was trapped in.

"Enlighten me," Hannah snapped, letting out an incredulous laugh. "How would you have handled it?"

Cammie, with absolute ice in her eyes, jerked her gaze to Hannah. "I would have been silent. There are things that are going on that are bigger than all of us, but that doesn't make us automatically exempt from the consequences of petty actions."

"Defending us isn't a petty action," Hannah replied, inching closer to Cammie. Hannah's tone was as bold as ever. She was uncaring of consequences, even now.

"It is when what you're doing could very well kill us all!" The sound spewed from Cammie's gentle lips in a way that made the very walls shake. She felt the thrumming in her bones, and her jaw set.

Hannah's anger morphed into shock, slowly softening into something that resembled guilt. "Cammie..." She reached out, but Cammie was too quick.

"No," she said softly, and she averted her eyes away. "You've proved so many times how reckless you are. We love you, Hannah, and I know that somewhere deep down, it comes from a place of love, but anger and love don't mix well. There's already a target on our backs here. The only option we have is to lie low and not ask questions. Not until the Council gets here." Cammie swallowed, her eyes flickering briefly to James before settling back on Hannah. "Prince Aamir has a target on his back. By association, we do too unless we can figure out who's behind all the killings. That way, maybe we have a chance of surviving long enough to prove our case to the Council. Until then..." Cammie trailed off, the words dying on her lips.

"You need me to stay out of the way," Hannah finished.

Cammie glowered her eyes, exasperated. "That isn't what I said," she exclaimed, throwing her hands in the air.

"But it's what you meant," Hannah uttered quietly, her face turning a shade of plum. Before Cammie could even utter another word, Hannah turned on her heel.

Suddenly, Darrian appeared out of the shadows of the hall. Cammie's stomach coiled with bile as Darrian began speaking, gesturing with a hand toward the rest of the hallway.

They had come that way before, after Prince Aamir had ushered them to a private sitting room. Cammie held her breath. Even the name was causing nausea.

She did her best to push it down, to will it to disappear out of sight, out of mind, but her stomach had a will of its own as it rolled yet again.

Her feet shook as she tried to move, and she felt a sudden tug on her arm. It wasn't hard enough to startle her, just enough to ground her. As she looked over, her eyes froze.

Somewhere in the commotion of Hannah and the other craziness, James had stepped in. He looked at her with a comforting expression that just barely made the nausea retreat but also made her heart flutter at a pace too fast to count.

"Are you all right?" His voice was barely above a whisper, yet it held the firmness Cammie had heard many times before in memories that were too far to touch.

She nodded, not trusting herself to speak. Despite everything, he still made her heart dance and her stomach twinge with something much different than nausea.

"Just keep your head up," he told her, before licking his lips. "I know there isn't a place for you to process here, but there will be soon. Keep Prince Aamir's words from poisoning your brain. Don't worry. You will be fine." He gave her a slight squeeze.

For a moment, Cammie almost felt like she had traveled back in time to a moment where death threats weren't on the table and Amarians were nothing more than some kind of fairy tale story.

As if her emotions were laid bare on her face, James' easy going expression faded. He removed his arm, darting his eyes away as he continued on his walk, but that didn't stop Cammie from feeling the ghost of his touch on her arm.

"The first rule is to stay in your quarters unless you are escorted out otherwise. To everyone else in this castle, you are under Prince Aamir's direct protection, but to me, it is a very different story. If even one rule is not obeyed, you will have me to answer to. The second rule is that you treat this castle and your corresponding rooms with the upmost respect. Whatever Prince Aamir asks of you, you will certainly do. Thirdly, do not comment on the articulation of words in the presence of help. They already know of the class system difference. They already know the common tongue of servants and soldiers and others differ. The last thing they need is humanity making them feel less than."

It seemed that with each step they took and each new turn of a corner, another rule came from his lips. There were far too many to count. This wasn't even under the guise of him being the one to tell them this protocol in a royal fashion. As of now, the girls were merely pawns in whatever plan the prince and his advisor were concocting. The break in constant dragging practically shocked Cammie from her daze. All the rules had blended together to where she knew there was no way she was reciting them. Absolutely no way.

Cammie felt eyes on her as she lifted her gaze from the floor, where she had traced a pattern on the section.

Darrian looked on at her expectantly, clearing awaiting an answer to a question Cammie did not hear.

Panicked, Cammie turned to Sabina, hoping the worry displayed itself clearly enough that her sister could identify it yet be vague enough that the advisor couldn't decipher the message.

Sabina's face lit up, and she cleared her throat. "We understand, Sir Darrian."

A ball of relief erupted in Cammie's stomach, and she reminded herself to thank Sabina once prying eyes and listening ears had turned away.

The response stalled Darrian in his tracks, and because of his movements, the entire group stopped walking. "I am happy to know that what I said registered."

Cammie swallowed the urge to laugh. This guy was pompous and arrogant. The only difference between him and the prince was that *Sir Darrian* did not seem to know it.

"Sabina was raised in a prominent family," Cammie explained instead, sending Darrian's eyebrows quirking upward.

So he was snotty *and* pleased. What a pair.

"It's true," Sabina quipped, the socialite side of her coming out of hiding. "My parents, or the people who raised me, taught me all they knew about proper etiquette, socialization, and the justified standing between socialite families and others who didn't have that status."

Darrian huffed, his side eye going straight to another person in the group. "Maybe you can use whatever limited skills you have from your realm to give the knowledge to others. I know some whom *desperately* need it."

The insult did not fall on deaf ears. Hannah's face reddened as she averted her gaze, and Cammie knew if no one was around, Darrian would have been beaten to a pulp. The embarrassed gaze on Hannah's face shifted to something that looked more like a steely resolve, but other than that, nothing was given away.

Sabina merely nodded to Darrian before giving a soft smile, one that Cammie wondered if she used often by how natural it looked. "I will do my best," she replied, angling her gaze back to Cammie. Cammie knew that as soon as Darrian took them wherever the destination was, Sabina would have questions. She always seemed to know when things just weren't quite "right," as she would put it.

Darrian continued on his monologue, pointing out the history of pictures on the wall. Several generations had portraits made by the most skilled Amarians of their time.

As he spoke, one portrait in question caught her eyes. She wasn't the only one. Caelan froze in his tracks, his entire body becoming rigid as his gaze remained glued to the couple photographed on the wall.

The woman was regal, with dark hair and midnight blue eyes, a shade that could have rivaled Hannah's. She was poised in her mannerisms, and her eyes and the rise of her cheekbones reflected nothing but kindness. Her skin contrasted with that of the man next to her. Where she was fair, he was olive, but together, the blend of the two fit together perfectly. He wore no expression on his face other than one that Cammie would have described as firm. Pride gleamed in his eyes, though, and it did on the woman's face as well.

Cammie questioned the picture with pinched eyebrows, the answer falling together perfectly as she grasped what the woman was holding in her dainty hands. *A newborn Amarian.*

Caelan swallowed, and it felt like the room grew all too quiet as the others passed by the painting.

"This is the last image we have of the late queen and king before Prince Aamir's father ascended the throne," Darrian remarked quietly. "After the assassination, our king thought it best to honor those who had passed, and if you would look a bit further back, you would see other portraits of previous rulers. Soon, I think, the king's will go up here as well."

Caelan's breath caught in his throat, and a constricted expression crossed his eyes. "When was this done?" he finally asked, his gaze never straying from the woman.

"They did the portrait about a week before the assassination," Darrian answered, folding his arms behind his back as he looked on at the picture thoughtfully. "The queen, I was told, wanted get the picture captured as efficiently as possible before the baby's next feeding. She was rather particular about things of that nature. Making sure her son came first was her main concern as soon as she fell with child."

An unreadable expression came from Caelan's face as he stared even harder at the portrait, letting out a quiet breath that didn't seem small at all. "I see," he said, his voice quiet amidst the hollowness in the room.

"If you would follow me," Darrian interjected, sweeping his hand back in the direction they had been originally heading to.

The others moved, but Cammie stayed back, lingering behind with Caelan, who watched, mesmerized, by the image on the wall.

Cammie raised a hand to his shoulder, hesitating. Should she touch him? Maybe he didn't want any form of contact.

"You don't have to stay," Caelan said, interrupting her thoughts.

Cammie decided to not let the thoughts in her mind win. She laid a hand on her father's shoulder, and he softened at her touch. "I want to stay," she said. "I can't even imagine how this must feel for you."

Another breath released from Caelan, and his shoulders tightened again. "In some ways, you can. Solenne kept you and your sisters hidden from me for your entire lives. There are memories I missed out on, milestones I never got to experience, all because I thought you were dead." His voice cracked on the last word.

Cammie felt a sudden tightness in her chest. As he tore his eyes away from the photo, she could see the unshed tears, and he didn't have to speak. She just knew he was thinking of her mother, the one person Cammie would never get to meet.

"If circumstances had been in our favor, and there wasn't a death wish on me since birth, your lives would have been much different. I would have been there, as best as I could, along with your mother. She made Solenne promise to keep you safe, and since she can no longer guarantee that, it is my duty, as your father and as the true king, to follow through with it. I don't know what Prince Aamir is encountering or who wants him dead, but I promise you this, Cammie, no harm will come to you anymore. As long as I am alive and breathing, I will find us a way out of this." Without warning, he crushed her in a hug.

She let herself fall into the arms of the one person she knew for sure she could trust, despite the hidden secrets and enemies that laid around them.

Caelan will keep us safe.

"Are you two coming along?" Darrian was at the end of the hall, waiting for them to follow the others.

Caelan let go of Cammie, wiping his eyes before putting on a mask, his expressions unreadable. "We are," he replied. Looking over to Cammie, Caelan whispered, "Do as he says, but trust no one. We have no idea who could be behind the killings. Stay on your guards and let me handle the rest."

Cammie nodded, wordlessly, following behind Caelan's determined steps toward their destination.

CHAPTER FORTY-NINE

SABINA

DARRIAN HAD TAKEN THEM TO their prospective rooms. Tony, Will, Trevor, and Marcus all roomed together at the end of the hall. Darrian said it was easier to keep them together, away from James and Caelan, because blending in would be difficult with so many people in the same room.

That left Sabina, Hannah, and Cammie together in the another room. It was spacious, a lot bigger than she imagined, a room for people who were once headed to the dungeons. Darrian had left the door open, just to make sure no *unnecessary* business went on.

"The wall color is disgusting. It makes me want to gouge my eyes out," Hannah remarked, gagging.

Sabina rolled her eyes at Hannah's dramatics, but she was right. The wall had chipped paint to where the aging stone was peeking out, but the color hadn't faded by any means. It was a mix of burnt orange and yellow. The room held no windows, leaving them trapped in this mass of color horrors.

"At least try to be positive," Cammie chirped, sitting on the much-too-large poster bed. If it wasn't for the circles under her eyes, Sabina would have said she looked almost relaxed.

Aside from the bed, there was a red chaise lounge, which Hannah plopped into promptly, letting out a sigh of contentment. "I can't speak for the crappy people, but I can speak for the comfiness of the furniture."

"The early ancestors did well to make sure everything in the castle was not only functional but comfortable," an unfamiliar voice said.

Sabina looked to the doorway, where a woman dressed in plain clothes stood, holding towels. Several other women behind her each held a bucket of steaming water.

Hannah sprung to her feet, her fists balling as she raised them. She was always ready for a fight regardless of the circumstances.

Sabina clicked her tongue, giving Hannah a pointed look. "She's not here to drown us."

"Precisely not," the woman said, giving Hannah a small smile. "I am here, by the instruction of Darrian, to make you look presentable to the members of society."

Sabina raised a brow. She knew little about Amarians, but she knew the hidden meanings when propriety was a concern. "You're here to make us blend in, aren't you?"

The woman's expression remained unchanged as she waltzed into the room. She headed for the door on the far end of the room, the other women following behind her. Sabina watched, puzzled until she heard water sloshing.

The first woman returned, while the others lingered in what Sabina assumed was the bathroom. "Whomever wants to go first," she said, gesturing to the room behind her.

Hannah scoffed. "It won't be me. If you can't even tell me your name first, there's no way I'm letting you *help* me get ready." She practically choked on the word. It made sense. Hannah had always been allergic to being aided.

The servant girl just smiled then bowed her head slightly. "I apologize. You are right. I should have given you my name. To redo, my name is Eirini. Now, will one of you please get into the tub? The ball will start soon, and I need to do my duty."

Cammie and Hannah both wore conflicted expressions.

Sabina threw her hands in the air. "I'll do it, so you guys don't have to."

Eirini bowed her head again, her smile turning gentler, as if that were even possible. "This way," she instructed, her hand guiding Sabina into the room before shutting the door.

They took off her clothes in a hurry before instructing her to get into the tub. Sabina's feet were unsteady as she lifted herself into the space. Hot water sloshed around her ankles and she settled in comfortably, bits of steam rising.

Two of the women worked quickly, grabbing the sponge on the counter surface and dousing it with a strange purple liquid.

Sabina pursed her lips, but Eirini was already one step ahead.

"The prince, ahem, has informed us of your *condition*." She spoke the word quietly, as if it would be too detrimental for anyone else to hear. "You are unfamiliar with how we do things here, and that is okay. What we are using is lavender based, blended with water and some other herbs. The liquid acts as a cleaning property, and it will help us get the dirt off of you and make you more presentable before the ceremony." One woman handed the sponge over, and Eirini etched closer to the tub. "May I?" Eirini asked gently.

Sabina realized this must have been normal in this world. Swallowing down the immediate discomfort, she nodded. *Just because it was different didn't make it bad.*

Eirini gestured to the women, and they also grabbed several more sponges, dousing them with the same liquid. They scrubbed at her body furiously, and her skin burned at the friction. Eirini said something Sabina couldn't decipher. Without warning, the scalding water gushed over her head, completely wetting her hair. Eirini barked orders yet again, and soon, the purple liquid was being massaged into Sabina's scalp at a pace that was almost relaxing, if it weren't for the force of Eirini's fingers.

All too quickly, she was lifted out of the tub, goosebumps overtaking her bare skin as Eirini wrapped a towel around her body.

"Grab one of the other girls," she told one woman as she pushed Sabina out of the bathroom and back into the room they had originally come from.

Eirini kept pushing Sabina to the edge of the bedroom, where another door was waiting. The door opened with the force of Sabina's body pressing against it, and soon, they were in another room. This one held a vanity with a hanging mirror, a vanity chair, and a small lounge. Several items rested on the lounge, including an elegant ballgown, silver heels, and a few paints and brushes, among other items Sabina couldn't place a name for.

Eirini pushed Sabina down into the chair with a nod and a resounding, "Sit." Eirini worked in a hurry, clutching this and that. She pulled Sabina's hair back and pushed it into a clip. It was still sopping wet, but Eirini either didn't notice or didn't care. She grabbed the several paints and brushes before sliding the liquid on Sabina's face. Eirini pierced her eyebrows together in concentration, murmuring under her breath.

"Is something wrong?" Sabina asked, unable to move her head fully because of Eirini's grip.

"It is nothing," Eirini assured, though Sabina's gut told her that was a lie. "I am just not used to having a human face for a canvas. Amarians are much more...so..." She stopped speaking, clearly trying to find the right word.

"Prettier?" Sabina offered, joking.

Eirini actually laughed, shaking her head. "You are pretty, just in a different way. Amarians are...." She pinched her eyebrows together. "They are strong," she decided on. "Our heritage is different, and we are proud, but we are all unique in our own way. Humans, to me, all seem to be the same, but maybe that is because I do not know any of them until now." She said the last part with a smile.

Sabina could already feel herself warming up to this strange, new woman.

Eirini, in Sabina's opinion, wasn't pretty in the way most would define it. She had a demure demeanor about her, but her eyes reminded her of Hannah's—wild and untamable, if provoked. Her skin was on the more olive side, and her eyes were a deep shade of brown that seemed to rest in thought more often than Eirini probably realized. There was an ethereal quality about her, and it wasn't just because of her pointy ears. Eirini seemed to be almost magnetic. Eirini's dark hair hung in curly ringlets and swayed as she moved, and the more Sabina studied her, the more curious she was. How did she end up in the castle, and what was life like living in this world and knowing nothing else?

"We are almost finished," Eirini announced proudly, taking Sabina's hand.

After Sabina moved, Eirini grabbed the chair and brought it to the hearth, where a fire was already ablaze. Putting Sabina back in the chair, Eirini let the clip go, and the heat collided with Sabina's hair. She could feel the wetness dissipating as the flame ran over the strands still drying. Even the goosebumps lessened with the heat of the fire nearby, and Sabina let out a small, satisfied sigh.

"Is this much different than the world you are used to?" Eirini asked.

"It is very different," Sabina replied, trying to find words to best describe a world where technology was the rave to a person who would never understand it. "Electronic technology runs the world. We have phones, which is like...a calling device to reach others if they aren't nearby."

"Do these phones fly?" Eirini asked seriously.

"No," Sabina muttered. "They're attached to you, I guess you could say. You press buttons, and then those buttons help you call someone."

"Hmm," Eirini mused. "That is interesting. Here, we just use the messenger birds. It takes a day to get the correspondence desired, but it has not done us wrong."

Eirini shook out Sabina's hair before having her move yet again. This time, she had Sabina stand away from the fire as she brushed through Sabina's waves with a comb. It felt soft against her scalp, and soon, Eirini's hands were moving of their own accord, braiding strands and pinning them up.

Eirini gestured for Sabina to drop the towel, and with a mortified gaze, she did, shutting her eyes. Eirini helped her dress, handing her a pair of clean undergarments, similar to the ones on Earth, before slipping on the dress. The material was like the same silky one Sabina had worn for Solenne's funeral, except it felt softer on her skin. Sabina peeled her eyes open, choking back a gasp. The dress billowed out at the waist, and if one peered close enough, they would see the tiny, encrusted jewels embellishing the edges. It swept across her shoulders, leaving no inch of skin bare.

"It's gorgeous," Sabina breathed.

"And so are you," Eirini countered, spinning her around to face the mirror.

Sabina found herself breathless as she stared at her reflection. Eirini had pinned her hair elegantly, spare for a few strands hanging near her earlobes. The makeup accented the emerald in her eyes and brought out the rose-hue in her cheeks, making her look lighter, brighter. She didn't look her usual pale, washed-out self. She looked like she belonged, except for one small problem.

Her hands clasped her earlobes, a red blush coating her cheeks. "You did stunning work, but what about my ears? Won't people notice we aren't Amarian? Human ears are pretty obvious."

Eirini moved around her to the vanity and pulled something out of the drawer. It was a simple herb, and she handed it to Sabina. "Take this before you exit the room," she instructed. "It will take care of the problem."

"But what is it?"

"It is something we give the baby Amarians with deformities. It will allow you to have Amarian ears for a short period, enough time that the women and men of the court and society will not suspect a thing. Prince Aamir will announce your arrival at the ball as Amarians who were kidnapped during the assassination and hid in the Earth realm to stay alive. This ball is your eventful return home, to a new world you aren't familiar with. It covers all the bases that people would question, and it keeps you safe until Prince Aamir decides what is best to do and how to proceed."

"Why are you doing this?" Sabina asked, noting Eirini's serious expression.

"I am loyal to the Crown," Eirini replied. Sabina didn't miss how she didn't say the prince or his family. "My parents were loyal to this kingdom long before I was born, and they died a wrongful death for a just cause. I have no family left and no husband to tend to.... I am married to duty, much like a royal is married to the kingdom. My life has always been to serve, and if this will help bring the Crown to a better standing, then who am I to stop it? Prince Aamir gave me orders, and my part is to follow them. That is what my parents have done, and it is what I will do, even unto death."

Sabina had no idea what to say in response to that, but before she could even think of a word that would fit, a commotion resounded from the next room.

"I'm not asking for something impossible," Hannah shrieked. "You want to fix my hair into something horrendous? Do something better. Cut my hair off, then. I don't care that you think it would complement me perfectly. I *don't* want flowers in it. I want nothing super girly. Just *stop*."

Sabina let out a laugh.

Eirini cocked her head to the side. "Your friend...is difficult, no?"

"You have no idea, and what might blow your mind even more is the fact that she's my sister."

Eirini laughed, her eyebrows pinching together. "Okay, then," she said, heading to the door that led back to the bedroom.

Sabina followed behind her shortly after, ready to tackle whatever mess Hannah had gotten herself into again.

CHAPTER FIFTY

HANNAH

THEY THOUGHT SHE WAS JOKING. The look of absolute horror in their eyes was evident of that. Here, in Natrellum, women apparently didn't cut their hair.

But Hannah guessed their horror was justified. She was holding a massive pair of scissors over her hair, and these women could not stop her if they tried. Not to mention, she probably was being the epitome of the "crazy human" stories they'd heard of during bedtime stories.

"You're going to hurt yourself," one of the servant women called out.

"I've wielded weapons before. I'm not an idiot," Hannah retorted, waving the scissors defiantly.

One of the servants gasped, clutching her chest, and Hannah had to bite her tongue to stop the mocking from going any further. Just to spite them, she clipped a strand of hair. Hannah watched as the dark section fell to the ground like a feather.

An actual shriek erupted from one servant, and she brought her hands up to her open mouth. "Stop!

Your hair is still functional. There is no need to cut off these beautiful locks."

Hannah scoffed, bringing the scissors up to another level. "It is if they're dead weight."

Snip. Snip. Snip.

Another sound of horror came from the servant. Nothing could help these women now.

Just before Hannah clipped another strand of hair, the doors to the far end of the room busted open, and Eirini entered first, followed by Sabina.

While Eirini's face was amassed with shock, Sabina's eyebrows knitted together, and her lips tightened. *She was disappointed.*

But she isn't the one who had flowers in her hair. And yet...

Hannah couldn't deny that Sabina looked regal—almost too regal. Eirini had picked the best dress for Sabina's skin tone. The green on Hannah would have made her look like some sort of olive. Sabina's hair was an ornate array, beautifully done, so why did these women want to dress Hannah in a tomato-red gown with puffy sleeves and make her hairstyle resemble a peacock with floral decorations? It was, to put it bluntly, unfair.

"Why are my ladies shouting for their lives?" Eirini asked, looking pointedly at the one woman who was still frozen in front of Hannah.

"She was cutting her hair, Eirini, even after we instructed her not to. We had a plan to make her look so pretty," the woman replied, going into a small bow.

"You mean, you were going to make me look like a circus baboon," Hannah muttered under her breath, earning a death glare from Sabina.

Sabina didn't make comments on the insult but asked, "Hannah, why cut your hair? There's no need to."

Hannah gestured toward Sabina, letting out a strangled sigh. "You look like an actual member of society. It's easy for you to say that. My hair is chaotic."

"If you wouldn't have cut it, Hannah, then maybe your hair would be fine." Sabina spoke the words like cinnamon, but Hannah did not miss the steely edge that was underneath them.

"Well," Hannah said with a grin, "it looks like I have no choice except to finish what I started."

And so she let the scissors do their duty, sending more and more clumps of hair falling to the floor.

Eirini pinched the bridge of her nose, shutting her eyes against the monstrosity that Hannah was becoming. "Has the other girl at least bathed yet?"

"The *other girl* has a name." Hannah sneered, crossing her arms over the towel she was currently wearing. *Obviously the dress is a no-go.* "It's Cammie."

Eirini huffed, letting out a slow, long sigh that seemed to last for eons. "Fine. Has *Cammie* at least bathed yet?"

"She's in the tub now, madame," the servant replied, her face no longer flushing with embarrassment.

The bathroom door opened, as if on cue, and Cammie stepped out, her hair sopping wet. Her skin was slick with water, and she wrapped the towel around her body tighter, completely unaware of the chaos unfolding outside her door.

But it didn't take long.

After adjusting to her new surroundings, one look at Hannah made Cammie's face lose all of her color. "What did you do to your hair?" she screamed, almost dropping the towel completely.

"I made adjustments," Hannah replied with a broad smile.

It didn't make Cammie's expression any better. If anything, it only made the concern in her cheeks worsen.

"We don't have the time for this," Eirini lamented, using her hands to steady herself. She opened her eyes, snapping her fingers at the servant behind Cammie. "Ariella, get Cammie dressed in the bathroom. Estellanie, take care of...*her*." Eirini spoke of Hannah with such distaste that it made her swell with pride.

Ariella took Cammie into the bathroom and shut the door quietly.

Eirini grabbed Sabina and gestured for her to exit the room. "Since you're the only one presentable, I will do my duty of showing you around the castle to kill some time."

Sabina smiled, and they headed to the bedroom door. Sabina exited.

Eirini lingered behind for a moment. "Estellanie," she warned, "don't dawdle. Get her dressed quickly despite her complaints. We cannot afford to be late to such an important event."

Eirini left swiftly after that, leaving the frightened Estellanie in Hannah's more than capable hands.

Hannah gave a Cheshire grin, and she swore that Estellanie's face lost a shade of color.

This will be fun.

Hannah should have had more faith in Estellanie. The girl, once she got over her fear of Hannah, was skilled with a brush and some paints, and she wrangled Hannah's choppy bob into a more form-fitting one.

Hannah did her part, too. She wore flowers at the base of her head as they'd asked. The flower crown didn't look terrible. The dress wasn't so bad, either, once Estellanie agreed to loosen the sleeves.

Looking into the mirror, Hannah actually felt she didn't look like a dumpster fire. The ballgown blended well with her skin, even with the off-shoulder balloon sleeves, now that the makeup was on. Her cheeks were flushed with a pink hue, and her eyelids were silvery-brown, Natrellum's version of a smoky eye.. Estellanie topped it all off with a plum lip, looking on at Hannah expectantly.

"Do you like it, miss?" Estellanie asked, her brow creasing in.

"It isn't half-bad, 'Stellanie. You did good. Actually..." Hannah tapped her chin thoughtfully. "...you did pretty great."

Estellanie beamed, her smile overtaking her face. "Thank you, miss," she said, bowing.

The bathroom door opened again, and Cammie exited, holding onto the ends of her dress, barely stumbling into the room. "Does this look okay?" she asked, biting her lip.

Cammie was always shyer than most with dressing up. Hannah was bold, so the idea of having eyes on her was never a problem. If anyone got too courageous with their gaze, all Hannah had to do was deck them to take care of the problem. It seemed the servants knew just how to dress them, in a way that fit their personalities, because Cammie would rather die than slap a man across the face.

Ariella had taken care with Cammie, dressing her in a primrose-colored ballgown, flecked with tiny clear star accents that blended into the gown. The capped sleeves fell slightly off the shoulders. Ariella had pulled Cammie's hair halfway, letting the top section fall into a decorated rose design while allowing the bottom half to flow freely down her back in loose waves. She looked like the quiet princess she was, and Hannah wanted to just hug her.

"You look gorgeous," Hannah assured her.

Cammie's nervous demeanor fell away. She stood proudly, looking around the room. "Is Sabina here?"

"She was taking a walk around the castle with Eirini, but she should be back any minute now," Hannah said, looking on at the door.

With a whoosh, the door opened, as if Hannah had commanded it, and Eirini and Sabina rushed in, shutting the door suddenly.

"People are gathering already," Eirini announced, clasping something tightly in her hands.

Sabina unwrapped her closed palms, revealing a small, green herb the size of a small leaf. "Eirini has given this to us to blend in better. It will provide us the illusion of looking Amarian and will last throughout the time of the ball. All that we have to do is take it, and the effects shouldn't take long to set in."

Hannah furrowed her brows, giving Eirini a once-over. "How do we know you aren't trying to kill us?"

"If I wanted to kill you, why would I have dressed you up? I am here to serve as that is my duty. Nothing more," Eirini said.

She has a point there.

"I trust her," Sabina said, "and I want to do what's best for us. Whatever will get us through long enough to plead our case to the Council is what we should do."

With a resolved nod, Eirini opened her palms, revealing two of the same herbs. Cammie and Hannah each took one, bringing it to their lips.

It tasted like peppermint on her tongue, dissolving almost instantly. Hannah felt a slight tingling on her ears that shifted to a burning until it completely disappeared.

Looking over, Sabina and Cammie were completely different. Their normally round ears had shifted to a point, making them seem as if they belonged here since birth.

"You are ready," Eirini said proudly, opening the door wide.

Hannah could hear the chatter traveling down the hall from the ballroom, and her heart thumped in her chest.

It's now or never.

CHAPTER FIFTY-ONE

CAMMIE

Her hands were laced with sweat as her heels clacked against the stone floor. Sabina and Hannah were ahead of her, hovering just a few paces near the destination of the ballroom floor. The chatter and laughter grew louder, ringing against her ears as her feet continued moving.

Cammie didn't know where the others were. She hadn't seen them since Darrian had brought them to the bedrooms.

"Just be aware of what the others are saying. Be kind and don't speak too suddenly unless addressed." Eirini was already rattling off instructions, allowing Cammie space to mentally make ample notes.

Soon, the ballroom came into view. People were talking animatedly with each other and dancing, the sound shrill and high in the atmosphere, yet it sounded muffled in Cammie's own ears, probably because of the anxiety that was thrumming through her eardrums.

The music came through, though, loud and clear. An Amarian, sitting on an ornate chair, with an endowment for music, was playing an instrument that looked like a violin. The song was soft and slow, blending and melding around the chatter throughout the room. The woman had her eyes closed in concentration, and for a moment, Cammie felt a pang of jealousy. *How lucky would it be to just disappear into the background?*

"You will be fine," Eirini reassured her with a pat on the shoulder.

"Can you read my mind now?" Cammie asked, half-joking.

"You wear your expressions on your face distinctly. It would be hard not to notice the emotions that are flickering behind your eyes," Eirini responded, following Cammie's line-of-sight back to the crowd of people on the ballroom floor.

James was in the middle of the crowd, his gaze fixated on the Amarian woman he was lost deep in conversation with. Her hair was blonde, wrapped into a magnificent braid, and her dress was the most detailed Cammie had ever seen, with a tight fit that accentuated her curves in a way that Cammie's dress surely did not.

"You've proven my point exactly," Eirini said softly. "You're infuriated at the guard over there, and you might deny it as much as you want to, but the care you have for him is detailed in more than just your eyes."

Cammie wanted to reply with a quick-witted rebuttal, but before she could even form one, Eirini gave her a slight push, forcing her to be in the ballroom instead of looking on from outside of it.

Hannah and Sabina went ahead, blending into a section of the crowd on the side.

Cammie's face flushed with panic as several Amarians stared at her in wonder, and some looked on in plain disgust. The stares tripled then multiplied. *Is there something on my face?*

The only people who didn't seem to be occupied with gawking were James and the annoyingly put-together woman. Heaving a breath, Cammie willed herself to move forward. James and his companion were so engaged that neither of them moved as she continued walking in their direction.

Cammie couldn't help but feel another spike of anxiety in the pit of her stomach. *Who is she? What are they discussing?*

"—you have until the end of the ball to think on your answer and then call for me once you've decided. That should be more than enough time to wager if your family's legacy is worth it," the woman hissed.

Cammie wasn't fortunate enough to catch the first half of the conversation, but what she heard gave her entire body chills.

When Cammie finally reached James, the woman had stopped speaking, turning on her heel. Cammie only glimpsed the woman's face—angry and resolved—before she disappeared back into the crowd.

James was frozen in time, his face pale. He didn't notice Cammie's arrival until she hesitantly put an arm on his shoulder.

He flinched, blinking rapidly, as if her touch finally broke his trance. "Hi," he rushed, the color coming back to his face.

"Hi," Cammie replied sheepishly, knowing full well her cheeks were red as embers.

It's a weird divide between sharing a kiss with someone to not even knowing how to react to them being around in the next breath.

"The ladies really made you look different," James said, giving her a once-over.

"I can't be that unrecognizable, can I?" Cammie teased, hating how uneven her breathing sounded in his presence.

"No," James said, voice rough with something she couldn't place. "I could never forget your face."

As much as she'd hate to admit it, she knew, after everything, she could never either, especially not on a night when he dressed like this.

Donned in some of the best clothes she had seen him wear, James looked nothing like the boy she had met in the bookstore. Where he once resembled a disheveled, lost person, he now wore the softest tailcoat in the shade of emeralds, looking like a member of the highest court. The material was some kind of velvet, Cammie realized, as her fingers still clutched the material. It went perfectly with the dark pants he wore, and she couldn't help but marvel at how the material brought out the green in his eyes.

Somehow, they looked brighter the longer she stared at them. Cammie couldn't decipher if it was the ballroom lighting or something deeper.

It was a different environment than all the others he had been in throughout the memories she had with him. The earth realm had given her an opportunity to have the upper hand in their relationship. She had been the one teaching, cultivating, leading, but being here in a stuffy ballroom, watching her sisters melding through the crowd and leaving her here with a different version of someone she knew, made her heart patter to a tune that refused to stop.

Sweat slicked against the palms of her hands. "That's... nice of you to say, I suppose. I really hope you wouldn't forget my face so quickly. I mean, you weren't the one whose memory was Erased." A chuckle was building at the back of her throat, but Cammie swallowed it down.

"Awkward formality isn't necessary, Cammie." He took a step forward, holding out a hand. "Dance with me?"

Cammie swallowed the lump that lodged in her throat. "I'm not sure if that's a good idea."

"Please," he said, barely whispering. The creases in his eyes crinkled, and the earnestness stunned Cammie into shock.

Questions of whether this was a show for the crowd rang loudly in her mind even as her palm contacted his. She felt the electric zap in her skin before her brain even registered what was happening.

Her shoes skidded on the floor as he led her to an open section. As they stood there staring at each other for the briefest of moments, her heart caught.

He was stunning.

His grip shifted then, moving slowly toward the curve of her back. Zips of lightning traveled up her spine as the palm of his hand rested flatly against the small of her back. The pressure made her lean in closer. She could feel his breath mingling against her ear, their torsos pressing together, her chest against his.

The simple feeling of how close he was caused every single hair on the back of her neck to stand, and slowly but surely, the goosebumps appeared at the sound of his voice against her ear.

"I have no other choice but to speak to you like this," he whispered.

James started swaying, and by some miracle, Cammie's feet moved along with his movements. She had never been skilled dancer, but somehow, she wasn't failing now in front of these people who were surely watching her. He did a turn, and Cammie felt her face flush with red. Several pairs of Amarians were talking, but like she had predicted, a few had turned to gawk. This time, there was no hiding from it.

"Why..." Cammie couldn't find words to speak aloud, afraid that her heartbeat was deafening enough to drown the rest.

"There's a lot to explain, but I want you to piece the picture together with me. I'm worried," James murmured, turning them around yet again.

Cammie furrowed her brows. "Worried?" she asked, closing her eyes. "What do you mean?"

"I think something's happened to Caelan and the others," he said, his voice low. "They weren't there when I was getting ready."

"They weren't getting ready?"

James shook his head slightly, his chin brushing against her cheek as he leaned in closer. The movement alone made her shut her eyes tighter.

"No," he stated. "They weren't getting ready at all. By the time I had exited the room after getting dressed, Caelan was gone. When I realized what was happening, I went to the other room. Tony and the others had vanished, too. I'm not sure what happened, but I haven't seen them since they escorted us to our rooms. I was hoping nothing had happened to you, and, well..." James trailed off, heaving a breath. "You're here now," he said finally.

"I am," Cammie said, her voice catching in her throat as her mind raced with the thoughts that were close to spilling into spoken sentences. She opened her eyes hesitantly, as if doing so would make all of this more real somehow. She kept them trained on the lapel of his jacket. "How can we find them?"

"I've been to enough parties like this one before. It was one perk to being a palace guard, I guess."

He sounded like he was smiling, but Cammie wouldn't dare move her gaze. By doing so, she might as well lose her breath entirely.

"Going to these enough times gives you an advantage to know the schedule of how this could go. Prince Aamir's focus is to have us blend into the background as much as possible because, in his mind, this will give us an advantage. Maybe the person who's been murdering for sport is waiting in the shadows, or maybe not. Either way, we will be out of his way, which is what he wants. He doesn't want you to rule, but I don't think he'd stoop so low as to kill you or the others. If he did, he would have done that the minute Sabina revealed you three to be a threat."

His words rang true.

"What are you suggesting?" Cammie asked, noting how the music had changed tune yet again.

Several others had joined in, swaying to the beat on the dance floor, but Cammie kept her eyes trained on James' collar. If she allowed herself to look anywhere else, she was sure they would see the anxiety painted on her face like charcoal on a canvas.

"Do exactly as he wants," James stated plainly, to which Cammie scrunched her nose in confusion. "It sounds counter-intuitive, I know, but just trust me. After this dance, find your sisters. Talk with them. Socialize with the other Amarians. Make things up if they ask questions. It doesn't really matter. Prince Aamir should give a speech soon. It's kind of customary in celebration of life ceremonies. Since it is for the king, it'll be longer, more elaborate. Because of that, expect more guards around, more patrolling. Also expect him to cover up what happened earlier with dragging us away. He'll probably say we're huddled in the dungeon and the matter was taken care of."

"And what will you be doing?"

"What I do best. Defying orders. I'm already under watch, so what I do now won't make the situation any easier, but I'm one of the few people here who know the ins and outs of this castle. If they're being hidden somewhere, I'm your best chance at finding them." James pulled away just enough to where she could see his face. "Can you promise me to be safe?"

Cammie nodded. "I can do my best."

His grip on her back tightened as he leaned in closer, next to her ear again. "Don't trust anyone," he warned. "There are snakes everywhere, and in this castle, everyone could be disguised as a saint."

"Even you?" Cammie dared to ask, looking up at him from underneath her eyelashes as he pulled away. She couldn't even believe the thought had left her lips. Considering how many times he had lied to her, she'd had no choice but to ask.

Cammie expected to see a flash of hurt across his face, but his expression was that of a calm that couldn't be bothered.

"Even me," he said cautiously as the music flowed at a much slower pace. "At one point, I would have agreed that it couldn't be me who would defy doing the right thing, but being under the pressure of duty—that can change a person. It wasn't until I was free from it that I realized I had choices." His voice quieted, and he cleared his throat, peering into her eyes. "So, to answer your question honestly? Yes. At one point, even me. I am trying to be different, better somehow, but, Cammie, no person is perfect. No person is exactly one side or the other, as much as Amarians try to pretend to be. We are all a blend of our failures and mistakes, and...leaving you, lying to you...those are some mistakes I'll live with for the rest of my life. I can't change it, but I can change what I do now." His gaze shifted from softness to a hardened resolve, and he drifted from her grasp, letting Cammie's hands fall to her sides. "Be careful," he murmured.

The music ended suddenly, and the violinist came to a stand, taking a small bow.

The crowd gathered on the ballroom floor replied with thunderous applause, and the sound echoed in Cammie's eardrums until it changed to ringing that refused to quiet. She could still feel the ghost of James' touch, even after his fingers were long gone, and she looked over at him, wondering if he was pleased with the response of the nobles and many others in the crowd.

But James had vanished without warning.

Cammie was on her own.

She squared her shoulders, doing her best to ignore the invisible hand that clutched her throat. Anxiety was trying to keep her in its stubborn grasp, but she had to do better. Her life depended on it, and so did her father's. Her sisters' too.

Scouring the crowd, Cammie did her best to zero in on her sisters. After several minutes, she found them in the corner of the room, whispering to each other.

Her feet couldn't move fast enough as she power-walked to them, trying to diminish the red that had heated her cheeks.

"That was some show," Hannah remarked casually, a smirk plastered on her face. The maid who dressed her did a perfect job. The dress combined with the dark lip made Hannah look even more authoritative if that were even possible. She looked regal, powerful in her own right, whereas Cammie worried she looked like the scared girl she was.

"No show happened," Cammie rushed, averting her eyes.

"Well, I wouldn't say nothing happened," Sabina said, her gaze bright. "You two looked cozy."

"There was nothing cozy about it," Cammie defended, crossing her arms over her chest. *Why can't they understand how serious this is?* "It was strictly about what we're doing here."

"I dunno," Hannah drawled. "Any more minutes together, I was worried I'd have to call an officiant to start a ceremony and get you guys a private room for a honeymoon."

"Hannah!" Cammie whisper-shrieked. "You can't speak like that. Not here, where people can overhear."

Hannah, ever unfazed, merely rolled her eyes. "Seriously? That's what you're worried about? People hearing that you could be married and in nine months have a baby on the way? There's no need to worry about people hearing it. The way you were looking at him was obvious enough."

Cammie wanted to scream. "Do you even care about decency?"

Hannah's expression remained unchanged as she let out a breath. "Not particularly, no, but if it means something to you, I'm more than happy to ask Prince Aamir for an officiant. I'm sure with James being a former guard in the castle, Princey can find some sort of discount to start a ceremony, and, even better, you can use one of the guest wings here. Look at that—ceremony and room booked all in one go. Maybe I should see if there's wedding-planning jobs around here. I think I have a real skill for this kind of thing."

Even Sabina snickered.

Cammie couldn't believe it. "Are you and Hannah actually getting along?"

"That remains to be seen," Sabina replied, a small smile on her face, "but let's be honest. There is no reason I could argue with her when the love you have for him and him for you is all over your faces."

The heat in Cammie's cheeks traveled to the back of her neck, and the room suddenly felt very warm. "That isn't why I came over here," she said, trying to redirect the conversation.

"If professing your love to James and trying to convince us it doesn't exist isn't on your agenda, then what is?" Hannah asked.

Cammie wanted nothing more than to throttle her.

"Caelan and the others are missing," Cammie rushed. "James went to find them."

Understanding passed over Sabina's features.

Hannah's face only hardened. "What?" Her eyes went dark, and if her gaze could kill, Cammie was sure she'd be dead instantly.

"We aren't sure where they are, but he told me we needed to blend as much as we could. Whether that's by talking or being silent is our choice, but Prince Aamir is going to be giving a speech soon. That's why James left to find them. Prince Aamir will be distracted then."

Hannah rubbed her temple, and Cammie did a double take at Hannah's chopped locks. It would take some getting used to her short hair. "If we're talking about a potential kidnapping situation, I'm going to need something stronger than this conversation."

"Do you care for refreshments?" A servant carrying a tray that held several chutes of some sort of wine looked on at the girls, his face soft despite the surrounding hardness.

Poor guy had stumbled into the wrong conversation at the wrong time.

Without responding, Hannah plucked one glass from the tray. She took a long drink, gulping the contents down. When she removed the glass from her lips, a little red dribbled down her chin. She wiped it absentmindedly with the back of her hand. "That should do it perfectly. "Thank you," she told the servant, who stared on in horror.

He stayed, blinking, until Cammie gave Sabina a pointed look.

Sabina refused to budge, and Cammie made her eyes wider, hoping Sabina would get the memo.

She shook her head slowly, and Cammie sighed. She couldn't be rude. James said to blend in, and if taking wine would help them, so be it.

Cammie grabbed two flutes, muttering a quiet thanks to the servant, who moved on to the next person. Cammie handed one glass to Sabina, who reluctantly took it.

"Why should we be intoxicated if Caelan is missing?" Sabina asked, shooting Hannah a glare. "Just because she's reckless enough to down the whole drink doesn't mean we need to follow behind her."

"See?" Hannah groaned, letting out a burp. "I knew Sabina agreeing with me was too good to be true. She's already ready to argue with me as soon as the chance presents itself."

"We have to be diplomatic and blend in," Cammie explained. "You should know that, shouldn't you?"

Sure enough, Sabina slowly raised the flute to her lips, taking a small sip.

Cammie did the same. She could taste the sourness of cranberries on her tongue as the cold liquid went down. Her taste buds burned with irritation . Despite every prodding, Cammie held back the urge to gag by holding her nose. It made the liquid go down easier. She took another sip, forcing the disgusting drink down, but she couldn't stop the cough that followed.

"That's definitely...an acquired taste," she said.

"Agreed," Sabina said, her eyes watering. It seemed the pungent taste wasn't lost on her.

"It wasn't too bad," Hannah said, a hiccup following. *Hiccup. Hiccup. Hiccup.*

Oh, no.

The sounds grew louder, to where people were staring.

"We have to get her hidden somewhere," Cammie hissed. "Prince Aamir wanted no attention drawn to us, and without knowing where Caelan is, we can't have people annoyed at us already."

James' words came back to her in a flash. *There are snakes everywhere, and in this castle, everyone could be disguised as a saint.*

"Everyone—anyone—can be an enemy hiding in plain sight," she added.

Sabina nodded, scanning the ballroom. Her gaze finally stopped at the edge of the room to a darkened hallway. "There should be an exit there," she said. "We can get as far as the hallway, and one of us can stay with Hannah while the other goes to find Eirini or some other maid, who can help us back to the rooms."

Cammie grabbed Hannah's left arm, and Sabina grabbed the other, and they started walking to the edge of the room.

The clacking of dress shoes on the floor made Cammie's breath catch in her throat. *Prince Aamir is making his way to the dais. His speech is starting.* Unlike the Earth realm, there was no microphone, but she was sure his voice would carry far.

"Good evening," Prince Aamir said, and every single conversation in the room quieted.

Shoot. All eyes will be on them if we move now.

"I am most pleased that you have made an appearance here today. Tomorrow, the rest of the country will become aware of my father's passing. Tonight, we will celebrate together the legacy the king left and partake in a feast, food that is soon to be done in the kitchen. For now, enjoy your drink, the king's favorite wine from our own vineyard." Prince Aamir raised his own glass, his eyes focused outward at the multitudes who raised their glasses in response.

They all took sips, and Prince Aamir was seemingly silent, lost in thought.

Cammie's knees shook, and her heart pounded. She couldn't tell if it was anxiety or the effects of the red wine stunning her.

Prince Aamir started speaking again. "My father was a good man. He ruled this kingdom the best way he knew how, and I know, without a doubt, Natrellum was better for it. His life ended far too soon, and I only hope that I can continue the legacy as gracefully as he had."

"We need to keep walking," Sabina instructed. "He's distracted. It is now or never."

Cammie knew Sabina was right. They needed to move, but her legs weren't listening. They dragged with each step in a manner that was far from graceful.

Sabina led the charge, but Cammie knew she was slowing them down. Nothing she did was working. *What the heck is going on?*

The sound of their shoes didn't seem to be heard as the girls dragged Hannah toward the corridor.

Cammie's vision began blurring the closer she got to the destination. Her arms began to tingle and prick with the feeling of a thousand needles being shoved into her skin, and she couldn't taste her tongue.

"With my father's death, things have changed. There are people who have asked what will become of the kingdom now, and I am here to tell you…"

The prince's words were far, distant, buzzing in her ears. The words blended and pulled apart, and soon enough, they weren't words at all. They weren't letters. It was all incessant noise that Cammie couldn't turn off.

Sabina's movements lagged, and it felt like hours until they reached the miraculously empty hallway.

When they finally stepped over the threshold, Sabina dropped Hannah's arm, swaying. "I don't feel so good," she whispered.

One by one, Hannah then Sabina fell to the ground in a heap.

"What's.... Hannah...what..." Cammie's tongue tingled once more, the words foreign and strange on her lips.

Her vision blurred, making the hallway look like a picture stained with water that was almost unrecognizable.

Cammie saw a dark shadow approach her, and then she saw nothing.

CHAPTER FIFTY-TWO

CAMMIE

She awoke to the feeling of cold against her cheek. Her eyes burned when she blinked, doing her best to assess her surroundings.

As she found the strength to push herself up, it became apparent that she had been sleeping on the ground. No longer was she in the comfort of the room Prince Aamir had "graciously" provided. One look around her confirmed the dread that rested in her stomach.

Cammie was in the depths of the castle's prison.

In the same cell, Hannah sat in the corner, resting her hands on her knees. The flower crown she had adorned was torn to shreds on the floor. Little bits of petals were strewn by her feet, and Cammie took in how her shoes were missing, and her dress had tears and tatters.

"You're awake," Sabina said, her voice quiet. It was void of any emotion other than just being observant.

Cammie tried to remember what exactly had landed her in this place. Sabina was the only person in the cell who looked remotely put together as Cammie took in her own dress that was stained with dirt from lying on the floor for what must have been hours.

"How long was I out? What happened?" Cammie's throat stung as she spoke, and her lips felt dry. She needed water.

"It was the wine," Hannah said. "Had to be. What else would have knocked us out so fast?"

More clarity followed, and memories flooded Cammie's brain. Eirini. The herb. The drink.

Her head was still spinning, and it felt like someone was taking a hammer and chopping away at her skull. She grasped her temple, rubbing the sides of her head with shut eyes.

"Could it have been the herb she gave us?" Cammie asked, taking notes to lower her tone. Sound, any sound, was too loud. Too much.

"If it was that herb, then Caelan wouldn't be here, either," Sabina remarked. "I had that same thought until they told me what happened."

Cammie's eyes peeled open, and she ignored the throbbing behind her eyelids. "Caelan is here?"

Rattling sounded, and Cammie turned her head back to the cell bars. Through them, there was a cell directly across from the girls. It was occupied with five people.

She felt her stomach sink. "What happened? How did you get here?"

With the light barely flowing from the lanterns on the wall, Cammie could hardly make out Caelan's face. She wasn't sure if it was him at first until he spoke.

"We were never able to get ready. It was all a trap." His words were hollow, and Cammie could hear the anger that was lurking beneath. Caelan's fingers gripped the bars so tightly his fingers were white. "There was some kind of drink in the room, something that would ease our nerves. I was stupid. Thought it was Aamir's way of a peace offering. We all drank it, and next thing we knew, we were here." Caelan shook his head.

Cammie's eyes began to adjust to the darkness. She noticed the circles under his eyes. He had been stressed. Or maybe it was worry?

"I hadn't heard from James," Tony spoke up. He was in the back, with Will, Trevor, and Marcus, his expression dark in the room. "I was worried maybe he sold us out just like Rigel did."

"There's no way," Hannah stated, rising on her feet. "If you saw what we did in the ballroom, you would know what we do. James *loves* Cammie. There's no doubting it. If you have another theory, let's hear it because this one looks like grasping at nothing."

"What about Prince Aamir?" Marcus asked. "He would have motive. He wants us dead or, if not dead, at least out of the way."

Cammie thought back to the prince's knack for ruthlessness and the fear he'd worn on his face as he had explained the attempted assassinations. He was a two-sided coin, and she couldn't get a perfect read on him, but did that make him a cold-blooded killer?

"He promised us a way after the ball to talk to the Council," she said. "He wouldn't be that cruel to just take back his words."

The prison doors opened suddenly, the sound creaking against her ears. "How very astute of you," a voice said. "I never knew humans could possess such knowledge. In all the stories we hear of, they're always so...dense." Footsteps followed, but Cammie couldn't see the face attached to the voice until the person rounded the corner to the cells.

As she took in the dark smile and how he carried himself, she wanted to slap herself for being so blind.

"*You've* been behind this the entire time," Cammie shouted. "You're nothing but a snake. What do you think Prince Aamir would say to you, knowing you're keeping us captive?"

Darrian's eyes flashed dark, and his smile grew. "Prince Aamir will never know. The prince has been too absorbed in his own matters, what with his grief. I believe it will quite occupy him for a while."

Cammie felt her stomach roil. "You're kidding," she whispered. *No one can possibly be this evil.*

"What?" Hannah looked over at Cammie, but she was too focused on slowing her own breathing to give Hannah any answers. "Tell me, Cammie. What's going on?"

Cammie reeled in the bile and looked up at the man. "You're a monster! You would kill your own king? For what? Power? Do you wish to kill Prince Aamir too?"

Darrian scoffed. Throwing his head back, he let out a sound Cammie couldn't place at first until after a few seconds. He was laughing.

"Seeing as you'll be *dead* in twenty-four hours, I am not sure why it matters."

Cammie felt the sickness return yet again. After everything they had survived, this couldn't be how they went out.

She scoured the room, hoping James would be returning soon.

Darrian followed her gaze. Judging by his raised brows, he was amused. "If you're looking for your friend, he is indisposed. It seems some family issue arose, and he cannot, at least tonight, be of help." He merely shrugged, as if he were talking about the weather and not their imminent death.

Sudden creaking resounded, and Darrian turned, looking for the direction of the sound. Thudding came soon after, and a *clunk* of armor hitting solid ground.

What happened to the guards?

Darrian was quick on his feet, ready to head to the door to see what had happened, but before he even could, a woman walked in, her hands clasped behind her back. "The guards at the entryway have seemed to have fallen ill," she said.

The voice sounded so familiar to Cammie. She had heard it before, earlier today.

Eirini. Is she behind the nefarious plot, the same as Darrian? Or is she here to rescue us?

"There is no need for you to be here, maid," Darrian spat, his voice wavering. He was nervous.

Eirini's eyebrows rose. "Oh?" A faint blush covered her cheeks, and she was breathing heavily. "But there is no need for you to be here either. The captain of the guard oversees the prisoners, not the royal advisor, but do not worry. I have made Prince Aamir aware."

Darrian's face lost all its color as footsteps resounded into the room.

Prince Aamir walked in with his head held high, his dark hair swept behind his ears, and his nostrils flared. He was furious. "Why do you have our *guests* locked up?"

Darrian said nothing, and Cammie swore she saw a smile on Eirini's face.

"Answer me," the prince pressed, practically seething.

"My mistake," Darrian murmured, bowing slightly to Prince Aamir. He flickered his hand upward, gesturing to a guard who had entered the room.

Something unspoken passed between them, and soon, several other guards joined them.

"You have an audience like you wanted," Darrian said to Eirini, "but now there is no need for you. *Go.*"

The prince's face altered, and his eyebrows furrowed. "Darrian, you might have some leeway, but you forget it is *I* who gives the order. Not you." The prince surveyed the prison, noting Cammie first, and then his eyes flickered over the others. "Do not speak to her in this way. Let our guests go."

Darrian changed position and, for once, let his gaze meet the prince. "I am afraid I cannot do that."

Barely suppressed rage twitched in Prince Aamir's cheek. "And why not?"

"Because your father's secrets must stay buried with him," Darrian replied, his voice holding no trace of humor. It was bitter, coarse, and resolved. His fingers fiddled against his side, and Cammie heard the *whoosh* of metal.

Before Darrian could even get a strike, Eirini rushed forward, gripping something in her hands. "For my family, I will defend their honor," she screamed, letting the object in her fingers fly.

A single knife impaled Darrian in his midsection, and Cammie held her breath. Eirini had thrown a knife into his stomach.

Cammie waited for the pool of red, but nothing came. Darrian's face was frozen in shock, and with one free hand, he withdrew the weapon from his stomach.

It came out clean.

In one fluid motion, Darrian pulled his arm back. There was the sickening sound of metal hitting flesh, and a garbled moan erupted from Eirini's lips as her body toppled to the ground. Blood protruded from the wound in her neck, and her eyes turned lifeless.

"For my king, I will protect his legacy," Darrian responded to Eirini's defunct form.

There was a scream. It took Cammie several seconds to realize it didn't belong to her but to the prince.

Prince Aamir huddled over Eirini's body, strangled gasps flowing from his lips. "What did you do?" he cried out.

Tears flowed down the prince's cheeks, and Darrian merely wiped blood droplets from his shirt that had splattered from the knife's impact.

"I made your father promise that his legacy would be protected, no matter the cost. That maid was a liability, whether you realize that or not." Darrian walked until his feet were next to Eirini, and he knelt next to her body, prying the weapon from her neck. More blood pooled out as he did so, but he remained unbothered, merely stepping away from the scene. "She was also below your station. Your father would have been so disappointed."

"Guards," Prince Aamir screamed, failing to suppress his sobs.

Cammie hadn't been sure the prince was capable of emotion. Even when talking of his father, his face had been stoic, but this...was an entirely different undoing.

Nobody obeyed his command. The guards merely watched as the prince unraveled in spite of himself.

Pursing her lips, Cammie made eye contact with Caelan. Caelan, though, focused on the scene at hand, and Cammie silently prayed that he was trying to figure out some way for them to escape.

"If you are awaiting help, there isn't any," Darrian stated, folding his arms behind his back. His fingers still had death grips on the weapons, and his tone was matter-of-fact. He wasn't lying. No one was coming to save them. "The guards have answered me for a long time. They are fully aware of what will transpire tonight, so there will be no deviating on their part."

We really are doomed.

"How? Why?" The prince cradled Eirini close to his chest, crimson staining his once-perfect shirt. His gaze was transfixed on the floor that was slick with blood.

"Your father had sins he died with. It was up to me to make sure those sins stayed hidden. He worked so hard to get to where he is, to make a difference not only for himself but for you."

The prince's entire back tensed, and slowly, he lowered Eirini to the ground. He rose to his feet, angling his body to Darrian. "The healer said that in all of his records, he had never seen markings on father's skin like those. The black veins, the hue of his skin, he said it was some resemblance of a curse." Prince Aamir ran his hand through his hair, leaving behind traces of red as it sent his locks spiraling in a million different directions. "But it isn't just something a curse could cause, could it? With the right dosage and the right knowledge in toxin appropriation, it could very well give off the same result, could it not?"

Darrian was silent, and his face gave nothing away.

"Darrian, answer me," Prince Aamir demanded.

Once again, Darrian said nothing.

"I command you to answer me!" The words ricocheted off the wall.

Cammie felt her back respond in goosebumps as the prince heaved heavy breaths.

Within seconds, Prince Aamir had Darrian's shirt clenched in his fists, his grip like stone as their faces were inches apart.

"I was loyal to my king," Darrian responded, his voice a hollow whisper. "Even if that loyalty meant driving him to his death, it was what I had to do, and if it were up to my hand again, I would have chosen the same."

Prince Aamir faltered, his grip loosening on Darrian as his face slacked. "You actually killed my father?" he murmured. "This has to be some kind of trick. Surely you are not being serious."

"With your father, there was never a joking matter." Darrian looked pointedly behind Aamir.

The guards who had been stoically watching finally moved. They grabbed Prince Aamir on either sides of his arms, pulling him back.

Fully restrained, Prince Aamir fought against the guards, but there was no use. "What do you plan to do with me?" he asked, his eyes daggers. "Kill me as well?"

"That all depends on your cooperation," Darrian said, turning away from the prince and back to the others.

"I'll have you killed for this," Prince Aamir seethed, spittle flying from his parted lips as his face contorted in rage.

Darrian merely shook his head, the action reminding Cammie of a parent looking on in disappointment. "Your anger will always get the best of you if you don't learn to control it."

Prince Aamir laughed darkly. "Oh, that is ironic, coming from you."

With a wave of his hand, Darrian gestured to the empty holding cell next to the girls. This one wasn't separated by a brick or stone surface like the far side of the girls' holding cell. It was clear enough to see the adjacent side through the tiny bars that lined the prison cell. The only vision blocker of it all was the wooden door.

"Throw him into the special cell there. I will do my best to delegate the nobles. They need to leave so we can finish what was started all those years ago. I'll return shortly." Darrian started toward the exit, Eirini's knife and his sword still in hand. He wasn't stupid enough to leave them.

The guards complied, pulling open the heavy wooden door and shoving the prince inside. He landed on his stomach, the wind knocked out of him. As he regained his breath, the guards were already slamming the door shut and heading toward the exit, most likely to stand watch again.

"Oh," Darrian instructed, letting his index finger linger in the air. "Before I forget, take care of the body."

Cammie watched with wide eyes as the men grabbed Eirini's lifeless body, dragging her along the floor like nothing more than a sack of goods.

Long after they were gone from the room, Eirini's expression burned behind her eyelids. If she thought hard enough, Cammie could still hear Prince Aamir's piercing scream.

CHAPTER FIFTY-THREE

CAMMIE

I⊤ HAD TO HAVE BEEN hours. It felt like hours.

Trapped inside a cell with little to do except for counting the stone bricks, Cammie felt numb. The prison was far too quiet. Aside from the constant breathing, noise was scarce.

Hannah's face remained impassive, her fists clenching and unclenching as they rested on her stomach. She was on edge, which was to be expected. In all the years that Cammie had known Hannah, sitting still had never been her thing.

Sabina stared outside of her cell, her gaze completely transfixed on Prince Aamir. She was kind, always putting duty ahead of herself, and she did the same in her thoughts of others. Whereas everyone else was focused on anything but what had transpired, Sabina was focused on the person who needed it the most.

Prince Aamir had not moved from his position on the ground. His hands were glued against the stone floor, his fingers clutching onto the surface for dear life. Wetness pooled from his eyes, dripping onto the slab.

Sabina reached her hand through the small section of space between the cells, tapping her fingernails against one of the bars, trying to get the prince's attention. "Are you okay?"

The prince didn't even stir. The only inclination that he had heard her was how his head was slightly tilted in her direction. Otherwise, he remained on the ground.

"Okay, this is so stupid," Hannah said, finally breaking the silence that had gathered in the room. "Someone tell Mr. Pompous to get off his butt and do something!"

"Hannah!" Caelan stated, his voice booming in the quiet. "We do not need to harass the prince on how he handles his grievances."

Hannah rolled her eyes, shifting position on the bench to where her chin was on her knees. "Maybe I would agree if this was some sort of procession, but let's be real. We are in a *freaking* dungeon. There's time to grieve. Later. After we find a way out of here."

Caelan already had another rebuttal at the ready. "You are so much more stubborn than I gave you credit for," he grumbled, running a hand over his face, "but would it kill you to have compassion? The woman he loves got slaughtered in front of him. That deserves a bit of compassion. Just because you are not crying does not mean he has to do the same."

"She is not the love of my life," Prince Aamir mumbled into the stone. "She never was."

He was trying to come across stronger than he looked, but Cammie did not miss how his voice cracked as he spoke. If not love, then something was definitely brewing under the surface.

"Then why is he laying on the floor? A normal person would just get up and keep going." Hannah was still spewing frustration, and compassion was nowhere near her tone.

"Just because you can handle seeing people bludgeoned and be fine doesn't mean the rest of us are like you," Sabina snapped, her eyes darkening. She turned her gaze back to Prince Aamir. "We need to be there for the prince. That is the only thing we can do now."

Hannah growled, gripping the remnants of her hair in her fists. "You guys have all the wrong priorities. We need to get out of here and get help. If only I had enough time to train and that damn Nyx hadn't forced me to shift before I could—" With a scream, she threw her shoe at the bars, watching as it slipped through the cracks. "Stupid Nyx," she huffed, her breathing picking up pace. "I can't do this." She got off of the bench, pacing the cell. "I'm getting claustrophobic. Small spaces suck."

"Shifting won't help us. Not here in this environment. Your wolf will lose control trapped here. It might do more damage than good," Tony told her, his voice strong and slow.

He had seen Hannah in many states like this, Cammie figured. No one was usually this calm when Hannah got riled up.

"It's why we didn't shift at Solenne's place," he continued. "It would be too easy to get distracted, and we wanted to be there for you then, to help you adjust. I am asking you to calm down, to let me help you now. Okay?"

Hannah was still pacing, but she slowly nodded, regaining her breathing. "Okay," she replied, sitting back down on the bench. She inhaled deeply, shutting her eyes. The prison was silent until Hannah spoke again. "Tell me what we need to do. We can't stay here, waiting for Darrian. He will slaughter us. The question isn't if but when. He won't let us go, and if me shifting isn't the answer, then what is?"

"We will defy the odds and await a rescue," Prince Aamir stated.

All heads swiveled in his direction.

"Darrian said there isn't a rescue coming," Cammie said.

"I have to have faith that not all of my men became traitors." Prince Aamir was sitting now, no longer held captive by the dark sea on the floor. "Your sister is right," he said, looking at Hannah. "We cannot just sit here and wallow in our sorrows. As harsh as she was, she spoke the truth."

A spark lit Sabina's eyes. "What about James?"

The anxiety that had been withheld came rushing back in Cammie's gut. "He hasn't come back," she said, the feeling of being abandoned hitting her all over again. "Maybe he isn't coming."

"You're forgetting the legion of soldiers under Darrian's thumb," Caelan replied. "He could be hiding for the right moment to strike. Don't discount him just yet."

Cammie wanted to believe James could be coming, but as she laid on her back, doing her best to come up with a plan, she couldn't stop her eyes from drifting into sleep, where she barely held onto hope.

Warm hands gripped her skin, and Cammie jerked awake. Her first instinct was to scream, but a hand covered her mouth, a hand that had reached through the bars.

"I need you to be quiet," the voice said.

She couldn't recognize the face as her eyes were still adjusting, but after several blinks, it became clearer. But that voice...

"If I'm going to get you out of here, then you can't make any sound." The man raised his eyebrows.

Cammie felt the flutter of relief in her heart. James had come for them, just like he said he would.

James removed his hand.

Cammie slowly got to her feet, noticing that the others were still softly sleeping. "How did you get in here? I thought—"

"That I had run away?" James interjected, and Cammie's face flushed with guilt. "I made you a promise to get you out of here, and I'm keeping to it."

He fumbled through his pocket until he found what he was looking for. Something silver glinted in the light of the dim room.

"How did you get the key?" Cammie asked him, her eyes wide and curious.

"I waited until Darrian fell asleep. I had some help, and let's just say...his wine was rather flavorful." With the mischievous grin James wore, it was hard to miss the implication.

"You drugged his wine," Cammie blurted. "How?"

"Like I said." He shrugged, looking more like the James she knew and recognized. "I had some help."

He worked fast, unlocking the door. It creaked open, the sound jarring in the quiet, and Cammie winced, hoping whoever was guarding the doors wouldn't come running in.

"Don't worry," James reassured her, as if her thoughts were fully on display. "We have the guards dealt with."

Cammie wanted to probe more at who he was speaking of, but there was no time. She had to wake her sisters quickly, before they were discovered.

Hannah was the easiest, as she was always guarded, but Sabina was harder. It took several minutes, and by that time, Caelan and the others were out of their cells.

"I was beginning to think you wouldn't show," Tony said, his face twisted in surprise.

"My duty is to my kingdom, and leaving you all here would relinquish that duty, and I cannot run from my calling again. I refuse to." James spoke proudly, and his throat cleared.

Prince Aamir was bloody, his hair in disarray, and his eyes were dark circles, but he wore a smile, one that Cammie wasn't sure could exist, but there it was. "You've done your kingdom a great service," he told James, resting his dried, crimson-stained hand on his shoulder. "I won't forget this."

"You can thank me later," James replied, focused on the task at hand. "Right now, we need to get you out of here."

He took the charge, and Caelan and the others followed behind him. Hannah's face wore the expression of war, and Sabina lingered with Cammie.

Prince Aamir was frozen in time, his eyes stuck on the puddle of blood that had stained the stone floor. Sabina gently grabbed his arm and tugged. Snapped out of his trance, Prince Aamir muttered something under his breath and took off after the others.

Cammie followed, Sabina not too far behind her. They ran through the exit, and Cammie looked down, doing her best not to trip over the guards who were lying lopsided on either side of the door. Whatever James had done, it had taken strength. More strength than he was capable of, she was sure.

They rounded the corner, and Cammie skidded to a halt. Everyone had stopped running. Why weren't they moving? They were almost frozen to the spot, and with the size of everyone, Cammie couldn't see what the commotion was.

But she heard it all the same.

"I refuse to go with him," Caelan protested. "You cannot be seriously asking me to trust him with my life."

"We had limited options," James stressed, his voice tense. "I didn't know who was against Darrian or who was with him, and I figured he would be our best shot. You have to understand. Darrian put on a show for the nobles, and next thing I knew, the guards were stationed at every door, looking for me. I didn't know what they were trying to do until I heard one of the guards saying the prince had been captured and that I couldn't be aware. Rigel was our best option at getting out of here."

"Best option or not, he can't be trusted. How do I know he isn't here to lead us to more deaths than he did last time?"

"Because last time was a contingency plan," Rigel said. "I didn't know they would take you captive for long. If I would have known that Darrian planned to get rid of you all, I never would have gone through with it."

"You're telling me you deliberately planned to put my daughters in danger? You knew the risk, and you still jumped at the chance?" Caelan was enraged, his skin turning a slight shade darker.

Rigel bristled at the comment but regained his composure. "We don't have time to argue about it now. I need you all to trust me."

Cammie felt every muscle in her body freeze, and she saw a flash of red. She stepped out against the crowd, and Rigel's eyes locked on her.

"Promise it," she said. She felt her throat tighten, but she ignored the burning feeling and pushed through it. "Promise me you won't lie to us again or keep us out of the loop."

"I can't fully promise what you're asking," Rigel said. "If telling a lie preserves the legacy of the true heir, then I will do it in a heartbeat, without question, but I can promise you that now I am going to lead you to your safety—whatever it will take." His words rang loud and clear.

Prince Aamir gave him a look, and it was easy to tell he was only slightly offended by how a shadow cast over his eyes. It passed quickly, and Prince Aamir cleared his throat. "Then how do you suggest we go from here? There could be very many guards who are loyal to Darrian. Staying here won't be safe. My status in this castle doesn't mean a thing now. They're willing to slaughter me for Darrian's gain. I can't offer any sort of protection."

"You can't offer protection, but you know the ins and outs of this castle better than anyone else here. You can find us a way out to stay undetected. I heard rumors in the castle that Darrian was trying to finish this before the Council arrived. There's something bigger going on. I can just feel it. So, lead the way, prince." Unlike when Prince Aamir spoke the title to Caelan, this time there was no hint of snark. Rigel was matter-of-fact and practically bouncing on his feet to find a way out of here.

Prince Aamir went first, and James was second. The group resumed their normal running positions, following the prince down the winding hallways. It was eerily quiet, like too soon, all hell would break loose.

Cammie couldn't ignore the feeling in her gut as they continued running, her dress almost torn to shreds. Her feet were having trouble keeping up with the pace, and briefly, she wondered if taking off her shoes would have been easier or better, but there was no time for that now. She had to let the burning pressure subside.

When they reached another hallway after taking several turns, Hannah stopped to take a breath. Her entire body was tense, and she leaned her head slightly, as if she was taking everything in even though the hallway was completely empty.

"What's wrong?" Cammie asked her.

Hannah held up a finger, and Cammie instantly quieted, her brows pinched in confusion.

"Do you hear that?" Hannah asked.

Cammie tilted her head, craning for a sound. Nothing resounded, and she looked on at Hannah in confusion.

"I hear it," Marcus uttered.

Tony nodded, and Will's eyebrows furrowed. Trevor inclined his head in acknowledgement, and Cammie felt a ball of frustration arise. What could they possibly be hearing?

"It's the Lunar gift of hearing," Caelan explained. "They can sense things we cannot before it even happens. We should heed their words. Be ready."

Cammie braced herself for something to pop out around the corner, but nothing showed. Right when she was beginning to think Hannah was being crazy, a noise came from the empty hallway a few paces away.

It was laughter from the palace guards, and there was nowhere to hide as they were moving too quickly.

"What do we do?" Cammie whispered. She shot a worried glance to Caelan.

"We fight," Caelan said.

"But with what weapons?"

James ran to the edge of the hallway, rummaging through something that Cammie couldn't see. Rigel must have stashed them before they were rescued somehow.

When he returned, with weapons in hand, Cammie's face paled. "I've never held a weapon before. What am I supposed to do with it?"

Sabina took a longsword from James, her face set. "I have," she said. "You just have to watch your opponent and strike. It's relatively simple."

Cammie felt like Sabina was speaking another language. Her jaw slacked open, and she fumbled for words. She watched as the others mindlessly grabbed weapons as if it were the most natural thing in the world. "There's got to be more to it than that."

"There is," James told her, handing her the last dagger, "but all that *you* have to do is defend as best as possible. We will do the rest."

The guards rounded the corner then, and all traces of laughter disappeared. When they caught sight of the group, their expressions shifted, and their hands flew to the hilts of their swords, unsheathing them.

"Be ready," Caelan yelled as the guards charged.

"Ready for what?" Cammie screamed back, her face frozen in horror.

Within seconds, the guards were within reach of the group, swinging their weapons without caution. Cammie let out a yelp and dropped to the floor as a guard jumped over her.

He aimed right at Caelan, bellowing out a yell, swinging his sword to the left. Caelan parried quickly, blocking the metal with his own.

The hard *clang* resounded in Cammie's ears, and she did her best to slow her rapidly flowing heartbeat. She closed her eyes against it, feeling the rush of blood to her ears, and her face burned with heat.

An annoyed grunt came from the right, and Cammie peeked to see Hannah pinning another guard to the ground with only her foot.

"You're weak and you disgust me," Hannah spat, plunging her sword in the man's chest.

Cammie couldn't believe Hannah's ruthlessness. As soon as the guard let out his last gurgle, Hannah ripped her sword out of his chest and moved on.

Sabina moved efficiently as more guards exited from that same hallway. She blocked their attempts, and not once did she receive any blows, but, boy, did she deliver them. The soldiers she struck all had some sort of deep-entry wound, one that a subtle healing herb wouldn't fix. Caelan was her spotter, their backs touching as they warded off more and more attempts to thwart them.

Prince Aamir held his own, James and the others following close behind. It was getting easier to tell who the winning side would be. They were actually surviving this.

Maybe standing up wouldn't be a bad idea after all.

Right when Cammie made a move to sit upright, she made eye contact with a soldier. *Oh, no.*

He bellowed out a war cry, coming straight for her. Bold fear gripped her throat, and she used her arms to block her face, slashing about wildly.

A gurgling, strained noise resounded above her, and Cammie dared to open her eyes. Her attacker hovered above her, dead. His lifeless eyes were haunting, and Cammie scanned his body, looking for the source of death. The small dagger she was still gripping had impaled his neck. She had saved herself.

With chaotic, shaky breaths, she pushed the form away, her head spinning.

A hand reached down for her, and she took it gratefully. Blood stained her skin, and she wasn't sure she could ever get it out.

James helped her to her feet, and without even thinking, she clutched him tightly. She had killed someone. Accidentally. But she still killed him.

Cammie was sure the image would stay ingrained in her mind of the dead guard. She was still seeing his face behind her closed eyes, and a strange feeling tingled up her spine.

"I am not as stupid as you make me out to be." The voice boomed in the open hallway, where bodies lay scattered, and blood was seeping into the carpet.

The tingling sensation returned, and Cammie placed it quickly—absolute fear.

"Did you really think that a bit of henbane flower would kill me? I'm not so easily swayed." Darrian's words were slurred, and his movements slow, but Cammie figured the effects wouldn't last forever. "I've been building up a slow tolerance to it for years. Your dosage just put me in a deep sleep."

He took a step closer, his grip like stone on another sword, and James shifted his body to where he was in front of Cammie, shielding her.

"You won't hurt us," James growled.

"You really mean her, don't you?" Darrian taunted, his eyes mischievous. "There is no need to lie, James. You can be honest with me. You value the girl's life more than you do your own." His eyes flickered to Prince Aamir as his lips settled into a line. "You are not the only one who places love above duty."

Prince Aamir's hands clenched around his weapon, and he raised it above his head, his arms shaking.

"You will not do it," Darrian stated, his words becoming clearer. "You do not have the willpower to take a life, not one so close to you. Now, your father, he had true strength. He was cunning and brave and true to his word. Even if it meant lives were lost, your father never shirked his duty. He was brave until the end."

"You caused his end!" Prince Aamir shouted, his grip on the sword faltering.

"For a greater cause," Darrian said curtly. "Your father had secrets that needed to die, and I honored my duty by letting them follow with him. I protected his legacy as king. Until you have secrets that must be buried, you will never understand."

"There is nothing," Prince Aamir cried out, "that you could tell me that will garner sympathy or understanding for what you have done. As of now, you are dead to me."

Darrian's lip turned upward. "I will relish in saying the feeling is the same."

With lightning reflexes, he let go of his throwing blade, his aim clear on Prince Aamir's heart. Time seemed to freeze as the weapon sailed in the air. Cammie braced for the impact, forcing herself to still her scream. Prince Aamir watched incredulously as the weapon dove straight for his chest.

And then the weapon stopped moving. Sabina's eyebrows were knit in concentration, her face tight. The throwing blade was mere centimeters from stabbing the prince's heart, fully under the control of her sister.

A flash of rage flickered over Darrian's face. "She can move weapons with her mind," he said. "How is that possible?"

Sabina's brows furrowed again, and the weapon changed direction, no longer aiming at Prince Aamir but directly at Darrian.

"You dare threaten me?" Darrian adjusted his position, his hands raised in defiance, but in his stare was another emotion. It was pure-blooded fear.

"You threatened us first," Sabina snapped, her face beginning to relax. The weapon fired away, but Darrian was quicker.

He ducked at just the right moment, and there was a loud *clang* as the weapon collided with the wall. Slowly, he rose upward, a shocked grin plastered on his face. "You actually tried to kill me. And here I didn't think you have the guts."

"You would be wise not to underestimate the descendants of the true royal line," Sabina replied proudly, determination etching itself around her eyes.

"Not giving them enough credit will be something I always regret." Darrian was still walking on shaky feet, but his eyes were manic as he spoke, spittle flying from his lips. "I should have done my duty better that night, but I let my king down."

"Stop talking nonsense," Prince Aamir said, his voice heavy with red-hot rage. "We've had enough of your lies."

Darrian's head swiveled in his direction. "You have been nothing but a thorn in my side since you were old enough to take on duties. You are so preoccupied with what you think is best that you do not even realize the sacrifices it took to get here. Those same sacrifices put you within reach of the Crown!"

"My father earned this Crown honorably," Prince Aamir seethed. "You talk of protecting his legacy, and here you are, tarnishing it in the same breath."

"Is that what you think happened? You believed the story you were told without question? Your father was a noble, but his parents would never allow him to have the legacy he needed to break free from their pathetic mold. I did what I had to. I did what no one else would do. I loved your father like a brother, and family does what it needs to do so it can survive." Darrian's eyes were wild, and his words unhinged the longer he spoke.

Prince Aamir didn't move. He remained expressionless as a wave of unease passed through the air.

"I was seeking a way out for both of us, and when the opportunity presented itself, I grabbed it. I would have been a fool not to take it. I turned my back on my country, but it was worth it."

"What did you do?" the prince asked, his voice laced with venom. When Darrian refused to respond, the prince let out a growl. "Speak, Darrian! What did you do? I will not ask you again!"

"I led the charge against the assassination of the royal family. I was tasked with finding the entrances and exits, knowing the routes of the servants and the royal family intimately. When a position arose at the castle, I was the first to take it. As the queen's right-hand personal guard, I knew her comings and goings almost instantly. I communicated this, and when there was an opening the night of the prince's christening, I knew there was no turning back. Your father tended to the wounded, and I vouched for him at the Council's apprehensiveness. After some encouragement, there was no question. He would be their next king."

For a moment, everything was completely silent, and then Caelan let out a battle cry, rushing toward Darrian. Pain rested in his face, and his hands wielded the sword without question or mercy, focused on his target.

"I think I will quite enjoy this. I should have killed you when you were a baby. Instead, I let another accomplice handle the job that should've been mine." Darrian's hand fumbled in his pocket.

Cammie saw a flash of metal. It was another knife.

Just before Caelan contacted Darrian, forceful hands pushed him out of the way. Caelan fell a few feet away, unharmed.

But another lay on the ground in his place, clutching their stomach as crimson began to fill against open palms.

"No!" Cammie screamed, rushing forward.

Time stilled. Her brain was finally catching up, but it was too late to stop what had occurred. The blood was still seeping, and Cammie tripped over her own two feet, kneeling at his side. She applied pressure to the wound, attempting to stop the bleeding. When that didn't work, her hands fumbled with the hilt of the sword still embedded in his abdomen. She had to get the weapon out of him.

"Don't," James garbled, bits of crimson spilling from his lips. "The bleeding will worsen if you remove it." His breathing was shallow, and he took several breaths in, raggedy ones following from his parted lips. Even his teeth were stained red.

Cammie felt a balloon grow in her chest. "You're already bleeding," she cried out, her mind racing. What should she do? How could she save him? "Caelan, do something," she pleaded, tears stinging her eyes.

Caelan rose to his feet, and his gaze was deadly as he found Darrian.

Darrian's eyes glimmered with fear, and his eyes darted left and right before he turned on his heels completely, running away. *Coward.*

Caelan started running.

Prince Aamir hurried after him. "I'm coming with you."

Caelan nodded. "It's as much your vengeance as it is mine. Let's go." He turned back to Cammie, the gentleness in his gaze. "We will be back quickly. Keep applying pressure to the wound, and do not remove the weapon by yourself. We don't want to cause any more damage than has been done already."

Their footsteps pounded on the carpet as they headed in the direction Darrian had retreated to, and in the silence, Cammie's worry only grew.

Sabina's hand rested on her shoulder, the touch tender. "Are you okay? What can I do?"

Cammie swallowed back bile, doing her best to control her breathing. "Go find help," she muttered.

"What? I couldn't hear you—"

"Go find help, Sabina!" Cammie shouted, her breathing ragged as the rage in her stomach remained unchecked. "Stop asking questions about how I'm doing and go find help. *Now!*"

Sabina stepped away as if Cammie struck her. Her eyes glistened as she turned on her heels wordlessly. She ran down the hall in the other direction, and Cammie felt a pang of guilt.

That left Hannah and the others, who watched silently as Cammie hovered over James with heaving sobs. Hannah didn't rush forward, offering to console her or tell her everything would be okay. Instead, she directed her on where to place her hands, certain areas not to touch, and she and the boys kept eyes open for Caelan and the prince's arrival. Hannah didn't hover, but she didn't completely disappear either.

"Please...don't cry..." James said, his breaths becoming slower.

There was still no sign of Caelan or Prince Aamir, and Sabina still had not come back with help.

Summon the Light. Will the Light. Summon the Light. Will the Light. Heal James.

Nothing happened.

Cammie's chest tightened as the tears still flowed down her cheeks, but she refused to wipe them. She had to keep her hands steady around the wound, careful not to accidentally swipe the dagger with her fingers. "Stop talking. You need to conserve your energy."

Weakly, James lifted his hand until it rested on Cammie's wrist. "And...I...need...you...to...be okay."

As he breathed, more crimson spilled, and Cammie felt another surge of panic. *Where is everyone? Where is Sabina?*

"You need to stop worrying. I...will...be fine."

Cammie took in his physical state and how his eyes were struggling to stay open, and somehow, she didn't believe him. She couldn't. Not when he was like this.

"Stay with me, James," she pleaded, her eyes never leaving his face.

He blinked at her words, his eyes unfocused. "I am...staying...right...here...with...you. I am never... leaving you.... again." He swallowed.

His teeth were still tinted, if not even worse, by this point. He moved his hand, trailing his fingers down her face, taking ahold of strands of her hair. His fingertips grazed the curls, entangling around his hand.

"I love you, Cammie," he whispered, his chest slowing. Breathing was barely there.

Cammie's heart shattered. "No," she whispered, as James closed his eyes. "No. No. No, no, no, no, no. Stay with me! James, please stay!" Her voice cracked.

Cammie felt the rage resurface. She wanted nothing more than to see Darrian's head on a silver platter. Desperate, Cammie pressed her hands tighter against James, thinking back to Solenne's instruction yet again.

Summon the Light. Will the Light. Summon the Light. Will the Light. Heal James.

Still, nothing erupted from her palms. She tried again. And again. And again.

Nothing.

Frustrated, Cammie let out a cry. She felt it in the recesses of her soul, as if a piece of her heart had been taken and stepped on, and there was no way of fixing or retrieving it. The cry turned into a scream so loud that her ears rang, but it didn't matter. She couldn't heal him. She couldn't stop the bleeding. If she couldn't use her gift to save the man she loved, then what was the point?

Something bright flickered underneath her palms. It was lilac gold, shimmering.

"You did it, Cammie," Hannah breathed in shock. "You're healing him."

Sure enough, the glowing spread.

Cammie let out a sigh of relief. Her gift was working. She was saving James. "I think I'm actually—"

A sudden blast threw Cammie backward, and her stomach leapt to her throat as she landed on her tailbone, her head smashing against the stone floor. When she lifted herself up on her elbows, Cammie held back a gasp.

James was completely covered by a lilac force field, untouchable. Droplets of gold seeped into the wound, and Cammie looked on in awe as the weapon dissolved. The force field was overpowering the wound.

After the blood was completely gone, Cammie let out a relieved cry. James lay on his back as if he were only sleeping. The wound and damage were completely gone.

Hannah's face didn't hold the same excitement as Cammie's and she wanted to question why, but Hannah's stance was too tight.

As Cammie followed her gaze, she understood why. Several men in tyrian-colored robes looked on at the spectacle, their faces covered by hoods.

Footsteps resounded from the corner. Sabina returned, heaving her breath. "I found out from one maid that they have apprehended Darrian. Help should come soon—" She paused, registering James completely healed on the ground. "You healed him." She turned to Cammie, shock in her features. "How did it work this time?"

"We'd like to know that as well," one man said, stepping forward from the group of men that had gathered.

CHAPTER FIFTY-FOUR

SABINA

SEVERAL MEN IN PURPLE CLOAKS rushed forward, hoisting Cammie up by her elbows. They dragged her forward, and she kicked her feet in defiance.

"Who are you? Where are you taking me?" Cammie proclaimed, her face wild with fear. She looked back at Sabina.

For a moment, Sabina felt her heart clench.

The men, either ignoring or not hearing Cammie, refused to respond.

Sabina had no idea that they hadn't come to help. They had been very forthcoming, wanting to know what was going on, but she should have known by now that appearances can be deceiving.

Two others came, grabbing Sabina in the same way. She held her breath, knowing it would be better to be compliant than put up a fight.

Which was exactly what Hannah was doing.

After Hannah threw several punches and dodged hands, a few of the other men in cloaks restrained her.

Following Sabina's lead, Marcus, Trevor, and Tony went along peacefully. Will walked alongside the men, and none dared touched him.

Sabina looked back at James, who was still lying on the floor with no change except for the fact that he was now fully healed. A few of the men stayed behind, forming a circle around James. As they rounded a corner, Sabina caught a glance of them lifting James up and taking him in the opposite direction.

A sense of doom thundered in Sabina's heart the farther away they got from the hallway. Darrian was nowhere to be seen, but Sabina didn't know these men. Nor could she tell whom their allegiance was pledged to. Their grip on her arms was tight, but it was nothing similar to the men who had been under Darrian's instruction. These men had a purpose. Sabina just couldn't quite fathom what it was yet.

As they passed through another corridor, a shroud of darkness appeared over her eyes, and she couldn't see anything other than hazy figures. A light was barely lit in the room ahead, and if Sabina peered closer, she could make out an outline similar to Caelan's and someone who looked like Prince Aamir.

They entered the room after what felt like eons, and they brought Cammie to her knees first. Her legs hit the ground with more force than necessary, and she breathed out in pain. Hannah was next and then her friends and finally Sabina. Her knees screamed in agony as they contacted the stone floor, and she mentally cursed at how feeble her legs were.

One look around the room told her that this was a different situation. Even Prince Aamir was on his knees, a sign of respect as his head bowed in reverence. His face paled even more than usual, and Sabina noticed how he shriveled in the presence of these men.

The one who had spoken to Cammie stopped in front of the group, the hood still covering his face entirely. His head turned until his gaze landed on Prince Aamir. It was hard to tell, though, exactly where the man with the hood was looking.

"Are we alone?" the man asked. His voice was hard to place, and Sabina's heartbeat bobbed in her throat.

"Yes," Prince Aamir whispered, still averting his eyes.

The man with the hooded cloak removed his covering, and his face glinted underneath the light of the lantern. He had to have been ancient, but Sabina knew enough to know how Amarian appearances could fool you. His features were flawless except for the scar underneath his left eye and his hardened gaze. He was scrutinizing them, and the weight of his gaze made Sabina have the urge to squirm, but she ignored it, staying put despite the goosebumps dancing on her skin.

"We were hoping to arrive on better terms than what we found," the man said. "Instead, after days of traveling, imagine our surprise to find several of your guards slaughtered and you on a killing spree of one of your best advisors." The tone was curt, but the arch of the man's eyebrow gave an entirely different view.

"I understand, Cazden," Prince Aamir stated, his cheeks turning a slight shade of pink.

Cazden paced back and forth, his hands laced together behind his back. "But you did not act alone." He turned his head, halting. His eyes scanned until he landed on Caelan. "You, rise on your feet."

Caelan nodded, his eyes darting to Prince Aamir before complying with Cazden's request.

"Is he friend or foe?" Cazden asked Prince Aamir, who had still not moved from his place on the floor. "I imagine you would have to tolerate so much if he is a foe, to team up and kill one of your closest confidantes."

"There is more to the story that you do not understand, Cazden," Prince Aamir replied, finally lifting his eyes to the man, "but I would consider Caelan to be amicable, so friend."

"Seeing as time is ripe, I am eager to hear the tale. Go on," Cazden prompted.

"Darrian is no longer my advisor. To be entirely honest, he is also no longer with us. He took his last breath when you found us and gave us a rather cryptic message that I am unsure I could decipher." Prince Aamir swallowed. "He mentioned, 'The phoenix will rise from the ashes, only to be swallowed by the sky's emerald song. In life, I have pursued the Emerald Calling, and in death, it will sustain me fully.' That alone was enough to make me question his involvement in some sort of rebellious cause."

Cazden's face revealed nothing. "Your advisor was involved in a nefarious plot. That was one reason we came here, and it wasn't just for proof of your father's celebration of life ceremony. There have been rumors of others involved, and I just needed confirmation with my own eyes, which you gladly gave to me, so thank you for that. However, that still does not explain why you felt the need to slaughter him."

"You say Darrian was involved in a nefarious plot? I say boldly that he was treasonous, and his crimes had to be dealt with. Justice wasn't something to wait for, and I feared if we did not act quickly, then he would run and hide for his life. No punishment would have been delivered."

"And what punishment was fit for death? You couldn't possibly perceive enough about the rebel cause with your limited knowledge." Cazden peered at Prince Aamir, shifting his arms.

"Darrian was involved in the assassination of the king and queen, and he also killed my father in his sleep. I'm certain he was behind the deaths of the other nobles as well. He tried to pin it on James, the head guard, but he was unsuccessful as the truth came to light. James had revelations of his own, which is how Caelan came to be here."

"And James is the man that was sleeping in the halls?"

"Sleeping?" Prince Aamir questioned. "No, James was on the brink of death."

"No," Cazden said, voice firm. "When we arrived, someone fully healed him. *A human.*" His tone turned murderous as his gaze swiveled to Cammie, who paled at his words. "Nothing like that is possible unless they are involved in the things of darkness. I've seen enough sorcery in my time to know the penalties of such things."

"I can assure you they are not involved. I questioned them fully, and that is not the reason."

"Then what is the reason?" Cazden demanded. "We have worked hard to make sure we, as the Council, stay hidden to oversee what is necessary to keep the royal family safe. After the killings of the original line, we did our best to be sure it wouldn't happen again. By closing off the portal to our world and theirs, we ensured it, and you are to let them wander here without a course of action to Erase or remove them?"

"They have a right to be here. Their abilities, I have seen nothing like it. In the history of Natrellum, no one has wielded such gifting. The prophecy foretold it. Could it be possible this applies to them?" Prince Aamir asked, his voice rising. "Without proper research, you cannot just dismiss it so easily."

"Do not forget your place!" Cazden bellowed. "You speak to me of a prophecy that our entire race depends on, but you cannot apply the words to anyone you deem suitable. Only a true test can tell who the words belong to."

"Then test them," Caelan uttered. "I believe in my daughters."

"Oh, really?" Cazden replied. "Bring them forward. I want them at my feet where I can see them."

The other men in cloaks shoved Sabina forward, and Cammie and Hannah weren't far behind. Pushed onto their knees in another compromising position, Sabina seethed. *Do these men have no manners?*

"The anger is ripe on this one," one man said as Hannah fell to the ground. Hannah merely spat at him, and the man wiped his face with disgust.

"Surely these undignified humans cannot be whom we mean to save the entire Amarian race. How can they be? They don't even have Amarian line in their blood, and only that of the true line *can* save us. Judging by that fact alone, the entire prophecy might as well be a farce. No one from the line survived the attack."

"I did," Caelan stated boldly.

Cazden whipped his head in Caelan's direction, his face tense. "What did you say?" he whispered.

"I survived," Caelan repeated. "My mother's lady-in-waiting saved me. She took me to the Earth realm and raised me as her own for the day I would be strong enough to come back on my own. She believed in the prophecy as strongly as I did. As she lay dying, I promised to do my duty, and I am here to fulfill that."

"You expect me to believe your mother was our beloved queen? And that you have human daughters when you, yourself, are Amarian? If your goal is to make a mockery of our kind, you are succeeding." Cazden shook his head, running a hand over his face.

"Wait," a voice called from the corridor.

Heavy boots stepped along the stone, and Sabina felt a surge of hope. *Rigel.*

"Hear them out," he pleaded. "I promise they will not mislead you. Caelan speaks the truth." Rigel walked to where Cazden was standing and took a knee.

"You look familiar," Cazden murmured.

"Yes," Rigel swallowed. "I am a Hunter, loyal to the Crown. What reason would I have to lie to you? I gain nothing by lying to your face. Just listen to what he has to say. Surely you have some sort of record to follow, being intricately aware the prophecy, to know what to look for?"

Another man stepped forward from waiting in the shadows and removed his hood. Unlike Cazden, his features showed a progression of age, with his graying beard and rugged face. "My name is Favian. That would be my job. If the girls would be so inclined as to show me their shoulders, I can find this for myself. Same for the man. Caelan, step forward."

On shaky legs, Caelan stepped away from Prince Aamir's side, and made his way next to Cammie on the far end. Slowly, he removed his shirt, allowing the man to see his bare back. Caelan's marking shone clearly, and Favian inhaled. He ran his bare hand above the skin, not touching it, and said something under his breath in the native tongue that Sabina couldn't decipher.

"It is real," Favian whispered, his voice on the verge of breaking into sobs. "We have waited years, and it is here."

"The prophecy mentions a triad," Cazden snapped. "Do not be delusional until we can make known of the others. Hope is pointless unless we have the full pursuit of truth."

Favian nodded, walking to Cammie next. Gently, she allowed him to remove her left sleeve, and Favian whispered the same words as earlier. Nothing. Favian corrected her lowered sleeve and moved to her right shoulder. Cammie cried out, clutching her back.

Favian moved to Hannah, who was less pleased but still complied. Hannah made no move as Favian repeated the process, her face impassive.

Finally, Favian reached Sabina, and she did her best to hold back the fear bubbling in her throat.

"What are you whispering?" she asked him, curious.

Taken aback, he didn't respond at first, his face contorted in shock. *He has not spoken to a human before; it seems.*

"I am merely asking for any Amarian qualities that may be hidden to come to light."

"How will you know if it worked?" Sabina asked.

"Under the right light, nothing can stay buried," Favian replied, giving a small smile.

With hesitancy, Sabina allowed Favian room to do what he was set out to, and she closed her eyes in anticipation. Favian whispered the same words again, and Sabina's heart pounded. At first, there was nothing. She could barely feel the ghost of his hand almost brushing her right shoulder, and then there was burning. It felt like her skin was on fire. She let out a cry, surprised to find tears stinging in her eyes.

"Why does it burn?" she asked, blinking away the wetness.

"Because it is hidden no longer." Favian's voice sung with pride.

Sabina didn't need to turn around to tell he was also tearing up. The area where he had run his hand over was beginning to have a cooling effect. The burning was wearing off.

"But why didn't anything show up when I waved my hand over it?" Prince Aamir asked.

"This kind of concealment could only be done by someone powerful enough with an Amarian duty. Once a promise is spoken this deeply—in this case, to protect—the purest of motives only can reveal it." Favian turned to Caelan, a question shimmering in his eyes. "Is there anyone you know who could possess something like this?"

"Yes," Caelan said, breathless. "My mother, Solenne, would have. She made a promise to my wife, who was human, about protecting our daughters. It would not fully reveal them until they were ready."

Cazden nodded. "You possess the markings of the chosen line. Your daughters are obviously gifted and half-Amarian, but how do we know the prophecy applies to them for certain?" he asked Favian.

Favian could hardly contain his excitement. "Do you not remember the words our originator spoke on her deathbed? Or the dreams several of our healers have had? It all connects, brother. Our saviors are *here*."

Cazden remained unconvinced.

Favian let out a sigh. "If I must reiterate the words aloud, then let me do so. 'Redemption, at its finest, will come when the skies are cloaked with envy and bleeding with despair. Vengeance will be the culprit that sets the land ablaze. One who has not will become prey to the intrigue of the Darkness, and nothing will stop it. The hearts of those affected by depravity will surely suffer, but only a heart of altruistic value will win the war. The Triad is the answer for it will be three in one who hold the key and open the door, making way for the Phoenix to come alive. In the framework of its design, death to the head of the snake will transpire, but in this, hope will be revived.' What do you make of our ancestor's words, Cazden? Do you make them out to be lies?"

Cazden pinched the bride of his nose, his shoulder-length hair swaying. "I am saying we need to intervene and discuss when they are not present. There are many factors to consider, and we must be open to all of them." He inhaled, shutting his eyes. "Do the girls have any known relatives in the Earth realm?" He directed this question to no one in particular.

"Their adoptive parents," Caelan said. "My mother separated them at birth to keep them safe. They're spread out everywhere."

Cazden's eyes shot open. "We will take care of the matter. Until we finalize our decision, no one can remember you. Your existence is now a threat to Natrellum itself, and we cannot risk any humans finding our location." Cazden turned his gaze on Rigel. "Hunters have the adept ability for Erasing. Is that correct?"

Rigel nodded. "Yes. We do."

"Very well. For now, your loyalty is to me. You shall find their parents, along with anyone else who might have known of them, and wipe their memories entirely."

"They cannot even say goodbye?" Rigel asked.

Sabina felt a rush of gratitude at the quick thinking of her earlier phone call. *At least I called mother while I had the chance.*

Cazden's face darkened. "That isn't your concern. You will do as I ask unless you want to face consequences. Is that understood?"

Rigel lost all of his coloring. "I understand."

"Perfect. Then you will leave immediately. Do not return until the job is done."

Without another word, Rigel stood and exited the room. A draft entered as he left.

Sabina held her breath to keep from crying. *Everything is surely changing.*

"Where do you want us to go?" Caelan asked. "It sounds like you do not want us here."

"Several of my men will escort you out of the castle. From there, we will take you to the edge of town, where the portal is. No one is awake at this hour. From there, you will stay hidden in the Earth realm until we summon you. There is no need to worry about the Erasing for those you'll meet. I'd rather you cause chaos on your homeland than ours until we come up with a story to tell." Cazden's face was tight, and his lips pursed.

"How will we know we've been summoned?" Hannah asked.

Cazden gave the briefest of smiles. "Believe me. You will know." He snapped his fingers, and several of his men returned to their position. "Take them. We have a mess to clean up."

"Wait," Cammie shrieked as they brought her to her feet. "What about James? Is he okay?"

"James is no longer a concern. He is in the hands of our healers, and if you want to have the best shot at receiving destiny, you will do wise to adhere to my words. Listen to what my men ask of you, and all will be fine."

Another grabbed Sabina, and she felt herself being pulled to the exit. Giving one look back, she glimpsed Favian's anxious eyes before the doors slammed shut.

They were escorted throughout the market once again, except this time, all was quiet. The marketplace booths were covered with ripped tarps, and all other Amarians were nowhere to be found, save for the hooded men leading them back home.

The word itself felt foreign, and Sabina wasn't sure whether or not it would ever feel normal again.

"Do not come back until we send for you," one man said, his face invisible through the shrouding of the hood. "And do not forget that we are always watching."

With a gentle nudge, he pushed Sabina through the portal before she had time to react, and Natrellum faded from view behind her.

CHAPTER FIFTY-FIVE

CAMMIE

FOUR WEEKS WAS AN ETERNITY.

Cammie sat on the porch of the elegant cottage as the breeze tickled her skin. With her eyes closed, it was easy to pretend she was back in the ballroom and the breeze was James' breath.

Even the act of thinking his name had pain blossoming in her chest so deep that she was sure it would stain.

If it weren't for the tainted memory of how she had left him on the floor, it would have been easy to think that Natrellum had all been a lie.

Cammie and the others had settled into a routine so blissful that disturbances were nowhere to be found. It was jarring, how quickly they had gone from slaying enemies to cottage living, but what else was there to do?

Grunting resounded from behind her, and Cammie opened her eyes, pushing herself off of the steps.

They had worked tirelessly to repaint the cottage, and all remnants of the earlier bloodshed were gone. In its place was a beautiful blue hue on the outside, and a brand-new window that brought in even more light when the sun was at its peak.

Cammie followed the sounds of pain until it led her to the side of the house.

Hannah was on her knees, wiping away at dried blood and spit that had stained her cheeks. "Again," she growled, coming to a stand. Her tank top drenched with sweat, and even her shorts held a similar sheen.

Tony was her sparring partner, a satisfied grin on his lips. "Didn't think I'd hit you that hard. Don't tell me you've gone soft?"

"The only thing that's gone soft is your belief that you can crush me," Hannah retorted, shifting her neck side-to-side. "Are we going to keep gossiping like Sabina and Cammie, or will you actually throw another punch?"

In the weeks they had been back at the cottage, every afternoon when it hadn't been raining had gone quite like this one. Hannah spent her time trash-talking Tony while he got in as many punches as he can.

The other boys were nowhere in sight, Cammie mused, probably because they were busy scavenging the woods for berries to throw at the loser. She didn't really understand the hype, but it kept them out of trouble, so she wasn't really complaining.

As Cammie left Hannah to defend herself, she began scouring for Caelan. As of late, his position had been by Solenne's unmarked grave, where he would spend his time talking to her about anything and everything.

Cammie found him in that very spot, on his knees.

He held a bunch of newly picked flowers, adorning Solenne's grave with as many as he could fit onto the little section of grass.

"I wish that you were here to talk me through this," he whispered. "There's still so much I need to learn. I feel like I have barely survived the aftermath. There's no word on whether we'll return home or what will become of the girls. Rigel hasn't come to retrieve us, and I worry it may be too late. Maybe returning isn't an option for us. How can I bear it, if the thing I have been made for will never be in my reach? How do I lead them in the way they desperately need? You said as their father all I had to do was love them, but, Mother, it is way more than that. I feel…" Caelan took a breath. "Sometimes, I feel I am too underqualified for what I need to do. I just wish that I had your strength." He sat there in silence for a moment until he rose to his feet. His cheeks were wet with tears, and he seemed completely unaware that he wasn't alone.

Cammie almost wanted to leave as quickly as she had arrived.

"Don't go. You're not interrupting anything."

Cammie froze in place, guilt flickering in her stomach. She shouldn't have been watching.

"It really wasn't my place to stay here and listen. It was a private conversation," she murmured.

"All the same, I am happy you're here." Caelan sniffled, wiping his face before looking up at the sky. "There's been no word yet. I've been searching the horizon for any sign of anything, but nothing has appeared. Where are your sisters?"

Cammie cracked a smile. "Hannah's still sparring."

Caelan couldn't contain the grin that appeared on his previously solemn lips. "As she would be. Has she bested Tony yet?"

Cammie shrugged. "I wouldn't know. I left during the match."

"Maybe we should go and place our bets. The winner can decide on dinner," Caelan said with a twinkle in his eye. He was back in somewhat happy spirits.

"As long as it isn't that disgusting stew Will made the other night, I am all for it." Cammie laughed.

A bright expression overtook Caelan's face. "I can agree with that sentiment. Have you seen Sabina?"

Cammie shook her head. "Could she be in the garden behind the house? You know how she loves being with the plants, away from all the noise."

"There's only one way to know for sure." Caelan approached Cammie and put an arm around her shoulder as they headed back in the direction she had come from.

When they rounded the corner, they saw Sabina in the distance. She was running full force, waving something in her hands.

"Guys," she called out. "You'll never guess what I just found!"

Thunder started in Cammie's chest. *Can it be?*

She removed herself from under Caelan's arm and started running in the direction of her sister. Caelan sprinted after her. Grass tickled her ankles as she willed her legs to move faster until she reached Sabina with rapid breaths.

"Why did you leave the garden?" Cammie asked, barely able to speak.

Sabina waved the item rapidly, excitement coming off of her in waves. "I *was* in the garden," she said, "but then I saw something in the distance, flying in circles while Hannah was too busy pummeling Tony. I was tired of hearing the curses and shouts, so I followed the thing in the sky. Only, it wasn't a thing. It was what Eirini mentioned, a messenger dove. I didn't believe they were real, but there it was, just flying in the sky. After a bit of circling, it dropped this at my feet. And I read it, and, well, just see for yourself!" Sabina shoved the letter into Cammie's hands, barely touching her. "I have to go tell the others the news," she rushed, her voice an octave higher than Cammie ever thought possible. Her feet pounded on the grass as she ran away.

Hesitantly, Cammie opened the letter. She felt a brief touch on her shoulder before the hand moved away. *Caelan.* Her lips felt dry as she read the words but not even that could contain her smile.

There, in swirly script, were words that seemed almost too good to be true.

We, the Council, anxiously await your arrival. Please, appear as promptly as you are able, for our decision has been made.

"It's here," Cammie whispered, the excitement clutching her throat. "It's really here," she shrieked. She shoved the letter in Caelan's hands, and she watched as his eyes devoured the written script.

A broad smile overtook his lips. "Come, let's get the others ready," he said. Caelan dashed back to the cottage, waving the letter in his hands.

With her heart in her throat, Cammie raced after him as fast as her legs could carry her.

For the first time, after these years of searching, they were finally going home.

END OF BOOK ONE

ACKNOWLEDGEMENTS

I've heard it said that it takes a village to make a book come to life. While I am not fully sure of that phrase in the way of traditional publishing, I can confirm this as an indie.

For those of you who don't know, this book has been with me for eleven years. By the time this gets published, it will be almost twelve. That being said, a story definitely shifts and changes with you, and this is one of them. What started out as a role-play kind of thing in middle school when *Twilight* and other things were super popular has massively changed into something so much more. This story—these characters— are my heart. They've been with me through some of the most challenging times of my life, and I am in awe that God allowed me to create them.

Before I had friends in real time, characters were my friends. They allowed me to piece together many difficult situations that aren't easy to process as a child, much less a young adult. So, as I am typing this, waiting on Mexican food, allow me to thank everyone who made this possible, in no particular order:

To *Saint Jupiter*, whose cover design blew me away, thank you for allowing the story in my head to come to life in a way that readers would appreciate at a glance. You've captured the essence of book one in picture-form, and I cannot wait to work with you for the rest of the series.

To *Nicole*, thank you for putting up with my constant fears and concerns and for allowing the space that was needed to write this draft, even though I pushed back the deadline at least four different times. I know my book, in your capable hands, will shine the best way it can, and I thank you for taking a chance on a newbie like me.

To *Qamber Designs and Media*, I am so excited for the work you guys are doing, and will do, for my book baby. The effort it takes to make formatting look exquisite is something my writer-brain cannot even fathom, but the hours and time you put into it do not go unnoticed. Thank you for making my book beautiful in the best way it can be.

To *Whitney*, you have been such an integral part in my writing journey. I am trying not to cry writing this, but it is so hard. When several people critiqued my work and my style to the point of me questioning my story and the depths of its origins, you were there to ground me not just as a writer but as a friend. Moving to a new town has been hard with making connections, but having you in my corner has made all the difference. I love you. You're the older sister I never had.

To *Maureen, Beverly, and Calista*, thank you for being in my corner and for praying for me when things got tough. You guys have been such a beacon of hope in the midst of the confusion and have been an encouragement as I follow this passion of mine.

To my *friends back home*, thank you for being my fans before being an author was even a thing. You believed in me before I had the courage to take the next step, and I am forever grateful.

To *Bri and Kiersten*, without you two, these characters might be entirely different. Thank you for playing along in my pretend phase in middle school. I don't think any of us knew at the time that the story would still live in my head long after I had graduated, but here we are.

And thank you to *Wesley*, my husband. Throughout this entire journey, you have been nothing but supportive. Thank you for taking my author photo and for being a shoulder to lean on when times are tough. Marrying a writer isn't easy, and you handle it selflessly, and I am forever grateful. I only hope that I can offer you the same support on your own artist journey. I can't promise to be perfect, but I can promise to do my best to love you however I can, even if that means acknowledging the things that aren't pretty that need to change. Marriage isn't always easy, and it takes time to learn to navigate, but there's no one else I want to do this journey with or have as my soundboard.

There's one more person I want to thank.

You.

Thank you, mysterious reader, for taking a chance on the dream of a thirteen-year-old. Thank you for escaping into my world with me, whether it be for days, weeks, or months. I appreciate you allowing yourself to be transported to a world of my creation, for sitting with me in these words and these people that I have done my best to do justice. It is for people like you that I write, for people like my younger self who found solace in the lives of make-believe people. I hope these words have brought something that you can take away from.

And I can't wait to see you on this next journey.

ABOUT THE AUTHOR

KATLYN DEROUEN is a multi-genre author who dabbles in science fiction, fantasy, and romance. Driven by her love of the written word, she penned her debut book of poetry in 2019, which received an outpouring of glowing reviews. Encouraged by the support of her readers, she allowed her imagination to take her to the stars and back with countless new engaging characters and compelling novels. She lives in Kansas with her husband and two fur babies, where she can always be found getting lost in a story.